CROWN OF EARTH AND SKY

Secrets of the Faerie Crown, Book 1

EMBERLY ASH

Copyright 2023 Emberly Ash, Cara Maxwell Romance

All rights reserved. No part of this book may be reproduced, or stored in a retrieval system, or transmitted in any form or by any means, electronic, mechanical, photocopying, recording, or otherwise, without express written permission of the publisher.

For permissions contact: caramaxwellromance@gmail.com

This is a work of fiction. Names, characters, places, and incidents either are the product of the author's imagination or are used fictitiously. Any resemblance to actual persons, living or dead, events, or locales is entirely coincidental.

ISBN: 978-1-964408-13-2 (ebook)

978-1-964408-00-2 (paperback)

Cover Art: Selkkie Designs

Beta Analysis: Made Me Blush Books

Map Design: A. Andrews

 Created with Vellum

*For the girls who were broken by those that should have protected them.
For the women we were forced to become all too soon.
May we all, finally, be free.*

CONTENT WARNINGS

Crown of Earth and Sky is a fantasy romance with elements of dark romance. While it is not a true dark romance, the themes are heavy and may be triggering for some readers.

Content warnings include: suicidal thoughts and ideation, child abuse, rape, murder, death of a loved one, explicit sexual content, and graphic depictions of death, violence, and torture.

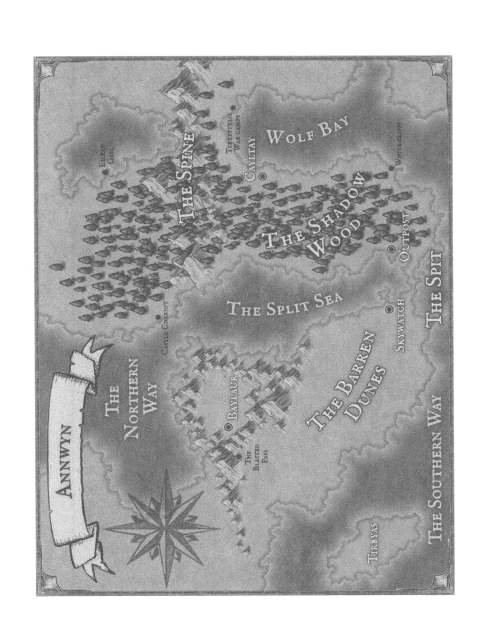

I
VEYKA

I should have died in the womb.

The wisdom of the Ancestors holds that the more powerful twin eats the other before birth, incorporating their power and growing stronger.

Our kind are vicious even before the first breath.

In the last millennia, only a handful of twins have been born to the elementals. My brother and I were among them.

The same brother stood over me now, Excalibur gleaming in his meaty fist, ready to strike the killing blow. He lifted one pale golden brow in perfect parallel with his smirk. His swirling storm-blue eyes —my eyes—sneered down at me. Superiority and satisfaction were twin beads of sweat running down from his temple.

"This is the end, Veyka," he crooned, shifting his weight subtly. I knew the stance, had seen him assume it dozens of times over the years. He was about to perform an execution.

"So soon? I thought you liked to play with your victims?" I ground out, hands aching for the blades that weren't there. He'd knocked one of my knives away, far enough it disappeared into a cloud of red dust somewhere in the courtyard. Out of reach.

But the other...

I knew my best chance was to get him talking. My prideful brother loved the sound of his own voice. How often had I heard him boast with his friends, rolling syllables around in his dark timbre, plotting which male or female he would pursue next?

"There is no sport in it when the opponent is so overmatched," he growled.

"And yet, that did not stop you from challenging me to begin with." The other knife was under my left hip, pinned. If I moved an inch for it, he'd gut me.

"A worthless opponent is an opponent, nonetheless."

The plan formed in my mind, each step as graceful and choreographed as a dance. "Only someone deeply insecure in their crown would think so."

His hand loosened on the golden hilt. Slightly. Almost imperceptibly.

But that is the thing about twins. We can perceive the imperceptible about one another. And I was faster than my brother.

I tightened the muscles in my abdomen and swung my legs outward, connecting hard with the sensitive insides of his knees. It wasn't enough to knock him down, but the half second it took him to readjust his grip on that Ancestors-damned sword was all the time I needed. My feet were under me. I palmed the knife that seconds before had been trapped under my body.

"Crafty bitch," he muttered, loud enough only for my delicately pointed ears.

"I am flattered," I said, darting a step forward and then back again, out of range. Reminding him just how fast I was—and how dangerous, now that I had a knife back in my hand. "Bow for me, dear brother, and I will let you walk away with your pride intact."

Murder shone in those sapphire eyes, turned dark with ire. I wondered if mine were the same just then, or if they'd taken on a gleam of their own. Our eyes were the only likeness between us, despite the accident of our birth.

But this was not the moment to ask.

He swung the monumental sword, a display of power and frustration. I was too far away to be in danger, but close enough to hear him growl, "The King of the Elemental Fae bows to no one."

I grinned. "As you like."

Then I struck.

Five breaths later, his back hit the ground.

"If I had half a mind for it, I'd have that pretty sword of yours as well," I said sweetly, flashing my knife to catch the sun beating overhead and reflecting it directly into his face. At least that infernal smirk of his was finally gone.

"Come and take it," he spat, blood mixing with spittle in the red dirt.

I shrugged, sheathing the knife at my side. "I'd rather not. I prefer my life of luxury."

"Vain creature."

"Your crown is crooked, Your Majesty."

"Your other knife is under the water barrel."

I cocked an eyebrow at the barrel, metal hoops gleaming. Even in the relentless heat, I knew the water inside would be cool and refreshing. Magic could be a convenient thing—if one was willing to pay the cost. I gave half a thought to wonder what the cost of keeping that water cool all day might be, and who paid it.

But instead of retrieving the knife, I strode forward and offered my brother a hand.

He stared at it, considering. Not at me, not at my face. Only at my proffered hand. For the space of a blink, fire danced at his fingertips. *Oh, he wanted to burn me, did he?*

That fire inside of him was always near the surface. Especially at a moment like this. I heard my father's voice in my head, counseling wisdom and patience as he always had done when he visited the water garden compound. When he promised me that someday soon, I would be freed.

But it was the brother before me who'd unlocked my gate.

What neither of them realized was I'd freed myself from that gilded cage long ago. But some knowledge was meant to live in the dark.

In the time it had taken me to think about it, the flames disappeared. When he reached for my hand, his fingers were warm with the remnants of his power. But then, Arthur was always warm. How he did not melt in the sweltering heat of the Effren Valley was beyond me.

"You ought to be nicer to me. No one else with spar with you," he said, dusting the red dirt from his close-fitting trousers. To no avail, as ever. Why he insisted on always wearing white...

"That is because your sentinels are cowards," I said, smiling sweetly at the guards standing at equal intervals around the perimeter of the practice ring.

An ice-cold wind whirled through the courtyard, catching me underneath my draped skirt. *Evander.* I ignored my brother's most hostile guard and his magical tantrum. His little wind felt nice against my sweat-drenched backside.

The others kept control of their magic. Gawayn rolled his eyes. Lyrena grinned even as she rubbed her forearm instinctively. The wound I'd given her while sparring days before had healed, but she was unlikely to forget it anytime soon. From the scowls on the other guards' faces, it seemed neither were they.

Arthur ignored their glares. "I ought to make you one of them. They could learn from you."

The strangled sound from behind me escaped neither of our notice. His cadre hated that idea even more than the prospect of facing me in the ring.

Arthur tipped the lid off the barrel of water, eyeing it longingly.

"Do not waste all that magic by pouring it over your head," I said, knowing instantly what my brother was thinking.

He wrinkled his nose and stuck out his tongue instead.

"Very kingly."

A half thought and two cups appeared in his hand. Whether he'd conjured them or summoned them or just quickly pulled them from their hiding spot, I didn't ask. I didn't care. His magic, his cost.

"Speaking of kingly... your presence is required tonight." His fingers touched mine as he handed me one of the cups, sending a spark of warmth into me. Even with sweat rolling down my back from our sparring, my fingers were cold. Always cold.

"Tonight?"

"Your attendance is requested," he said, dipping the cup of water and drinking deeply. A convenient ploy to avoid any explanation.

I didn't dip my cup. "Requested by whom?"

Arthur swiped a hand over his mouth, covering his telltale smirk as he said, "The terrestrial delegation, of course."

A lie—and one I did not need my status as a twin to detect.

"What need does the terrestrial delegation, here to arrange *your* joining, have of the spare?" I asked.

"Heir as well as spare, until my new bride accomplishes her duty," Arthur said.

I nearly choked on the cool water and succeeded at sloshing it down the front of my tunic, plastering the thin gossamer to my chest. The cooling magic wouldn't hold long now. It would turn sweltering in seconds.

"I was under the impression you'd been educated, even cloistered away in your little compound." Arthur set his cup down neatly on top of the barrel. I'd never seen him throw it to the side, as so many of the warriors were wont to do. Who cared, when you weren't the one to clean it up?

Arthur did. Arthur cared.

Which was why he was meant to be king.

He'd been training for this moment since we'd come squalling into the world twenty-five years ago. No one had expected him to ascend the throne so young, not when a powerful fae like our father could live past a thousand years. But Arthur was fourteen the first time he'd led forces into battle. By the time he was eighteen, he'd won over the people of Baylaur, our capital city, by capturing smugglers and distributing their wealth to the citizens rather than keeping it for the crown. He was destined by his very crown of golden hair to be a great and mighty king.

Mighty king, annoying as shit brother. He was trying to bait me, and I was tempted to let him. The knife holstered against my thigh had returned to the same temperature as my body, warm and close as a limb. He wanted another go at it. I could see the desire to win written in his eyes. That alone stilled my hand.

If we fought a hundred times, I'd win the majority. Being left on your own for twenty years has its advantages. But in any given match, my brother might best me. And today, I refused to give him the satisfaction.

"Well-educated enough to know the spare has never ascended, not in seven thousand years. A perfect line of succession straight from the Ancestors down to you, King Arthur," I said, bowing low. Exposing my neck. Offering submission—to the only person who would ever be worthy of it.

I felt a flicker of warmth. Not from the sun overhead or the exertion, but from flames. Arthur's fingertips hovered above the nape of my neck, exposed by the long plait of white hair draped over my shoulder. Tonight, if I had to attend this ghastly event, my braid would be woven with stands of pearls and diamonds. Now, the mass of shining white that fell past my shoulder blades was adorned only with a bit of gold rope—strands of precious metal braided together before being twisted into the long plaits favored by elemental fae females.

Arthur loosed the flames just a little until they singed the tiny hairs still curled with sweat and heated the gold rope where it was knotted at my nape. Then the heat was gone, and my brother stepped away.

A time-honored tradition. A show of my acceptance of his power and his reign. After the Joining, when he was finally crowned High King of Annwyn, every member of his court would step forward to repeat the same ritual. But here, in the privacy of the training ring, with only his guards looking on, it was just ours. Not an act of subservience, but protection. My brother was the only one who had ever protected me—but only once he had come of age.

Before that, I learned to protect myself.

"What are the odds I can convince you to wear something appropriate this evening?" Arthur asked, beginning to shuck off his leather armor to reveal the softer, flowing white tunic beneath.

Gawayn stepped up, taking my brother's sweaty discards. Captain of the Goldstone Guard, but also a glorified handmaid. I bit my lip to keep from pointing it out. Gawayn tolerated me on my best days.

"I wasn't planning on wearing this." I motioned down at my clothing, dark with sweat.

Or at least it would have been if it was not already dark to begin with. Black gossamer silk draped in layers to form a tunic that left my shoulders and a swath of my stomach exposed, held in place with a brown leather harness. My skirt was a similar style, secured with a belt and falling from my hips in clever panels so I could move and fight. Like the metallic strands braided into my hair, the buckles and loops of the harness were gold. I did not look entirely uncouth.

"I would settle for that," Arthur sighed. "If you would condescend to wear it in white."

"Pale colors do not suit me," I teased, sheathing my second knife.

Arthur was down to tight knee trousers and his billowing shirt. The tight leather belts holding my garments in place were starting to itch.

"You are made up of pale colors."

He was right about that, at least. White hair, alabaster skin, pale blue eyes.

Arthur crossed his arms over his chest, rising to his full height—trying and failing to intimidate me. "Seafoam green," he ordered.

I countered. "Hunter green."

"Turquoise." Counteroffer and a sigh of brotherly frustration.

It was stupid, really. He was the King of the Elemental Fae and me, the Crown Princess. And we were arguing about what color I would wear to dinner.

To Arthur, it was political. The terrestrials were here. The tenor of the elemental court was stilted on a normal day. On a night such as this...

But when you'd spent twenty years without choices, even the small ones mattered.

My brother must have remembered that, for in the next breath, his jaw softened.

"Emerald," he offered.

"Done."

That was the real reason Arthur would make a great king. Not because of feats of bravery defending Annwyn or tossing gold to peasants. He was empathetic. While most elemental fae were worried about hiding their true emotions so they could manipulate a situation, Arthur truly let himself feel his. Which meant when he saw someone struggling, he could feel that too.

Maybe it was a side effect of being locked away for so long, or maybe he'd simply stolen all of those traits away from me in the womb. But I was wary, sarcastic, and too proficient with a blade to make friends.

Arthur raked a hand through his golden hair, stance loosening. He turned for the corridor which led back into the goldstone palace but froze a step from the blessed shade. "You *will* be in attendance," he said.

Damn. How had he known? I'd agreed to wear emerald, but I hadn't actually agreed to attend the dinner—

"Veyka."

"I will be there," I ground out, stalking in the opposite direction.

I ignored my brother's self-satisfied laugh and began plotting how I could slip hellroot into his aural tonight. It would serve him right to be flatulating while trying to talk up the terrestrial delegation.

"Careful. If you plan something too malicious, I'll be forced to take you into custody," Lyrena said, effectively reading my mind.

My favorite of my brother's Goldstone Guards followed me into the shade, making for the blank expanse of goldstone bricks on the site side of the courtyard. Her eyes were glowing—not for me, of course, certain. She'd just been watching my brother spar.

"I wouldn't want to put you in a position to pick favorites," I said, letting her come around me, push open the latch to the hidden door, and check the passageway for dangers.

Someday, the guarding would become cumbersome. But today, it was still new. Not to be guarded, but protected. Having someone care about whether I lived or died, instead of what threat I posed.

Lyrena winked as she motioned me through the hidden door. Her grin was unremarkable—only because she was always smiling. But no one could question her beauty, even without the cheeky grin in place. She was perfect in every way our people measured beauty. Lithe, with golden skin burnished by hours spent in the sun training. Unlike me, muscular but soft, Lyrena was all corded muscle and flat stomach. Even her golden braid, styled almost identically to my own, looked decadent just because of its glowing color.

I could see why Arthur chose her, again and again.

But all that would end when his terrestrial bride arrived.

With an unnecessary snap of her fingers, Lyrena's fire magic lit the torches lining the passage. The flick of her gleaming plait as the door closed caught my eye, a second before she was gone. A second was long enough to spy the jeweled band securing the tail of her braid: a band of gold and emerald. Arthur's colors.

Glowing eyes—the curse of a passionate race, unable to hide lust and passion when it literally changed the brightness of one's irises—and my brother's colors in her hair. Their affair was still going strong, even after all these months.

Perhaps things would not change as much as I supposed. A thousand years was a long time to share only one female's bed, especially if it was a joining of duty rather than passion.

I shuddered at what awaited my brother. I'd sooner cut off my left hand than suffer such an arrangement. For what must have been the tenth time that day, I offered a prayer of thanks to the Ancestors for the precious four minutes my brother had entered this world before me.

2
VEYKA

By the second round of toasts, I regretted not letting my brother gut me in the practice ring. The Court of the Elemental Fae was known for three things—opulence, heat, and deception.

Every goldstone pillar was gilded in gemstones the size of my fist. Literal fountains of aural poured from the walls. Though only those seated well below the dais were foolish enough to indulge in more than one pour.

The folds of my diaphanous emerald gown hid the beads of sweat rolling down my back. The delegation from the terrestrial court was not so lucky. Their thick woolen tunics were soaked through and darkened embarrassingly at the necks and armpits. Their quarters would stink like a decaying animal by the end of their visit.

But the toasts—those were what chased me from my cushioned seat on the dais. Another round of false, honeyed words and I'd likely try to drown myself in one of the aural fountains.

Unity, friendship... sweet deceptions to make everyone feel better, feel as if the accords between us were anything other than a pea balanced on a knife's edge. A balance that I, thankfully, would not be tasked with preserving.

I took up a post on the perimeter of the throne room turned banquet hall, leaning against one of the goldstone pillars. Even it was warm. Couldn't someone be bothered to cool the damn hall?

A horribly selfish thought. All magic had a cost. Cooling a cavernous room such as this, open to the elements, would take several less powerful fae. Even shared between them, they would likely be comatose by the end of the evening. Or worse, if the Ancestors demanded a steeper cost. A fire at home. A sick child. One never knew the cost until the magic had been expended.

My eyes flicked to Evander, second-in-command of the king's Goldstone Guards. He lurked in the opposite corner behind the dais, looking cool and comfortable as ever. Easy enough to use your own magic to cool yourself; less risk there, more control.

Not all of us were so blessed with ice and wind in a land of perpetual heat.

I jerked my gaze away from him. If Evander caught me staring, I'd have to deal with him smirking at me for the rest of the night. Then I might be tempted to stab him. Which my brother would not appreciate, given our guests from the terrestrial fae court.

Thankfully, said brother chose that moment to rise. He drew all eyes to him effortlessly, glowing like the golden, sun-blessed ruler he was.

"We welcome our terrestrial brethren, come to make our kingdom whole once more," he began.

"A whole lot of nonsense," I muttered under my breath, swirling the aural in my glass.

No one could hear me. I was far enough away that even the predatory sense of hearing bestowed upon the fae could not detect my words. Even so, Arthur glanced in my direction, if only for a moment.

"They have braved the Spit between our two kingdoms, crossed the Split Sea, to bring us news of the terrestrial heir," he continued, voice thundering.

Had he charged someone with amplifying the sound? Carrying it on the breeze so it echoed among the goldstone pillars? I flicked my gaze to Parys, my brother's closest friend and sometime lover. He appeared to be chewing on a bit of candied pear, but...

My eyes narrowed on the pulsing vein above his temple. He was holding his concentration, even as he tried to appear casual. From a distance, I could see the gold glow in his warm brown eyes. Parys adored Arthur—as a friend and a lover. I could have snorted—if I was not a delicate, lovely princess on display. The two of them had surely planned this, to make Arthur even more impressive to the delegation.

As if that was necessary.

We were all stuck with this arrangement, this Offering of brides and grooms, by the blessing and curse of the Ancestors. It was the cost of peace. Though my brother described it a bit more eloquently.

"Once every generation, our two fae kingdoms come together in the Offering to renew our promises of peace and prosperity once more," Arthur continued.

Promises of peace and prosperity made by the Ancestors, seven thousand years ago. My own ancestors, as a matter of fact.

Two powerful fae races—elemental and terrestrial—doomed to occupy one realm and kill each other in endless skirmishes and retaliations for a million years. Until it all exploded into the Great War.

Until the Ancestors—the fucking perfect, revered Ancestors—came up with their scheme to unite the elemental and terrestrial kingdoms under one throne.

How many of these same fae had been here for the last Offering? My mother, obviously. The Dowager. If I was an accident, what was she? A monster, my mind answered. I suppressed the shiver that slinked through me despite the heat. Turning back to my brother, I forced myself to focus on him instead. Not on the past. It was too dangerous.

"A High King and Queen to rule all of Annwyn, one elemental, one terrestrial. United, as our kingdoms are and shall ever be.

Terrestrial brethren, the Court of the Elemental Fae are honored by your presence." Then Arthur did something unexpected.

He bowed his head to the delegation below the dais. I nearly spit out the aural in my mouth. A few courtiers didn't manage quite so well. The advisors, my brother's Royal Council, were horrified.

But Arthur looked at none of them. He stared directly at the terrestrial fae delegation, meeting each of their eyes in turn. Showing respect. "My court welcomes you. *I* welcome you."

My heart swelled with pride. The crown of the elemental fae was hereditary. Anyone might have set upon that throne, myth or monster. My mother, for example.

But my brother was meant for this, made for it. He was the sort of king legends and epic poems were written about.

One by one, to almost everyone's surprise, the terrestrial fae dipped their heads in recognition and respect of Arthur's offering.

He lifted his aural in a toast. "For all that has been, and all that will ever be."

"For all that has been and all that will ever be," the room recited back to him.

Then they all drank.

If I had been anyone else, I would have ignored the invitation—nay, requirement—to sip. But I was Veyka Pendragon, Crown Princess of the Elemental Fae. Whether I liked it or not, and I certainly did not, the half of the crowd that wasn't watching Arthur was watching me.

So, I lifted the aural to my lips, like a good little princess.

Even though I knew it was all a farce. All that has been—the past the Ancestors so meticulously crafted. All that will ever be—the future of the fae we were charged with protecting. For those things, I'd been locked away in the water garden compound for most of my life.

But I was not trapped any longer, I reminded myself as the silky sweet liquor rolled down my throat. I was free. Arthur was the king. All was well. With Arthur as king, maybe—just maybe—it could be a different sort of world.

Across the cavernous room, my brother's eyes found me. He knew, of course, what those words meant to me. He alone knew and understood. I held his gaze, refusing to let my eyes slide past him down the dais, to where my mother sat. She could not have this moment. Or any other. Not after all she'd done to us.

I see you. You are safe, my brother's eyes promised me.

I could not incline my head, not with so many spectators. But I knew Arthur could read the thoughts in my head. Another anomaly of twins. The shared language of our souls spoke to one another across deserts and goldstone palaces alike.

When Arthur turned back to the terrestrial delegation, my pulse was steady once again.

But—What was that?

Behind him, a shimmer of light slipped between the goldstone pillars. A shimmer of darkness. No, of light. Ancestors, it changed with each second that passed. It almost looked like the flapping of wings.

What was it?

I blinked rapidly, over and over. Perhaps I'd drunk too much aural. It had been months since I'd partaken, and my brother's vintner might make a more potent blend than my father's.

When I opened my eyes fully again, it was gone. No light, no darkness, and certainly no wings.

Arthur's bellow filled the hall. "I am pleased to announce that negotiations have been successful. In one month's time, our court shall be whole once again. My power," he paused.

Fire bloomed at each fingertip, joining together in a ribbon of flame that he twisted around his fingers, unburnt. Always a show-off.

"My power will join with the terrestrial heir at the Offering, and Annwyn will be secure for another thousand years."

Whispers started immediately. What sort of power would the terrestrial heir have? Would she be a shifter like the king who had come before? Or another Queen of Roses, like the legends?

I didn't particularly care. As long as she left me alone and was kind to my brother, I'd accept whomever the terrestrials conjured up to fulfill their half of the Offering.

Arthur pulled Excalibur from its sheath at his hip, raising it high above his head. "Power. Power is life. Power is safety. Power is—"

In the next breath, all the light extinguished. Every single flame went to nothing, blanketing the hall in darkness. Even the stars in the sky beyond the open arches of the goldstone pillars seemed to wink out. He must've had someone summon cloud cover. That would be costly. I fully expected to see one of Arthur's councilors pass out from the sheer force of power required—whenever my brother deigned to reawaken the flames he'd doused.

But another moment passed. And another.

My stomach tightened, the aural inside it threatening to revolt. *Revolt.*

A wet sound slithered through the dark air, a snake uncurling itself. A second later, the whispers began anew.

"You've made your point, my liege."

"—showing off for the delegation."

Then the yells.

"Enough of this! We know you're damned powerful!"

"Ancestors, watch where you are walking!"

Then, just as suddenly as the darkness had come, it lifted. I heaved a sigh, resigning myself to cross down to the low tables where the terrestrials waited, to soothe tempers instead of stoking them with sarcastic comments.

But everyone was standing. Every fae in the throne room was on their feet.

And Arthur—

Where my brother had stood a minute before, a mischievous glint in his eye... there was nothing.

Whatever Arthur had planned, it had gone wrong.

Complete chaos gripped the room. The guards rushed the dais and I couldn't see anything. Ancestors, why had I gotten up from my seat? I shoved aside a servant, shot a glare at a terrestrial who was approaching me—as if I had any more answers than he.

I took a step forward, then stumbled backward as if I'd run straight into a wall. The scent filled my nostrils, my chest, searing a terrible pathway right into the inner confines of my soul.

Blood.

Someone screamed. Not someone—Lyrena.

Another someone grabbed my arm. Even as I spun, allowing myself to be pulled along, to give my captor a momentary advantage, I drew the dagger from my calf and swung it upward.

Gawayn did not spare me a word as he dragged me from the throne room. Nor did he flinch from my blade at his throat. One look at his eyes and I knew—he'd let me slit his throat before he released my arm.

He was willing to die to protect me.

I clung to that thought as he dragged me out.

Where was Arthur? Was this some sort of jape to entertain the terrestrial delegation? No one seemed amused. Cries—I was hearing cries now.

I recognized the desperate sounds even as a gust of warm wind hit me from behind, pushing me through the goldstone arch to the jewel-encrusted filigree door beyond. Gawayn's wind was always warm, the heat to Evander's frigid winter blast.

Someone was dead.

Gawayn's summer breeze slammed the door closed behind us, his hands rough on my bare shoulders where they were exposed by my gown, shoving me forward.

"Keep going," he instructed, voice gruff.

Gruff. Not calm, not taciturn, not stoic. But racked with barely contained emotion.

Realization clanged through me, sharp and painful as any sword. Gawayn was with me. He was captain of my brother's Goldstones. But he was with me. Which could only mean one thing.

"Gawayn, we have to go back." I planted my feet in the narrow corridor, bracing a hand against each wall. But my guard was bigger, and I still had my dagger clenched in one fist, preventing me from holding tight to the goldstone.

"Take me back," I demanded.

"No, Your Majesty."

My heart stopped. The arms that I'd pinned to the walls dropped to my side, slack. The dagger clamored to the ground. I couldn't think. I couldn't breathe.

But I could hear.

I heard Gawayn say the words that would doom me forever—

"King Arthur is dead."

3
VEYKA

What do I want?

A quick death. Barring that, I only dream of one thing—revenge.

Growing up closeted away in the water gardens, I'd dreamed of freedom. I'd yearned to walk through the goldstone palace at will, to eat and drink as I wished. Such silly, childish dreams. Now, all of my dreams were dead.

"More wine, Councilor Teo?"

Teo did not even look at me. His palm glided over the top of his goblet, a silent negation. The only indication he deigned to give that he'd heard me at all.

I didn't grit my teeth at the slight. I knew exactly how Teo felt about me, the queen that was never supposed to be.

"Councilor Roksana?" I asked, keeping my voice light and soft.

"No, thank you," the older female said, pale gray eyes flicking over me. "Your Majesty," she added, one dark brow arching.

I did not curtsey. They bowed to me now. The reprimand in Roksana's eyes was clear. She did not approve of the Queen of the Elemental Fae filling the role of cupbearer to her own Royal Council.

"The terrestrial delegation arrives in a week," Councilor Esa reminded us from her post near the head of the rectangular table.

She wouldn't dare to actually seat herself on Arthur's throne, but she was as close as she could manage. And as *donna* of the Royal Council, Esa was more queen than I at this point.

"Have they made their selection for the Offering at last?" Teo scoffed.

"Yes," Roksana spoke up before Esa could.

Esa might be the council's *donna*, but at eight hundred years old, Roksana was its oldest and most experienced member. She was also the emissary to the terrestrial court.

"Do not keep us waiting," Teo grumbled. "You are as bad as the terrestrials—"

"Councilor Teo!" Elora was on her feet, ice spreading across the table from her hands at the insult.

"Councilor Elora, please mind your—" Esa tried to intervene.

Just like that, the Royal Council, charged with ruling the Kingdom of the Elemental Fae, descended into chaos.

No sign of Roksana's own ice magic, though her daughter, Elora, was still allowing hers to spread. Soon the entire council chamber would be coated in frost. Teo's thunder rumbled beyond the open archways, while Esa's water magic attempted to douse the flames simmering from Councilor Noros on her right.

I just kept pouring wine.

"Councilor Teo, if you would prefer my role as emissary for yourself, you are welcome to it," Roksana said, her voice cutting smoothly through the chaos.

Esa stilled, annoyance dripping off of her like the errant water droplets that coated her hands. She was *donna*, but Roksana commanded the room.

Teo's thunder still rumbled in the distance. But Roksana gave not an inch, her dark skin and darker hair unruffled by wind or water or fire.

"Who is the new terrestrial heir?" Esa interceded. I heard the splash of water—Teo's empty wine goblet filling.

Teo looked like he'd rather splash it in Roksana's face, but he took Esa's silent directive instead and lifted the goblet to his lips.

Roksana turned back to Esa. I took that opportunity to slip back between the goldstone pillars framing the council room.

"Arran Earthborn," Roksana said, voice clear and cold as those gray eyes.

"The Brutal Prince," Noros murmured, speaking for the first time.

The words crashed over the room like an icy wave. And me, I should have been hit the hardest. It was why I was hiding between the pillars—because I was still terrible at hiding my emotions, even having lived at court for almost a year. My closeted upbringing had inhibited me from learning an elemental's most treasured tool —deception.

But the announcement that the cruelest, most dangerous and powerful fae male in millennia was to be my groom? It stirred nothing inside of me.

Esa recovered first. "He is old to be selected as heir."

Roksana wasn't fazed. "Indeed. But as we have discussed, the terrestrials were expecting to provide a female heir. Therefore, they have begged us to accept their choice."

Begged. The terrestrials had done no such thing, and everyone in the room knew it. But clever Roksana managed to make it seem as if we, the elementals, were in control. Nothing could have been further from the truth.

The court had been spiraling since a pack of humans snuck into the goldstone palace and beheaded my brother.

It was the only sure way to kill a fae. The humans had planned well.

And this council had done nothing to punish them for it. They may be content to spar with words, but I—

The anger died within me. As it always did. *Had it lasted longer this time?* No, I did not care enough about that to wonder. I did not care about anything any longer. Not since that moment six months ago.

"Annwyn needs a strong leader," Teo mused, drawing his index finger and thumb down his cheeks to meet at the base of his receding chin. "Perhaps the Brutal Prince is precisely what is required after the... upheaval."

Elora snorted. "A king of peace and hope exchanged for one of cruelty and bloodshed?"

"We still have the Princess of Peace."

My back hit the warm goldstone wall.

Roksana's words hung in the air. No breeze, warm or cool, came to brush them away. They could all see me, even as I attempted to disappear into nothingness.

"In any case," Esa said, breaking the silence. "We must face events as we find them. The terrestrial delegation arrives in seven days. Perhaps sooner, if they have flying shifters among them."

The meeting descended into logistical concerns. No less contested, thunder still groaning occasionally as the afternoon dragged on, but monotonous enough I resumed filling wine goblets.

The sunset gilded the goldstone pillars with pinks and reds when Esa finally called the council meeting to adjourn. It was time for my other role.

My hands were steady enough as I set aside the wine and came to stand at the head of the table.

I did not sit. I never took Arthur's seat at the table, even as laws and precedent demanded I assume his throne. I even avoided touching the table's stone surface. Teo caressed the sapphire embedded in the stone that marked his spot. But I didn't even glance down at the amorite that marked mine. Arthur's emerald was gone, just like he was.

Just like that legendary sword, Excalibur. Disappeared in the confusion after Arthur's murder. Meant to be presented only to the worthy wielder, it had passed hand to hand from High King to High King for a thousand years. Until Arthur died, and Annwyn was stuck with me.

"Thank you for service, councilors. I adjourn this meeting." Simple, formal words. But they must be spoken by me, the Queen of the Elemental Fae. Even though I had no intention of governing. I'd surrendered that right to the spineless council.

I had other matters to attend to.

"Your Majesty," the council murmured in response, several already halfway to standing.

They respected me no more than I did them. The spare who had inherited the throne was a disappointment to everyone.

"Your Majesty," Roksana said again—an entreaty this time. "Perhaps you would join me in my chambers for dinner. I can tell you what else I have learned about your betrothed." She shot a look across the table at her daughter, who watched us closely even as she listened to Esa droning on about menus. "Elora will not be joining us."

This time, Elora managed to keep the frost to her fingertips. Like me, she had not yet mastered the crucial elemental skill of hiding one's emotions. If Roksana noticed as well, I could not tell. Her intent eyes had returned to me.

I opened my mouth to decline, but Roksana held up a hand.

A bold action to one's queen.

"Before your refuse, Majesty, allow me to reassure you. I will not ask you to speak of anything you do not wish. I merely offer company," she said.

Damn if she didn't look earnest.

Once, I might have walked gratefully into the mentorship and mothering she offered.

"I am promised elsewhere," I said instead.

For a second her lips parted, as if she might argue. But she only inclined her head. "Good evening, then."

I nodded tightly. Esa lingered in the periphery of my vision, her conversation with Elora concluded. But if she wanted my ear next, she was about to be disappointed.

I strode directly past her, my pewter skirts trailing behind me. With a shove, I was through the filigree doors. Silence hit me like a wall.

The antechamber was full of courtiers, but every whisper ceased at my appearance. I ignored all of them.

Gawayn and Lyrena closed ranks at my shoulders. The council chamber and my bedroom were the only places they left me alone. Perhaps I ought to be grateful.

Twenty-seven long strides and I'd reached the corridor. After that, I didn't need to count. I was practically running. Through the courtyard. Past the Dowager's wing. Another corridor.

Evander shoved open the door to my apartments. I ignored the dinner laid out on the table. Gawayn and Lyrena peeled off to take up positions on either side as I threw open the double doors to my bedroom.

I did not bother to close them behind me. Not as I unclasped my skirts or tugged off the cropped tunic top. Not as I reached the bed, planting a hand on Parys' chest to shove him flat on the sheets.

If my guards had any thoughts as I straddled by brother's best friend, they kept them well hidden. And as my hips drove forward, riding him forcefully, the sensation wiped away any feelings or grief that had managed to work their way into my head.

I fucked Parys hard. Until no painful memories were left in either of our minds.

Until one word remained, its letters etched in my soul.

Revenge.

4

ARRAN

"They all must die."

Her exhale was barely perceptible. But my wolf-like hearing caught it even before she said, "There is such a thing as mercy."

"After what happened to the elemental heir?"

The man on the left clasped his eyes closed, not wanting to see his final moments. The woman at his side pissed herself.

Guinevere bit her bottom lip hard, the scent of blood hitting my nostrils a second later.

"I would think that I, above all others, would be entitled to an opinion on the matter," she said, voice lethal.

I could sense her anger. I did not need to glance down at her knuckles to know the feline claws must be slipping free. Perhaps she was right. The humans had murdered her betrothed.

All the suffering she'd endured to win the title of terrestrial heir had been rendered meaningless when King Arthur died and a terrestrial female was no longer needed to complete the Offering. She'd watched friends and relatives brutally cut down; had to deal the fatal blow herself, not just to emerge victorious, but to survive.

But she was not the only terrestrial fae whose life had been irrevocably altered by the gruesome beheading we'd only heard stories of from our stronghold on Wolf Bay.

And we were not yet in the Kingdom of the Elemental Fae. Until we crossed the Spit, we were firmly in terrestrial territory. Until the new High King and Queen of Annwyn were officially crowned, the laws of the individual territories held sway. Which meant that as the highest ranking terrestrial fae present, the decision of what to do with the prisoners we'd caught lurking in the Shadow Wood lay with me.

"They must die," I said again, though this time my voice was softer. An invitation to my companion to express her thoughts.

"They have broken the human-fae treaty, so by rights, you are entitled," Gwen agreed. She was attempting to control her emotions. "But we do not know why they have come to Annwyn, nor through which rift. This information could be valuable."

She wasn't wrong. But humans were a waste of time, they always had been. "We do not have the time to delay in questioning them."

Gwen's gold eyes glinted, the only hint of the wild cat hidden within her brown-skinned beauty. "I can make quick work of it."

That was my decision made.

She wanted to torture them—to use these three humans, most likely marketeers looking to collect fae goods to sell in the human markets—to relieve some of the anger simmering in her veins.

If I let her, she'd hate herself later. Unlike me, my friend was still good. Beneath her anger and her rage at the future the humans had stolen from her, she was kind and honorable. This sort of torture was my specialty. My soul was already heavily stained.

Gwen was panting now. The need and excitement flowed through her strongly enough even the silent human was cowering on the ground.

On my next inhale, I drew the battle axe from my belt. As I exhaled, I swung it forward in one precise motion.

Three human heads hit the ground. A second later, their bodies followed.

Gwen shifted so quickly, the humans would have missed it.

The raven-haired beauty who'd stood beside me a moment before was replaced by a lion nearly twice the usual size, thick black mane wild in the wind and brown fur glistening in the sunspots that filtered through the canopy of leaves overhead.

She threw that massive head back and loosed a roar so loud I had no doubt they'd hear it on the other end of the Spit at Skywatch. Then she turned and bounded away through the trees.

"Should we send one of the winged sentries after her?" Osheen asked, appearing silently at my shoulder.

I shook my head. "She will find us again when she is ready. Hopefully, before we reach the goldstone gates of Baylaur."

5
VEYKA

If I stared long enough at the ring of mountains that encircled the Effren Valley, and Baylaur by extension, I told myself I could see the water. The wide balcony that jutted out from the goldstone palace gave me an expansive view across the valley to the eastern half of the mountains. The Tower of Myda loomed at the edge of the city, near the center of the valley, as if guarding the citizens from the fell beasts that lurked beyond. A cunning illusion, like most things in the elemental kingdom.

Several levels below, I could see the courtyard and other balconies attached to apartments occupied by elemental courtiers. If I looked left, I imagined I could see the Northern Way, with its choppy gray waves. Straight ahead, and I would glimpse the Split Sea, its legendary still sapphire blue surface.

But the truth was, I'd never seen a body of water larger than the turquoise pools of the water gardens where I'd been raised.

From the way my council watched me, half of them wished I'd never emerged from my tranquil prison. While the other half worried I might retreat back to it and never return.

How was a fae princess who'd been kept hidden away for most of her twenty-five years of life to rule a kingdom?

The answer was easy—I didn't mean to.

The Royal Council could have at it. The Brutal Prince, when he arrived, could fight it out with them for control. Me? I had other matters to attend to.

My eyes flitted down from where I stood on the edge of the palace, built into the side of the mountain, to the city beneath. A strip of desert separated the edge of the city from the base of the mountain, a stretch of innocuous open sand. I felt a smile curve the edge of my mouth.

Maybe when I finally caught the villains who'd murdered Arthur, I'd take them there. Drag them into the middle of that open expanse, beneath the unforgiving Annwyn sun, and watch as they were devoured alive by the Gremog.

"What are you planning?"

Parys' voice cut into the very enjoyable vision I was constructing for myself, full of blood, gore, and begging.

"Why do you think I am planning anything?" I asked, raising one eyebrow in his direction.

He rose from my bed, reaching his hands above his head and stretching so that every muscle of his lean body was outlined in the midmorning sun. He didn't bother to cover up his cock, soft and spent from the punishing ride I'd taken him on just an hour before. When I woke with my blood threatening to boil me from the inside out, the physical release of climax was the only thing that could calm it.

Still naked, he strode toward me, taking up a position in the middle of the balcony.

Whispers reached our fae ears, their words clear enough I wondered if Parys had summoned them on his wind.

"The Queen and..."

"Such a specimen..."

"...arrival of the terrestrial delegation..."

"—Brutal Prince."

Parys' gaze slid to me even as his wind encircled the balcony, ensuring that no one would hear our words as easily as we'd listened to theirs.

"They are wondering what you will do with me once the Brutal Prince arrives," Parys said.

I shrugged. "Perhaps he will be interested in a threesome."

That earned me an eye roll. "Clever."

Parys stepped back inside the bedroom long enough to return with sustenance. The male was always thinking of food—always hungry. For food and flesh, it seemed. He tossed me the shining red apple at the same time he spoke.

"We both know this cannot continue, Veyka."

He called me clever, but he was the one with a mind crafty enough to make every elemental jealous. Parys' brain seemed made for the intrigues of this court, while mine was perilously one-track. Throwing me the apple so my hands would be busy when he dropped that little tidbit of his into the void between us. *Clever, indeed.*

"Maybe you are my mate," I joked, digging my thumb into the rich red flesh. But even I knew it was a useless attempt at humor—one I didn't even feel.

"Grasping at folklore and fairytales now, are we?" Parys said.

"I am the queen," I pointed out, taking a bite.

"Whose king is set to arrive any day now," Parys said between mouthfuls.

As if I needed reminding. My eyes drifted southward to the Blasted Pass. There were very few ways in and out of the Effren Valley. Coming from the Kingdom of the Terrestrial Fae, there was only one possibility for the terrestrial delegation.

"It will be months until the Joining," I said mildly. By which point, I planned to be gone, my mission accomplished.

Parys scoffed, his apple nothing but a core. He chucked it over the edge of my balcony carelessly. My heart pulled at the memory.

No—I reminded it sternly. Dead things cannot feel.

He stretched again, arms overhead, using the motion to glance from side to side and quickly survey the surrounding balconies populated with other members of the elemental court breaking their fast or already drinking aural. I knew canty Parys was filing all his observations away for later. He would make a good royal councilor, someday.

Hopefully, the Brutal Prince would recognize his value.

Then the clever bastard turned his eyes on me. "I do not relish finding out how the Brutal Prince feels about finding an interloper in his betrothed's bed."

"I never took you for a coward, Parys," I said with a sigh, letting the hand that held the half-finished apple drop to my side.

I was not as naked as Parys, but not far off. The gossamer dressing gown I wore was little more than a wide strip of iridescent violet fabric with a hole cut out for the head. I knew that from the other balconies adorning the eastern side of the goldstone palace, my courtiers' sharp fae eyes could see the rounded curves of my hips where the fabric failed to contain my generous figure.

But if I did not care the court knew I was bedding Parys, I certainly was not bothered if they saw my partially clothed body. I'd belonged to them since the moment of my conception. Queen of the Elemental Fae I might be, but nothing in this realm was truly, individually mine.

"I'd rather be a coward than be dead," Parys said, casually striding back into the bedroom and toeing around the bedsheets in search of his tunic.

I watched him dress, no desire or interest rousing in my body. This thing between us, it wasn't love or even lust. It was desperation, both of us driven by the voids in our chests.

But knowing the keenness of his fae hearing, lacking his wind power to shield myself, I waited until he disappeared into the bathing room before I murmured, "That is how you and I are different, my friend."

6

VEYKA

"There are reports of birds circling the mountain," Gawayn said, face stern.

"Birds," I repeated, biting my lip to keep from scoffing aloud. "And you've come to me with this report because…"

"They could be terrestrials," he bit out.

I knew that, of course. The implication was as clear as day. But that did not make torturing him any less fun.

Was it still called fun if you felt no joy in your belly? I teased Gawayn out of habit now. Because during those first few weeks, when I could barely rise from my bed, I hadn't liked the version of him I saw then. So, I forced myself to jest and joke, so that even if I was clearly broken, at least he wasn't trying to suffocate me.

"Do you think the Brutal Prince is among them?" Charis said, voice brimming with awe and excitement.

"He doesn't take the form of a bird, Charis," Carly said disdainfully, nudging aside her sister's hand so she could take over plaiting my hair.

"You do not know what form he takes," Charis scoffed back, reaching for the braid herself. Her sister swatted her hand away.

When the third sister appeared, Gawayn sighed audibly.

"Your Majesty," he said, pointedly ignoring the copper-haired eldest of my three handmaidens. "The terrestrials will arrive imminently. But if they are circling like common carrion birds, we need to know why."

"They are probably just scouts," Cyara said, holding up two long jeweled strands, one diamond and one opal, for me to choose between.

I shrugged, eliciting a little mewl of displeasure from Carly, still at work on the intricate plait. When I was a child, there had been no one to plait my hair so ornately. I'd dreamed of an army of handmaidens. As an adult, I'd learned three was more than enough.

They were older than me, though one would hardly know it. All in the vicinity of fifty years old, they were still young to have earned places at court. But I enjoyed them—as much as I could enjoy anything. Mostly, I found the way they annoyed my Goldstones into relaxing their guard to be useful to my purposes.

"I am certain they are scouts," Gawayn agreed tersely. "But if they are spying on us, then we need to be spying on them."

"They are a party of goodwill, come to make Annwyn whole once again," Cyara argued, handing over the opals to her sister. "Spying on them sets the wrong tone."

"Trusting them is idiotic. Or have you forgotten—"

Cyara slapped him.

Ancestors below, she was bold.

"Mind your tongue in the presence of the Queen," Cyara warned, stepping back and out of easy range of Gawayn's grasp.

The Captain of my Goldstone Guards stared at the handmaiden as if he'd like nothing more than to drag her over to my balcony and drop her off of it. As if my thoughts were carried on the wind, her delicate, white feathered wings twitched. Little good it would do him.

He could have bested her in a second. But instead, he glanced in my direction. I avoided his gaze in the reflection of my mirror.

"I seek to protect the Queen," Gawayn said.

"As do we all," Cyara said back instantly. The response had clearly been poised on the tip of her tongue.

Protect. So many people intent on protecting me.

Gawayn blamed himself for my brother's death and had become insufferable in his duties since the moment he shoved me into that passageway to safety. Cyara refused to even let Arthur's name be spoken within my earshot. She was afraid it would unhinge me.

Maybe if they'd all protected Arthur so diligently, he would still be alive.

They were as culpable as the rest of us.

I shook my head, ripping the tail of white hair out of Carly's grip and ruining her last several minutes of work. The string of opals hit the tiled floor with a hideous clash.

"Go. All of you."

Not a single one of them dared to look at me. They stared at the floors, the goldstone pillars, the gems mounted on swords and rings. But none of them could look at me. I preferred it that way. If no one looked too closely, no one would realize my plan.

"Out," I rasped, nothing more than a hoarse whisper.

In the next breath, I was alone.

Just like always.

7
VEYKA

Out. Out. Out.

The word drummed an unbearable demand with every beat of my heart.

I had to get out.

To the balcony, where everyone could see but no one ever noticed. Through the secret panel.

Secret. Our secret. But not ours any longer. Not when there was only one alive to keep it.

My secret. But not my most dangerous one.

Down the staircase. Wait behind the door. Dash across the hall. Staircase. Staircase. Staircase. Down. Down. Down.

Into the bowels of the mountain. Into the depths whose secrets were now forgotten.

I could smell the freedom; taste the brightness of it on my tongue.

Five more steps. On my belly, cursing the layers of soft flesh slowing me down, slithering through the tunnel. Then air.

So much air. I gulped it down, greedy for every breath.

I rolled to my back, my skin trembling with exertion and need and pain. But the sky—the yawning pale blue void the same color as my eyes—as Arthur's eyes.

There were indeed birds circling above.

8
ARRAN

We were two weeks past the Spit, the human dead in the Shadow Wood long forgotten. Guinevere had given up her sulking when we reached the base of the mountains. On the other side waited Baylaur, the Queen of the Elemental Fae, and my future.

Gwen had remained in her dark lion form, scouting ahead on the ground while the winged shifters among us took turns in the sky. The delegation was forty terrestrial fae strong, but less than half were fauna-gifted. The flora-gifted had been nearly stripped of their powers as we crossed the Barren Dunes, with not a stem of plant life to draw upon.

But now, on the other side of the Blasted Pass, I could see the signs of their powers strengthening. The patch of dry grass where Osheen rested was now a lush green. A trail of daisies followed the young one, Maisri, who'd been sent to tend to the cooking and washing.

Gwen's shift was silent, but the subtle backward steps of those on the other side of the fire told me easily enough who approached.

I snapped a stick in half, staring into the fire. "Report."

I felt her shrug as she folded herself lithely onto the rock beside me.

"The same as the airborne scouts, I expect," she said, pulling a hare from behind her to hand over to the daisy fae.

"Have you heard their reports?" I asked pointedly. As I spoke, the two splintered ends of the stick fused back together.

I snapped it again.

"There is nothing out there," she groused. "That is what they will say as well."

"On the contrary—these mountains are filled with any number of fanged beasts that would like to make a meal of us." The stick regrew.

Snap.

We'd all sensed them, lurking beyond the perimeter of our camp each night. So far, none had tried to test our defenses. But with each passing day, that feral creature within me strained, hoping one would just so I could rip it to shreds.

Regrow. Snap.

"The only fanged beast I am concerned about is you," Gwen said. I felt the heat of her gaze upon me.

When I flicked my eyes up from the fire, the gold orbs were solid. No ring of glowing desire. A small mercy, that.

"How long has it been?" She was the only one in all of Annwyn who would have dared to ask.

"Too long."

Regrow. Snap.

She uncurled to her feet, that feline grace never truly leaving her. Planting a hand on each hip, she surveyed the camp.

"Go now—"

"No. We are just through the Blasted Pass." I'd anticipated this argument. By the wide berth the rest of our party was now giving us, I was not the only one.

"The elementals are going to eat you alive," Gwen scoffed humorlessly.

"Your input is not appreciated," I said. Though I knew she was right. If I did not get a handle on this tension, the court would see it as a weakness to prey upon. In a court famed for its subtle intrigues, a volatile temper was not an asset.

How had Uther Pendragon managed so well? I'd only set eyes upon the former High King twice before his death. I'd been a small child when he'd been sent to the Offering to wed his own elemental queen.

The second time had been at the once-a-century summit held on either side of the Spit. Another legacy bequeathed to us by the Ancestors seven thousand years before, when they'd written these bargains in blood to bring peace between the warring fae kingdoms of Annwyn.

Both times, he'd been a golden-haired enigma. A terrestrial, yes, but the High King of Annwyn. No longer tasked just with upholding the traditions of one half of the kingdom, but the peace and tranquility of the whole.

That first time, when I was very young, I had imagined what it would be like to be high king. Before I was captured, before I became the Brutal Prince. Later, those imaginings had ceased to matter. A female heir was needed from the terrestrial fae to seal the treaty.

Until the golden king's son had been murdered.

The life I'd built for myself had not been pretty. Bloodshed rarely was. But, as commander of the terrestrial armies, at least my magical gifts had been put to good use. I'd earned the title of Brutal Prince with every throat I ripped out and opponent I tortured over the course of three hundred years. I had a hard time imagining my brutal methods of maiming and killing would be as well used in the goldstone palace.

I shook my head, tossing the two halves of the stick into the fire.

None of this mattered. It was in the past. The future was what I needed to concern myself with.

My duty was to Annwyn, as it always had been. No matter what it cost me.

So, I'd sit on a throne and join with a mysterious queen and I wouldn't be needled by a lion shifter.

"The elemental court—*my* court—will learn to mind its place or pay the price in blood."

Gwen's gold eyes looked away. If she had been offered in my place, Annwyn might have faced a different sort of future.

"You intend to live up to your moniker, Brutal Prince?" she asked, eyes fixed on the flames now.

"A gentle king will not survive on the throne of Annwyn," I said, knowing the words would pain her but letting them pass my lips anyway.

Her shoulders shook, either from a suppressed sob or a mirthless laugh. "Let us hope our new queen is sturdier than her brother," Gwen said, bitterness lacing every syllable.

I left her then, knowing she would keep the watch.

Because even though I had heartily protested, I knew she was right. If I didn't shift soon, the need to let my beast run free would consume me. I had to be in control when we stepped into the legendary goldstone palace, or it could mean not just my own destruction, but that of the kingdom I'd sworn my miserable life to protect.

9
ARRAN

The wind howled in my ears, their fae keenness even sharper in this form. With each bound of my powerful legs, I cleared several yards of the mountains, outpacing even the flying fae scouting above.

I was the fastest. I was meant for this. This was my true form.

None of the foul beasts of the mountains dared to approach. I caught their scent, my wild heart surging after them. But the remnants of my mind, the little control I had, kept me on pace. I needed to see it, then I would go back.

I trusted Gwen to keep the delegation safe. She was the only one—the only fae I'd met who came anywhere close to being my equal. Though that, too, was a fallacy. Even now, in this brutal beast form, I could feel the trees and bushes bending to my will, curving out of the way of my huge leaping strides.

No one was this powerful. No one else carried this curse.

The trees were thinning. I'd dodged the aerial scouts, bending the canopy high above to hide my movements. None needed to know that I was not at camp. A traitor could lie even within the midst of the trusted fae who'd been assigned to my delegation. For all they knew, I was asleep in my tent, Gwen sitting on a log outside to keep guard, as usual.

But the trees would not shield me much further.

In the next breath, I shifted, landing on my two feet with the same ease that I ran on four.

It must have happened in the second that I shifted. That mere second that I was vulnerable to the world around me, caught in between. That was when she appeared.

In that second, I'd lost my advantage. Any advantage beyond my superior power and magic. At least I'd had time to shift. From the frown on her face, rather than terror, she had not seen the beast.

There was a chance, if she hadn't seen my animal form, she did not know who I was.

Her brows knitted together, a furrowed line of silvery white that I'd only seen on the oldest among us. Yet the woman before me was young. Impossible to tell her exact age, long-lived as the fae were. But her coloring was unusual—pale porcelain skin, silver white hair in a mussed braid hanging off her shoulder, and eyes so blue—

"You should not be here."

Her voice was sharp as a blade. Not the cool, soft thing I expected from her wraith-like coloring.

"Nor should you," I countered, my hand going to the handle of the axe sheathed at my side. I couldn't murder an elemental in the woods, a stone's throw from the goldstone palace.

I'd done more killing for less, a voice whispered.

Her brow softened, revealing more of those eyes. Mesmerizing, the same color as the waters around Eilean Gayl. Beautiful, but not a hint of glowing cerulean ringing the irises. I hoped my own were similarly unchanged.

But, as I looked her over more closely for any clue as to her identity, any advantage, I was less certain. Her gown hung on her as if by magic. Maybe it was, though it would be a wasteful expenditure. But she was elemental; perhaps they had no care for such costs. Besides, a body like that was a weapon all its own.

She took a step to the side, circling the edge of the clearing. I mirrored her, maintaining the distance between us.

With each movement, the translucent folds of her pewter gown shifted, revealing the generous curve of a hip or toned calf. I could easily imagine them wrapped around me. I tightened my hold on my mind, willing my eyes not to give me away. Sex was transactional at best. But with only hours separating me from the elemental queen, such a transaction was unwise.

I would not risk angering my betrothed before I even met her.

But the female before me, her breasts swaying with each measured step, had clearly been sent by the Ancestors to test me. Maybe after the Joining, when an heir had been produced and peace secured in Annwyn, the queen and I would have the freedom for our own dalliances.

The inhale of her chest drew my eyes up a second before she spoke. "Are all of your kind so rude?"

Not amenable to my interest then.

"Only when threatened," I said, wondering what I might learn from her response.

Her tongue slid slowly over her bottom lip. She was pleased to think me threatened by her. There were two blades sheathed on either side of her wide hips. I'd assumed them decorative, given the bejeweled scabbards glittering with amorite. But from the casual way one of her hands landed on her hip, making a show of toying with the bare skin above her navel, moving into a better position for curling around a hilt, I realized I'd assumed wrong.

"You are a long way from your delegation, terrestrial," she said, scraping an idle fingernail over one rounded hilt.

"How do you know where my delegation is?" We'd seen no sign of elemental scouts.

But more powerful elementals could carry away sounds and scents on the wind, masking their presence. I was already calculating how to reorganize my guards when she spoke again.

"The fowl in the sky are circling. Unusual for this time of year. Unless they aren't birds at all," she said, followed by another idle motion, this time a shrug.

She was very good at maintaining a ruse of casualness, as if she was not at all concerned by the information she gleaned or divulged. But I ought to expect no less and assume more from every elemental I met. Already, a headache was forming at the base of my skull at the prospect.

It would be easier to live up to my name than to play these games. My hand curled around the axe handle at the prospect.

She'd vex me no more if her head was separated from her body.

"I am scouting ahead. Our leader wishes to know how long before we reach Baylaur," I said.

Still, she showed no fear. Her long fingers were unapologetically curled around the hilt of one dagger. Apparently, she thought that would be enough to fell me. How easy it would be, to cut my way through this treacherous court, if they were all as pridefully presumptuous as this female.

Her bow shaped lips pursed, but she didn't pull her weapon from its scabbard. Amusement glinted in her eyes as she stepped to the side. Her fingers curled around a branch, pulling it with her to reveal what lay just beyond the clearing.

There it was.

The goldstone palace gleamed in the falling light, the towers transformed to a glittering burnt umber amidst the undulating sides of the Effren Valley.

"Aren't you going to remark upon its beauty?" she asked. The hollowness in her voice drew my eyes away from the glittering palace and back to the cipher before me.

A beautiful female, but all fae were. Comfortable with weapons, though scantily armed and dressed like a courtier rather than a guard. Aggressive about my presence, but there was derision in her voice when she spoke of her home.

I cocked my head to the side, strands of dark hair falling across my vision. But I didn't flinch to brush them away. "Who are you?"

She dropped the branch, letting it snap into place. It streaked across her cheek, but she didn't move even as it left an angry red scratch over her pale skin.

"Nothing. No one. Pretend you never met me," she said,

backing away toward where I'd first spotted her. I could see no path, but this was not my territory.

"But I have met you." I relaxed my hand on my axe, trying to bring her to ease, suddenly desperate for a name.

She licked her lips. "Have you never told a lie? Never omitted something?"

"I cannot lie," I said simply.

She rolled her eyes in time with a gruff growl in her throat. "Ancestor's be damned, are all terrestrials so infuriating?"

I barked out a dark laugh. "Only an elemental would remark upon it."

Her face hardened. "You know nothing about me or my kind."

"A bold statement," I bit back. I knew enough. They called me the Brutal Prince, as if I was the only one with blood dripping from his hands.

"One of your precious truths," she said, voice nearly disembodied as she melted into the shadows of the scrubby trees.

In the distance, bells began to chime, their sound amplified beyond possibility. Elemental magic carrying the tune on the winds, where it would reach the terrestrial delegation waiting in the mountains. They knew we were close. The time to hide and plot had come to an end. The real game was about to begin.

The elemental female's eyes disappeared entirely from view, her creamy skin shrouded in wisps of black the last I saw of her.

"We never met," she said softly.

Then she vanished. Fast enough, it must have been magic.

What had it cost her?

Why was it worth the price?

10
VEYKA

If my coronation had been a farce, the Offering was destined to be something closer to disaster. The princess who'd been raised in near secrecy, revealing herself to a terrestrial scout—and a surly one at that.

Though from the tales that had been schooled into me from birth, it was a characteristic of the rival fae. My father was the only terrestrial fae I'd met until the delegation arrived six months ago to discuss my brother's Joining.

Neither my father nor his kin had impressed me. Not that I held any love in my heart for the elementals. The one person I'd ever allowed myself to love was dead. I would never again allow myself to make that mistake.

But I had made the mistake of lingering too long beyond the palace walls, drinking in the only freedom I had—that which I took for myself.

Careless.

My outburst would keep Gawayn and my handmaidens away from my chambers for a time, but not indefinitely. I was the queen —privacy unheard of and impractical.

The terrestrial delegation was close. My betrothed was probably already through the Blasted Pass, if scouts were venturing this near to the goldstone palace.

Not *that* close to the palace, an irritating voice inside my head that sounded decidedly like Parys reminded me.

I broke into a run.

The palace guards would be back by now, making their report to Gawayn. Then he would make his—to me. If I was not in my apartments, I'd be in a whole new realm of trouble. Gawayn had not discovered Arthur and I's secret passage. If he did, my most reliable route out of the palace would be eliminated. And another connection to Arthur, severed.

But that was only one of my current problems.

My thighs began to chafe in the heat. I hadn't thought to change into the billowing pants I usually favored when slipping out of the palace. I'd been much too desperate to escape. But I ignored the pain and the sweat pooling beneath my breasts.

Even if I reached my rooms in time, another problem remained —the terrestrial scout.

He hadn't recognized me. Little surprise. Until a year ago, I'd only been trotted out for the most formal state occasions— Samhain, Beltane, Yule. My own citizens hardly knew my face.

But when everyone descended on that throne room, that same one where my brother had been brutally murdered, my last traces of anonymity would be wiped away.

And that terrestrial fae now held one of my secrets. Not the most dangerous, but one of the most precious.

If he betrayed me to the Brutal Prince...

No. I would not allow it.

I would bribe him. If necessary, silence him in less tasteful ways. A missing tongue would regrow, but the pain would be a powerful message and reminder.

I could not expose any weakness or secret to my betrothed. I could not allow him power over me. The risk was too great.

Nothing could stand in the way of my revenge. Even the fate of Annwyn.

My slippered feet found new purchase, my honed muscles flexing and rising to the speed I demanded.

I hit the ground hard, knowing the red-orange dust would irrevocably stain my clothing. It did not matter. I was under, through the tunnel, grabbing the walls and pulling myself up to stand.

Up the stairs. Up, up, up. Nearly a thousand of them. But my body was strong, even if my heart was broken.

I hurled myself through the secret door, onto the balcony, no time to worry if there were onlookers on the nearby verandas wondering at my sudden appearance. Let them attribute it to my mysterious powers.

Gawayn's voice carried from the antechamber. Evander's too. My stomach recoiled at his presence, as always. But I didn't have time to dwell on my loathsome guard.

I willed my hurried steps to be silent. Across the bedroom, past the bed where Parys and I tried to fuck away our pain, and into the bathing room. A second later, naked, I dashed back to toss my ruined clothing into the ever-burning hearth. I did not wait to see if they caught flame. Lyrena's voice had joined the chorus; I was nearly out of time.

Only when I was fully submerged beneath the scalding water of my bath did I pull the bell to summon Charis, Carly, and Cyara.

A bath—that was what a normal female would do to relax.

But I hadn't been normal since the moment of my improbable conception.

11
VEYKA

"What do you mean, they are here?"

I must have water in my ears. I could not have heard him correctly.

"The terrestrial delegation has arrived," Gawayn repeated, staring at the ground rather than my naked body.

Not quite naked—I'd allowed Charis to drape a dressing robe over my shoulders before Cyara admitted Gawayn with a poorly masked glower. But the perfumed water of my bath still dripped from my body, turning the gossamer robe almost useless in hiding any of my curves. I didn't care, not about that.

"How can they have arrived so soon?" I demanded.

Surprise flickered briefly over Gawayn's face before he hid it, ever the consummate elemental soldier in utter control.

"I sent out my guards hours ago, Your Majesty," he said.

Ancestors above and below, I was going to damn myself through my inability to keep my tongue in check. He had sent them out nearly two hours before, with my permission. Before I'd escaped into the woods and found the terrestrial scout. I'd assumed the delegation was still a day or two behind him, but clearly I was wrong.

If only I'd seen him before he shifted, I might have known how quickly he could travel.

But there was no way to know if the dark-haired, surly terrestrial fae was blessed with the flora or fauna gifts of his kind. Maybe he hadn't shifted at all.

"Of course," I said, turning away. I was showing too much—caring too much. That was why Gawayn was surprised. I hadn't cared enough about anything in the last six months to demand it from him or anyone else.

But the possessiveness in that male's eyes, dark and brooding...

Glowing. I had not missed the ring of black fire in his eyes as they raked over me. Elementals were famed for our ability to dissemble, but the cursed fae eyes spanned both our kingdoms. Desire was the one thing that could not be hidden.

"Your Majesty, would you like to receive the messenger yourself?" Gawayn asked. I didn't need to hear the tone of his voice to know he was relieved he no longer had to avoid looking at my barely covered breasts.

"Of course not," I shot back, too quickly. I forced a deep breath in. "It would be inappropriate for the queen to receive a mere messenger. Esa can do it."

Lyrena snickered from the doorway, where she and Evander were standing as silent sentinels. Not so silent, in Lyrena's case.

Esa would take it as a slight; anyone might receive a messenger. As the *donna* of the Royal Council, she was supposed to be *someone*. But I did not care enough about Esa or any of the rest of them to orchestrate such a thing. She imagined herself in charge of the Kingdom of the Elemental Fae? She could deal with the delegation's early arrival.

I had other concerns—primarily, what I would use to bribe or threaten the terrestrial male who had seen me in the mountains. His price would not come cheap, I could tell that from our brief minutes spent together. The way his fingers had curled around his battle axe... taking his tongue would not be as easy as I hoped, either. He'd put up a fight, cause a scene.

I would need to be more cunning—more elemental—to silence him.

"Very well, Your Majesty. We will deliver your edict." Gawayn jerked his head in Evander's direction.

The latter did not bother to hide his grumble as he opened the door and stalked out, little more than an errand boy. That suited me fine. I would never understand what my brother had seen in Evander, to approve his appointment to the Goldstone Guards. The less time that I had to spend in his presence, the better.

A chill swept in from the open veranda doors, sending a shiver down my spine.

Carly moved at once to close them, but I forestalled her. "No. Leave it."

I couldn't tell her that when the veranda doors closed, it was like I was being trapped inside the water gardens once again. I could not tell any of them that since Arthur's death, even walking through the inner halls of the goldstone palace, the ones that were entirely closed in, was a trial.

Gawayn cleared his throat. "The Dowager has also sent word."

The blood in my veins turned to ice, no chill breeze required.

If Gawayn had any notion of the pain, if Arthur had ever confided in him, he did not let it show. "She wishes an audience with you."

"No."

Gawayn did not argue. It was not his place. But from the way Cyara tilted her head, avoiding my eyes, I knew some silent conversation was passing between them. They were supposed to hate one another, not pass silent messages about my well-being, as if they knew better.

"Your Majesty, perhaps it would be best to entertain her now, in private, before the terrestrial delegation arrives," Cyara said, holding out a goblet of wine I hadn't seen before.

She did not possess conjuring magic. Later I would wonder where she'd gotten the wine from. But in that moment, I saw fire and ice and stars and the very pits of damnation.

"No."

Cyara bit her lower lip.

"The Dowager can make a fool of herself before the terrestrial delegation if she so desires," I said, venom dripping from every word. I might have been startled by my own show of emotion, were it not for the burning in my chest that made it impossible for any thoughts at all. "She no longer holds any power in this court or this kingdom. Nor in all of Annwyn."

That calmed me when nothing else did. My mother held no power over me, not any longer. I was the Queen of the Elemental Fae. She had been stripped of all powers other than those gifted to her by her heritage. Not unsubstantial, but no threat to me. Especially with Gawayn and his Goldstones guarding every breath I took.

"As you wish," Gawayn said, bowing.

"Take that message to her," I heard myself say.

Gawayn froze in a half-bow. "Your Majesty?"

"Go to the Dowager and repeat my words to her." It was cruel. But if I was capable of such cruelty, my mother was the one who'd shaped me into such a creature.

I hated her.

The moment that my Joining was sealed, my betrothed's blood mingling with my own, I would be the High Queen of all Annwyn. And then I would banish my mother straight to hell.

12
ARRAN

I was ready.

Shifting had softened the rage, the hunger of the beast prowling just beneath the surface. Even if the female at the edge of the forest had gnawed open something else inside of me.

There was no more use waiting. As soon as I arrived back in camp, I sent Gwen ahead to the goldstone palace to announce our arrival. She'd grinned, taken her fierce feline form, and disappeared into the twilight.

The rest of the delegation sprang into action, packing up the tents and dousing fires. They did not question. Just as they had watched me behead the humans on the other side of the Spit, they followed my edict without hesitation. Even if my brutality had never been inflicted upon any of them, the whispers were enough to motivate even the weaker fae among us.

Moving with all the speed our fae heritage promised, we were at the edge of the city, the gates of goldstone palace visible across the strip of falsely calm sand, before full dark had descended upon the Effren Valley.

Gwen stood at the edge of the strip, a feline smirk upon her face. I did not ask how she'd crossed the notoriously dangerous expanse of sand, the home of the Gremog.

"Will we be received?"

"Tomorrow," she said, flicking her dark braids over her shoulder.

I'd expected as much. No one allowed their foe into the keep under the cover of darkness, even when they'd been invited.

"We camp here," I said, loud enough to reach all the fae ears in the delegation.

My eyes flicked upward. Was the female from the forest on one of the verandas above, watching us? It was too far away to make out any individuals. But somehow, I felt that if she was watching, I would know it.

But there was no burning in my gut. Only that cold flame where my heart was meant to be, fueling every decision I made—to keep the flame going, to keep the Kingdom of the Terrestrial Fae safe. Now, all of Annwyn.

If any of the delegation questioned my choice of location, so close to the realm of the legendary Gremog, none of them voiced it. They wouldn't even dare to whisper those thoughts in the confines of their tents.

I was the Brutal Prince.

I'd faced horrors much worse than whatever lurked in the sand, guarding the goldstone palace. It was best that the elementals knew exactly who was about to become their king.

❦

The lines formed before the sun was fully in the sky. Arranged exactly as I'd drilled them during the long journey through the Shadow Wood, across the Spit, and into the lifeless hills of the Barren Dunes. I'd had three centuries to hone my skills as a battle commander, trying out various formations of flora and fauna gifted fae until I knew precisely how to balance them.

I could not have explained it to anyone. But as my eyes scanned up and down the neat columns and rows, reviewing each individual's gifts and relative strengths, a sense of calm settled over me.

Osheen was the strongest flora gifted aside from myself, able to drag life from the most bedraggled plant and grow it into something powerful. He would guard the rear. In front of him, another flora gifted female with much weaker magic but unparalleled sword skills. To her right, a hawk shifter who could also control other birds, if only briefly. On and on it went.

There was no explicable method to it, other than the animal instincts that roared beneath my skin. I knew that if I led this unit into battle, they would fight valiantly and defeat almost any foe.

Would they fare as well in the throne rooms and gilded halls of the elemental fae? That remained to be seen. We were about to wage a battle unlike any we'd ever fought.

We stood in formation, ready to meet our new foe.

And we stood.

And we stood.

For three hours, as the sun rose above our heads and the sweat began to drip down our backs, every terrestrial fae stood in perfect form.

Not a single one of them protested. I'd instructed everyone to dress as lightly as possible. A tall order, given the proclivity for woolen knits and layered linen. This was not the Shadow Wood, with its shaded glens and icy burns. Everything about the Kingdom of the Elemental Fae was hostile—we'd learned that the moment we stepped clear of the Spit. It appeared our welcome would be no better.

In the third hour, I began to contemplate who I would punish.

Not for me. I would stand in the heat indefinitely, the least of the tortures I'd endured in a cursed immortal life. But for my companions...

Peace, I schooled myself. Anger must be exchanged for reason. I was not the war commander I'd been before. I was to be king of this wretched place. Peace mattered above all else. So I would limit the number of heads that went rolling across the goldstone floor from the swing of my axe. But I would not spare them entirely.

The smirking Goldstone Guard who appeared on the other side of the desert expanse was a fitting candidate. His cropped dark hair lifted with an eerie wind, the gilded goldstone clasps at his shoulders, elbows, hips, and knees gleaming beneath the sun.

Behind me, one of the females in the delegation sucked in a breath.

It was beginning already—the deception. They'd sent this pretty young warrior out to distract us.

If only I could peer into the minds of my companions, warning them not to fall for these antics... but that power had been lost long ago, at the same time as the void power.

"What are your orders?" Gwen said from beside me, eyes trained on the elemental warrior. "He's a Goldstone Guard."

"I expected your tone to be less reverent, considering how spectacularly they failed to protect your betrothed."

Guinevere's face hardened instantly, her posture shifting subtly. Every weakness she had, crated up and contained, already a master of the control required by the elemental court. She would have made an excellent queen.

Instead, they had me.

I stepped out in front of the unit, perilously close to the territory of the Gremog.

"I am Arran Earthborn," I said, my voice loud and clear.

True to his elemental heritage, the guard's face did not shift at my declaration. But a second later, the breeze that had lifted his dark hair found my own, brushing across my cheek and pulling the long strands loose from the knot at the back of my neck.

Bastard.

The wind increased into a gale. Around me, I could hear the subtle shifting of my companions as they steadied themselves. I would not turn my back, even as my eyes began to burn. If they kept this torture up, I'd give the order to shift. Let's see how that elemental poise faltered when confronted with the true beasts of our race.

But then the wind stopped, whispering away into a breeze and then nothing. The sand was gone, pushed up onto banks on either side of a narrow goldstone path, laid into the very ground itself.

The elemental inclined his head.

Our way across.

"Don't step off the goldstone," I commanded as I took the first step. Hardly wider than my two booted feet beside one another, I knew what it would mean to deviate from the path—death.

One step into that sand, and your foot would be ripped clean off, lunch for the Gremog. If you were lucky. Unlucky, and you'd be pulled down into the sand, either to be suffocated as those red-gold granules filled your lungs, or to bleed to death while the Gremog ate through you limb by limb.

Only on the goldstone path, so long as we did not disturb the sand and alert the Gremog to our presence, would we be safe. A brutal but efficient line of defense for the goldstone palace, the warrior in me recognized. But not how I'd have my delegation begin their sojourn in Baylaur.

When the last of our delegation had cleared the sand, the breeze returned. I did not turn to see the sand sweeping back into place. But I did hear the soft, preternatural rumbling as we mounted the stairs of the goldstone palace.

There, beneath the arched pillars gilded with more gems than I'd ever seen in one place, stood a tall female dressed in shimmering blue so light, it almost appeared white. Her dark hair fell in an intricate plait over her shoulder to her waist, sapphires and blue tanzanite woven into the thick strands. She was nearly as tall as I, with all the bearing of a queen.

But a queen she was not.

Greeted not by the Queen of the Elemental Fae, but a proxy.

That fire within my chest crackled in protest.

What sort of queen would not meet us herself?

"Welcome to the Court of the Elemental Fae, Arran Earthborn.

I am Esa Lyonesse," she said, though she did not bow. To her kind, our appointed titles meant nothing. For an elemental, blood and lineage were everything.

But I didn't care what the ancestors who bore her surname had done in this court.

I waited until I felt Osheen and Gwen at either shoulder before I demanded— "Where is the queen?"

Her serene demeanor did not falter. "You shall meet Her Majesty at the Offering."

"What elemental maneuvering is this?" I snarled.

"It is tradition." She kept her head held high. A smidgen of respect took form inside of me.

"Your traditions, not mine." I drew my axe free from the holster at my waist.

Still, her deep blue eyes were unmoved. "Are they not one and the same now, Your Highness?"

From my left, I heard a snicker. Nearly imperceptible. But I was the most powerful fae born in millennia.

With an effortless swipe of my axe, I relieved the dark-haired, smirking Goldstone who'd cleared the sand of his right arm.

I fixed my glare on the female, not bothering to wipe the blood from my blade before returning it to its sheath. "Not yet."

13

VEYKA

A slow, subtle pressure across my stomach roused me from a dreamless sleep to greet the morning. I thanked the Ancestors for every night that I did not dream of the horrors of my past. The water gardens, Arthur's death...

But it was not morning, I realized as my eyes cracked open. The sunshine that spilled across the balcony and into my bedroom was the bright gold of midday. Before I could lurch upright, that insistent pressure increased.

I was not alone. Parys' hand slipped down over my belly, past my navel, tangling in the hair above my cunt.

The nightmares I hadn't had in sleep danced at the edges of my waking consciousness. I arched my hips, urging Parys' fingers lower, hoping as always that the sensation would drive away the other thoughts that tried to crowd into my tired mind.

He obliged, slipping one finger inside of me while his thumb massaged over my clit.

His thumb drove a strong, steady rhythm. We'd been doing this for months, chasing away our demons. By now, we knew how to bring one another to the thoughtless oblivion of climax.

I reached across the bed, letting my eyes skate over his golden form. Parys was lithe and strong, always in motion. Just like his wind magic. Even now, his cock was hard, pressed against my hip, subtly shifting in time with his finger inside of me.

I reached for it just as a cool breeze flicked up to tease my nipples to tautness.

Sweat beaded on my brow as I pumped him once, twice.

I pulled my hand away long enough to coat it with my own saliva before sliding it down again, the moisture making my motions slick and smooth. Again and again, I moved my hand up and down his shaft, that repetitive motion that I knew would bring him release. A squeeze at the base, a long stroke up, then a subtle twist as my tight fist reached down to bump against his throbbing balls.

He made that sound, low in his throat, that he always made when he was getting close.

I paused, waiting for my own release to rise within me. This wasn't lovemaking, this was a transaction. Climax for climax, one escape to oblivion traded for another.

Parys did not disappoint me. He slid two fingers inside, abandoning my clit and increasing the speed as he fucked me with his hand. My hips rose to meet him, my hand resuming its motion on his shaft.

The pressure in my navel built, my release edging closer and closer. Parys cried out, rolling to the side and taking himself in his other hand, careful to avoid spending himself on me. His queen.

In the next second, my own climax flooded over me, my pussy clenching tight and forcing Parys' hand out. But unlike my companion, no sound fell from my lips.

We lay there in silence.

I tried to close my eyes, willing the oblivion of climax to put me to sleep, where I could hide from my reality for a few hours more. But I'd already slept an entire night and half a day. While my mind might protest, my body was ready to rise.

Beside me, Parys' breathing evened out. I knew without looking over that he'd dozed off. *Bastard.*

I also knew that if I looked over to the other side of the bed, there would be an empty gilded chalice, drained of the sleep-inducing tea that Parys had poured down his throat day after day since Arthur's death.

My brother's best friend had been more than half in love with his king, though I doubted Arthur had realized it. He'd probably taken the desire glowing in Parys' eyes at face value. Everyone adored Arthur. I wondered how often Parys, Arthur, and Lyrena had all shared a bed. A beautiful, golden trio—now fractured into nothing but broken pieces.

At least Lyrena seemed to be managing. Her role as one of my Goldstones gave her something to focus on beyond her lost lover. Meanwhile, Parys and I were adrift, clinging to each other in a sea of darkness.

But this too would end. Parys was right—the Brutal Prince was near. Some instinct in my gut told me that my betrothed would not take kindly to another male sharing my bed.

I was not in love with Parys. But I would certainly miss his companionship and the mindless escape he offered.

Staring up at the ceiling, I traced the outlines of the golden arches with my eyes. The goldstone was painted in shades of twilight. Pale blues danced with streaks of amethyst and burnt orange, swirling and glittering. It was beautiful. But I wished I could see the sky, rather than a painted facsimile of it.

Only when I was free of the goldstone palace, underneath the scorching hot skies of Annwyn, did I truly feel safe.

Safety, I reminded myself ruefully, was not the objective.

Quite the contrary. I would willingly sacrifice my own safety if it meant bringing Arthur's killers to justice.

My one official edict as Queen of the Elemental Fae, before formally surrendering control of my kingdom to the Royal Council, had been to order the execution of the humans who'd beheaded my brother. They'd been easy to find—as if they hadn't thought of how they would escape the goldstone palace after their deed was accomplished.

The human deaths had satisfied my court.

But instead of walking to the dais and assuming my brother's throne, I'd written a missive to the Royal Council, claiming my heart too broken to rule. Esa and her peers had been only too happy to take control, albeit short-lived.

Once the Brutal Prince was announced as the terrestrial heir, there was no doubt the council's reign would be brief.

The Brutal Prince.

My betrothed.

The monster of bedtime stories the elemental fae told their children to frighten them into compliance.

Lucky me.

My sharp, pointed ears heard the footsteps, recognizing them moving in triplicate, a few seconds before the knock rang out.

I could hide no longer, it would seem.

Swinging my feet to the perpetually warm goldstone floor, I reached for the dressing gown I'd abandoned sometime the night before.

"Come," I called, raising my voice even though it was unnecessary. My handmaidens' fae ears could hear my movements as well as I could theirs.

By the time the three of them glided in, led by Charis, I'd managed to fasten the clasp at the front of my deep turquoise silk dressing gown. Nestled just above my belly button, the emerald clasp held together the cool silk as it cascaded down my body. Layers and layers of it. So much silk it would have swallowed a smaller female. But over my curved form, with my blue eyes sparkling, I knew it was striking. Such things mattered to most elementals. I could play along—for now.

"Your Majesty," the three sisters said in unison, sinking into identical curtsies.

I rolled my eyes. Cyara rewarded me with a look of reprove.

"If you are going to insist upon tending to yourself in the evenings, then you must actually do something with your hair rather than letting it become a tangled mess," Cyara said, eyeing my ruined braid. "Your Majesty," she added as an afterthought.

She was not incorrect. The intricate plait, this one made by twisting several smaller braids together and interlacing them, was nothing more than a bedraggled shadow of the fine work Carly had wrought the evening before.

Cyara snapped her fingers. Carly and Charis both jumped, their delicate white feathered wings twitching in surprise.

"Charis, make the tea. Carly, fetch a comb," she ordered.

"I will make the tea," I said quickly, walking to the ornate circular table nestled in the corner.

Cyara did not argue, though I guessed that if I turned around, I would see her eyes rolling toward the painted ceiling as mine had moments before. I couldn't just sit and stare at myself while they meddled with my hair. If I made the tea, at least my hands would be busy.

And if I was turned away, no one would be able to see my face when Cyara worked up the nerve to read the missive she was holding in her hand.

"Very well," Cyara said. "Charis, can you see about tossing Master Parys from the bed? I'd like to change the sheets sometime today."

"I'm up!" Parys shot to his feet, sheets entirely forgotten, not a shred of clothing on him. Nor a shred of embarrassment either, even though Charis and Carly began twittering immediately.

I'd often wondered if there had been a bird shifter in their family bloodline, on account of the wings. The way they giggled and tittered only made me more curious.

"Master Parys," Cyara sighed heavily.

"Just Parys," he said. He managed to pull a tunic over his head, the long-cut style finally covering his male bits.

"Charis, go fetch lunch for Her Majesty and... Parys," Cyara ordered.

There was a bit more squabbling, but I gave them all my back, reaching for the mortar and pestle.

I tipped open one little pot, its lid encrusted with a pattern of blue and white gems to look like crashing waves. I pinched a few leaves into the well of the mortar as Carly appeared at my back. She tugged gently on my braid. In answer, I shrugged it back over my shoulder so she could begin untangling.

"Esa has sent word," Cyara said from behind us. She paused, waiting for a directive from me.

Instead, I added several whole leaves from a solid gold pot to my tea mixture.

"Your Eternal and Royal Majesty," Cyara began to read, her voice a passable imitation of Esa's formality. "The Heir of the Terrestrial Fae has arrived in Baylaur. In accordance with your wishes, I have received His Highness and welcomed the terrestrial delegation to the goldstone palace."

"Esa doesn't care about anyone's wishes but her own," Parys grumbled from somewhere in the vicinity of the veranda.

I selected a tiny purple flower, its petals shriveled to nearly brown, sprinkling in two pinches. I reached for a third. Carly tugged sharply at a knot in my hair.

Coincidence?

Perhaps not.

It didn't matter. Two pinches were sufficient for my purposes.

"Since His Highness is now in residence..." Cyara's voice faltered. I began grinding the herbs mercilessly.

"Since His Highness is now in residence, the Offering has been set for tomorrow evening at sunset," Cyara read, no quaver in her voice this time.

"Tomorrow? That cannot be." Parys' steps echoed across the goldstone floor. The swish of paper told me that either Cyara had handed over the missive or he'd ripped it from her hand.

My head handmaiden exhaled sharply. The latter, then.

"It's hardly enough time to confer with the priestesses," Carly commented, her warm breath skittering over my shoulder. All three sisters were always warm.

Did those wings turn to flames when they took to the sky?

The blend of flowers and herbs in the mortar was breaking down, the scents tickling my nostrils with promise.

Carly's hands did not tighten in my hair. If she recognized the scents, she gave no indication.

Cyara sighed. "The priestesses can be persuaded—"

"Have you heard?" Lyrena's laughter filled the room, mingling with the heavy footfalls of her fellow Goldstones. I glanced over my shoulder to note—Lyrena, Gawayn, Evander.

I wrinkled my nose and turned away. Lyrena and Gawayn I could tolerate. But could and would were different matters just now.

I lifted the mortar to my nose, sniffing again. Something was missing. I cast a hand over the sea of intricate pots, looking for just the right complement to what I'd already assembled.

My hand passed over the herbs that I brewed into a contraceptive tea each evening in favor of the chocolate powder Cyara sourced especially for me, a brew usually found only in the terrestrial territory.

It had no medicinal properties, but it would make the concoction palatable.

"Gawayn," Cyara bit out. "Are you not Captain of Her Majesty's Goldstone Guards?"

All three sets of footsteps halted.

"Yes."

"Then why did you sanction such unceremonious and indecorous behavior in my Queen's bedchamber?" I couldn't see Cyara's wings twitching, but I could certainly imagine it.

"We bear urgent news for Her Majesty," Gawayn said gruffly.

"Normally you at least manage to knock before barging in—"

"It's the Offering," Lyrena interrupted, earning irritated exhalations from both. But her footsteps were towards the corner. Towards me.

"It has been set for tomorrow," she finished softly.

"So we have heard." Parys sank back down onto the bed, the rushes inside the mattress shifting under his weight.

"Why the haste?" Cyara wondered aloud, closer to me now.

A sudden burst of heat, and the flame beneath the teapot leapt to life. From the corner of my eye, I watched Cyara rub at her wrists. The aches she always felt there... most likely the cost of her magic. And yet, she never hesitated to expend it in my service.

I pushed back the guilt and ground harder.

Carly pulled her fingers from my hair, her work done, as I added the tea mixture to steep.

"Esa must be insisting," Parys said.

"But why would she? The longer the Joining is delayed, the longer the Royal Council can hold on to power." Cyara wandered back toward the center of the room. A bit of pressure in my chest eased.

"The Brutal Prince did not appreciate being made to wait outside the goldstone palace overnight. She is attempting to appease him," Gawayn offered, his voice tight. Cyara must be standing close by. They were always ill at ease with one another.

Parys laughed, acid coating each syllable. "He's the Brutal Prince. He is not famed for his patience."

I knew what they were doing. These conversations should have been conducted in whispers, or not at all. None of them were courtiers—except Parys. But I'd always thought his noble birth the least interesting thing about him.

They were trying to engage me. Trying to make me care.

But they—my handmaidens, my guards, the nearest things I had to friends—they ought to have known better than anyone that I was far past being interested in petty court posturing.

"Nor his mercy," Gawayn added.

Lyrena began giggling again.

"It is hardly a laughing matter," Cyara chided. As she spoke, a frigid wind swept through the room, threatening to smother the flame that heated my tea.

I moved instinctively to protect it with my wide body.

"On the contrary," Lyrena snickered. "I will be using this morning's scene to lift my spirits for years to come."

Another icy blast. Then a wave of heated flame and a very unattractive grunt—from Evander.

"What happened?" Cyara asked, her voice carefully neutral.

Gawayn answered before Lyrena could. "He seemed to think Evander did not need his sword arm."

I turned quickly from my hiding spot in the corner, disbelief choking the scoff from my throat.

Evander stood at the door, his short-cropped dark hair disheveled but otherwise the rest of his armor and clothing in place. Except for his arm. His arm was missing, taken from just above the elbow.

My surliest Goldstone Guard glared as all eyes in the room turned to him.

"I granted the terrestrial delegation safe passage across the Gremog's territory. It is nothing more than the cost of the magic expended," Evander sneered.

I could almost see myself liking the Brutal Prince—if I had the capacity to like anyone anymore. If there was anyone who I'd enjoy watching suffer, knowing that though the arm would regrow, it would be brutally painful... yes, Evander was on my list.

The rest of the room continued to stare in awkward silence. I turned back to my tea. It was done steeping now. With steady hands, I poured the steaming concoction and walked back to the bed. Charis would be back soon with food.

"I cannot wait to see what the price is of this," Parys said drolly, flopping back onto the bed.

Whether he meant the gossiping, his presence in my bed, or something else, I did not contemplate. I was too focused on the tea. It burnt my tongue and the roof of my mouth. The glands at the back of my throat protested. But I was fae. The small hurts eased almost instantly, fast enough that when I took another gulp the liquid burned new tissue.

I could have drunk it either way, healed wounds or not. I'd suffered much worse pains than hot tea.

Make it stop.

The searing tea, at least, was a temporary pain. It would stop once I'd finished the cup in my hand. One cup was more than enough.

"We would all do well to remember that the Brutal Prince is not just the terrestrial heir, but our future king and Her Majesty's future—"

"I serve the Queen—"

"—do not be obstinate—"

Gulp. Gulp.

"Should I ask Her Majesty to brew you some special tea, Evander?"

"—I wouldn't accept—"

Make it stop.

The white porcelain at the bottom of the teacup stared up at me.

Already, my limbs were becoming dangerously heavy.

I managed to set the teacup aside. If it clanked unnaturally loudly on the little table beside my bed, what did it matter? I would only be conscious for a few more seconds...

"Your Majesty?"

"What is wrong with her?"

"Veyka?"

"It's the Ancestor's damned tea."

Their voices slipped away into a pleasant hum as I lay down, tucking one hand between my head and the pillow.

Make it stop.

No one else would, so I did.

14

ARRAN

I was a very efficient killer.

The first had been messy. A bread knife thrust into the throat of a guard. I must have hit an artery, for his blood sprayed everywhere, coating my face. Sometimes, when I raised my battle axe all these centuries later, I could taste the blood of my first kill upon my tongue and smell it in my nostrils. I was eleven years old.

Now, I only tasted my victims' blood if I desired it. Or if I was in my beast form, ripping out their throats.

Perhaps it was the mess of that first kill which had led me to select the axe as my primary weapon. I was more than proficient with a sword, even better with a bow. But the axe... I could make it do things that terrified beings on this continent, this realm, and far beyond.

I could slash it at an angle, cleaving my opponent's head from their body. Or bring the blade downward and bury it in their chest —no finesse was required for such a kill, the blunt damage of the brutal weapon doing most of the work. Fighting close, I could feel the crunch of bones as they yielded to my blade, sense it as the lifeblood of one immortal warrior or another ebbed away to nothing.

But on those days when the killing made my stomach turn instead, I could throw it across a battlefield. I could inflict death on those too far away to even see me properly. I could choose to be the face of justice or its silent coconspirator.

Today, I was neither.

Today, I was a prince and a future king.

My growl of disgust was muffled by the knock on my door, in the same moment as the inlaid wooden handle slipped from my hand.

The thump of the axe nestling itself in wood was apparently all the invitation that Gwen needed to enter.

One look at her had me stomping across the room to retrieve it.

"I see you've finished dressing," she observed drolly. "Here I thought that I might offer you help with your vestments."

I growled.

She'd traded her usual gray wool vest and linen undershirt for much finer versions. The dress she wore was still wool, despite the heat, but the emerald green had been marbled with various other earthly shades to bring movement to the otherwise stiff garment. The hem fell to the floor, though wide slits were cut up the front and back—I presumed for air flow.

I'd never seen her in anything but trousers.

Against her skin she wore an underdress of a thin, slightly shimmering golden fabric that highlighted the warmth in her dark brown skin. She looked regal—like the queen she'd been meant to be. Except instead of a crown, she wore a simple gold braid circlet.

Gold and emerald. The colors of her dead betrothed.

King Arthur.

This was her Offering ensemble, I realized.

Hers, not mine.

This was what she would have worn when she walked across the goldstone throne room, kneeled before the priestesses, and pledged to fulfill the arrangement made by the Ancestors to preserve peace in Annwyn forevermore.

Beside her, I looked like exactly what I was—a rough warrior ill-suited to politics and ruling. I was built for killing. I'd known it since I was eleven years old.

The power that thrummed in my veins—both flora and fauna—had never been seen before. I could command the trees and grass, bend any plant within a hundred yards to my will. My vines were as lethal as my blade, choking the breath from an adversary or holding them in place until I could strike the death blow.

But I could also shift. When I did, it was not into the graceful lion that the female before me embodied even in her fae form. Mine was a beast of death.

Gwen waited until I'd launched my axe across the room once again. There was a lack of targets in the rooms I'd been assigned, and I'd already destroyed the frame of one historical painting. At least my aim was good enough that it was only the frame, rather than the art itself, that was in splinters.

"I brought you something," she said.

I said nothing, crossing the room to retrieve my axe.

"It is from your mother."

I paused with my fingers curled around the handle.

I had not seen my mother since before King Arthur's murder. Before the series of events that had set my life on this path. Nor had there been time for me to return north to Eilean Gayl before fulfilling my duty as the new Heir of the Terrestrial Fae.

During all that time, Gwen had been at Wolf Bay.

"How?" I said, shoving the axe roughly into the holster on my belt. I doubted I would ever feel comfortable walking the halls of the goldstone palace without it.

"She brought it to Wolf Bay."

My hearth clenched. Why hadn't she stayed? We must have only missed each other by days.

"She felt it was not wise to linger. I do not know if..." Gwen paused, choosing her words carefully. "I do not know if the rest of the court realized she was there. She appeared at my window late one night."

"As a hawk," I said, already knowing the answer.

She hadn't felt safe enough to formally visit the Court of the Terrestrial Fae, even with her son newly named as its heir. The longing in my gut turned to rage.

Gwen unwrapped the small parcel she'd been holding, no larger than her palm. I recognized it from the first glint of silver. My family crest. Not the entwined Tree of Life and Serpent of Wisdom that symbolized the Kingdom of the Terrestrial Fae, but the single rose rising from the ground.

Earthborn. What I was—what we all were. My mother's words echoed in my memory.

"Will you wear it?" Gwen asked quietly.

Her body was already half turned to the door when the sound of a thousand murmuring voices found my ears. We were out of time and we both knew it. The Offering was beginning.

"Get on with it," I said roughly.

I had only the time it would take for her to pin the crest to my own wool-covered chest to compose myself. There was no way in hell I would allow the elementals to see my misery.

15
VEYKA

My head was still pounding from the tea. Too much nightbloom flower and too few of the willowood leaves to ease the pain. But at least I'd been spared from the arguments and posturing in my own damned bedchamber.

I knew what they were about. They hoped that if they talked about court politics enough, if they discussed the matters in detail, I would eventually show some interest.

None of them realized that most of the time, I just wanted it all to stop.

All the noise, all the talking, all the Ancestors-damned attempts to draw me back to the world of the living. I hated all of it. And I hated them a little bit for not realizing that and leaving me be.

But this, I could not avoid.

The Offering.

For seven thousand years, since the original treaties were signed between the Elemental and Terrestrial kingdoms of the fae, each generation an Offering was made.

Each kingdom produced an heir, an offering of solidarity and peace in Annwyn.

For the elementals, the right was inherited. My mother, my

grandfather, my great-grandmother, back and back, an unbroken line of elemental fae since Nimue, the first elemental heir and one of the Ancestors.

Among the terrestrials, the honor was won. Through death and bloodshed, naturally.

But always, the Offering took place here, in the goldstone palace.

I had no idea how the Ancestors had determined it, and if rumors were true, the terrestrials resented that the High King and Queen always resided in Baylaur, rather than the terrestrial capital on Wolf Bay.

Nor did I really care about the why of it. I needed to be in Baylaur, in the goldstone palace, to seek revenge.

"Veyka?"

Cyara's gentle but firm voice cut me off as my thoughts turned bloodthirsty.

She never called me Veyka. Always 'Your Majesty.'

Her turquoise eyes met mine in the mirror. Carly had just finished with my hair, the silvery white woven with strands of gold and blue tanzanite to complement my eyes. Every female in the elemental court would be wearing her hair like this today. The more finery one could weave into the long braid, the better. A stupid, vapid status symbol.

I was tempted to shake out the whole thing and leave it loose just to be petulant, but Carly had dedicated more than an hour to it.

Cyara was still staring at me in the mirror.

"What?" I asked, lifting a hand to my temple.

She didn't bother to hide her amusement as I tried to massage away the side effects of my own actions.

"Councilor Roksana has sent a request on behalf of the Royal Council."

I sighed. "Esa thinks that if it comes from Roksana, I'm more likely to comply."

The grim line of Cyara's mouth confirmed as much.

I leaned forward on the dressing table, resting my elbows on the gleaming mirrored surface so I could massage both my temples at once. "What is it?"

Cyara cleared her throat delicately. "In keeping with tradition, the Royal Council requests that Her Royal and Powerful Majesty select a gown which reflects the customs of her court and the elemental Ancestors who have come before."

A laugh peeled from my throat, a humorless and cold sound. "You know what they really mean."

"Indeed," Cyara said.

She turned away for a moment, reappearing with a diaphanous white gown draped over her arm. I could see the scalloped edges of the hem, gilded with gold. Beautiful, angelic. A statement of purity, peace, and power.

As if our court, our entire kingdom, had not been torn to shreds just six months ago.

As if Arthur had never existed.

The Royal Council requested I wear white?

They could go right to hell.

I'd given them the power to rule my kingdom. They would not have another damn piece of me.

"No."

Cyara nodded. "I suspected as much."

Charis appeared over her shoulder and the white gown disappeared.

When Cyara turned back to me once again, she held an altogether different option.

My hands fell away from my temples. "Yes."

※

I turned away from the mirror when Cyara placed my mother's crown upon my head.

The Dowager would be in attendance at the Offering, there was no way to avoid that.

It doesn't belong to her.

It is the crown of our court. Of the elementals, worn by Nimue herself and every heir after.

But I didn't care about my court. All they'd ever done was cause me pain.

The same as my mother.

Arthur had worn this crown, my father's massive sword at his side, when he'd been crowned King of the Elemental Fae. At my own coronation, I'd managed to wear the thing as well. Though my memories of that event were foggy at best. Hastily executed in the days after my brother's murder, my coronation had been a farce—an opulent show by the elemental court that although their king was dead, all was well.

All was not well.

Not then, not now.

When I was crowned High Queen, I would have this crown melted down and scattered to the winds.

At least I didn't need to worry about what to do with my brother and father's sword. Excalibur had disappeared in the minutes after Arthur's death.

I had real worries, I reminded myself.

I would not look at the Dowager, not even a glance. She'd be positioned near the throne—my throne—but luckily, the ceremonial Offering would take place in the center of the room, so I would have my back to her for most of it.

My eyes would be scanning the terrestrial delegation. Not for the Brutal Prince—there would be no missing him, I was certain. But for the terrestrial brute I'd met in the forest. The one who held my secret. The one who must be silenced.

Ancestors, how I hoped he was nothing more than a lowly scout.

I could fake a slight and sever his head from his body. It would be unfortunate, but some things were more important. Namely, revenge.

A knock rang out on my door.

My time was up.

Cyara murmured something to Gawayn as she opened the door. Charis and Carly fell into line behind me, their white gowns and neat plaits lovely and perfect. I felt like a trussed-up chicken. At least I wasn't wearing white.

Gawayn's face was stoic as he held out his hand to motion me forward. Lyrena winked as she took her place on my other side. Evander fell back to guard my back; though I wondered if he would rather stab me in it.

Together in procession, we made our way to the throne room.

The halls and courtyards of the goldstone palace were empty, every courtier and servant gathered to watch the once in a generation moment. Palace guards lined the goldstone walls at regular intervals, only a few feet separating one from the next. So many more than usual.

Had Gawayn or the Royal Council been responsible for the change?

It didn't really matter. The message was clear. They'd lost one Pendragon heir. They would not lose another.

We walked past the Dowager's wing. I didn't let my stride falter. She wasn't there, anyway.

Then we were there. I could see the dais we'd been seated on that night all those months ago. Unlike then, the hall was empty of tables, cleared of all furniture except the two thrones. Courtiers lined the walls fifteen deep, crowded together to leave a wide swath of empty goldstone tiles in the center of the room.

A lone priestess waited there to perform the ceremony.

I could not see to the other side of the throne room, where the Brutal Prince no doubt waited. But someone must have sighted me, for a murmur whipped through the already buzzing crowd.

If I'd tried harder, I might have been able to make out some of the words. But I didn't care what my courtiers thought of me any more than I did the Royal Council or the Brutal Prince I would be forced to join with. All of this was a farce, to buy me time.

This will end. This will end. I'd chanted that to myself so many times in the last six months.

I forced my hands to relax. A dagger hung on each hip in the bejeweled scabbards. I could handle whatever happened next.

The priestess in the center of the hall raised her hand, signaling silence.

High among the arched columns, an owl hooted.

My heart clenched, my eyes rising, searching.

Father.

I'd never seen another creature grace this hall. Only him, gliding down from the rafters, shifting into his fae form in a flourish as he landed before his throne.

But there was no flap of white wings among the goldstone arches.

I slowly exhaled, my gaze falling to the crowds, wondering what the crowd made of it. But they were all staring at the priestess, eyes transfixed as she began her show. She possessed water magic and was using it to tell the history of the Offering. A brilliant display of forms and bodies created out of water.

She was powerful, yes, but...

Had no one else heard it?

My stomach rolled uneasily as I glanced upward again.

As I did, a shadow glided between the two arches high above the priestess. Massive wings stretched wide. But when I blinked, it was gone.

I searched the crowd again, hoping someone would be looking upward as well, that someone else had seen...

But all those sharp fae eyes were trained on the waterworks in the middle of the hall.

It must have been my imagination. The remnants of the tea I'd made the night before, too much nightbloom flower—

The priestess' voice swirled through the room, carried on a dozen winds of elemental magic: "Her Royal and Powerful Majesty, Veyka Pendragon, Queen of the Elemental Fae."

I stepped forward, past the dais, into the void of space left just for me.

"The Heir of the Terrestrial Fae, Brutal Prince and Protector of Annwyn, His Highness Arran Earthborn."

From the knot of earth-toned wool at the other end of the throne room, a massively tall male stepped free. The dark-haired, surly fae scout stared at me across the expansive throne room.

Realization slammed into me with more force than the combined wind magic of every elemental fae in that hall.

He could not betray me to the Brutal Prince. He *was* the Brutal Prince.

16
ARRAN

Veyka Pendragon, second born of Uther and Igraine, the female dubbed the Princess of Peace by a kingdom stunned by her very existence, stepped onto the dais.

She'd been beautiful in that clearing, sweat rolling down her limbs, her white hair matted against her face. But in all the finery of the elemental court, she looked like she'd come through the rift from another world entirely.

Her hair was styled similarly to every other elemental female watching from the wings, in an ornate plait that hung to her waist. But the color was unique. Not a pale platinum blonde or the silvery gray of old age so rarely seen among our kind, but a true white.

Her gown was revealing, showing off all the soft curves of her body. A golden brassiere held her breasts in place. They were nothing short of magnificent, barely contained by the forged curves of metal, begging to be touched. I knew that if I turned and surveyed the courtiers, I would see many eyes burning with desire.

A new flame lit inside of me.

Mine.

That soft stomach revealed below the gold brassiere—mine. The ivory pale skin of her navel, framed by the deep V of the belt that held the silky, translucent folds of her skirt in place—mine. Those strong, muscular legs revealed by the slits cut up to her hips had one purpose—to be wrapped around my waist while my cock was buried inside of her.

Thank the Ancestors my eyes were so dark that no one would be able to see my lust unless they were standing right in front of me.

The only person in front of me was Veyka Pendragon.

She looked like the queen of hell herself.

Every elemental courtier, dressed in all their jewels and flowy finery, wore soft pastel shades gilded with gold and silver. But not the Princess of Peace.

She wore black.

When her eyes landed upon me, I could feel the burning from the other side of the throne room. And it had nothing to do with desire.

She was incandescent.

In a sea of beautiful but carefully indifferent faces, the fury poured off of her.

I'd deceived her, and there was not a single shred of doubt as to how she felt about that.

I had as much right to be angry as she. What business did the Queen of the Elemental Fae have sneaking out of the palace? Her own brother had been murdered mere months ago in this very throne room. Did she not care even a little for the stability and safety of Annwyn? If she died, the process of tracing lineage and finding the next elemental heir would be too much. Annwyn would fracture, the tentative peace between the fae realms dissolving. I had left everything I had ever known—my family, my home—for this spoiled, selfish princess.

Despite the fact that my cock was hard, my chest tight with the desire to claim, I bared my teeth. The crowd gasped.

Veyka rolled her shoulders, loosening her muscles as if she was about to join a battle.

She was going to lose. I would ensure that.

But the priestess at the center of the hall was having none of it. The priestesses had been stripped of most of their power at the same time that the Ancestors put the accords into place. The priestesses had meddled in crown politics and, as punishment, lost their power over anything but the most formal ceremonies. In Wolf Bay, we hardly bothered with them at all.

But this priestess was reminiscent of the stories told about the Great War. Powerful, canny, and clearly desirous of remaining in control of the Offering.

The water the priestess had summoned for her little history lesson coalesced into a sphere the size of a large melon, rotating slowly in the center of the room several feet above her head.

The elementals were not as impressed by the magic as my own terrestrial fae brethren behind me. Most had never met an elemental until we crossed the Spit. Fewer still had seen such a display of power from one.

I used the moment to examine Veyka more closely. She wore a jeweled belt with two scabbards and two daggers. Weapons, even to a formal, peaceful ceremony. My blood heated in appreciation.

But my mind noted what was missing—the sword. The rumors were true, then. Excalibur was missing, had not presented itself to the new queen. It didn't bode well for any of us.

"Heirs, approach," the priestess ordered.

The hate bleeding out of Veyka's eyes was palatable. I met it with my own.

I hadn't held out much hope that my betrothed would be a worthy ruler. But I assumed after witnessing her own brother's murder and living through the turmoil that followed, she'd at least be concerned about preserving peace and consistency in Annwyn.

Instead, I was betrothed to a selfish twenty-five-year-old brat who snuck into enemy-laden forests without a guard in sight. Lucky me.

Now we stood face to face, the length of a body separating us. I wanted to grab those muscled upper arms and shake her like the child she'd proven to be. I wanted to drag her mouth onto mine and see how she tasted before I leaned her over and took her from behind to punish her for her foolishness.

Instead, I looked at the priestess.

Her dark hair was straight as a line, falling in a perfect waterfall over her shoulders and down her back. Her clothes were similar in style to the loose, airy fabrics preferred by the elementals. The priestess, however, wore blood red.

Was it meant to be a reminder of how this would end? At the Joining, when she would drag a knife across each of our palms and seal me to Veyka Pendragon with the blood oath?

Or she wanted to stand out. It would have worked well, if the Queen of the Elemental Fae herself had not shown up to the Offering spitting in the face of her kingdom's traditions by dressing in midnight black.

The color of my eyes—something that was known across Annwyn. Eyes the color of a demon were fitting for the Brutal Prince. Maybe her courtiers thought she'd dressed this way in homage to me, to show alliance. But I knew nothing could be further from the truth.

She was being petulant and childish.

The priestess waved an elegant hand at the space between us and a gleaming golden chalice appeared. Surprise bloomed—water magic and the ability to conjure. She was powerful, indeed. From the satisfied look upon her face as she heard the audible sounds of admiration from the crowd, she had the potential to become a problem.

But that worry would have to wait.

The priestess stepped forward, her spindly fingers closing around the base of the goblet. She looked to me.

"Do you, Arran Earthborn, son of Pant and Elayne, Offer yourself as the Heir of the Terrestrial Fae, to seal the accords made by our forbearers, the revered Ancestors?" Her voice boomed across the hall.

Over her shoulder, an elemental female collapsed, power expended. The other courtiers dragged her away.

I knew my part. I held out my hand and said the words: "I, Arran Earthborn, do Offer myself."

The priestess drew a small knife from the folds of her gown. She lifted it high above her head in a dramatic flourish, and then sank the tip into the mound of flesh at the base of my thumb. My thick, red fae blood trickled out in a single line. The priestess caught the stream with the golden chalice, letting several drops fall before pulling the knife away.

My wound began to knit together instantly, the blood flow stemming before even a single drop hit the goldstone floor.

The priestess turned to Veyka. At the Joining, our blood would be truly mixed, shared between our bodies. For now, it would mingle symbolically within the golden chalice.

"Do you, Veyka Pendragon, daughter of Uther and Igraine, Offer yourself as the Heir of the Elemental Fae, to seal the accords made by our forbearers, the revered Ancestors?"

I expected Veyka's eyes to be defiant, angry—blue storm clouds. But she was not looking at me, nor at the priestess. She stared at the golden chalice. When she lifted her hand, it was shaking.

"I, Veyka Pendragon, do Offer myself," she said, her voice strong and clear despite the tremble of her fingers.

The priestess pressed the knife into the base of Veyka's thumb.

Nothing happened. Her skin did not yield, no blood sprang forth.

We were isolated enough at the center of the room that none of the spectators could see what was happening, though their senses were sharp enough to recognize that only my blood had been drawn so far.

The priestess lifted the tip of the knife, examining it, looking back at my half-healed hand, the blood already in the chalice.

If it weren't so strange, I might have been amused at her discomfiture.

With a slight shake of her head, her red gown quivering around her, she pressed the blade into Veyka's hand again.

Veyka breathed in sharply and I felt my chest relax, expecting blood to burst forth.

But none did.

"Ancestors," the priestess huffed in frustration.

"Ancestors be damned," Veyka cursed.

In the next breath, she drew one of the daggers resting in the twin scabbards on her hips and plunged the blade into her hand herself.

The blood gushed out of her hand, spraying over the priestess' gown, as well as her own. If she'd have been wearing white, it would have been ruined. The priestess was blinking owlishly, as if she couldn't comprehend the sequence of events. I couldn't either.

Veyka rolled her eyes and tipped her palm over the chalice, squeezing it into a fist until her blood ran down to join mine.

She sheathed her weapon and then let her hand fall at her side.

The priestess was still visibly shaken, but she managed to step back and hold the chalice high for the surrounded audience to see. "Our heirs have made their Offerings in blood. As their life forces mix and join together, so may our kingdoms be joined in peace and prosperity."

As she swirled the blood in the chalice, the ball of water above our heads loosened. Long, graceful tendrils swirled outward until they encircled Veyka and I completely in a ring of glowing, moving water.

The priestess looked to us, inclining her head almost imperceptibly. What did she want? For us to join hands? Kiss?

I shot a look to Veyka, her hands fisted at her sides, distaste practically dripping off her like the blood moments before.

My own blood began to boil again, the formality of the ceremony giving way to the anger and frustration I'd felt before.

The priestess cleared her throat, clearly deciding we weren't going to humor her further. "The Joining will take place on the eve of Mabon, to symbolize the balance of light and dark being restored to Annwyn at long last."

I'd expected that much, at least. The Joining always took place at the equinox. Mabon was closer than Ostara, a mere three months away.

The ropes of water encircling us turned to cool mist.

Applause filled the room, spilling out the open archways carried on the wind of the powerful elementals assembled. Those words would be carried all across Annwyn, through the rifts into the human realm. A reminder that the united kingdoms of the fae were strong. We were death to any humans stupid enough to test us again.

I would personally dismember anyone who attempted to disrupt that peace. My entire life had been an act of sacrifice to my kingdom. I would not let it be in vain now that the crown had landed on my head. Ill-fitting though it might be.

But the applause suddenly fell away, replaced instead by murmurs and gasps. I saw a few elementals faint away outright. Veyka's eyes were trained over my shoulder, her luscious lips parted in disbelief.

A chill slid down my spine as I turned to see what was capable of holding the entire court in rapture after the spectacle of the Offering.

A stag.

At the head of the hall, where I'd stood minutes before with my travel companions, stood a large white stag. Its hooves were caked with the red dirt that blanketed the kingdom of the elemental fae, but its coat was pristine.

The moon white creature gleamed, its coat the same color as Veyka's hair, I thought absently. The same color as my—

Before I could finish the thought, the creature lifted its magnificent head and bellowed, the sound loud enough to echo through the throne room without any magic at all.

The stag exuded a magic all its own. I counted thirteen points on its impressive rack, that instead of brown or tawny, glowed bright gold. As if it had been gilded by the Ancestors themselves.

To my right, the priestess began muttering some sort of incantation.

Veyka took a step toward it, her hand brushing against mine.

Heat exploded up my arm, as if a hot poker had been shoved in through that already healed over cut. I jerked my hand away, shaking it out, trying to dislodge the sensation.

The stag's bellow filled the space again, drawing my eyes back.

It reared up on its hind legs, taller than the tallest fae in the room—me.

When it landed, everyone in the room took a collective breath in.

Then it charged.

I did not think. Not about my own life, or the strange heat that Veyka's touch had sent ricocheting through me. I thought of Annwyn. Of peace. Of my mother.

I threw my body against Veyka's, catching her around the waist and dragging her out of harm's way. We shoved past the priestess, knocking her to the ground. She could be trampled. I did not care. But not Veyka.

Chaos took the hall. Magic surged, twirls of water and strong winds trying to corral the animal. The stag appeared impervious to it all, a true being of legend. A being that needed to die. I saw Gwen a second before she shifted.

Sword drawn, she was halfway across the hall but struggling to get through the moving mass of elementals. She dropped her sword to the goldstone floor, her dark skin gleaming in the evening sunlight, and shifted.

Her roar filled the throne room. Elementals fell back, aiming their magic in her direction, not understanding what was happening. They were as unused to us as we were to them.

But Gwen was the best of my warriors. She dodged the blasts of water and flame, her sinuous feline form weaving between bodies until she found her prey.

"What the—" Veyka shoved me aside, a knife in each hand, struggling to her feet as she tracked Gwen.

As Veyka watched, the lion launched herself across the room, soaring over the heads of her courtiers and catching the stag's throat in her jaws, tearing it out in one motion. Bright red blood, thin and viscous, sprayed across the hall, covering the courtiers nearby.

The hall went absolutely silent.

The lion shook her massive head, black mane flowing around her as she turned to face us, the future High King and Queen of Annwyn, her maw dripping blood.

Veyka's hand closed around my arm, tight as steel but without any of that otherworldly heat.

"Let's go."

Before I could process her words, she was dragging me across the throne room, past the crowd, and through a cleverly camouflaged golden door set right into the goldstone itself. As the door closed behind us, pandemonium erupted.

17

VEYKA

"I do not understand," he growled, refusing to move away from the door even if he had allowed me to shut it.

"She killed it!" I shook my head, the golden rings dangling from my ears chiming, mocking me with their melodious song.

He gnashed his teeth. "As if you elementals would not have done the same—and hoped it was a terrestrial as you did. How did a deer even get into your precious goldstone palace?"

Precious? I'd raze it to the ground if I could. But that was his second error.

"A white hart."

His thick, dark brows knitted together. I could almost have enjoyed the shade of uncertainty on his otherwise smug face—were it not for the disaster I had just watched unfold around me.

"The Quest of the White Hart?" I said.

This had to be a joke. Though the terrestrial brute had shown no signs of even knowing what one was. Humorless? Too soft a description.

Soulless.

I ought to have been glad to meet someone who was just as dead inside as I was. Instead, I found it infuriating.

The imbecile did not even know the Quest of the White Hart? And he was to be High King of Annwyn?

Slam! Slam! Slam!

The door burst open, blades flying. The Brutal Prince had his axe out of his belt in half a heartbeat. Gawayn's sword was raised and ready, Lyrena in a fighting stance at his right. The cool metal of my own dagger kissed my palm.

Gawayn's eyes slid from the Brutal Prince, axe raised, to me posed with my own weapon a few steps behind.

"Your Majesty," he said carefully. "Are you well?"

"Am I well?" My voice cracked. I was hysterical. "His feral beast killed the white hart! The first one that has been seen in a thousand years! The herald of peace and prosperity!"

"If I recall, it is meant to be killed and served at the Joining feast," a feline female voice said.

She must have slunk in behind Gawayn and Lyrena. Now she lingered beside the door, no apology in her dark face.

"Today was the Offering, not the Joining, in case you failed to notice," I ground out.

I didn't need any of this. The council would be in fits. Gawayn and the Goldstones would be on edge. Every move I made was already watched; after a disaster like this, the eyes of the elemental court would be fixed upon me, waiting for me to stumble.

I didn't care what any of them thought.

But I did care if it got in the way of my one true goal.

"I noticed, young queen." The female stepped forward, gracefully sidling past Lyrena and Gawayn.

She was unarmed, but I recognized a fellow warrior when I saw one. The lion shifter would be as lethal with a blade as she was with her claws and fangs. Elegantly dressed for a terrestrial, she looked a queen in her own right.

But I'd spent enough of my life on my knees. I would not be cowed by her.

I lifted my chin, holding my body in its offensive stance.

Her golden eyes raked over me. Anger—such anger.

I'd seen it only once before.

In my own eyes, staring back at me in the mirror in the days after Arthur's murder.

Whether she saw that anger reflected back now, or my understanding—which might be worse, a low growl slipped from her lips. "The Quest of the White Hart is to be undertaken for the Joining. The priestess just declared your Joining will not take place until Mabon. What message does the white hart that comes at the Offering and then disappears send to your kingdom?"

My heart hammered in my chest as I sifted through her words.

"I have spared you the rumors, Your Majesty," the female said, unflinching. Then she sank forward into a bow so low her long black braids grazed the goldstone floor. "Now you can blame it on the stinking terrestrials."

Lyrena gasped.

"Gwen, that's enough." The Brutal Prince lunged forward, grabbing the dark-skinned female's arm.

My pounding heart stopped.

"Gwen," I repeated, looking the regal female over with new eyes. "Guinevere."

I was the imbecile.

She stood before me in emerald and gold, regal as a queen, because she was meant to be one.

I should have worn emerald and gold. I should have been the one paying homage to my brother.

Guilt rose in me like bile.

I spun away, desperate to make the pain stop.

This was why I refused to let emotion in. If I cared about my court, if I cared about anyone or anything, I would never survive. The pain of it would choke me until I was as dead as Arthur.

Not yet. I could not give in yet.

"Why are you here?" Lyrena's curious voice sliced through the tension.

I opened my mouth but had to close it again just as quickly. What tea I'd choked down that morning threatened its revenge.

"I wished to speak to my betrothed in private," Arran said, his voice full of gravel and menace.

Was he... trying to spare me?

Was I so transparent?

Of course I was.

I was turned away from everyone else in the room, choking on my own vomit. It did not take ethereal magic to sense my distress.

"My duty to Annwyn did not die the day that Arthur did," Guinevere said.

His name on her lips had me turning.

Arran's hand on her arm had softened, offering comfort rather than a reprimand.

"I asked Arran if I could join his delegation. He was smart enough to accept my offer," the stunning terrestrial female said, her eyes flicking up to where the Brutal Prince towered over her. The warmth in her words was obvious.

He had not responded to Lyrena to spare me, but her. Guinevere.

The true High Queen of Annwyn.

I really was going to be sick.

"I will retire," I said, irritated beyond measure at the sharpness of my own voice.

Gawayn stepped forward instantly. Lyrena lingered a breath longer, her eyes still considering the terrestrial female. Was that a subtle glow—

"We can take the passageways, Your Majesty," Gawayn was saying, already opening the gold filigree door at the back of the chamber.

The passages wound throughout the goldstone palace so the royal family and council could move without being pestered by courtiers when needed. I wanted to avoid that throne room full of calculating eyes almost as badly as I wanted out of this chamber.

"Thank you, Gawayn," I said. I nodded in Arran's direction, avoiding looking too closely at the familiar picture he and Guinevere presented.

Lyrena moved past me, ready to lead the way into the passageway.

"Hold a moment."

I froze, half turned between the Brutal Prince and my escape. I felt him cross the room, each step a brutal echo over the goldstone floors. He was too large to be real, even in a palace of soaring ceilings and a land of cavernous valleys.

But his eerily dark gaze fell on Gawayn, rather than me.

"In the future, if I close the door behind myself and my betrothed, that door shall remain closed." His words cut through the air with a ruthlessness that left no doubt he deserved his moniker.

Gawayn did not melt. He stared down the Brutal Prince, a swirl of heated wind coalescing around him.

"My only concern is for the Queen's protection," he finally said.

"Good." Arran stood before me now, his dark eyes sharp and unforgiving as they stared down the Captain of my Goldstone Guards. "Trust that I will safeguard her life above all else."

An order.

For a second, the wind threatened to coalesce into a cyclone. Then it disappeared entirely.

"Of course, Your Highness." Gawayn bowed. Just a nominal bending of the waist, but enough. When he rose, he looked to me. "Your Majesty."

I stepped forward, ready to slip back into my mindless oblivion. Perhaps Parys—

But a hand caught my arm.

My entire body pulsed in response. Every grain of my being was suddenly aware, awake.

I could not think. I could barely keep myself upright as the force of that contact and the events of the last hour threatened to drag me under.

Then the Brutal Prince pulled me in, his mouth grazing my cheek.

All a show, a performance for the assembled audience, so that he could whisper against the delicate point of my ear—
"We will speak again soon. You will explain yourself, *Princess*."

18
ARRAN

Her scent lingered on the warm breeze even after she disappeared into the darkened passageway. Plum and primrose, mixed with something darker that I couldn't identify. Probably an herb indigenous to the elemental kingdom.

"If you want her that badly, just go after her."

"Want her?" I scoffed, the sound scraping across the back of my throat. "Want to strangle her, maybe."

Gwen sighed heavily, her long wool skirt dragging across the goldstone floor as she drifted to the window, a wide turquoise and white painted arch overlooking the red valley below. Her eyes moved over the undulating curves of orange, burnt umber, deep brown.

"This was always meant to be my home. I wanted this—to be here—more than anything," she said, eyes faraway.

It wasn't a question and I couldn't pretend to have an answer.

This future had been thrust upon me, the crown of Annwyn as well. But somehow that did not seem as bad as having expected those things your entire life, only to have them ripped away. I'd seen Guinevere in many stages of life through our hundreds of years of shared history. Regal, wrathful, covered in the blood of her enemies. But never melancholic. Not until Arthur's death.

"Thank you for killing the white hart," I said, my attention still half trained on the golden filigree door my betrothed had disappeared through. I hoped the change in conversation would break the tension—or the melancholy, at least.

Gwen rolled her eyes, turning her back on the scenery below. "Your queen was not as thankful."

"She will be in time."

Gwen's dark brows rose slowly. "You think so, do you?"

"I will make her," I growled, for no one's benefit but my own temper.

I had little to claim as my own in this life. I would not inherit Eilean Gayl. I would take the throne of Annwyn as its High King, yes. But while the power was absolute, it was shared with the queen —Veyka Pendragon.

The secretive female who was too free with her tongue.

"Ha! No one will make that female do anything." Gwen shook her head. "Her first instinct is to accuse, rather than listen."

I didn't care for this conversation any more than the first.

"Will you give her your father's table?" I asked.

Gwen's arms dropped to her sides. "I do not know."

It would arrive soon; Gwen had mentioned when we left Wolf Bay that it was being packed and readied for transport. Her family estate was on the southern side of the Spine, meaning the massive piece of furniture would not have to cross the jagged mountains. Though it would take a troop of airborne fauna-gifted terrestrials to get it through the Blasted Pass and into Baylaur.

Gwen toyed with the golden cap at the end of one of her braids, her eyes drifting out the window once again.

"Arthur promised to be a king of strength and prosperity. She..." Gwen's face contorted, holding back any manner of angry epithet. Finally, she finished, "I do not know what she is. Not yet."

19
VEYKA

Another day, another Royal Council meeting.

Another opportunity.

I'd begrudgingly admitted to myself that Guinevere's reasoning in bringing down the white hart was sound. But I would die before I admitted as much to her or the Brutal Prince. Luckily, I'd had no reason to see either of them. After the Offering I'd returned to my rooms. If I was truly lucky, I wouldn't have to deal with another terrestrial until the Joining itself at Mabon.

I hadn't sighted any more owl-shaped shadows, either.

The Royal Council, however, was something else entirely.

I'd surrendered control of my kingdom, but I'd agreed to be their cupbearer. For my own reasons, though I know that when Roksana suggested it, she'd hoped that hearing the near daily discussions would provoke interest in doing some ruling for myself.

I was interested in what they said—to a point. The point that it served me.

That was best accomplished if I blended in.

I'd selected a gown of burnt umber, nearly the color of the goldstone palace itself. If my unusual hair and less than willowy body made me stand out, at least the color of my gown could be nondescript.

My twin shadows walked on either side of me, a half step behind.

On my hips, my twin blades in their matching scabbards.

Rather ironic, considering I was a twin missing her other half.

I passed through the audience chamber where fae courtiers loitered. I'd never worked up the stomach to linger in this room, to try to hear what was being said outside of the council room. A court of treachery, I knew.

Someone within this court had plotted my brother's death.

Whether that person stood here in the audience chamber, even now sipping tea and plotting, or whether I would be pouring them wine in a few minutes' time, I did not know. But I would find out, and then I would exact my revenge.

Imagining the brutal ways I would torture and maim was my nighttime lullaby.

"Hold a moment."

The blood in my veins turned to ice. The fury and fire I'd felt moments before was replaced by cold. The sort of deep cold that killed, that froze your organs in place and sucked every bit of air from your chest.

There was only one person who could summon that response in me.

My mother.

We were in the middle of the audience chamber. Elemental courtiers stood all around us. I'd even spotted a few terrestrials near the aural fountain, keeping to their own, but still *here*.

There were too many witnesses to say or do what I truly wanted.

I stared straight ahead, refusing to look at her as her soft footsteps approached from my right. Lyrena shifted closer to me. I wanted to kiss her for it.

"My messages must continue to go astray. I have sent many requesting an audience," Igraine said, her voice like silk.

A snake in silk, ready to sink its fangs in at any moment.

"You have been told not to leave your wing," I said, struggling to keep my voice from trembling.

A soft, melodious chuckle. As if this were an actual conversation rather than a battle all its own. "The magic sealing the doors has faded since Arthur's death."

"Then perhaps it is time to reseal them," I said, moving instinctively a half-step back towards Lyrena. Her fire magic was strong. If she banded together with Cyara and my other handmaidens, it might be enough to seal her in.

Igraine stepped in front of me. I didn't flee, though every instinct inside of me screamed to get away, to make it stop.

A beautiful lie, that's what she was. Her lithe frame, draped in cream-colored silk and bands of gold that matched her hair, was the opposite of my well-rounded one. Only our skin was the same, that pale alabaster. Even our eyes were different. While hers were blue, like most blessed with water powers, they were very pale. The cerulean in mine tended to turquoise or sapphire, given the lighting. Igraine Pendragon was the perfect image of elemental femininity.

She'd also been my captor.

"You are not welcome at my court," I said curtly, not caring who heard it.

A wan smile peeled back her lovely pink lips. "The court was beginning to wonder where I was, why I was absent. I have mourned your father and your brother. I cannot remain sequestered from court any longer."

It was a fucking lie. No one around us thought that there was anything but enmity between Queen and Dowager. With my father's death, her reign as High Queen had come to an end. She did not want to give up the power. She did not want to be irrelevant. That was why she was here, trying to torture me still.

I'd been tortured enough. I still bore the scars on my skin and my soul. The ice inside of me started to melt away, giving way to a dark, howling void—

"You will remain in your wing, or I will—" I snarled, stepping forward. Free of my guards, just me and Igraine.

Her eyes fell to my waist, where my hand hovered over the hilt of my dagger. "You will do what, Veyka? Kill your own mother? You are not capable. You are weak. You have always been weak."

My fingers curled around the hilt. The leather welcomed my hand with a familiar kiss.

I could do it.

I'd swing upward, underneath her rib cage, shoving my blade straight through the withered organ that she called a heart. Once the last dregs of consciousness faded from her face, I'd take Lyrena's sword and remove her head from her body for all the elementals and terrestrials to see.

When I killed my mother, it would be final.

"Your Majesty," I heard Gawayn say, the words muted as if spoken underwater.

I blinked, the world around me clearing.

"The Royal Council awaits your arrival to begin proceedings," Gawayn said.

Neither I nor Igraine moved.

"Step aside, Dowager," Lyrena said, the warmth of her fire at my back. I suspected if I turned, I would find her sword drawn, the blade burning.

Igraine chuckled soundlessly.

Then she stepped away. But not before I heard a soft hiss behind me—the sound of her water magic extinguishing Lyrena's flame.

"By your leave, Your Majesty," Gawayn interjected, keeping either Lyrena or myself from doing or saying something rash.

I felt my legs move beneath me, some part of my brain moving my body to function when I could hardly drag in the next breath.

The crowd of courtiers in the assembly chamber parted instantly to make way for us—further proof the hate seething off of me was a secret to no one. Hate seemed to be the only emotion I could feel.

I preferred the apathy.

Two palace guards opened the door to the council chamber. Gawayn and Lyrena took their spots, sealing the room behind them. Without pausing, I grabbed a bottle of wine from the sideboard and stalked to the head of the table to say my pretty bit of fluff and begin the meeting.

But the words died on my lips.

The glass bottle shattered in my hand, deep burgundy wine staining the front of my gown and covering the floor.

Sitting at the other end of the table, directly across from Arthur's throne, was the Brutal Prince.

20

ARRAN

Clumsy as well as late.

My betrothed's list of flaws was growing by the hour.

"Are you well, Your Majesty?" The stately dark-skinned female seated about halfway down the table asked.

She wore her black hair in braids similar to Gwen, but much smaller, and then braided together in the more intricate multi-stranded plait that all the other females of the elemental court wore. Diamond clips studded the long plait. They also dripped from her ears, around her neck, gleamed at her wrist. Whoever this elemental was, she was important.

There was also no doubt of her gifts—someone dressed so obviously wanted everyone to know that she possessed ice magic. A lot of it.

"I am fine, Councilor Roksana," Veyka bit out, her voice edged in ice.

Perhaps that was the magic she was so keen to keep a mystery. If she had such a powerful ice-gifted elemental on her Royal Council, and her own gifts were minimal, it could be another reason she chose not to demonstrate.

"I did not expect the Brutal Prince to join us today," Veyka said, bending to pick up the shards of glass herself.

Before she could reach the floor, two servants rushed forward to clear it away instead. Annoyance flickered in Veyka's eyes, but she stepped away and allowed them.

"I invited him," the female called Esa said. She stood behind her seat. We all stood, waiting for Veyka to call the meeting to order.

Not the entire truth—typical elemental posturing. I'd sent Osheen to the female who'd introduced herself as the *donna* of Veyka's Royal Council, with orders to bring her to me. She'd tried to demur—using this meeting as an excuse. The invitation to join had only come when I offered to reschedule it entirely.

I was already sick of this. How had Uther Pendragon—a powerful terrestrial from the Spine itself—managed for 300 years?

I'd been here a week, and I was ready to shift into beast form and disappear into the mountains.

"How industrious of you," Veyka said.

For a moment, her eyes glanced down at the gem marking her seat at the head of the stately table.

Amorite. An interesting choice. Each seat was marked with a gem—typical of the opulence of the elementals. Esa had explained when I arrived that I must convey my request for my own seat, at the opposite end from Veyka. For now, the stone before me was empty and smooth.

Veyka let out a very slow, measured breath.

With that, the nonchalance that I'd glimpsed earlier snapped back into place. She cast her eyes beyond the table of councilors to the goldstone wall above my head. "I call this meeting of the Royal Council of the Elemental Court to order."

All the challenge and argument, the anger that had flashed in her eyes upon seeing me sitting at the end of the table, all of it was gone. I half expected her to melt into the stately throne-like chair in front of her, the energy of her rage snuffed out.

But instead of taking the seat with the amorite before it, she walked back to the sideboard and selected another bottle of wine. I watched with horror as she filled not her own glass, but Esa's.

My ears filtered out every other word being said, every voice except Veyka's.

Wine, Councilor Teo?

Wine, Councilor Elora?

"Wine, Brutal Prince?"

"No," I said, trying to meet her eyes.

But they were trained studiously on the ground, away from me, away from all the other members of the Royal Council.

Veyka moved past me to pour wine for the one she'd called Roksana.

"We have much to accomplish before Mabon," Esa began. The cloudy pale blue stone before her seemed to glow slightly as she spoke. "It has been weeks since the court has received petitioners. I will—"

"Forgive my intrusion, Councilor Esa. But I believe with His Highness now in residence, that is no longer under your purview," Roksana said, drumming her fingernails against the table, giving the appearance of boredom.

Esa's face remained calm, unlined. I waited to interject, despite the direct reference. I'd told myself I would observe this meeting, rather than interfere with it.

I tried to read the expressions of the other councilors assembled—Elora, who bore an uncanny resemblance to the forward-speaking Roksana; Noros, who was observing it all with eyes akin to a fox; Teo, whose heavy brow ridges had been fixed in the same brooding frown from the moment I entered the room.

Each of them was in perfect control of their emotions. Or at least enough to fool me, an outsider. Even if I ruled here for five hundred years, I doubted I would have that sort of control over my temper. The beast inside of me would not allow it.

"The Queen has not requested that the ruling of our fair kingdom be returned to her charge," Esa said, each word measured to the fraction of an inch.

I felt the disbelief as it etched itself across my face.

It could not be true.

Veyka Pendragon had never expected to be Queen of the Elemental Fae or High Queen of Annwyn—no more than I had. But this... to surrender control of her kingdom...

That nonchalance on her face... it was not because she was trying to hide her emotions. It was because she did not care.

The sound of wine splashing into Councilor Noros' cup pierced into my consciousness.

Cupbearer. Veyka was not a participant in the meeting.

Not only had she given up any responsibility for the Kingdom of the Elemental Fae and the fae residing within it, she'd lowered herself to pouring the drinks of those she'd given it up to.

I'd seen enough carnage on the battlefield to wreck the stomach of a much stronger male. Ancestors, I'd been the one to inflict it.

But this was the closest I'd felt to my stomach turning over in the last hundred years.

And the cause of it? She refused to look at me, refused to look at anyone. When she finished pouring the last goblet of wine, she retreated to stand against the wall. Even the color of her gown matched the goldstone—as if she hoped she might disappear right into it and be absolved of any responsibility.

Hate was not a strong enough word. Utter loathing. For her, for what she'd done, and for the fact that I was going to be saddled with her for the rest of my immortal life.

The discussion about petitioners continued. I forced myself to listen to it. This was a power struggle I'd walked into, I began to realize.

Veyka had given up her ruling powers to this council—which was why Esa had tried to keep me out of it. When we were Joined, Veyka and I would be crowned High Queen and King of Annwyn. This council would dissolve to be replaced by another of Veyka and I's choosing. It only existed now to rule the Kingdom of the Elemental Fae in the interim since the death of Uther, then Arthur.

But Veyka should have sat at its head. Not demurring against the wall.

Esa would retain her power only until the Joining, or until I could convince Veyka to demand control back sooner.

"What do you think, Your Highness?" Roksana said, turning her eyes to me expectantly.

I needed time to think—time to decide how to get Veyka to give a damn. I wished I'd let Veyka pour me some wine just so I would have some reason to delay a few moments.

"Veyka and I will receive the petitioners," I said slowly.

Veyka straightened at her name, her eyes narrowing. There was the fire, the rage I'd seen in the throne room and after when she'd eviscerated me and Gwen over the loss of the white hart.

She did care about something—just not her citizens or her kingdom.

"If that is Her Majesty's wish."

All eyes swung to Esa, mine included.

The *donna*, however, looked to the silent queen.

Such bold words. Such a blatant attempt to cling to power.

She'd taken a gamble and misplaced it.

Veyka Pendragon did not care about her court or her kingdom, why would she care about putting herself between her power-hungry *donna* and myself?

She did not disappoint.

How could she? When she'd already shattered all of my expectations like that bottle of wine.

"As the Brutal Prince wishes," Veyka said quietly.

A beat of silence. Then the fox-eyed councilor, Noros, wisely launched into some other topic. But Veyka...

Her eyes were pinned to me.

Slowly, I let the beast a little closer to the surface. Carefully, because I could not let him have control here. But I could let him show a little, let his menace shine out through my eyes, the color of death.

I might never have the cool, calm composure of the elementals.

But I was a terrestrial fae, the most powerful in millennia. The beast that lived inside of me was something to be feared. Apparently, Esa needed reminding of that. Maybe Veyka did as well.

I pushed back from my seat, saying nothing.

Let them watch me, warily, like the rabid beast I was.

I rolled my shoulders and worked my jaw so that my prominent canines were visible. Whatever shared lineage we elementals and terrestrials shared, their more animal features had long been bred out. But as a full-blooded terrestrial, mine remained. The sharp canines once meant for ripping out throats—the size, larger, stronger. The ability to shift.

I left my chair out but swiped up the empty wine goblet—my pretense for approaching Veyka.

She glared at me as I approached, holding out my cup.

I would not have been surprised if she chucked the bottle at my face.

"What do you want?" she hissed.

I held up my empty goblet. "I would think that obvious."

Her hand on the wine bottle did not move. "You said no."

"I changed my mind."

"Go to hell." She turned her eyes back to the council, currently debating the granting of a lordship to someone named Pellinor, and pretended I did not exist.

"I am already there," I said with complete honesty. Whatever the humans imagined, this had to be the fae version.

Veyka continued to ignore me.

I turned so that my back was to the table of councilors, my eyes fixed on the rolling red hills and valleys beyond the goldstone arches. I spoke so quietly, even the keenest fae ears would not be able to hear me.

"Why did you give up your rule?"

From the corner of my eye, I watched the pulse jump in Veyka's throat, her nostrils flare. "I am in mourning."

"For who? Your father? Your brother?" I pried.

I doubted she'd grant me the knowledge, I hardly knew her and the foremost emotion we'd exchanged was mutual hate. But I was desperate. I wanted to be wrong about her and her motivations.

"My father at least had the honor of dying in his bed. My brother was murdered in cold blood," she said, her breasts moving up and down faster now.

Such beautiful breasts, barely concealed by the flowy orange fabric of her gown. I wanted to tear it off with my teeth, expose her body and soul so I could see exactly who I was dealing with.

I huffed a mirthless chuckle. "Don't you think six months is long enough?"

Brutal.

The pain in her eyes, in her mouth, in the breath she dragged in...

When her eyes cut to me, it was easy to see. She hated me as much as I did her.

I had earned my name on the battlefield and now here in the goldstone palace.

"Ask your partner, Lady Guinevere. She ought to understand," she bit out.

It was cruel and painfully true, but I only latched onto one word. "Partner?"

Veyka's sharp laugh was as cold as my own. "Companion, ally, advisor, *lover*. I do not care what you call her. She seems to have all the answers."

Oh, but she did care. The heat in my loins started to burn. "Is that jealousy I sense, Veyka?"

She snorted, her laugh near hysterical now, barely keeping her voice low enough not to be overheard. "I would rather sleep with a pig than with you."

It might be true. Her eyes were not glowing. They remained a flat cerulean blue, no telltale glimmer of desire. But that was jealousy in her voice, whatever her eyes said.

It should not have pleased me. I hated that it did—revulsion rising in my throat. I was appalled at her lack of duty, her complete selfishness. Yet my cock could not have cared less.

Veyka had apparently had enough of me. She dumped wine into my cup unceremoniously, not caring about how it sloshed over the rim onto her dress, and then turned away. I caught her arm, dragging her back.

Her bare arm was corded with muscle. Soft, yes, like every part of her was soft and inviting. But there was steel beneath. I wanted to battle that steel with my own, to feel her wrapped around every inch of me. I hated her for it, and I hated myself.

I yanked her closer, close enough that my lips could have brushed against the delicate pointed shell of her ear. "Sneaking out of the palace with no regard for your own safety... playing cupbearer to your Royal Council instead of ruling it... you are a shameful waste of the crown that sits upon your head."

"For once, it seems we agree on something," Veyka snarled, wrenching her arm free from my grasp.

She strode to the other side of the table, to Roksana, to begin her round of pouring wine once again. If any of the council members had overheard us, they kept their eyes averted and their faces clear—in true elemental fashion.

I took up Veyka's post against the goldstone wall, the wind of the Effren Valley sweeping in between the open archways to cool my ardor and my temper.

They were saying something about the Split Sea. Unusual weather patterns, unease between the elemental settlements there which might be to blame. I listened with only half an ear.

When the meeting adjourned, Veyka practically ran from the council room.

You can try to run, Princess, the beast inside of me growled.

But I will always find you.

21
ARRAN

"Why are we walking through the halls in the middle of the night?" Gwen grumbled. "Isn't this the job of those useless Goldstones?"

"The Goldstones are the queen's personal guards," I said, though Gwen was perfectly aware of the fact.

She was well versed in the histories and customs of the elemental fae. As a terrestrial female of the appropriate age, she'd been brought up by her family with the hopes that one day she would be selected as the next High Queen of Annwyn. My parents had once held similar hopes for me and my brother. But once Arthur's birth was foretold, there was no need for males. Males could not ensure another generation of peace for Annwyn. So, we were trained as warriors rather than scholars.

I hadn't wanted for an education, but it had been focused on other things.

Bloodshed, for one.

Mercy had not been in the curriculum.

"There are palace guards as well," Gwen observed as we passed one standing sentry at the intersection where two hallways met and opened onto an expansive, roofless courtyard. "Though I'm not sure what good they are," she added when we were still well within earshot.

I ignored her questions. I was busy making observations. She ought to be as well. A king had been murdered in this palace six months ago. The Royal Council had found the human culprits and punished them. They'd declared the goldstone palace secure.

After that disastrous council meeting, I knew better than to trust them with mine or Veyka's life.

The courtyard was open to the sky, which meant it was vulnerable to aerial attacks. But while a more powerful elemental might send a cyclone or a thunder storm rife with lightning, the possibility for damage was minimal.

But not for the terrestrial fae. An aerial regiment of winged shifters could land here with little trouble, kill the elemental fae guards posted in each corner, and storm the goldstone palace. The guards were not even equipped with bows.

I added it to my mental list. I already knew who from my delegation I'd like to post here. But not all of them had indicated a desire to stay in Baylaur. It would be a waste of time to train a team if half of it would return to Wolf Bay after the Joining.

"We'd need a half dozen," Gwen observed, as if she could read the thoughts in my head.

"Are you sure you don't have hidden ethereal powers?" I asked, turning down the next corridor. We were getting closer.

"Ha!" she scoffed, tossing her thick black locks over her shoulder. "A queen is meant to fulfill the Ethereal Prophecy. A queen, I am not."

I didn't argue with her. She'd trained her entire life to sit on the throne that was now occupied by a despondent, selfish female with wide hips and even wider breasts. Veyka Pendragon would not be fulfilling any ancient prophecies. She could hardly be roused to be interested in the running of her own kingdom.

Gwen tossed her hair again, the gold-studded tips of her braids catching the firelight that flickered from the torches lining the goldstone corridor. The eternally burning flames danced against the glowing burnt orange color of the goldstone, the glittering dust particles caught within the stone sparkling bright. Goldstone, yes, but totally different than the yellow gold that held Gwen's black locks in place.

I glanced back over my shoulder to where the guard we'd passed earlier stood, face emotionless, posture rigid. What was his power? All fae were born with magic, but he was a palace guard, so he must be relatively strong.

He'd better not be responsible for the torches burning in these adjacent corridors. It was a waste of magic. A useless expenditure for a guard, when that well should be reserved for defending his queen, in a world where all magic demanded a price. Sometimes it was as simple as an aching joint or a leaking canteen in the brutal desert. For a soldier, the price was often steeper.

If the goldstone palace was attacked, the price would likely be death.

"This place will be a bloody nightmare to defend properly," Gwen observed as we entered yet another uncovered courtyard, this with a series of fountains in the middle and multiple verandas overlooking it.

"Yet defend it we must," I sighed.

The throbbing headache in the back of my head had returned. The need to shift thrummed through me, making its demand once more. But the beast inside of me would not be satisfied with a mere change in the throne room, to the amusement or horror of the courtiers. My beast wanted blood—always.

"Osheen could—"

"Osheen has already studied the perimeter of the palace. Over the next few weeks, he will shore up those defenses. Tonight, it is the internal mechanisms I am concerned with." I cut her off, curving around the fountain so she was forced to fall into step behind me.

I felt sorry for her, I did.

But I also was not in the mood to have my plans questioned.

The night sky winked above us, not a single cloud covering the bright stars. It was light enough that if any courtiers had remained on their balconies, they could have easily seen me walking through the night in the direction of the queen's apartments.

And if they did?

By Mabon, Veyka and I would be joined. The blood oath was the show of unity, not whether we shared one another's bed.

As we reached the other side of the courtyard, Osheen appeared.

"Report," I ordered as he fell into step beside me.

"All the flora within the palace are potted. Not a single thing with roots in the ground. It would be difficult to mount a significant defense here using flora gifts," he said, no hint of regret in his words. Unlike most males, Osheen was perfectly satisfied with the gift he'd been given and its strength. He did not long for more.

I'd once longed for less.

But that was a different time.

Only children bothered to hope for the impossible.

"Then you will be stationed outside, starting tonight," I said, glancing his way. Osheen nodded; he'd already been expecting this order.

"There is plenty of foliage there to use. The plants are different, to be sure. But they are just as powerful as those in the Shadow Wood," Osheen said.

"Good. Work out a schedule and report daily—" My head snapped forward; as if an invisible string had yanked on my chin, my consciousness.

Osheen inhaled sharply. "What is that..."

I scarcely heard the soft purr of Gwen's shift. I was already sprinting down the corridor.

The Queen.

22
VEYKA

Drip. Drip. Drip.

My ears twitched, pulling me to wakefulness instantly. We imagined ourselves so evolved, but fae were only a few steps above the animals that so many of the terrestrials could still shift into. Like a mother wolf protecting her den, my ears heard the sound of blood hitting the tiled floor.

Only fae blood made that particular sound.

The veins of the fell creatures that haunted the Blasted Pass ran with thicker blood that turned sticky in a matter of moments. Humans were the opposite. Their blood was so watery, spilling over the ground in waves of crimson.

The pattern of the human blood, as it spilled from the humans who'd killed my brother, was burned into my mind. Even though it had long been scrubbed away, I doubted I would ever forget the peculiarities of human blood—bright red, coppery.

Not like fae blood. Thick, scarlet, vibrating with its own magic. It seemed to call out to the fae bodies around it, as if some shade of the fae life force remained within.

Those drops hitting the floor were fae.

There was no doubt in my mind.

And they were coming closer.

From the direction of the veranda. Half of the time, Parys fell asleep on one of the reclining lounge chairs there, claiming he liked to feel the breeze upon his face. A believable claim, for an elemental fae blessed with wind powers. Some nights, I joined him, staring beyond the tiered balconies to the star-bright sky beyond.

But not tonight.

Tonight, the balcony was empty.

Which left an opportunity for the assassin.

Drip drip drip drip drip—closer together. Faster.

The assassin had already killed once, their weapon dripping with blood. The cost of reaching my bedchamber—another fae life.

I didn't have much time. My fingers closed around the dagger that lived beneath my pillow.

One slow breath in, letting the air fill my body and call every muscle to attention.

On the exhale, I sprung from the bed.

23
ARRAN

The sound of the heavy doors crashing open was nothing compared to Veyka's deafening roar as she leapt over the bed, shoving someone bodily aside.

Her dagger caught the light as she slashed, but the assassin jumped backward out of her range. Veyka rolled off the bed, head over feet, landing in a crouch with teeth bared and blade ready.

The assassin, clad in clothing so dark it seemed to swallow the light spilling in from the antechamber, took one look at her and turned to flee. The balcony was open. If they could shift, they'd be gone in a minute. I lunged forward, swinging my battle axe overhead in a motion that was as natural as breathing.

Something zinged past my ear, but I didn't pause, not with the threat of escape steps away from the assassin's grasp.

Until the black-clad form crumpled, two paces short of the ledge.

I drew myself up, raking my gaze over the assassin's limbs, searching for some sign of a feint. But I knew what I would find.

Veyka's knife—buried to the hilt in the center of the assassin's back.

Before I could lean down to check that they were really and truly dead, Veyka herself was at my side. She kicked the figure hard in the gut. When that elicited no response, she aimed for the head. Nothing.

Only then did she lean down to retrieve her weapon. She held it loosely in her hand, but her muscles were still taut as she nudged the figure over onto their back. Without a glance back at her audience, swelling by the moment, she slit the male assassin's throat.

She stared at the vacant face for several long moments.

Then she straightened, turning to survey the other occupants of the room. Her gaze swept over the female who'd been asleep in her bed. Delicate white wings, a simple white silk nightgown, and neatly plaited copper hair. Two more females, similar in appearance, huddled against the wall next to an open door on the other side of the bed. Handmaidens, I guessed. And the one in the bed had been a decoy.

With a shaky snap of her fingers, the winged woman in the bed lit the braziers on the walls. The ever-burning hearth, which had been at a low simmer, roared to life once more.

Veyka's sharp blue eyes swept over the guards—hers and mine—much more quickly. Before they landed on me. They were fathomless, unreadable.

The elementals were famed for their ability to hide their feelings, to present a lie to the outer world. But Veyka had seemed less capable of it, her passion and temper showing through like it had after the Offering and in the Royal Council meeting. Now, though, she had that indifferent mask in place.

Indifferent? A small voice inside my head asked. Or disappointed. If Veyka had been the one in the bed, would she have bothered to defend herself?

"You are bleeding."

Suddenly, I could feel it. My battle-worn brain had been trained to ignore small hurts. But I could feel where her blade had nicked the tip of my ear and shaved off several strands of hair.

I did not reach up to stem the flow.

"Who is he?" I asked instead.

Veyka bit her lip, but did not answer. She looked past me, to the three Goldstones who always seemed to be near.

"He is not a member of the elemental court," the blonde one said, stepping forward. Gwen had told me her name—Lyrena.

I recognized the dark-haired one I'd relieved of his arm the day I arrived in Baylaur. He glowered at me, no circumspection evident. Clearly still bearing a grudge. But I didn't have time for that now.

Gawayn, the captain, stepped forward. My elder by at least two hundred years, his light brown hair already shot with gray. I wondered how much of it he had gained since tending to the new queen.

"Is he a terrestrial?" he asked.

Gwen growled, shifting in the blink of an eye to say: "We do not travel with assassins."

Osheen offered a more diplomatic approach. "He did not come with our delegation. But it is possible."

There was one way to find out. The eyes of all the elementals in the room swung to us, their terrestrial counterparts. They were all just as capable as us at stepping forward to make the determination. There were only two races of fae in Annwyn.

But not a muscle moved among them; not even the twitch of a delicate white wing.

Presumptuous, haughty, entitled. Every single one of them.

But I forced those thoughts to remain in my head, stepping forward and kneeling beside the assassin.

The dagger he'd wielded hung half out of his limp hand, the blade scarlet with blood. He'd injured or killed someone on his way in. A palace guard, most likely. But that was a worry for later.

I reached for his sleeve, a black knit fabric similar to the wool I wore myself. But as I pulled it away, it was featherlight. I'd never felt anything like it—almost like a spider's web woven into clothing.

When I laid my hand upon his skin, my entire body tensed.

Cold swirled through me. Colder than the peaks of the Spine in my homeland. Colder than the midnight waters surrounding Eilean Gayl in the dead of winter. The cold reached inside of me and tried to touch what lay at the very center of my being—my power.

Only then, in the face of that blackness that lived inside of me, did the cold recede.

My fingers returned to normal, the blood in my veins warm once more.

I waited for a comment, waited for those around me to say something. But no one seemed to have noticed. It was just me—only me. Confined to my person.

Swallowing back the concern that was yawning awake in my stomach, I refocused my magic. I was meant to be reaching inside of him, the assassin—not the other way around.

It took concentration, even for a fae as powerful as I. That was why none of the others in the room suspected anything was amiss. Summoning the two twin tendrils of my magic, flora and fauna, I willed them through the outer layers of the male's skin, past the physical boundaries to where his soul lay beneath. Or at least, what remained of it. Magic was not always easy to detect, but dead as he was, the male had no defenses.

I found what I sought quickly then, rocking back on my heels and pulling my hand away. Despite myself, I felt relief as I stood. I was glad to no longer be touching him.

"He's terrestrial, flora gifted," I said grimly, already anticipating the gasp that ricocheted through Veyka's handmaidens. Her guards were more stoic.

A wicked smile curved toyed at the corners of the queen's pretty mouth.

Of course, she would be amused to find her would-be assassin was terrestrial.

"That explains how he gained access," Osheen said. "There are climbing vines along this side of the palace, on the outside. He must have been powerful enough to strengthen them enough to climb."

Lyrena, the golden-haired Goldstone with the quick smile, walked over to the balcony and peered out.

"None of the other verandas are lit; everyone else sleeps," she observed. "Once he was within the palace walls, a steady sense of balance could have gotten him here without much trouble."

I turned my gaze to Osheen. "Your patrols—go, now. Work as long as you can, then choose your second best to take up while you recover. I want all of the adjustments made to the flora by sunset tomorrow."

Osheen bowed and left without a word.

The Captain of the Goldstones watched him go with a furrowed brow, but he did not countermand me. He turned instead to Veyka.

She was a study in contradictions. Her white hair, nearly silver in the evening light, was in a loose, casual plait. No trappings of diamonds or pearl, no intricate styling. Her nightgown was the opposite of the simple white one her handmaid wore, translucent black fabric with a neckline cut in a low square, showing off her breasts. The straps were nothing more than black ribbon, delicate enough that a sharp tug would tear them and have the whole garment falling away. A nightgown made to be seen by a male.

And in her hand, her blood-drenched dagger.

Bloodthirsty, buxom, beautiful. *Mine.*

My stomach clenched. The urge to shift, to chase every other male from the room—and females, for that matter—threatened to overwhelm my rational mind.

The corner of her mouth twitched.

The damn witch knew exactly what I was thinking.

My eyes must be glowing. Thankfully, no one was close enough to me to tell.

Except, perhaps, Veyka.

"Your Majesty," Gawayn said, clearing his throat gruffly. "I will post Lyrena and Evander at your door. Inside, starting now."

Her wicked smile melted away. "Gawayn, we have discussed this at length—that is not necessary."

"But Your Majesty—"

"I agree with the queen."

The captain's surprised eyes swung to me, rebuff on his lips.

But I forestalled him, looking directly at Veyka as I said, "I will guard your door."

24
VEYKA

"*I* will guard your door."

Panic seized me. "You most certainly will not. My Goldstones—"

"Failed to protect you tonight."

I waited for Gawayn to interject, but he said nothing.

"I can protect myself, as I've shown quite well," I said, waving my hand at the bloody evidence laying on my balcony.

Arran did not bother to look. "At least you were wise enough to use a decoy."

I had not wanted to. Gawayn had insisted. But I did not feel like sharing that information with Arran just then.

"But if you used a decoy, then you knew there was a threat." His voice was menace wrapped in velvet.

My instinct was to raise the blade, still dripping blood, and cut off the entire damn ear I'd nicked minutes before. Instead, I forced myself to keep my arms at my sides.

"Indeed," I said, willing every drop of elemental fae blood in my veins to help me keep my voice even and clear of emotion.

Arran's eyes said what his mouth did not—*You should have told me.*

Instead, he said, "Leave us."

Guinevere, back in her fae form but still looking as dangerous as a lion, moved for the door immediately. My own servants were slower. Of course, Carly and Charis had been cowering against the goldstone wall since the moment the Brutal Prince had entered the room. But Cyara was not so easily cowed. Her white wings were quivering with defiance on my behalf.

She'd never been in any real danger, I told myself. She'd insisted, along with Gawayn. But I would never do it again, even though the threat had proven true. I would not let her die for me.

Arran cleared his throat impatiently. The urge to stab him returned.

I inclined my head with what I hoped was agonizing slowness, my eyes fixed on Arran's. If this was a struggle for dominance, he would know that I was not his to dominate. I belonged to no one but myself.

"Go," I said quietly.

Cyara slid from the bed, clucking her tongue as she shooed her sisters through the door to their adjoining rooms. At least Cyara would be able to sleep in the comfort of her own bed tonight, I thought wryly. If she could sleep after a near death experience.

Gawayn jerked his head toward the door to the antechamber, summoning Evander and Lyrena. I resisted the urge to stick out my tongue at the former. The latter winked at me. Only Lyrena could find amusement in a scene like this.

Not true, I reminded myself. I'd enjoyed catching Arran's stare.

He tried so hard to rein in the temper, the passion. But he was a terrestrial, and a powerful one at that. The most powerful of all. He'd told me himself, that first day in the forest, that he could not lie.

All the doors shut in unison. Leaving me very much alone with the Brutal Prince, once again. Well, besides the dead assassin.

Every time before, we'd argued.

But now, standing before him in nothing but my nightgown, the lust of battle and bloodshed pounding through my veins, my body yearned for a different sort of sparring.

"I will guard your door, Princess."

Oh, but he'd already figured out how to get under my skin.

If he called me princess one more time, I was going to sink my dagger into him and watch him bleed for a solid hour before I removed it and allowed him to begin the painful healing process.

The Princess of Peace had died the same day as Arthur. There was no room for her in Annwyn.

"You will do no such thing. Lyrena and Evander will be sufficient guard—from the outside," I added. I could not allow Gawayn's notion of guards in my bedroom to take root. I would never be able to sneak out with fae ears two steps from my bedside.

"Your Goldstones are not sufficient. This evening proved as much. You are vulnerable from too many directions," Arran argued, stepping closer.

"You've seen to the perimeter," I said, cursing myself for not recalling the name of the flora gifted fae he'd sent away to guard the exterior of the goldstone palace.

"The veranda is vulnerable. The entrance through your handmaidens' quarters," he said, brows knitting together into a nearly solid dark line.

Everything about him screamed of darkness. Dark eyes, dark clothes, dark hair. But he'd switched his knit undershirt for a cream linen in recent days, I'd noticed. And his hair stuck out a bit, where my blade had caught his ear on the way to do its deed.

It made him seem... softer? No. There was nothing soft about Arran Earthborn. Completely out of my control, my eyes swept downward—

"Then set one of your flying friends to circle the courtyard," I said, sharper than I'd intended. "There is no exit from my handmaidens' quarters. They can only leave through this room."

"My flying friends have other occupations," he said, eyes flashing. There was no softness in him. Not even a hint. "Every courtyard must be secured. Every entrance watched. This palace is a nightmare to guard, even with the wards in place to prevent outsiders from entering without escort. The only way I can assure your safety—and the security of Annwyn—is to guard you myself."

He did not sound happy about it. I hated that the shredded remains of my heart took offense. I should be glad that he cared so unwaveringly for the peace and safety of Annwyn. Someone needed to.

I suppressed the guilt that threatened. *I* had other concerns.

"I do not want you guarding my door," I said plainly.

I regretted the word the moment I said it. His brows eased apart, his stance shifted. The words slid from his mouth in a dangerous purr.

"What do you want, Princess?"

My hand tightened on my blade. "Queen."

"Queen." He said the word slowly, drawing it out over his tongue. The dark stubble on his chin gleamed in the low firelight mixed with stars and moons as he tried out the syllables. As he said, "My Queen."

There was only one answer.

"You," I breathed.

There was the real truth.

I hated him.

He was the symbol of everything that had been stolen from me.

Freedom.

I should have been a princess in waiting my entire life, centuries spent sparring beneath the sweltering Annwyn sun while my brother reigned on high.

Choice.

Princesses in a realm of brutal beings held together by tenuous traditions had few choices. But before Arthur's death, with my mother locked away in her wing, at least I'd had those few to cherish. The Queen of the Elemental Fae had none. Wed. Rule. Reproduce.

I wanted more.

I wanted less.

I wanted.

I wanted him.

Despite what I'd lost, I wanted Arran with every breath I took.

I wanted his mouth on mine, his large hand curled in my hair. I'd touched myself to the thought of what his cock would feel like inside of me.

Despite the objections of my mind, his body called to mine.

Now. Now. Now.

"I want you," I breathed, catching Arran's arm.

He didn't try to pull away, allowing me to drag him closer. There were no illusions of who would win a battle of physical strength between us. If Arran had not wanted to be there, he would not be.

He was close enough now that I could see what I wanted.

His eyes were not glowing.

The curse of a passionate race—desire could not be hidden, even among the treacherous elementals.

They were burning.

The legends told of a male with eyes darker than night, the irises enveloping the pupils until they were nothing more than ominous black orbs. But I could see their beauty.

They were black, like the soul he'd shown me again and again since our first meeting. But in shades. His pupils were the darkest, the color of forgotten desert pits where only death and decay awaited. But the irises were a softer shade of black. The color of a starless night.

A color I recognized from those first nights I'd snuck out of the water gardens. In the deep of winter, clouds came to the Kingdom of the Elemental Fae. While in summer the stars were so numerous one could walk without a lantern or magic flame to light the way, in the winter the night took on a different shade.

But just there, almost imperceptible, where the irises touched the pupils, danced a glittering black flame. A flame that lit every desire within my body.

Arran wanted me.

Maybe it did not consume him, waking and sleeping.

In all likelihood, he did not sip his tea and imagine it was my mouth on his.

But he wanted me.

And he could not deny it.

"You will not sleep at my door," I said.

Arran's eyes burned into mine. Searching, surely, for the same hint of desire in my own eyes.

But he would not find it.

"Would you rather I sleep in your bed?" He couched the words in sarcasm, but I recognized them for what they were. He was searching for what he could not see. He was chalking it up to a trick of the light, that my eyes did not match my words.

Oh, my poor Brutal Prince.

If only you knew.

But he had not earned access to that part of me, even if he thought himself entitled to be the protector of my physical body.

"If you come to my bed, there will be no sleeping," I promised.

I dragged my tongue over my bottom lip, tilting my head to one side.

He could make whatever excuses to himself that he needed to about my eyes and their inexplicable lack of lusty glow.

I was close enough to see the burning in his eyes flare brighter as he leaned in. His breath slid over me, warm and musky, down the sensitive skin of my throat toward my breasts.

His lips grazed the corner of my mouth, that tender indent where my lips met.

"When I come to your bed, it will be because you beg me for it," Arran breathed. "Not because you are trying to distract me to get your way."

Then he stepped past me, brushing me to the side. Every point of contact, every place where his clothed body brushed against mine burned with need. But pride pressed my lips together, kept me from telling him that the want I felt was for myself.

I would never beg for him.

Leaning over, Arran tossed the limp male body over his shoulder. "I trust your Goldstones know how to dispose of him."

I said nothing. It was not a real question. I'd sent my blade through his heart and slit his throat. But given enough medical attention, if the power in him was strong enough, the male could possibly recover. The only sure way to kill a fae was to behead them. My Goldstones understood that without question.

Arran walked to the door, not bothering to look at me even when he paused to say, "If you want me, I'll be right outside your door."

He closed it just in time for my knife to embed itself in the thick wood—rather than his back.

25
VEYKA

The terrestrial brute stayed awake until past midnight, every single night.

I dismissed my handmaidens early, not even bothering to have Carly untangle my mass of hair still braided from dinner. Luckily, I'd built a habit of seeing to myself in the evenings. I could have done without a handmaiden at all—had done, for all those years of seclusion.

I could draw my own bath, fold my own clothing, and plait my own hair. But a queen was meant to have handmaidens.

When they'd first been assigned to me, in the weeks after my father died and Arthur assumed the throne, I'd tried to dismiss them. Arthur had persuaded me to keep them on—playing at my guilt. It was an honor to be selected to serve the princess. It would bring shame upon their family if I dismissed them. They would be turned out from their home.

I did not know if any of it was true. Though the more I learned about the elemental court, the less I doubted my brother's veracity.

Charis, Carly, and Cyara had become my friends, of a sort. At least, they had started to become such, before Arthur's murder had shoved me into my pit of despair and apathy.

But they took their evening dismissals in stride, smiling and nodding. They passed into their connecting chambers to spend the evening at their leisure. I wished I could have housed them elsewhere, both for their sakes and my own. They deserved to partake in the pleasures the court had to offer, even if I was determined to lie listlessly in my bed. But they could not leave me, their only path to freedom through my bedchamber—a path they would rather die than tread.

So it was only when the sounds ebbed from their shared chambers, when my betrothed ceased moving and his breath came in regular intervals, that I slipped from my bed to the secret door on the veranda.

This time I was clad appropriately. I wore the same deep amethyst tunic I'd worn earlier in the day, gossamer held in place over my torso and breasts by silver clasps. But I'd exchanged my flowing skirt, open at the hips to reveal my legs, for billowing pants that whispered in the wind.

I was no more than a phantom as I descended the thousand stairs below the goldstone palace to the forested mountains. It was a slow path, but a secure one. As I moved through the clearings of stunted desert trees, every step brought me closer to vengeance.

Until a sound pricked my delicately pointed ears.

Behind me, I heard the brush of wool against wood.

I was not alone.

"Very clever."

Arran's voice sliced through me. It might as well have been his battle axe.

I forced the tension from my shoulders, channeling Parys' cocky smile as I turned around, one hand planted on my hip.

"You're the clever one, it would seem," I said wryly.

My hand closed around one of my knives by instinct, though I knew by now that Arran would not harm me. It would endanger his precious peace and stability, his absolute dedication to peace in Annwyn. But that did not mean he would not try to drag me back to the palace and lock me inside.

"How did you get past the wards?" he asked with feigned casualness.

He leaned against a barren tree, his face half in shadow. The dark eye that was illuminated glittered. Even now, he wanted me. Maybe I could use that against him, finally.

There was nothing casual about the game we were playing now. Arran had discovered another one of my secrets—my route out of the palace through the secret door. I could not give him another.

I pulled my knife free, testing its weight in my hand. "How did *you* get past the wards, terrestrial brute?"

His eyebrow twitched. He was getting better at hiding his emotions, but that temper of his was always so near the surface. And the more we were together, the easier I could spot his tells.

"I am the most powerful fae in thousands of years. Or have you forgotten?" As he spoke, the tree groaned behind him.

I darted several steps forward into the clearing, away from the perimeter of trees. Arran's dark chuckle filled the air around me. I was closer to him now, within half a lunge.

"Bastard," I swore under my breath. He'd driven me right into his clutches, no better than an animal being herded by a predator.

I would not be his prey.

He'd untangled the complicated wards protecting the goldstone palace. Difficult, but as he'd pointed out, the creators of the wards had never anticipated someone of his power. But I knew exactly who stood before me.

I flipped my knife into the air.

"You followed me," I said, meeting his black fire eyes.

"Of course."

The hilt of the dagger landed in my palm. "Why?"

He gifted me a humorless chuckle. "Did you forget the part where I am meant to be protecting you?"

I stepped to the side, dagger loose in my hand once more. "I can take care of myself."

"So you say," Arran sighed, pushing away from the tree. He was tiring of my antics.

Time to make my move.

I dragged the tip of my dagger down the center of my chest until it touched my navel. The deep amethyst gossamer fell away to reveal the curves of my breasts.

"Or perhaps you would rather take care of me," I purred.

The glimmer in those dark eyes intensified. He looked like a demon from the very pits of the hell humans were so afraid of. Despite my precarious position, desire unfurled in my belly.

"If you'd rather beg me to come to your bed instead of forcing me to sleep on the floor outside your door, I'll not refuse you." Arran stepped forward, hands flexing toward me.

Something inside of me growled—*yessss*.

"So you'd have another excuse to haunt my every step? I think not." But my actions belied my words, my fingertips drifting down to skim the barren curve of my breast. I held my ground as Arran stalked closer.

He was near enough to reach me now. A jerk of his hand, and he'd be dragging me back up the thousand stairs to the goldstone palace. I couldn't match his powers. He had every growing thing in the clearing at his command—and the beast I'd yet to see.

"We will be joined eventually," Arran breathed.

The end of my braid twitched.

I sucked in a breath, my eyes falling. The moonlight didn't reach the close space between us. But my sharp fae eyes could see enough without it.

Arran's wide, powerful hand gripped the tail of my plait, one fingernail scraping over the strand of lapis lazuli I hadn't bothered to remove before pretending to go to bed. What would that hand feel like cupped around my breast, the fingernail scraping over my taut nipple...

A nighttime breeze stirred the warm air, lifting away the gossamer hanging off of me in shreds and teasing my tortured flesh. And on that breeze—a fetid, stomach-turning stench.

The warning ripped from my throat at the same time as Arran's roar, the space where we'd stood moments before now a writhing mass of fur and fangs.

As the knife left my hand, I was already drawing the slender blades from my back. Longer than daggers, not as hefty as my brother's sword, forged especially for my use.

"Get back!" Arran yelled, his battle axe catching a sliver of moonlight.

The creature it illuminated made my fae blood run cold. Nearly as tall as Arran, its blue-black fur gleamed in the moonlight. But the real threats were the sharp white extremities—pointed spikes down its back to the tip of its tail and wickedly curved horns that could pierce fae shields. At least those wielded by the elementals. I belatedly wondered if the magic that forged terrestrial shields was stronger as Arran raised his.

The shield shattered instantly, knocking Arran back onto the ground.

I screamed as loud as I could, the sound wrenching through the short trees. The skoupuma turned at the sound, giving me only a half second of regard before attacking.

It was enough—I was fast, if nothing else.

I jumped clear, landing hard against one of the trees at the edge of the clearing. Absorbing the impact to my shoulder, I used the force to shove myself in yet another direction.

But the skoupuma wasn't fooled, its lithe body curling to face me. A cloud covered the moon. I couldn't see Arran in the dark, though I could sense his gathering power. I could not wait and hope for him to save me.

Nor did I want to.

I launched myself forward with all the anger and rage I'd suppressed for the last six months.

One blade swiped for the eyes, dangerously close to those fangs, while I aimed the other for the base of its horn. If it impaled me with one of those horns, it would corkscrew its head from left to right, digging deep into my flesh. Not enough to kill me, but to subdue me until its fangs—and the malodorous venom dripping from them—could end my life.

My blade found one eye, but the skoupuma's vicious yowl, its head rearing back, sent my other blade skittering away. A massive paw hit my chest, the force of it sending me careening backward even as sticky green blood flowed down over my forearm.

But I didn't stay down, could not. It was a second behind me, the stench of those fangs filling my nostrils as I dragged myself up into a crouch. I would not die here, now. I could not—with Arthur's murder still unavenged.

I crossed my blades in front of my face, ready to shove the beast back and counterattack.

But I didn't get the chance.

Blades of grass sprung up all around me, as tall as my face where I crouched waiting for an attack that did not come. I shoved them aside, pushing to my feet. But the skoupuma was already falling back, the long blades curving around its legs, pulling it down and pinning it to the ground.

I watched in awe. It ought to have been impossible. It was grass, for the sake of the Ancestors. My swords swiped through dozens of blades as I unraveled to my feet. But hundreds, thousands, maybe millions of blades of grass were twining around the creature's body. It could do nothing but roar its displeasure.

I saw Arran then, standing on the other side of the clearing where he'd been felled. No shield or axe in sight. Only his empty hands, flexing before him, controlling the plants in the clearing. Not just the grass, I realized. He'd peeled back the very treetops themselves, so that the entire clearing was bathed in moonlight as clearly as if it had been day.

And the expression on his face?

Boredom tinged with annoyance.

That was power.

He flicked his eyes to me, the glow of desire gone but a different sort of lust in his eyes.

"Finish it," he said.

I didn't argue with his order. I stepped through the long grass, now tall enough to reach my waist. I sheathed one blade behind my back, then shifted the other so I held it between my two clenched fists.

I did not look up to see Arran's expression as I drove the sword down between the skoupuma's horns.

It died in silence, no yowl or roar or ceremony.

I supposed that most of us could hope for no better.

Arran kept the grassy manacles in place for several minutes, until even the fetid stink of the creature's poison faded away.

"What is it?" he asked.

I raised an eyebrow. "Didn't they drill you on beasts of the elemental kingdom before sending you here?" I certainly knew all about what lurked in the Shadow Wood. But then, his training had been practical while mine, closeted in the water gardens, was mostly theoretical.

He glared at me.

"A skoupuma. The fangs are coated in poison. If it enters your body, you'll need a skilled fae healer faster than you'll be able to find one," I said, looking closer at the beast now that it was free of its emerald cage. "They do not usually come this close to the palace. I have never encountered one."

Arran shot me a disapproving look—how often had I been among these trees at night, to know such things?

I ignored the question in his eyes.

Which was a mistake, because he asked a more difficult one instead.

"Why did you not defend yourself?"

I forced a wry smile to my face and held up my blade, quite literally dripping with the creature's blood.

He eyed it grimly, but did not flinch. "Not with that. With your magic."

Too close, too close, my insides screamed. "Magic has a cost," I parroted, as I must have a thousand times in my short life.

He shook his head in disbelief—and blatant disapproval. "Surely your life... or mine... warrants the cost. Or do you truly hate me so much? That you would leave me upon the mercy of that thing?"

"I do not hate you." The words sprang so quickly from my chest I had no chance to stop them, to weigh their worth in this fraught game we'd been playing for days. Weeks, now. Years, if the Ancestors were to be believed.

He shook his head again, dismissing me with a look of derision.

Part of me yearned to tell him.

How could that be? I'd spent my entire life guarding this secret, closeted away in the water gardens by my mother, to protect the realm. The same reasons that poured from Arran's lips at every turn —peace, security, safety.

Why should I want to tell him?

To share the weight, my bruised heart answered. With Arthur gone, it was mine alone.

I could not keep it a secret forever, could not keep it from him when we were destined to spend eternity together. But until our Joining... until then...

Until then, I had to protect myself. I had to stay alive long enough to avenge Arthur.

He could hate me. I could stand it. Had I not borne those same looks from my mother since my awakening?

Willing ice into my veins, I lifted my arms and sheathed the blades down my back. A drop of that dark, revolting green blood fell onto my cheek, dripping from the steel. I felt his eyes note it, though he was pretending to ignore me now. But I did not flinch.

"We must return to the palace before we are missed," I said, stepping around him. I heard his predatory steps behind me, stalking me through the forest like the hunter that he was. But I did not glance back over my shoulder. And I did not wipe away the blood until I was alone in my chambers once again.

26
VEYKA

My mouth was sticky with the chocolates my nursemaid snuck in. My mother disapproved of sweets, her comments about my soft tummy ringing in my ears long after she floated away from the water gardens.

The water gardens. My first memories were of crashing waterfalls, ebbing rings of ripples, and terror.

Suddenly it wasn't chocolate in my mouth, on my fingers. It turned white and milky before my eyes. I wasn't a child. No, I was. A child still, even if they insisted I was not.

My nursemaid was screaming—Ana. She was horrified. They were always horrified at first, before they became complacent. What escape was there? That was the Queen of the Elemental Fae looking on, her water magic increasing the crash of the waterfalls into a roar loud enough to cover my screams.

Ana wouldn't stand quietly in the corner or slip away to the nursery. She was fighting her way toward me, past the wall of water my mother summoned. She tore at it with her wind, trying to divert the swell, but her power was nothing to the Queen.

"Stop that howling."

Whose? Mine? My mouth was open, screaming, tears running down my face. No matter how often it happened, I couldn't stop the tears. The pain—it wrung every bit of control from me.

The wall of water surged higher, then plummeted down in a graceful swirl.

Graceful, if it hadn't been horrific. If that twirling rope of water was not shoving itself down Ana's throat, silencing her screams.

Drowning her.

I pressed my eyes closed.

Make it stop. Make it stop. Make it stop.

But it wouldn't. I was old enough to know that, to know that when my mother came—when she brought him with her—they wouldn't stop until he was satisfied.

I choked, sputtering, my body fully out of my control.

Make it stop.

It wouldn't stop.

Make it stop.

Then he withdrew, the intense pressure ripped from my body. Every orifice aching, my stomach clenched, the bitter emptiness inside of me somehow hollower than it had been before.

My eyes were still closed.

The roar of water couldn't cover the things happening within the room, my fae hearing too sharp even if I was deficient in every other way.

Fabric shifted back into place, as if nothing untoward had happened. A satisfied male sigh.

"Well?" my mother demanded in her low whisper, cold and calculating, always.

"I have filled her as best I can."

My stomach lurched. I was going to be ill.

Not now, I urged myself. *Not until they are gone. Not until they leave us.* If I could hold out that long, Ana would pull me into her lap. Maybe she, finally, would help me escape this never-ending torture.

"When will we know?" the Queen asked.

"We must give the seeds of magic time to take root."

I couldn't contain it. Bile spewed from my throat, onto the stone floor before me. My knees trembled with the force of it. I collapsed to them, hardly *feeling the pain of my joints hitting the ground. Everything else hurt too much.*

My mother's disgusted scoff filled my ears.

They walked away, out the door which closed with a soft sweep of hinges. The crash of water softened until it was nothing but the natural fall of water into a still pool. I stared at that door for several long beats, never truly believing the torture was over.

Magic would never take root. Not in me. No matter how many times they tried to pump me full.

Finally, I allowed myself to look to Ana, a whimper escaping my throat.

A whimper that turned to a scream, with no crash of water to cover it.

She lay on the cold stone floor, no breeze left to lift her hair away from her cheek. Her once warm brown eyes stared at me, unseeing.

I collapsed forward, scrambling across the ground to reach her. Crawling through my own vomit, through the liquid evidence of my torture. But no matter how much I begged, she did not rouse.

Make it stop.

But there was no one who would.

<hr />

I jolted awake, straight up in the center of the bed soaked with my own sweat. Droplets ran down my face from my temples, mingling with the moisture on my cheeks. I might be crying. If I was... at least there was no one there to see my weakness.

I had not dreamt of the water gardens in months. In those first weeks after my rescue, they had haunted me nightly. But with Arthur's love, with his companionship—with my mother banished to her wing of the goldstone palace—I had begun to heal.

Since Arthur's murder, it had been a different nightmare that haunted my dreams.

Arthur, who had walked into the water gardens after my father's death and killed every guard and servant who'd played a part in my imprisonment. Arthur, who had done what my father had always been too passive, too afraid of my mother to do. Arthur, whose raging flames had sealed my mother inside her suite of rooms as punishment for the torture she'd overseen. Arthur, the last person who knew my secret.

That despite my mother's years of trying, no magic lived inside of me.

I was utterly powerless.

I came into the world that way—and if I was not careful, I would leave it very soon.

27
ARRAN

Veyka was not the only one sneaking out of the goldstone palace.

I didn't dare leave her at night. She hadn't fought my presence outside her door even after I followed her out that secret passageway. The thought of that hidden door on her balcony kept me from sleep for the rest of that night. If there was one secret passageway, there were more.

Which meant there were more routes into the palace than I'd accounted for so far. Another assassin would come. But the next would not get into Veyka's bedchamber. I'd searched her rooms the next morning, under the guise of listening to Gawayn give his daily report. No more hidden doors to be found.

Was the attempt on her life connected to the successful one on her brother six months before? It was possible, but the humans responsible had been beheaded.

Humans could continue to slip through the rifts, a few at a time. They always would, so long as the passages between realms remained open. Our world was a mirror of their own, though Annwyn was filled with magic, while the human realm was a pale imitation.

I had never passed through one of the rifts myself. There was no shortage of worthy foes in this realm—why would I seek out the weaker human ones?

Even now, I doubted the humans were the true threat. They'd gotten lucky once. But twice was impossible.

More likely, someone within the Annwyn saw an opportunity.

Veyka was young at twenty-five years old, but her twin had been as well. Arthur, however, had been raised from birth to be High King of Annwyn. Guinevere, while not selected until adulthood, was part of the generation of powerful terrestrial fae females raised with the goal of becoming High Queen.

But Veyka had not.

Neither, I hated to admit, had I.

She was the spare. Second children were not unheard of among the fae. But we were so long lived, so damn difficult to kill, that one had never ascended the throne of Annwyn. There was no reason to prepare her for an impossibility.

Who knew what education she had received. I knew very little about her. The Princess of Peace, she'd been called at her birth. I recognized it for what it was—the priestess' attempt to put a positive spin on an impossible occurrence—the birth of twins to the royal family.

My own education had been in battle and brutality, not statecraft.

Yet, here we were. Set to become the High King and Queen of Annwyn.

A powerful fae might think us easy to dethrone. If they could get to Veyka before the Joining, it would throw Annwyn back into the chaos our Offering had only just forestalled.

Veyka had been careful never to reveal her power to me. Another secret between us. Whether she kept it from her entire court, or it was some intricate elemental ploy to keep the terrestrials off balance, I didn't know.

Most assumed water. It was her mother's power. And she had those mesmerizing blue eyes.

Perhaps she was weak. It would have been considered an embarrassment. The High King and Queen were traditionally powerful. The elemental bloodline was kept pure for that very reason. The terrestrial heir was always selected for their strength. But I knew enough history to know that there had been less gifted rulers. By only using her powers minimally, she could keep the illusion and mystery alive.

But when I closed my eyes, the female that clouded my mind was anything but weak. She was cunning and dynamic. Frustratingly headstrong, she had seemingly no regard for her own well-being. I could not say what motivated her. But when that passion entered her eyes, when it overtook the despondent façade she tried to wear... No. Whatever Veyka was, she was not weak.

Good.

When I finally got her under me, when she begged for my touch, I wanted to fuck her hard enough to shake the walls of the blasted goldstone palace. I wanted her strong thighs wrapped around my waist and her chest heaving those gorgeous breasts up and down for my own sole enjoyment.

The beast within me roared.

Veyka was not the only one who needed a route out of the palace. By revisiting the entrance to the monumental staircase, I'd found my own.

It was trickier to sneak out during the day without the darkness to shade the way. But until we were joined, and I was officially High King, the Royal Council of the Elemental Court was more than happy to exclude me from their daily dealings. I'd decided to grant them a reprieve—for now.

Only because I needed to keep an eye on Veyka. I trusted her judgment even less than the Royal Council.

The strange, shallow-rooted trees that populated the mountains surrounding the Effren Valley were easy enough to pull together, to hide me from airborne eyes as I slipped from the goldstone palace under the sweltering Annwyn sun. Once I was out of earshot of the sensitive ears of the terrestrials Osheen had patrolling the perimeter, I shifted.

My strides lengthened, the wind whipping at the layers of pale fur that covered my beastly body. I'd never seen myself in this form, but I had read a few descriptions written of my battlefield terrors. The eyes black as death. The fangs as long as a child's forearm.

I was a giant in my fae form, towering at seven feet tall when most fae males never reached six and a half. But as a beast, my eyes were level with where the spiky fronds started to branch off from the thick trunks. The deeper I ran into the mountains, the taller the trees and the better the cover.

I was so much faster in this form. So much freer.

My mother had once told me that she felt most herself soaring in the skies as a hawk—more than she ever had as the Lady of Eilean Gayl.

I could understand what she meant. When I ripped an enemy's head from their body... felt their lifeblood drain away... in my beast form, the guilt left me. All that mattered was the beast's need to kill.

The wisp of a scent filled my nostrils as I bounded over the next rise. I'd have missed it in my fae form, even as powerful as I was. Perhaps the beast knew—this was his fight, not mine.

I lifted my head to the sky, the burning orb of fire hovering at exactly high noon, and howled. It echoed through the red canyon below, over the hills from where I'd come... perhaps all the way back to the goldstone palace.

But those worries were, for the moment, behind me.

Now to find the skoupumas.

28

VEYKA

I wanted to kill and maim. After nights of fitful sleep, I'd woken that morning with bloodlust on my tongue. I donned the twin scabbards that Arthur had gifted me on our twentieth birthday and stalked to the training courtyard with only a mouthful of eggs and a sip of tea for nourishment.

My rage was enough to fuel me.

"Ah, ah, ah," Lyrena clucked her tongue, easily dodging the swipe of my dagger. "You're fast, Veyka, but never feint unless you're ready for it to become a true attack," she advised.

I let her think that I was taking her lessons in stride.

She was a fine warrior, there was no argument from me. When she sparred with Arthur, they'd both coated their blades in flame. But my first rule of the ring had always been no magic.

Actually, Arthur had made that decree. When he freed me from the water gardens, he'd told his Goldstones that he wished to measure the extent of my skill without magic. After that, no one had dared question why I never wanted to test my powers in the ring as well.

They assumed my power was over the element of water, like my mother.

I would rather have my organs extracted from my body through my throat one by one than share something with the Dowager.

Besides, magic had a cost. The greater the use of magic, the greater the cost. If I was a powerful water wielder as they all believed, having grown up in the water gardens would have given me plenty of practice. What need did a queen have to show off when there were servants to attend to my every need and bear any unfortunate consequences?

I let them come to all of those conclusions, played into them whenever I could, just as Arthur had. The one thing Arthur, the Dowager, and I all agreed on—my lack of magic must be kept a secret at all costs. If the Royal Council, my courtiers, if *anyone* knew... it would tear the kingdom apart. Perhaps even invalidate the treaty signed by the Ancestors seven thousand years ago that ended the Great War between our two kingdoms.

Lyrena parried forward, catching my blade low.

I tried to hold on, but she was strong and the angle was bad.

I had no choice. I dropped the dagger, spinning away fast before she could nick me and draw blood.

I darted around one column. I used the second I was out of sight to pull the other dagger from its scabbard and slip it down the front of my bodice.

A benefit of having such large breasts was the gap between them. They were a hindrance to my movements most of the time. But they were also a superb hiding place.

As I stepped into the open archway between the next two pillars, I pulled one of the slender curved blades from across my back.

"Hiding?" Lyrena teased, circling her wrist rhythmically as she spoke. Her sword moved faster and faster, a dangerous spinning scythe moving closer to me with every falsely casual step she took.

I shrugged, matching her easy manner. "Do you think I ought to hide from you?"

"I think it has been a long time since you've been bested in the training yard. It makes you cocky," Lyrena said. Her voice rang with sincerity.

I wondered who had been the one to knock her down a few pegs. For her sake, I hoped it had been Gawayn or Arthur, rather than Evander. He was my least favorite, and the cruelest opponent among my Goldstones, by far.

But Lyrena's assessment of me was a mistake. I wasn't cocky, I was confident. I knew her abilities and I knew my own.

She thought I was tired.

In a second, her casual stance morphed, a battle cry tearing from her lips. She charged, hoping to catch me off balance. I'd barely slept in days, I'd already faced two opponents, I ought to have been tired—my reactions slower.

I wasn't tired. I was wide awake, this clang of metal on metal pouring energy into me more efficiently than sleep ever would.

I waited until she was close enough to hear my sharp inhale before I dashed to the side, spinning again. Lyrena caught herself before she careened into the wall, coming up with a brutal slash I had to twist to dodge. Even so, she caught the edge of my loose gauzy trousers.

I drew her out, across the courtyard, into the middle of the ring.

She accused me of hiding? A wicked idea formed in my mind, my mouth curving as it took root.

Around and around I drove her, our feet loosening the packed red dust in the center of the courtyard. I could sense her frustration growing. She wanted this to be over. She would make her final attack soon.

I waited patiently.

And when she lifted her sword above her head to strike the powerful blow to end it all, I ducked underneath and used all the breath in my chest, blades swirling in each hand, not towards her flesh to draw blood, but across the ground and up.

The red dirt we'd kicked up in our sparring swirled into the air, clouding it instantly. Lyrena's choking cough filled the ring. But she recognized immediately the danger of it, swallowing down dust so she was silent.

It was too late.

By the time she found me, the tip of my curved blade was pressed against her throat.

"Do you concede?" I said with mock sweetness.

She laughed, even with my blade pressed to her throat. "It seems that I have no choice, Your Majesty."

I released her, indulging myself in the pleasure of a small smile as I sheathed my weapon and gave her a gentle shove.

"Who's next? I won't be the last one to be embarrassed!" Lyrena crowed, pointing her sword in a wide arc at her fellow Goldstones, as well as the palace guards further back.

Not a one of them spoke out.

Evander's nose crinkled as if he smelled something unpleasant.

Coward.

I reached one arm above my head, catching the wrist in the other hand and stretching before repeating the stretch on the other side.

Slow, methodical claps rang out across the training ring.

As the red dust cleared, settling back onto the ground, I saw him.

His thick dark hair was tucked back, secured at the base of his neck as if he might have to spring into action at any second. The lines of his jaw, so broad and strong, promised mercilessness in battle. The flame of hate in my belly crackled and burned, but it was not alone. It danced with lust, just as hot and even more dangerous.

My gut clenched. How long had he been lurking in the shadows, watching? One match? Three?

Maybe, after the night with the skoupuma, he'd finally decided to see just what I could do for myself.

Everything, I wanted to scream at him.

I released my arms slowly, knowing that raised over my head like this my breasts must look amazing. I was much too far away to see that burning desire in his eyes, but I knew it was there, nonetheless. I'd use it against him every chance I got.

If that made heat pool between my legs that had nothing to do with the sweat of exertion... well, I'd already admitted that I wanted him. Both to Arran and to myself. But I would not beg, ever.

He could go to his death in a thousand years with his hand around his own cock for all I cared.

Arran stalked closer, eyeing Lyrena, her chest still rising and falling heavily. Then he looked over the rest of the guards, granting Evander a particularly nasty sneer. At least Arran and I could agree on one thing.

"Will none of you take her on?" he asked, stopping in the center of one of archways, arms crossed. His head nearly touched the center stone, painted a glowing cerulean blue.

Even though he'd been here for weeks, I did not think I would ever grow used to seeing him in the goldstone palace. His dark hair, dark clothes, dark aura were so at odds with the airy heat of this place. What was his body like, beneath all of those layers?

"She's that terrifying, your queen?" But as he spoke, Arran was not looking at the guards any longer. He was staring at me.

"If you step into the training yard, you have to fight her," Gawayn advised from his post against one of the pillars.

Arran ran his thumb along the head of his battle axe, still holstered at his waist. "Is she bound by the same agreement?"

His lips pouted out slightly, considering me.

His eyes asked—*will you fight me, princess?*

I flipped my long braid back down my back, unsheathing my twin curved blades in answer.

"Well, then," Arran murmured, his eyes never leaving mine as he stepped into the ring.

In the periphery of my vision, I saw Guinevere walking over to the water barrel, saying something to Lyrena I could have surely heard if my ears were not pounding with my own blood.

The glance in their direction was a mistake. In that half a

breath, Arran had unfastened the buttons at the top of his black wool tunic.

What was he doing?

"Not everyone is as adequately dressed as you are for the weather," he said to my questioning eyes.

I frowned, realizing what was happening a second before he tossed the wool tunic to the ground.

"I see you've adopted a lighter undershirt, at least," I said. Thank the Ancestors, the words were not as choked as they felt coming out of my throat.

But Arran did not stop at the woolen tunic. He pulled open the laces holding the linen undershirt in place, bearing a wide triangle of deeply tanned, golden brown chest. I could see the sweat already gleaming across his sculpted pectorals, the top of his etched abdomen peeking out... a promise of what lay beneath that billowing linen undershirt.

Standing in the middle of the sparring yard, staring at the most magnificent male specimen I'd ever seen, my hands began to sweat.

I was in such deep shit.

29
ARRAN

I couldn't see her eyes glowing, pale blue that they were in the afternoon light, but I could see the subtle tremble of her hands around the hilts of her blades. She'd admitted she wanted me. The Ancestors knew I dreamed of that luscious body of hers nightly, imagining what it would be like to push through the door that separated us and take her body for my own.

But this was battle.

Our bodies may burn for one another, but our souls sparked with loathing.

Just then, I wanted to punish her for her recklessness sneaking out of the palace. I wanted to remind her that she was not invincible.

She needed to understand the danger her cavalier attitude implied for all of Annwyn.

I also wanted her at my mercy.

I could not have her in my bed, so I'd bend her to my will the only other way I knew how—through battle and bloodshed.

I would use her desire for me against her. She'd never seen me in anything other than the customary clothing of a terrestrial male. Close-fitting trousers covered with knee-high boots, a knit undershirt—oftentimes more than one in the winter or when traveling north of the Spine. I'd traded that for a lighter linen base layer since coming to Baylaur. But even that was always covered with my wool tunic, buttoned at an angle across my chest.

Now, I was barely half-clothed before her.

And she was trembling.

I would enjoy having Veyka Pendragon at my mercy.

"See something you like, princess?" I said for her alone, though I knew the words would be heard by all the sharp fae ears around us. Let them hear; Veyka and I would be joined soon.

"*Like* is not the word I would use," she said, her grip tightening. She shook her head slightly, as if trying to clear it.

Little good may it do her.

She lifted her blades, rocking on her heels to settle her footing. "To first blood?" she asked coolly.

"To surrender," I said, feeling the excitement beginning to heat my blood.

I waited for the cool calm that always descended upon my consciousness, that part of my mind that shifted towards the beast even when my body remained in my fae form.

She favored her right hand, but she'd be deadly with both. It hadn't come into play in her duel with Lyrena, but I knew from how easily she'd killed the assassin in her bedroom that she was accurate with her throwing knives. This would be a duel fought close at hand, then, where my size and experience in hand to hand combat would be an advantage. She may be well trained, but I'd been killing my way across battlefields for three hundred years.

Sparring in a ring was not the same thing.

In the few breaths it had taken me to make my assessments, Veyka had moved into position. She thought I expected her to wait. So the instant my axe was in my hand, she attacked.

I was ready.

Veyka was quick—her rapid, precise movements in our squabble with the skoupuma had been no fluke. She really was an accomplished fighter.

But Arthur had been too.

One mistake, and she would be as dead as he.

Her flowy, iridescent elemental clothing left her vulnerable. There were no thick layers of leather to protect her as I swung my axe around to parry. She was wicked fast, knocking my sword aside and ducking away.

The loose pantaloons she wore, gathered at the hip with a belt then left open from hip to ankle where they gathered again, let her move swiftly. That was her main advantage, I decided.

Veyka caught my next swing, trying to force my blade up and away. She was faster, but I was stronger. I shoved her back, the blade falling from her hand. I heard the crunch of my elbow against her shoulder as she stumbled away.

I could finish this now.

I would bend her to my will, knock her flat on that beautifully rounded ass, those shapely legs sprawled around her.

What would it feel like to catch that smug lower lip of hers between my teeth and tug—

But instead of taking a moment to catch her breath, Veyka leapt forward.

She brought her blade up, quick as a flash, catching me at a bad angle. All I had to keep myself armed was my brute strength. The force of her attack ached through my wrist, then I felt the sharp burn that always meant blood as she drew away.

Ancestors... I'd never been distracted like this while sparring.

She'd managed to draw first blood. I could smell it, dripping from the tip of her curved blade, seeping through the thin linen of my shirt.

But I would have her surrender.

I darted forward—parry, slash, feint.

I was fast as well. Veyka matched me.

Heat began to build in my gut, just below my belly button. Respect. She was a formidable opponent, perhaps even Gwen's match. Who had trained her? Why had she even been trained?

Magical ability was expected, as was the basic ability to wield a weapon.

But this?

Veyka was a warrior.

Despite all her other flaws—which I catalogued for myself nightly to try to cool my ardor—she was a warrior. I could see the gleam in her eyes.

And for the first time, a more difficult question occurred to me. Not the who—but the why.

Why had Veyka Pendragon not just trained with a blade, but with throwing knives? With wickedly curved rapiers clearly made for her personal use? Why was she good enough to best her own Goldstone Guards?

Why did the Princess of Peace need to be a warrior?

Cold prickled at the back of my neck.

For half a second, I suspected foul play—perhaps she had ice magic after all.

But the determination in her eyes, the lack of pause or distraction as she twirled her body, bringing that curved blade toward me in a gruesome corkscrew, killed that supposition. I bent my right knee and swiped my sword upward, knocking her blade to the side.

I had to end this before my own distraction got me wounded enough to leave Veyka vulnerable. I would trust no one else to guard her door.

She was back, a knife in her left hand now. She jabbed the knife upward, forcing me to jump to avoid it. As I did, she brought her curved sword in from the other side. A half second slower, and she'd have succeeded in getting her blade against my throat.

But I'd watched her enough from the shadows to know what was coming. My fingers curled around her wrist, digging into the sensitive pressure point. The rapier clanged to the ground. I twisted her arm up above her head, the blade of the axe in my other hand pressed against the pale skin above her breast.

She still gripped her dagger but was powerless to wield it.

I was bleeding. She was not. But I had no doubt she'd be sporting her own bruises come the evening.

"Do you surrender?" I said, staring straight into those endless blue eyes. There was certainly no glow of desire now, though I knew my own were burning. This close to her, both of our blood running high, my cock was as demanding as my lungs gulping greedily at the air.

Veyka bit hard on her lower lip, refusing to speak.

"I'll make you a different bargain, rather than admit defeat," I said on a whim. "Let me see that wicked smile, princess," I crooned.

The one she had as she stood over her opponents in victory, the curve of her luscious mouth when she was about to land the winning blow... that look would fuel the next several weeks of fantasies. But I wanted it for myself.

"You don't deserve my smiles," she sneered, flexing her fingers around the hilt of her knife.

I pressed the blade down a little harder into the soft skin above her breast. "And why not? I will be your husband."

Her eyes flashed. "You'll find I do not put much stock in titles as the due for affection."

"How quaint, for an elemental." My grip on her wrist, still above her head, tightened. "Yet you are so irritated when I call you princess, rather than queen."

Her lip curled up to reveal her teeth. "My brother died for me to have this title."

"Died *for* you?" What a way to phrase it.

"One smile, princess, and you're free," I reminded her, letting my gaze travel down her face to her chest, to where the swell of her breasts spilled over the loose bodice. Did she wear one of those spectacular golden brassieres beneath? Or nothing at all?

I let her feel the proprietary lingering of my gaze. Felt her squirm at the hips as she tried to get away, uselessly. It only served to inflame me further.

"What smile do you want?" she bit back.

"The one I wear for the courtiers?" She forced her lips upward into a strained, almost painful expression. "Or the one for my lovers?" This one was lazy, sensuous, but bored.

"I want the one you wear just before you make the kill," I said softly, letting the heat of my breath spill across her cheek and down the column of her neck.

"This one?"

The brief flash she gave me would have to suffice. Because in the next second, she drove her knee up into my balls.

30
VEYKA

Arran Earthborn could go straight to hell.

The pits where the Gremog bred, deep in the desert beyond the Blasted Pass? The perfect place for him.

Right through one of the rifts into the human world—exactly the sort of destiny he deserved.

So long as he wasn't anywhere near me. Not in my kingdom, not in the goldstone palace, and certainly not sleeping outside my bedroom door.

"Your Majesty," Gawayn called after me, jogging to catch up.

"Veyka," Lyrena huffed, coming up alongside of me, her gold braid bouncing against her shoulder. "You cannot run off without—"

"Do not tell me what I can or cannot do," I snapped, rounding a corner.

Ancestors below.

Courtiers—everywhere.

What the fuck were they doing here in the middle of the day?

"Having afternoon tea," Lyrena answered.

I hadn't even realized I'd spoken aloud.

I threw up my hands, turning and nearly crashing into Arran.

"Leave me alone," I said, shoving hard against his chest.

Little good it did me. I was like a hummingbird beating its wings against an iron wall.

"I should have expected you to be a sore loser," he said sardonically. Though he did shift his hand to cover his balls. Satisfaction flared through me.

"Sore loser, unfit to wear the crown, you're compiling quite a list," I said as I shoved past him. It was a mistake. I should have ignored him altogether. I'd practically invited him to follow me with that comment.

Which, of course, he did.

Lyrena and Gawayn fell back. Apparently, I could not be trusted to guard myself, but Arran was sufficient. I'd have it out with them later about that. I'd bested half of my own Goldstones in the training courtyard today. It was time for them to give me some damned space.

"You could stop giving me things to add to it," Arran said. "You could start giving a shit—about anything other than fighting and fucking."

"Just because fucking is always on your mind does not mean it is on mine," I yelled over my shoulder.

It was a lie. I thought about fucking Arran day and night. I'd told him as much, after I'd killed the assassin and he declared he'd be my personal ghost.

But thinking clearly was not on the menu at that particular moment.

I was all fire and brimstone.

I threw open the doors to my suite of rooms before anyone could do it for me.

"Liar as well," Arran murmured, low enough that I knew it was meant for my ears only. Too bad we had an audience.

"Add it to the list!" I yelled back, throwing a hand up into the air.

Charis nearly upended the tray of food she was carrying to the dining table. Carly ducked behind a curtain—as she'd taken to doing whenever Arran showed up. I didn't see Cyara, she must have been in the bedroom.

Good—I wanted a bath, and for once I wouldn't mind letting her wait on me. My body was going to start aching soon. I'd let Arran land too many blows. I should have taken him down early, instead of letting that duel drag on.

But I'd been too damn busy appreciating the flashes of muscle I kept seeing beneath his billowing shirt.

My hand was raw from holding weapon after weapon for hours on hours today. Every blister screamed as my fingers closed around the handle to my bedroom. Maybe it was a night for Parys' tea—

"Get out of the way!" Arran roared, shoving me sideways across the room.

My hip hit the bookcase hard, the impact of my considerable weight sending several volumes flying.

"Have you lost your mind?" I yelled, staggering back to my feet.

Cyara screamed as Arran leaped for the bed, his sword above his head. I knew what was coming next—the vicious sweep of death.

"What is it?" I scrambled forward, grabbing the edge of the bed to lever myself around, a knife already back in my aching hand.

Another attack. Another assassination attempt. Maybe this was as serious as Arran and Gawayn seemed to think. I clenched my muscles, ready to throw or stab or—

My knife dropped to the bed, lost among the bedsheets.

An unhinged laugh tumbled out of my mouth.

There in my bed, frozen in what must have been casual repose mere moments before, looking like he was about to piss himself, was Parys.

"He is my friend," I repeated for the third time in as many minutes.

Arran was still brandishing his sword, though he'd retreated to the floor rather than standing on my bed with his dirty boots like the feral beast he was.

Parys' tawny skin was nearly as white as mine. His dark curls, usually framing his handsome face, were raked back. He'd just raked them back, I corrected. Several times. In between raising his hands, palm up, in the most ridiculous gesture of submission I'd ever seen.

"I have no weapons," Parys said, also for not the first time.

"You can do harm without weapons," Arran said, glaring.

I rolled my eyes. "What is he going to do, tickle me with his wind?"

"Or steal the air from your very lungs. Carry in a poisonous smoke through your open balcony. Your kind are crafty." Arran did lower his sword, though.

"At least that could be somewhat construed as a compliment," I said, my own knife already safely returned to its scabbard. "Add it to your ridiculous list." As I spoke, I unfastened the belt that held the twin scabbards in place and tossed them onto the velvet-upholstered bench at the foot of the bed. "Now get out."

Parys scrambled to his feet. I rolled my eyes. Again.

"Not you," I said, looking past Parys to the Brutal Prince. "Him."

Arran cocked one dark eyebrow. He was as sweaty and caked with red dust as I, but whereas I was certain I looked like a hag, I found myself wanting to lick his throat just to feel his stubble against my tongue.

That, or stab him.

Instead, I pulled loose the gold pin holding my bodice in place and began unwinding it from around my midsection.

Arran's eyes flickered. I knew if I looked closely enough, I'd see that black fire that burned just for me.

Just for me.

I wish.

Why did I wish that, precisely?

I forced down that thought, refusing to examine it even a teensy bit.

But despite the argument inside my own head, Arran's eyes were watching as inch by inch, with each pass of the sheer fabric falling away, I revealed more of my body to him. Cyara appeared at my shoulder, catching the end of the fabric and taking over the task.

"Why is your friend waiting in your bed, Veyka?" he said slowly.

Danger.

Every instinct inside of me—warrior, female, fae—all of them screamed in unison.

"Excuse me, Your Majesty," Cyara murmured, the last of the bodice falling away to reveal nothing but my thin laced bustier that held my breasts in place while I trained.

She melted away, her footsteps quietly retreating toward the door. Parys went as well, giving Arran a wide berth as he joined Cyara. They closed the door behind them.

"Parys is my friend," I said, suddenly aware that I stood before Arran in very little clothing, in very close proximity to a bed. My bed.

Whatever emotions were welling in my chest, my body did not care.

Come, it called to Arran's. *Take what is yours.*

On some other plane, down low, so deep I could almost feel it, I thought I heard the rumbling growl of an animal in return.

Arran lingered at the side of my bed, his fingers reaching down to toy with the slightly rumpled bedsheets where Parys had been laying. "Are all of your friends so comfortable in your bed?"

I swallowed hard. I should lie. "Only those I invite into it."

Arran's blade sang as it slid back into its sheath. His eyes were down, staring at the pillow, the coverlet, the traces of another male.

"You do not deny a physical relationship?" he asked, voice low and casual. He was getting better at this game.

As if we were discussing what would be served for supper. But I was not fooled. This was about to become a battle on par with the duel we'd just had in the training courtyard. The only difference was that this one would be fought with words rather than blades.

I shrugged, trying to match his tone. Knowing it was all fake. "Parys and I understand each other."

"I see." His fingers closed around the coverlet and with a sharp yank, he stripped it from the bed. Then the sheets. The pillows. All of it, until only the mattress remained.

Ancestors, at least it wasn't stained. Parys and I had never... well, we'd satisfied each other. That was the most I could say. But the kind of bed play that left behind traces of gratification after the fact? I'd never had that kind of pleasure.

I opened my mouth to protest. I *liked* my sheets and my coverlet. I'd selected them myself, when Arthur freed me from the water gardens and I finally had the freedom to choose the minutia of my life.

But the sound died in my throat as Arran stalked across the room with predatory grace and speed, and dumped the lot into the ever-burning hearth.

My anger flared. "How dare you! Those are *mine*."

"*You are mine*," Arran growled, suddenly in front of me. Suddenly cupping my chin, dragging me closer to him.

"Not yet," I managed to ground out, even as my traitorous body arched to reach him. Even as my cunt began to heat with desire.

Mine. No one had ever wanted me—not really. From the moment of my birth, I'd been the perplexing extra. Only Arthur had ever made me feel loved. But that was the love of a brother. This... I would not pretend that it was love. But it was heady all the same.

And I wanted it. I wanted him more than I wanted my next breath.

My mind and body made war inside of me, the loathing and hate crashing against the heat and desire. I was powerless before my own needs. I had no control over what my mouth or body might say or do. Nor was I really trying to reclaim that power. Not yet.

Arran lifted my chin to the side, as if examining the planes of my face. "You said your friend—"

"—Parys—" I inserted, knowing it would rankle him, pushing my lower lip out petulantly as his eyes flashed.

"*He* understands you," Arran said, twisting my chin the other way now. "What precisely does he understand, Veyka?"

I did not have an answer. Not one that I could articulate to myself, determined as I was to stay far away from the pain of my own deeper emotions. Certainly not one I was willing to articulate to the Brutal Prince.

I'd give him my body willingly. But my soul? Never.

Finally, bringing my chin back to center, he lifted it up, up, up. I was a tall female, but he was huge. Taller than any male I'd ever been with. I felt myself rise onto my toes—ready, finally.

But his mouth moved past mine, the stubble on his chin scrapping against my cheek as he spoke into my ear.

"Does he know how to make you quiver?" he breathed into my ear, raking his sharpened canines over the sensitive pointed tip. A shiver ran all the way down my spine right to my cunt.

His hand was no longer on my chin. He bracketed my hips, dragging me closer. I arched against him, eager to feel the heat that fifteen minutes ago I'd been so keen to connect with my knee. Now I wanted to feel him pressed against me. I wanted to know if that cock inside his tightly fitting terrestrial-style trousers was every bit as massive as I'd dreamed.

But Arran's hands gripped my hips harder, lifting me up off my toes as if I weighed nothing. That alone had my pussy drenched. I'd never been with someone who was my physical match. But Arran, my Brutal Prince...

He ran his tongue from the lobe of my ear, studded with jewels, along the column of my throat. There was no hiding from him how I felt, he could feel the hammering of my pulse with that tongue. Slightly rough, like an animal.

His thumbs dug into the soft flesh of my belly, just above my navel, pushing their way under the narrow ribbon waistband holding my billowing pantaloons in place.

"Does he see the warrior that lives inside of you, the beast that you try to hide?" His mouth was on my chest, his tongue teasing along the curve of my breast exposed by the half-corset.

One careful movement of his mouth, and his canines would tear through the ribbon holding the bustier in place. He'd said I would beg for him. This was all a game, a punishment for having let Parys into my rooms. But I would not beg.

But I wasn't stupid enough to push him away, either.

Ancestors, his mouth. His tongue moved along the top of the bustier, closer to the center where the lacings were. I could not control the little yelp of pleasure as one canine pricked my skin. No scent of blood, but Ancestors, the pleasurable pain of it...

Then he swiped one hand lower. "Does he fill you with his fingers until you come all over him in tidal waves of pleasure?"

Arran cupped me through the layers of thin fabric that covered my legs. His soft chuckle poured over me, the warmth of his breath sliding beneath the bustier until my nipples ached.

There was no mistaking my desire. Whatever my traitorous eyes might have said—they were closed—the pool of heat between my legs spoke loud and clear.

I'd kept my hands firmly at my sides, clenched into fists so tight I knew I'd have bruises where my fingernails pressed into my palms. But as his fingers began to stroke me, playing me like a musical instrument, I could keep my hands to myself no longer.

I went straight for his hair. I'd dreamed of tangling it around my fingers, pulling it from the neat bun he always kept it in.

I slid my fingers past his temples, the heat and sweat and scent of him nearly melting me into a puddle on the tiled floor. His bun was loose from our dueling, some strands already falling forward. I stroked with my thumbs across his temples, weaving my fingers between the strands.

Ancestors above, if this was how he smelled, how would he taste?

Arran paused, tipping back his head to look at me.

I opened my eyes hesitantly. Some part of me worried that if I did, all of this would end.

"Because I understand, Veyka," Arran said softly, slowly pulling his hand away from my pussy.

I had just enough pride to keep from clenching my legs together in a desperate attempt to keep him there. I slid my hands from his hair, letting them rest on his shoulders as he drew his mouth away from my breasts and lowered me to the floor, looking down at me.

His words were soft. Like the promise of a lover... but with the threat of death.

"You are hiding something, Veyka. I will find out what it is. Even if it means taking you to the edge of pleasure, until you are wet and hot and willing to give me anything. Then, you will tell me, Princess."

I shoved him backward as hard as I could.

He did not stumble. Because of course he did not. Whether I admitted it—and I certainly would not—he'd won this duel as well.

He smirked as he rolled his shoulders, loosening himself up after a battle well fought and won.

"Find yourself some new sheets," he said, glancing back at the bed.

My anger flared in time with the flames in the hearth, which had so thoroughly consumed my coverlet and sheets. My knives were in their scabbards on the other side of the bed. So I swiped up a beautifully wrought clay pot off the nearest table and threw it at his head.

My aim was excellent.

But he was too fast.

He chuckled again, and damn him, but all I could think of was how that warm chuckle had felt against my tortured flesh.

"See that no other male spoils them," he added as he continued toward the door. "From now on, the only male in your bed is me."

"What about a female?" I asked flippantly.

Arran's eyes darkened, the corner of his mouth lifting. It might have been the first genuine smile he'd ever given me.

"Perhaps someday, Veyka, we shall invite another female to our bed. But not until I have charted every crevice of your body to my satisfaction."

The second pot hit the center of his back. But the bastard acted as if he hadn't felt it at all.

31

ARRAN

She was very adept at sneaking out, I had to give her that.

I'd been sleeping outside of her door for weeks on the same bedroll I'd traveled with for the last hundred years or so. Tiles weren't the most comfortable bed I'd ever had, but they were far from the worst.

In that time, I'd come to recognize the sounds of her handmaidens. The younger two, Charis and Carly, were always jabbering—until I entered the room. That was fine; the less female drama I had to contend with, the better. The Ancestors knew that Veyka created more than her fair share for someone only twenty-five years old.

The best part of their constant talk was that they made it easy to track activity in the room. Their elder sister, the senior handmaiden, was much more circumspect in her interactions. She was the voice of reason. Often, the only way I knew she was in the room was by the shuffling of her wings.

Veyka was near silent, even when she wasn't actively trying to sneak out.

Why?

She'd been raised in seclusion, I knew that much from listening to casual court conversation. Uther and Igraine only trotted her out for important state occasions and festivals. Until Uther had died and her brother Arthur assumed the elemental crown—then she had become a fixture at court. She took over these lodgings, was often seen sparring in the training courtyard, and frequently walked through the winding courtyards arm in arm with her brother.

Not a single part of that simple history told me why she snuck out of the goldstone palace. Nor did it speak to her skill at doing so.

She was twenty-five years of age. From what I knew of the human realm, women of her age often already had spouses and children. But in the fae realm, she was young. Less than a decade past her awakening. Fae her age were known for being reckless, loud, and graceless.

Veyka was the first, at least.

But the second two... no. She moved as gracefully and soundlessly as a mouse.

Not a mouse—far too meek for my moonlight-haired vixen.

A cat.

Not the kind you trained and kept for a pet, sleeping meekly on your pillow.

If Veyka had been born a shifter, she'd have been a forest predator, strong and sensual.

Lethal.

But as quiet as she was, she could not sneak past me.

I didn't hear her, exactly. It was that pull again, as if someone had stretched a line from Veyka to the center of my chest. The same one that had summoned me to her chamber the night of the assassin's attempt on her life.

A chill snaked down my spine at the memory of the assassin's skin, the way the darkness inside of her had reached out, trying to touch me. Veyka's hands were always cool to the touch, but it was an entirely different sensation. Touching Veyka reminded me of dipping my fingers into the streams that ran down from the glaciers in the early spring, fresh and sweet. Not the sort of mind-numbing cold that threatened to steal my very soul.

My eyes flickered open, summoned by the pull in my chest.

Go back to sleep, I silently willed her. If she'd ever been asleep at all. I certainly had been—and I did not appreciate being roused.

But I could sense her moving away, across the room.

With a sigh, I sat up, pulling the strip of leather from around my wrist and using it to tie back my hair. Whatever she was up to, the last time it had ended with a skoupuma attack. I grabbed my axe from beside the bedroll and fastened that to my belt as well.

There was no one else in the antechamber to disturb. Gawayn had his Goldstones posted outside the door, in the corridor, deeming my presence protection enough outside Veyka's actual bedroom.

Careful to keep my own movements silent, even to sensitive fae ears, I slipped through the door into the bedroom—which was empty. But the faint scent of primrose and plum told me enough about where Veyka had gone.

This time, she didn't try the door. She decided to scale the veranda itself.

I paused long enough to give her a head start. This time, I would find out where she was going before I dragged her selfish ass back to the goldstone palace.

My feet silent, I moved to stand on the edge of the balcony. Overhead, I heard the soft caw of a crow—a sound of acknowledgement. One of Osheen's airborne guards, circling the courtyard. I wondered if they'd seen Veyka as well. I made a mental note to myself to confer with Osheen tomorrow—when I'd gotten some damned sleep.

But if I'd noticed the terrestrials circling overhead, Veyka had too. Which meant she'd gone the other direction—down.

With a sigh, I rearranged my axe so that it was strapped over my back instead of around my waist. Then I swung my leg over the edge and began to climb.

She was not as quiet as she made her descent. I tracked her

footfalls easily enough. Twice, she slipped, and a soft gasp of frustration escaped her luscious lips.

Stop thinking about her lips.

I'd been thinking about nothing else since that afternoon I found the sniveling elemental in her bed.

That's a lie.

I'd been thinking about her breasts and cunt, too.

But now was not the time for either.

Though maybe I'd spank that round ass of hers as punishment once I had her safely back in her bedroom. She'd probably enjoy it. My cock hardened at the thought.

I gritted my teeth and forced myself to focus on softening the sounds of my own foot and handholds.

Veyka scaled three levels of balconies before she swung herself down, landing with a *thump*. I didn't have that luxury, losing precious time trailing her as I worked my way down to a silent landing.

It was an empty suite of rooms. Mine, I realized as I followed her inside.

Crafty bitch. She was using the fact that I was now sleeping in her antechamber to her advantage. My hand ached with the desire to smack her bottom—hard.

She sauntered right through them, though her steps were still quiet. I followed her easily, staying well-hidden. She lingered for a moment by the bed—just a breath longer than she should have, not quite breaking step. But enough that I noticed. Alone as I was, I didn't bother to stop the smirk that I felt come to my face.

I would have Veyka—and soon. The game we were playing would not last much longer. One of us would break. I just had to make sure it was her that ultimately surrendered—not me.

It was a brilliant escape route, really. The elemental court was too afraid of me to come too near my suite of rooms, especially at night when they believed I was occupying them. My own terrestrial companions knew better than to wake me unless there was an emergency of truly dire proportions. Limbs must be missing—

important ones—to warrant waking me. Otherwise, I'd remove a few just for spite.

Gwen, of course, knew where I truly spent my nights. She'd ribbed me about it often enough. When I had to leave, to sneak from the palace to let my beast run free, Gwen was the one I left to watch over Veyka.

Veyka cleared the goldstone palace with stunning ease. She avoided guards, slipping through doors that were so well camouflaged in the walls I hardly recognized they were there. Once she reached the secret passages reserved for the royal family and councilors, she started to jog. Her steps echoed with confidence—she was certain that she would not come upon anyone here.

I followed her as swiftly as I could without alerting her to my presence. A few times, the scent of her on the lingering breeze was my only hint as to where she'd gone. But my senses had memorized her weeks ago, imprinting her on my consciousness whether I willed it or not.

Unlike the long, winding staircase from her route that first night, we descended by levels. Only my vague animal senses were able to keep track, to tell me that we were close to the base of the mountain where the goldstone palace was perched over the city of Baylaur.

Sure enough, I heard the soft click of a door followed by a rush of fresh air. As fresh as the humid desert air of this blasted place could ever be.

I took a brief moment to examine the lock. It latched internally. Which meant that not only was Veyka putting her own life in peril by sneaking out, she was endangering everyone within the palace as well. I'd learned how to move through the magical wards, by shattering them apart. Veyka had as well. What was to stop another powerful interloper?

I would circle the perimeter and tar the doors shut myself if Veyka could not be trusted. Willful brat.

As I stepped through, I heard the subtle snap of a vine.
Clever.

Turning back to the door set behind a thick drapery of ivy—probably courtesy of Osheen—I understood immediately what Veyka had done. She'd threaded some of the vine across the door, through the handle, so that anyone coming in or out of the door would have to break the vine. She couldn't lock it behind her from the outside, but she'd know if someone entered or exited other than her.

My estimation of her nudged upward, just a little.

Of course, she'd failed to account for a flora-gifted terrestrial.

With a flick of my hand, the vine was back in place, fused together as if it had never been torn apart.

Ahead, a tall sand dune blocked the Effren Valley from view. Veyka was already near the top of it. The moon shone brightly above our heads. Once I stepped out of the shadow of the gold-stone palace, I'd be clearly visible if she turned around.

I forced myself to wait, even as my blood thrummed with anticipation in my veins. Beyond the vines hanging from the palace walls, there was little vegetation here to call to my aid. Only sand.

Veyka reached the top.

For a moment, she paused. I imagined I could see her eyes closing as she let the breeze skitter over her skin. Her dark clothing billowed behind her in the desert wind. Silhouetted against the moon, she looked half female, half ghost. Long strands of her white hair had worked loose from her braid, swirling around her with her clothing.

A mythic queen of legend, that was how she looked. All that wanted was a crown and a swirl of elemental magic.

She could be that queen, a voice inside of me said.

I bit my lip to keep in the scoff, even though I was sure she was too far away to hear it.

Veyka cared only about herself. She'd proven it again and again.

A queen that might have been, that's what she was. The supposed Princess of Peace, who was so concerned about herself that she did not care if she risked bringing her kingdom back to the brink of implosion.

She disappeared over the other side of the dune, and I was glad of it. If she had lingered another moment, I might have lost my resolve to find out where she was going and dragged her back to the palace.

My temper rearing and raging at my attempts to bridle it, I scaled the dune. When I reached the top, I knew where we were going.

Baylaur gleamed in the distance.

Maybe by the end of the night, I would know why.

She took a circuitous route around the edge of the valley, avoiding the strip of barren desert where the Gremog made its home. When she finally did cross, I hesitated a moment. She took no apparent precautions as she walked across the desert toward the city. I could only assume we were out of the Gremog's range.

I was tempted to shift—for the speed alone.

But Veyka was getting smaller and smaller in the distance. I could not lose her now.

One hand on my axe, I sprinted across.

From there, I followed her into Baylaur itself. I hadn't ventured into the city yet. I figured that terrifying the elementals inside the goldstone palace was sufficient until after the Joining. At least then, I would be High King of Annwyn rather than a foreign prince, in title, if nothing else.

The streets she chose were narrow, no more than alleys. She was trying to avoid notice.

She'd pulled a hood over her head, her white braid disappearing beneath it.

Was her appearance well-known in the city? It certainly wasn't beyond it. I'd known next to nothing about my betrothed until I'd seen her across the throne room. If one ignored that first meeting in the woods.

Which I did not.

We were working our way toward the heart of the city. The alleys slowly became dirtier, busier. I had to dodge refuse being dumped from windows overhead. Even this late at night, children darted across the alleyways.

Poverty was as alive here as it was in my own kingdom, despite the presence of powerful magic.

Veyka stopped only once, to drop something into the hand of a sleeping figure huddled against the wall.

I paused long enough behind her to see—a jewel. One of the amorite gems she wore in her ears, pressed into the palm of the sleeping fae with grizzled gray hair.

With a sigh, I turned back to the end of the alleyway.

Veyka was gone.

Ancestors below, she was so fucking fast. I was at the edge of the alleyway in half a second, but it met a much bigger street. Busy, even now that it was well past midnight. I supposed in a city of this size, the hour didn't much matter. Veyka's scent mingled with the other elementals crowding the street. I tried harder, summoning the beast within me. I caught a whiff of terrestrial magic—one of my own from the delegation, probably. I'd given them no orders binding them to the goldstone palace. A traveler was possible, though the citizens of our two kingdoms rarely intermixed, especially this far from the Spit.

But no hint of Veyka.

Fuck. I spun for the alley, my furious strides eating up the ground. I had to catch her essence on the breeze again, see if I could follow—

"Who's the clever one now?"

The tip of her dagger touched the artery just below my clavicle.

I inhaled deeply, letting the smell of her flood my nostrils and mouth, all the way into the empty cavity of my chest. Despite the anger that was still rushing through me, the distaste that I was even out of my bed for this selfish princess, my beast rumbled a little growl of satisfaction at having her near once more.

"How did you hide your scent?" the beast asked in my own voice. He didn't plan on letting it happen ever again.

"That is none of your concern," she said. "Why are you following me?"

I ignored her question. "When did you realize I was trailing you?"

Veyka snorted. I hadn't expected her to divulge that information. "I have told you—and shown you—that I can defend myself."

She pressed her knife a bit harder against my chest to make her point.

"I could have you on the ground beneath me in the time it takes you to stab that knife into my chest," I crooned, soft like a lover.

"Then do it."

I jabbed my elbow back sharply, feeling the force of the air leave her as I buried it in her soft stomach. Her hand didn't falter, the blade pressing down hard. But not hard enough—and she knew it.

I knocked her hand away, my other arm reaching for her wrist.

She let me catch it, anticipating that I would try to throw her bodily over my shoulder to the ground. She threw one leg around my waist to prevent me, landing her heel dangerously close to my balls. I swung her laterally instead. Her bottom ought to have hit the ground, but she miraculously got a foot under her, which she used to shove herself up and me off balance.

I stumbled backward. She managed to untangle herself and get a few feet of space between us, dagger up and ready.

"We can do this all night," I said, brushing the red dirt off my trousers.

I'd enjoy it, too. Almost as much as I would enjoy fucking her afterward.

The alleyway was lit by a single torch, but we were almost directly beneath it. Enough golden light scattered across the ground that I could see Veyka roll her eyes.

"I have places to be," she said, shoving her dagger back into the empty scabbard at her waist. She glanced back toward the busy street at the end of the alley.

"When you threaten to stab someone, do it," I said, drawing her eyes back to me. I was not letting her go.

Her brow furrowed, drawing the shadows to cover whatever light might have been in her eyes. She yanked her hood back up into place.

"I shall remember that next time," she said before spinning on her heel.

Veyka Pendragon was going to be the death of me.

She was fast, but I was still able to get a hand on her.

I dragged her back into the light, dodging the dagger already back in her hand.

As promised, she did not hesitate this time. I just barely managed to arch away. But her knife caught the front of my shirt, ripping it open in one swipe so that it fell away to reveal my chest.

There hadn't been time for my woolen tunic. Only the linen undershirt, which I hadn't bothered to tie at the neck.

In the torchlight, she could see everything.

Her eyes went wide with shock, my stomach tightening protectively in response as she stared.

"I thought it was a myth," she said softly, eyes fixed on my bare chest.

Her gaze raked slowly over the sprawling tattoo inked on my chest, the tips of the farthest branches right above where my heart beat beneath my skin. Her eyes lingered over my abdomen, following the downward slope of the branches where they joined a detailed trunk, then spread again into reaching roots that disappeared beneath the waistline of my pants. For the barest second, I thought I saw a glimmer of desire in those blue eyes.

"We are marked with the Talisman when we come into our full power." I watched as she stepped closer, fingers outstretched. As if she would touch me not in anger, but in reverence, desire, almost... almost with emotion, as if she wished to caress the black ink that was a part of my very being.

"You were a child when they did this to you?" Her hand jerked back in shock.

"Terrestrials reach majority at age twenty," I breathed, at once thankful for and hating that space between us, physical and metaphorical.

Veyka and I could not have been more different. We shared the pointed ears and magical powers of the fae race. But our kingdoms, our priorities, our ages... there was not a single similarity beyond the physical.

Veyka's eyes were on mine, but then flicked down again, as if she could not help herself. A pulse twitched in her throat. "Did it hurt?"

"Yes." I tracked her stare, waiting for her eyes to settle upon me once again. When they finally did, I met them with my own. "I have endured much worse pains than this."

Her eyes darkened, any hint of bright blue completely erased. The emotions she might have shown were shuttered completely.

"Honor to the Ancestors," she said. But her face remained hard. As if she too knew that the Ancestors were to blame for this bargain and the pain that had come before. And all of the pain that would come after.

She turned away once more.

"Veyka, where are you going?" I asked. An entreaty, rather than an order.

I did not expect it to work. But she paused.

"I am meeting someone," she said, back still to me.

I pressed my luck. "Who?"

She half turned, the torchlight casting her pale white profile in sharp contrast to the darkness around her. I could read the frustration in every line of her body. Whatever this was, she cared about it deeply.

Good. Until tonight, I wasn't certain Veyka cared about anything.

"If you are determined to trail me like an Ancestors-damned shadow, then I have conditions," she said.

I raised one amused eyebrow. "I do not think you are in a position to bargain."

"If you try to carry me back to the palace, I will kick and scream and make a scene. I will disrupt your precious peace." Her voice dripped with distaste at the word. "But if you can keep your mouth shut, and not interfere, you can accompany me."

"I am protecting you," I reminded her. I had no intention of doing any of the things she'd said if I felt she was in danger.

She fingered the hilt of her dagger, most likely restraining herself from throwing it at me.

"You will watch," she ground out. "That is it. You don't speak, you don't pull your axe. Promise me."

"Fine."

"Say it," she insisted. I realized then what she was doing. She knew I would not lie. She was as cunning as the elementals in her court, in her own way.

"I promise I will not interfere unless your life is in danger," I said.

She lifted her head skyward and muttered something that sounded like an appellation to the moon herself.

"Keep up. You have wasted enough of my time tonight," she said before jogging away.

32
VEYKA

If he so much as breathed in my direction, I was going to fucking kill him.

Arran Earthborn thought he was so sneaky, so stealthy, so clever. The Brutal Prince thought a whole damn lot of himself, even after I'd shown I was more than capable of taking him on.

Three hundred years of experience and he still couldn't scale a balcony in silence. Once I'd realized he was following me, there was little point in covering my own footfalls. The bastard seemed to have some sort of extra sense where I was concerned.

But getting the jump on him in the alley... I shivered in satisfaction. That would be fueling my daydreams for the next week, at least.

We reached the intersection, my giant shadow looming behind me, and I had a decision to make. Arran would stick out no matter where we went; he was huge, for one. He also exuded the sort of power that even the weakest among our kind would be able to detect. At best, he might be mistaken for a bodyguard. At worst... had the details of his physical description made their way down from the goldstone palace into Baylaur yet?

I would have to chance it.

I couldn't risk losing this contact. It had taken me months of sneaking out, making shady connections in the alleyways of Baylaur, to infiltrate the Shadows.

The illusive society responsible for smuggling banned goods in and out of Baylaur had earned its name by operating in near complete secrecy. They killed anyone who asked too many questions. They killed their own members when they got sloppy. I'd made more than a few of them bleed to obtain the information I wanted.

I turned back to Arran, frowning at his chest. Those tattoos would be a dead giveaway as well.

"You have ten minutes to acquire a cloak," I said to his chest, trying to view the hard planes of it before my eyes as nothing more than another layer of clothing.

One dark eyebrow rose. "A cloak?"

"Yes. I cannot have anyone seeing your talisman. It will mark you as a terrestrial immediately," I said. That was as much explanation as I planned on giving him.

"There are a fair number of us in Baylaur now," Arran pointed out, looking over my shoulder to the busy street in front of us as if he would conjure up one of his companions with merely a thought.

"Stop. Arguing." I bit down on my tongue but a growl still gurgled low in my throat. "We don't have time for it. Buy it, steal it, I do not care. But when you arrive at the tavern, make sure the hood is up."

The struggle playing across Arran's face would have been humorous to watch if the moment wasn't so dire. He had a million questions and a million and one arguments. But somehow he managed to stuff them down.

His black eyes glittered with warning even as he inclined his head in acceptance.

I gave him brief directions to the tavern and then merged into the flowing crowd on the streets without a backward glance. The less that people saw us together here in Baylaur, the better.

He was an unqualified pain in my ass, but at least he was on time.

Clever too, despite my less than flattering thoughts to the contrary. Arran waited for me in the shadows just beyond the tavern. I might have missed him completely if I had not been on the lookout for an uncomfortably tall brute hidden beneath a too-short cloak.

His ankles stuck out, but his head and chest were covered. It would have to be enough.

"Who are we meeting?" Arran asked.

"I am meeting—you are sitting on a barstool in the corner and keeping your mouth shut," I reminded him.

I glanced downward. He'd moved his belt to the outside of the cloak, axe and sword visible. In a tavern after midnight, it was probably the wise choice. But I didn't share that compliment. I adjusted my own daggers inside their jeweled scabbards and pushed into the tavern.

The place was crowded to bursting, even this late. In the summer months, the citizens of Baylaur often stayed up into the wee hours of the morning to avoid the worst of the heat, sleeping through the afternoon to compensate. In the goldstone palace, we had the breezes off the mountains to cool us, as well as the magic of ice and wind wielders.

The benefit of being a courtier was you could use your servants' magic, with no thought to the cost it might inflict. I thought of Cyara and her aching wrists. I'd told her time and again I didn't need that damn ever-burning hearth. But short of dismissing her, I could not force her to stop.

I spotted my mark immediately.

At first glance, he might have been mistaken as some relation of Arran's—dark hair, dark eyes, powerfully built. But as I wound my way through the crowd, I could see the differences emerge. His dark hair was in a bun at the nape of his neck, similar to how Arran wore his, but it had streaks of brown in it where Arran's was pure black. His eyes were a dark brown as well.

His eyes immediately reminded me not to be fooled—the male was handsome, but he was a Shadow. Which meant he was as likely to stab me as share the information I wanted.

Arthur had made it his personal mission to stop the smuggling in and out of Baylaur. He'd caught many individuals, even smaller rings, disposing of them and redistributing their wealth to the poorest fae in the city. I didn't know for sure if he'd threatened the Shadows, but it was easy to guess they could have had a vested interest in his death. Which meant I had a vested interest in them.

"Thank you for saving me a seat," I said as I slid onto the empty stool beside him.

I couldn't see Arran, but I hoped he'd faded into the crowd. At the very least, I did not feel his overbearing presence directly over my shoulder.

"They told me you were barely more than a child," the male said, raking his eyes over my layers of translucent clothing. "But you are all female."

The hood still covered my hair, though I'd thrown the cloak back over my shoulders. If my breasts helped me get what I wanted, I'd happily put them on display.

"They told me you would answer my questions," I said pointedly, though I tucked one arm under my breasts purposefully.

Behind me, a low growl cut through the din of tavern goers. My hand curled into a fist, but I kept my eyes on my new companion, ready to try to defuse his reaction. But none came. Was I the only one who could hear it?

"A drink, first." The male lifted his hand to the barkeep. "Two cups of—"

"Ambrosia," I cut in.

It was a poor imitation of aural, but potent still. Outside of the goldstone palace, it was the strongest spirit available. Only the strongest, most powerful fae dared to drink it. I had no powers, but I was willing to wager that if I could handle aural, I could take this.

The male raised his dark brows but nodded to the barkeep. Two roughly carved cups were set in front of us, the swirling pink liquid within giving off a faint rainbow mist.

My new companion lifted his cup. "To beautiful females named..."

"I will tell you mine if you tell me yours," I said, not waiting for him before taking a sip. As I suspected—strong, but nothing compared to the golden aural.

The male's smile curved over his cup.

"Jax," he said, offering a hand.

"Gwen," I said as I held out my own.

The growl behind me came again—though I wasn't sure if it was from the use of Gwen's name or the way that Jax was holding my hand, rubbing his thumb over my knuckles twice before releasing it.

I tucked my hand into the folds of my loose pants, near enough to grab my dagger if needed. The growling faded away. But several patrons behind me were leaving in a hurry, pricking my suspicions.

"Who's the muscle?" Jax asked, eyes drifting over my shoulder.

I had no choice but to turn and look. To see Arran, back against the tavern wall, glaring at the pair of us.

I thought that Jax looked like Arran? I could have laughed at my own foolishness. Jax was a handsomer-than-usual elemental fae with dark features and an easy smile.

The Brutal Prince looked like death itself. Even in a cloak that was too small, his eyes glared out. Sinister black holes that threatened to swallow me up—to punish me for every wrong I'd ever committed. My blasted body thrummed with desire at the thought.

I spun in my seat, determined to give him my back. This was too important to be distracted by my own ridiculous lust.

I waved a hand dismissively over my shoulder. "A bodyguard. My employer wishes to ensure that his information is returned safely."

"There was no mention of a guard," Jax said, splitting his gaze between me and Arran.

"I was promised information. And yet so far, all you've done is waste my time," I said sharply. That earned back his gaze.

"Ask your question," he said.

"I want details about your shipments."

Jax laughed loudly into his cup of ambrosia. "When? What? Where? I cannot give you that information, and well you know it."

I took a daintier but long sip. Let him think I was loosening up. "It's the who I'm interested in, and only one particular shipment."

"Your *employer* is insane if you think I'll reveal identities. It is called the Shadows, for Ancestors' sake. No amount of gold is worth what they'll do to me," Jax said. There was no fear in his eyes, but there was conviction.

"I imagine the Shadows are very good at disposing of bodies." I fingered the hilt of my dagger.

His eyes flashed. "Indeed."

Setting down my cup, I shifted my weight and hooked a thumb around the hilt of each dagger at my waist. "I don't care who is doing the shipping, I want to know *who* is being shipped."

Understanding dawned on his face, as well as panic.

I was getting close, then.

"We don't trade in human cargo."

I slid my elbow across the bar top, leaning over and resting my head casually atop my fist. I summoned the lazy smile I'd so often seen Parys wear when talking court gossip out of his fellow courtiers.

"We both know that there is what is said, and there is what is *done*," I said, my voice just above a whisper.

Jax adjusted the collar of his coat, avoiding my eye as he asked, "Is the Queen of Secrets cracking down on illicit imports?"

I choked on my ambrosia. "The Queen of Secrets?"

Jax scoffed derisively, clanking his cup down on the bar top hard enough to splash some of the flowery scented liquid over the edge. "Isn't that what she is? She hides up there in her goldstone palace, reigning on high above us all. But we know nothing about her."

All the air was being sucked out of my chest, my throat.

Closing. My airways were closing.

"Old Uther and Igraine kept her well-hidden. It seems not much has changed now that she sits the throne." Jax shrugged, as if it hardly mattered.

Queen of Secrets.

It should not have mattered, not after all that I'd endured.

But those three words punctured deep into the shreds that remained of my heart.

Queen of Secrets. He had no idea how true it was. How the secret I kept would unhinge the delicate peace that held Annwyn hostage. A terribly timed reminder of why I was there... and what I stood to lose.

I knew I was not destined to be a sovereign of fairness and grace, like Arthur would have been. He'd deserved to have legends written about him. After the way things had ended... he probably still would. I suppressed a shudder at the thought.

But to hear that not even my own subjects thought me worthy, those who had never known me... it cut so much deeper than it should have.

For someone who was supposed to care about nothing.

No one.

Except revenge.

That was why I was there, in a tavern in the bowels of the Effren Valley.

I took a deep drink of the ambrosia, pretending it was revenge in liquid form. I willed it to sustain me, flood my senses, give me purpose.

"I have no idea what the queen has planned." That was the truth. Everything hinged on the information Jax would give or withhold. "I want to know about six months ago—were there humans smuggled in around that time."

"Around the time of King Arthur's death, you mean." Jax was looking right at me now.

I had to tread this line very carefully.

The rumbling growl began again, lower this time, but no less ominous. I silently prayed to the Ancestors that Arran would keep his promise. One misstep, and all these months of work would be for nothing.

"Humans do not belong in Annwyn," I said, pulling one dagger from my hip. I lifted it until it was even with my head, then let it fall straight down so the tip embedded in the bar top. "They need fae help to get through the Blasted Pass."

Jax tried to keep his eyes on me, but they slid again and again to my dagger. He was likely weighing how proficient I'd be with it.

"The Blasted Pass is not the only way through the mountains," he said with a casual shrug. As if he had not just dropped a wrench into the machinations of my mind.

My hand tightened around the hilt of my dagger, my entire stance changing. I felt Arran surge to his feet behind me, felt the heat of him inches from my back.

"Sit down," I ordered over my shoulder, not taking my eyes off of Jax.

I could feel Arran's hesitation; he lingered another breath longer.

When he finally retreated, I let a sigh of relief slip out.

"Your bodyguard is quite protective," Jax said, leaning forward to admire my dagger.

It was a lovely thing, with its jeweled handle. A wolf was carved in the silver pommel, a black diamond glittering in its eye.

"He is well paid," I said. "As you shall be, in thanks." I pulled loose the little bag of gold tied at my belt and dropped it onto the bar top in front of Jax. He stowed it away with a slight nod.

"It's too bad, really," he said, eyes still on my dagger. "I am curious to see how well you wield it. But alas…"

Jax's eyes never left my dagger as he buried his own in my gut.

"I shall use it in your memory, sweet Gwen," he said into my ear.

Then all hell broke loose.

33
ARRAN

I tried to honor my word. I really did.

Even if the beast inside of me raged when that elemental trash touched her hand and ogled her breasts. I was determined to stay out of it, so long as no actual danger befell her. I'd gotten what I wanted out of this endeavor. I knew where she went. I listened to every word they said, determined to find out why. By the time she dropped her dagger into the bar top, I had pieced enough together to have suspicions. At least enough to question her about later.

We might have returned to the goldstone palace without incident.

Then he pulled a knife.

I shifted in a second, my roar shaking the rafters.

Fae of all ages and abilities ran screaming from the tavern. Someone threw up a wall of ice to protect themselves. Another used wind to break open the windows, other elementals scrambling out behind them, heedless of the broken glass. Only knowing one thing—fear.

I saw none of it.

My beast, dark and feral and free, had eyes only for Veyka.

The three males that stood between me and Veyka? My jaws

closed around whatever part of them was in reach, whipping them to the side. If they were dead, I wouldn't regret it.

The male called Jax, the one who took her gold and gave her a gut wound in return? I ripped his head from his body.

His skull crushed between my teeth, soft and pliable as a plum. I could taste his magic, flowing in his blood as it coated my tongue. Fire-gifted. He'd have been better off trying to burn the tavern down around us than to stab her.

Veyka. *Mine.*

My animal eyes found hers, blue and bright even in the dim midnight tavern.

Her chest heaved up and down.

Up, down, up, down.

For once, I didn't notice her breasts.

No, my beast was smelling for blood. Without thinking, I touched the tip of my dark nose to her shoulder, nudging her, seeing if she was truly all right.

There was no wound in her gut, no blood wetting her dark clothes.

Her eyes slowly lowered, staring down at the long snout. My snout.

I saw it as she might have. I realized—I'd shifted.

Fuck. I hadn't meant to do it. But the moment she was threatened, the beast and I became one and the same. There was no thought, no conscious decision, only the need to protect what was mine—ours.

Now I stood before her, on four legs, a beast. The reality of the Brutal Prince.

Fuck.

I didn't wait to see the horror written on her face. I shifted, thankful that when I did, the blood and gore dripping from my teeth would disappear along with my beast form.

There was not a single soul left inside the tavern.

Just Veyka and I, standing there staring at each other with a thousand questions and no answers between us. For what was only the second time in my entire life, I felt helpless. It was the one thing I had vowed to myself never to feel again. And yet this selfish slip of a princess had brought me back to the lost, scared child I had once been.

It was unacceptable.

She was not worthy. Beautiful, brutal, brazen—yes, yes, yes. But even if what I suspected was true...

No. No one was worth this feeling in my gut.

Especially not her.

"Show me your wound," I commanded, ignoring the roughness of my voice. I could still taste blood on my tongue.

Veyka turned away, sheathing her two daggers back in her belt. "I'm fine."

My patience was nonexistent. I grabbed her arm, dragging her back around to face me.

"He stabbed you. You are not fine," I growled.

"He didn't even nick me. The knife got tangled in the folds of the gown, hit my brassiere," she hissed, trying to yank her arm away. She glared when I didn't release it. "It didn't help him that by the time he tried to stab me, I'd already slid my own dagger between his ribs."

My eyes went to the body of the elemental male on the ground, missing his head.

There was indeed a deep red stain on the left side of his chest.

One dagger on the bar top—a distraction. The other must have been in her hand. The male—Jax—had been a fool to underestimate her.

But hadn't I done the same?

No.

I would not feel sorry for her. I would not let her wrap me up in her web of lies. She was the one in the wrong. She was sneaking out of the palace, getting into tavern brawls, putting all of Annwyn in danger for her own ends.

I didn't look back as I strode for the door, letting my own righteous anger fuel me. "Let's go."

For once, Veyka did not argue.

※

We were nearly back to the goldstone palace when my temper got the better of me.

She'd gotten nearly everything from me—the talisman inked on my chest, to see the beast I kept so carefully hidden unless absolutely necessary. And what had she offered in return? Nothing. Not a damn thing.

I blew apart the wards protecting the palace without a second thought. She was reaching for the vines that covered the doorway back into the palace. Once she opened that door, silence must reign.

I could not allow it.

"How could you be so selfish?" I spat, every syllable laced with loathing—for her, for myself, for this lot in life neither of us had wanted. For the very crowns destined to rest upon our heads.

Veyka paused, her body hidden in shadow, no moonlight permeating the overhang of trees and vines on either side of the door.

She did not respond.

So I pushed her more.

"What happens if you die, too?" I nearly yelled, stalking closer.

She spun on me so fast I almost didn't get my arm up in time. Even so, she used the surprise and her momentum to pin me against a tree.

But her smaller body could not hold me for long. And the tree had been a mistake. I reached for my power without thinking, the branches already curling to my will—

Until I felt the tip of her knife nick through my shirt.

Ancestors, she was quick.

"Perhaps I shall kill you and see if that improves matters," she hissed, twisting the blade.

I leaned forward, just a fraction, just enough to breathe into her ear, "You can try."

The roots surged up from the ground and wound around her ankles, yanking her from her feet and dragging her across the ground.

Veyka cried like a skoupuma, hissing and fighting. I felt her cutting away at the vines with her daggers. Each severed vine was like a cut to my own flesh. But I didn't retreat, summoning more, summoning the sparse grass to curl around her.

Somehow, she managed to roll onto her stomach.

Good, easier to slam her face against a tree root. I was merciless. I wanted to punish her, to make her see that she was not invincible. That if she'd been a half second slower, if I had not been there, Annwyn would have been without a queen. I would have been without Veyka.

"Enough of this!" she roared, driving the dagger into the root of the tree where it connected to the trunk.

It forced me to loosen my grip, the shock of it ricocheting through my body. That was all the time she needed to get back on her feet. Her blue eyes, dark as midnight sapphires now, bored into mine, daring me to try again.

When no vines slithered up around her, she tipped her head back until the moonlight shone on her face, gilding her features in an otherworldly silver glow. "They killed my brother."

She spat on the ground, eyes shining with the stars. "There is nothing I will not do, nowhere I will not go, to avenge him."

"The elementals are not known for their loyalty." I expected her face to crumble, but she sneered instead.

"No, we are not. But Arthur and I were something different." She turned away, sliding her blade into its sheath on her belt with a fluid grace that still caught me off guard.

I had to stop underestimating her. It was likely to get one—or both—of us killed.

"That is why you've been sneaking out of the palace," I said carefully.

Veyka snorted. "I have been sneaking out of the palace since I was ten years old."

I did not ask her how she untangled the wards—I knew she would not tell me. This little bit of information she'd offered... why would a child sneak from their home? A princess, at that? A new thought occurred to me.

"You were upset when he called you the Queen of Secrets," I said, forcing my eyes away from her even though I wanted to watch and read every line of her face.

She ground the toe of her shoe into the ground. "It is a fair name. I have been absent—first as a princess, by my parents' doing. Then as a queen, by my own."

I reached deep down inside of myself, quelling the parts that urged me not to say the stupid, stupid words.

They spilled out anyway. "It does not have to be like this."

Her eyes rose.

"You could be the queen they need. The sort of ruler that Arthur would have been," I said softly.

It was true. I would always be the Brutal Prince. Three hundred years of killing would not be forgotten, even by the long-lived fae of Annwyn. But Veyka, she could be anything, anyone. She could be the Princess of Peace, the Queen of Peace, the future of a stable and prosperous Annwyn.

As I watched, all the vulnerability in her face melted away. Until all that remained was a hard, angry mask. Was it an improvement on the devoid nonchalance? I couldn't decide.

"The only thing I want is revenge," she said, raising her chin. Not a hint of regret or remorse. "I want them all to pay. Every single one of them."

"The humans who killed him were beheaded."

The laugh that ripped from her throat was hysterical, unearthly. "If you think mere humans were responsible for killing the greatest king Annwyn has ever seen, you are as stupid as every one of those slimy, traitorous hypocrites on my Royal Council."

There it was, finally.

The truth.

It hung between us in the warm, lifeless air, heavy as the mountains around us and as ephemeral as a scent on the wind.

I said nothing.

What was there to say? Veyka had just blamed her court for her brother's death. As much as I hated to admit, I wasn't inclined to disagree with her assessment.

Which meant that the elemental court was much more dangerous than I'd initially imagined. And the threats could not be kept out by sealing the entrances and setting a competent patrol. The threats lurked within.

Veyka sighed heavily, her shoulders drooping as she stomped past me. "Come. I am done for the night. Escort your queen back to her gilded cage."

So I did.

34
VEYKA

I did not sleep.

I lay alone in my bed, counting the breaths, letting the heat flood my skin.

The heat that had nothing to do with the sweltering summer night and everything to do with the fae warrior asleep outside my bedroom door.

I'd seen the Brutal Prince for the first time tonight. The scars inked upon his flesh, a brutal reminder of the powers he carried. The vines of his talisman—a curse, as much as a gift.

And the beast...

That was what growled for me, not Arran Earthborn, my betrothed. But the beast that lived within him, the beast that *was* him. The beast that had claimed me as his own. I'd felt it when his nose touched my shoulder. Proprietary, inescapable. I wondered if Arran felt it too.

I could not forget, could not scrub the image from my memory.

I did not want to.

As my hands skimmed over my body, tweaking my nipples, nails dragging over my inner thigh, finally coming to touch my clit, hard and needy with arousal, I knew the truth.

I had finally seen the Brutal Prince.
And I was not afraid.
I wanted every inch of him.
Male.
And beast.

35

VEYKA

Queen of Secrets.

The citizens of Annwyn would not be able to accuse me of hiding myself away any longer. The doors to the goldstone palace were open, several wind-gifted guards keeping the way open over the Gremog's strip of terror.

Any resident of Annwyn, be they terrestrial or elemental, rich or poor, could enter the goldstone palace today and make their plea to the queen and her prince. I smiled smugly to myself, knowing that in a few minutes I would be introduced as the Queen of the Elemental Fae, and Arran as His Highness, the Brutal Prince.

The terrestrials had no royal family. Their heirs for the Offering were selected each generation for their strength. Which meant that until we were joined, Arran remained a prince by courtesy only.

He appeared at my side, and I was reminded of how fucking childish that line of thought was. Only an idiot would think a title mattered to someone like Arran Earthborn. He didn't need one to exude power.

Whatever words Esa used to introduce him, the male standing beside me looked every inch a king.

He'd freed some of his dark hair from its customary bun, letting it hang loose around his shoulders. Thick and dark, black as the night, it gleamed beneath the low lights of the antechamber where we waited. For once, I could see no stubble on his chin.

The sleeveless tunic he wore was deep burgundy, made of a tight-knit wool like all of his clothing. But there were shots of gold thread woven into the fabric that glimmered when he shifted his weight. The buttons, cutting at an angle across his chest to finish up at his shoulder, appeared to be carved bone. Which fell terrestrial creature that bone had been taken from, I couldn't guess. Each one was carved to depict a different horrifying creature in the midst of a roar, jaws hanging open.

He'd traded the white linen undershirt he'd taken to wearing for a black one instead. Was that for me? A tribute to my own preference for dark colors? Or simply a better complement to the crimson tunic and dark trousers he'd chosen to wear today?

After the way we'd fought outside the palace walls, the hatred and loathing in his eyes, I couldn't imagine the former.

What would the courtiers and citizens of Annwyn make of us? I glanced down at my own clothing. I'd chosen a deep pomegranate skirt that covered my legs entirely, held in place by a jeweled belt at my waist. My daggers in their scabbards were there as well, of course.

The tail of my elaborate white braid hovered near my exposed torso. The matching pomegranate silk of my top was held in place by gold braids that looped underneath each of my breasts, twined around my arms, and then attached to a jeweled collar at my neck. Long, sheer sleeves billowed from my arms, falling in long panels to the ground before being gathered into golden bangles at my wrists.

I looked like a queen. Maybe even a Queen of Secrets with my unusual hair white hair and nontraditional dark clothing. But I'd eschewed the crown—my mother's crown—when Cyara had offered it. I was more than a little relieved to find that Arran, too, had foregone any such overt symbolism.

He stood staring directly forward, eyes fixed upon the door to the throne room. This was the same room I'd dragged him into after the Offering. How much things had changed since then—and how little.

Arran—that was how I thought of him now. Yes, he was the Brutal Prince. But he was more than the dread warrior of legend. I liked him no more than I had that first day. Did I hate him less? Maybe.

His feelings for me were quite clear. He could not even look at me.

Some small part of me had thought that once he knew the reason for my actions, my need to avenge Arthur, that he would understand. Not approve, I did not expect that. But surely someone whose life and legacy had been forged in bloodshed would understand my bloodthirsty need for vengeance.

But still, all he had for me was loathing.

I shoved the rising emotion in my chest back down to the dark pits of my soul. Emotion and wanting and hoping... there was no room inside of me for such foolishness.

I opened my mouth, my tongue burning with words of contempt and pain.

But the door to the throne room opened and Esa swept in, a shimmering mist swirling around her.

"It is time," she said, looking us over.

Her eyes lingered on Arran's chest, tracing the breadth from side to side. Loathing rose to my tongue once again, but not for Arran. My chest burned. He was *mine*, and Esa damn well knew it.

Unable to control myself, I stepped close to Arran and put my arm through his. He stiffened so slightly, I knew only I had felt it. Then his hand came down to cover mine. A show of unity—and a show it was, I was certain—but Esa's face closed instantly.

But she could not hide the gleam of desire, the ring of blazing deep blue around her pupils. Desire for my betrothed.

"Get on with it, then," I snarled, my fingernails digging into Arran's arm.

The beast rewarded me with a low, subtle growl. For my ears only, I realized now.

Arran may hate me, but his beast did not.

Esa took her silly little magical mist and disappeared through the door. A heartbeat later, Arran and I followed.

So many eyes.

More than had ever seen me before, all at once.

Every inch of the throne room was crammed with occupants. I vaguely recognized the courtiers who made their homes in the goldstone palace. Esa went to join Noros, Elora, Teo, and Roksana where the other royal councilors waited on the far side of the twin thrones.

Gawayn, Lyrena, and Evander stood at the foot of the dais. No one would approach closer than that stalwart line, I knew. Not even the royal councilors.

Parys lurked near a pillar about halfway down the throne room, a goblet of aural in his hand as he laughed with another elemental courtier.

A group of terrestrials stood all together to the left, the same side as the throne traditionally occupied by the king or queen hailing from the terrestrial fae. Guinevere, surprisingly, was not among them. I did not see her at all, I realized.

I turned to ask Arran about it, but his face was hard, hewn from granite. I knew intuitively that I'd be ignored if I said anything to him now. Which made me want to even more.

"Where have you sent your feral feline?" I asked softly as we climbed the stairs of the dais.

He ignored me, turning to face the crowd.

They all watched, taking in the spectacular, regal sight we presented. I hated every bit of it. It was a lie, and a painful one at that.

I dropped myself down onto Arthur's throne with no ceremony at all. As one, the crowd blinked in surprise. Arran's eyes flashed with annoyance as he inclined his head respectfully at me and then took his own seat.

The crowd parted. The petitioners formed some semblance of a line. I stared into the sea of faces, hardly processing their existence as I said to Arran, "If she intends to come roaring in here again, I'd appreciate fair warning this time."

Still no reaction.

"Will she maul one of the other courtiers this time? Or perhaps one of your airborne companions will come swooping down from the rafters instead of lurking in the shadows like the last time we were here," I said, recalling the shadowed wings I'd seen above our heads during the Offering.

That earned me a strange look.

"Perhaps she—"

"Would it kill you to act like the queen you are? Even for an hour?" he barked, black eyes burning with an intensity that would have melted any other member of this court.

Satisfaction flooded my chest. I turned to him with a lazy smile. "This is the queen that I am." Then I faced the crowd. "Let them come."

※

The afternoon wore away to early evening. Most of the concerns were easily managed—a complaint between neighbors farming the steppes beyond the mountains ringing the Effren Valley; a squabble between elemental courtiers about needing larger quarters for expanding families.

Esa watched it all with a void expression on her face. She'd never dare to sit in one of the thrones, but I could easily imagine her standing on the dais in her shimmering rainbow mist and doling out judgments. Arran had been right to take this away from her. She tried to hide it, but the frustration simmering off of her was delicious.

The sun had dipped below the mountains, bathing the throne room in shades of pink and gold, the goldstone walls shimmering, when three fae males approached the dais.

They looked vaguely familiar... something about the set of their shoulders, the proud arc of their chins...

To my surprise, Gawayn stepped away from his station at the foot of the dais to join them. Understanding flooded my brain instantly. Beside me, Arran shifted forward, resting one elbow on his knee as he considered the four brothers standing in line.

"Your Majesty, Your Highness," Gawayn said, formal as ever, sinking into a bow. "I present my brothers: Agravayn, Gaheris, and Gareth."

The resemblance was there in spades. The proud lift of the chin, the glint of the sandy brown hair. Agravayn was taller than Gawayn, but not quite as broad. Gaheris was shorter but wider. The one I assumed to be the youngest, Gareth, might have been Gawayn's twin, minus the streaks of gray.

I couldn't help but smile at Gawayn's clear discomfort. He'd never made a request of me in his life. Yet here he stood with his brothers as if he was any other petitioner.

"You did not need to make your family wait in line, Gawayn," I said, smiling at each of the three newly arrived brothers in turn.

Gawayn coughed uncomfortably. "It would have been improper to rely upon my position as the Captain of your Goldstones for favoritism."

I rolled my eyes. Gareth chuckled. I felt the corner of my lips climbing higher. His brother's twin in looks, but not in taciturn nature, it seemed.

"What issue have you brought to put before us?"

Arran's stern voice drew all the eyes in the room, including my own. He'd hardly spoken all day, other than to murmur a few thoughts during certain petitions. Though I suspected that if he'd disagreed substantively with any of my decisions, he would not have hesitated to make it known to the whole damn court. My feelings had never been of particular importance to him.

I ignored Arran, knowing it would annoy him. "Welcome to Baylaur, brothers of Gawayn. You have come to me as petitioners rather than visitors. Let me hear your request."

If a feral growl slipped from my betrothed at that word, *me*, I pretended not to hear it.

The male called Agravayn stepped forward. His face was as serious as his eldest brother's. But where I often detected worry and affection in Gawayn's sternness, I saw none in this male's. He was not amused by his queen.

"We have come on behalf of our family and the surrounding villages. Our estate is situated on the edge of the Split Sea, beyond the mountains," Agravayn said. He looked directly at Arran—as if I were not even there.

Ancestors. Was this going to be my entire life? The next thousand years spent being looked over in deference to the Brutal Prince who sat at my side?

You don't care, I reminded myself.

This won't last. Not forever. Not even a year.

I forced myself to listen even as my mind clouded with plans. Plans that I had thought set in goldstone. Plans that all of the sudden felt ephemeral, hard to pin down.

"There have always been disappearances. It is inevitable, given our proximity to the Split Sea. But in recent months, they have increased. What used to be a disappearance twice or thrice a year is now nearly weekly," Agravayn was explaining.

My eyes went to Gawayn. His face was unreadable. A disappearance a week? And he'd said nothing to me? He must have known, these were his own brothers standing here. But he had not said a word... had not trusted me enough? Had not believed I would care.

You don't care, a voice that sounded like Arran's whispered in the back of my mind.

For six months, I'd cared about nothing but fucking, sleeping, and planning my revenge.

This was my fault.

Every single disappearance could be laid on my doorstep.

I was paralyzed, unable to think or breathe, even as Arran asked intelligent, probing questions. *Where were they taken from? Noble or poor families? Was there a certain pattern they'd yet discerned—weather, moon phase, tide?*

"What about age? How old are the ones that are disappearing?" Arran asked.

Agravayn leveled a glare at me that matched the self-loathing in my own soul. "Children."

Fuck.

"We will send someone to investigate," Arran was saying, his eyes immediately scanning the crowd. He didn't bother to lean in and consult me. Why would he? I could decide petty squabbles between courtiers, but no one would trust me with the safety of the kingdom. I'd proven I didn't care enough to deserve it.

"Gawayn," I said, my voice hoarse. They all looked to me, each brother, every courtier, my own betrothed. I forced in a breath, cleared my throat, and continued in a stronger voice. "Gawayn, you must go. You are the best of my Goldstones, the most powerful. You must see to this at once."

"Veyka," Arran's voice warned, low enough for me alone.

"Children are being taken, Arran. *Children.*" I felt the flood of tears, the helplessness.

This was what I'd been trying to avoid. This terrible emptiness, uselessness inside of me was why I was void of feeling.

Make it stop.

"You cannot send Gawayn, he is your captain, your best protection," Arran said.

I could feel the eyes of every courtier upon us. I felt a warm wind encircle us, carrying away the sounds of the court, keeping our voices in. Gawayn, I thought. The stray strands of hair around my ear lifted, tickling the side of my neck. Parys—he was still among the other courtiers, but his eyes were fixed upon me.

I felt a surge of gratitude for them both.

But it was still nothing to the despair clawing at my chest.

"We have to do something," I insisted, clutching Arran's arm. "We must send someone who will actually do something, not a vague gesture, not a committee. This must be fixed." My breath caught in my throat. "Please."

Arran stared not into my eyes, but down at where my hand

clasped his arm. My knuckles were as white as my hair against my already pale skin. The contrast of the light against the dark of his shirt was stark. He was warm and steady, the muscles of his forearm strong beneath my icy fingers.

Fingers that were trembling.

He covered my hand with his. Hiding my vulnerability. Not from the rest of the court, too far away to see it, but from myself.

He turned back to face the four brothers, the invisible cyclone of wind dropping away instantly. Parys relaxed back against a pillar, taking a long drink from his goblet. Gawayn was as immovable as always.

"Evander," Arran said sharply, his words cutting off any side conversations.

I jerked in immediate and negative reaction, but Arran held me fast.

Evander stepped forward, the fabric of his Goldstones attire swirling around him in what I was certain was an icy wind of his own making. When he faced the dais, his expression was solemn. No sneer in sight—for once.

"You will return to the Split Sea with Agravayn and his brothers. End this travesty, or do not come back at all." Arran's edict rang out across the throne room, spilling through the open archways.

I expected a challenge, an argument from Evander, whose very arm had been cut off the first time he met the Brutal Prince. But to my utter shock, he sank to one knee.

"Of course," he said.

I felt like I might vomit.

"You are dismissed," Arran said to the kneeling male, then lifted his eyes to Gawayn's trio of brothers. "You as well."

It was for me, I realized.

Gawayn was my captain, my foremost protector after Arran. Lyrena was the closest thing I had to a friend. But Evander, I could hardly stand to share a room with, even if he was skilled and competent and powerful.

Arran had made this decision for *me*.

"Your Majesty," Gawayn stepped forward, his head bowed respectfully. "This will leave a vacancy in your Goldstone Guards."

"Do you have a replacement in mind, Gawayn?" Arran asked.

"Perhaps—"

"I submit myself, Your Majesty, for consideration."

My nerves could not take much more. I certainly was not prepared for Guinevere, former heir of the terrestrial fae and slighted future high queen, to step forward and offer herself as one of my personal bodyguards.

Ancestors, I hadn't even realized she'd entered the room.

Arran must have, because his eyes glittered with amusement.

I shifted uncomfortably in my seat. "I don't—"

"Done," Arran said sharply.

I blinked. Once, twice.

"Gawayn, do you have any objection?" Arran asked, ignoring me once again.

Gawayn shook his head. "None at all, Your Highness."

"Good. We are done for the day." Arran was already standing, tugging me to my feet.

I had no desire to fight him now. Guinevere wanted to be a Goldstone Guard? Fine with me. I wanted out of this throne room. I wanted to drown myself in the aural fountains.

I wanted someone to fuck my brains out, and then I would sleep for a year.

Anything to avoid the clamoring, clawing emotions eating me alive from the inside out.

"There is one more petitioner," said a voice from beyond the dais. Not Esa, who'd been bristling to take control all day. But Roksana.

The wizened councilor stepped apart from the others. She looked past Arran directly to me, her eyes full of meaning.

Something in her stance, in the tilt of her chin, filled me with dread.

I slowly turned back to the center of the room to see the crowd parting. A lone figure walked toward me. Shorter than every other being in the room, steps slower and more hesitant. His clothing was rough, dull browns and grays, rips evident. I could smell the scent of his unwashed body from where I stood, my feet unable to move. But it was not the scent of his body odor that kindled rage in my already tumultuous soul. It was the smell of his humanity.

36
VEYKA

The human stopped well before he reached the foot of the dais. He sank into a bow so low his forehead touched the floor. He thought he understood his place here, his powerlessness. He thought he could survive the ruthlessness of our kind if only he prostrated himself before us.

How very wrong he was.

"How did you get here?" My voice sounded foreign, like it came from someone else entirely.

The man lifted his head a few inches off the floor, his eyes rising to me. "I have come to beg sanctuary, Your Majesty. The human realm—"

"How did you get here?" I asked again. I was not shaking any longer.

He slowly lifted his hands and chest from the floor, coming back to rest on his heels.

"I passed through the rift—"

"Which one?" I demanded. Arran tried to grab my hand. I shoved it away, descending the stairs in a flourish of pomegranate silk.

Fear flashed in the man's eyes.

He had no idea what fear was. Or pain. But he would once I was done with him.

"The... the mountain..." he stuttered.

"You are in violation of the treaty between our realms. By rights, I should have your head," I said.

"B... but... I come in peace," he said.

"Peace? What do humans know of peace? You take and you kill and you maim." I was towering over him now. I felt Arran behind me, heard his footsteps on the stairs of the dais.

"I have done nothing," the man begged.

"Nothing?"

Rage took over.

For everything that had been taken from me, every pain I had endured for the last year and beyond. Finally, one of the treacherous humans was within my grasp. Finally, I was in control. I would make him pay.

I drew a dagger from my waist. Arthur had given them to me; it seemed fitting.

"Veyka." Arran caught my wrist, holding it back. I hadn't even managed to get it up to my shoulder.

"Let me go," I cried, wrenching my arm away, twisting my entire body.

"This human comes in peace," Arran said, circling me, trying to put his body between my blades and the quivering human.

Our argument on the dais had been private, this one would play out before the entire court.

"They have done nothing but wreak death upon this land, upon me," I snarled, drawing the other dagger. There were so many ways to kill, to torture, with two blades.

I'd start at his ears. Cut free the two most obvious human characteristics. Then his nose. He'd be screaming by then, but his blood would blend into the deep color of my skirts. He was sobbing already. Begging. So many words.

As if words could compensate for what had been stolen from me.

"Move, Arran," I said, laying out a plan of attack in my head. I could see the graceful spins and arcs it would take to get past Arran long enough to sink my blades into that tender human flesh. "Move out of my way, or I will make you bleed as well."

"I am not afraid of your blades, Veyka."

I flashed that wicked smile he'd teased me about in the training courtyard. "You may not be. But he is."

Then I launched myself forward.

Like the blinded, bloodthirsty idiot that I was, I didn't see Guinevere coming. She knocked the human away, sent him flying across the goldstone floor without even needing to shift into her dark lioness.

Arran went for me. I slashed at him, the scent of his thick blood filling my nostrils. But he did not wince. I felt the blades slip from my hands, heard them clatter to the floor.

Then I heard nothing at all.

37
VEYKA

Heat.

Every limb was suffused with it.

I was burning—not from the ever-burning hearth, but from the force of my own rage.

A lifetime of torture had taught me to come to consciousness slowly. I didn't suck in a desperate breath of air or stretch my arms above my head.

I listened. I noticed.

I smelled the scent of him, so near.

I could hear his breathing, too. Steady.

Inhale, exhale, inhale, exhale.

Maybe he was asleep. Maybe I should feel bad about killing him while he slept.

But I did not.

The weight of my belt and daggers was missing from my waist. They might be within arm's length, they might be on the other side of the room. The seconds it would take me to locate them would mean the difference between life and death—*his*.

Fine. I could rip him apart with my fingernails.

Three breaths, then I would move. I counted each one.

I would pivot on my knee and pin him down. *One.*

With enough force, I'd be able to sink my thumb nails into his jugular. *Two.*

Only when his lifeblood was drained from his body enough to immobilize him would I fetch my blades and sever his head from his body. *Three.*

"Don't even think about it, Princess."

Too late.

I was straddling him, one knee planted on either side of his hips, my hands coming down for his throat.

He caught my wrists, slowing me down, letting my hands close around his neck, but with enough force in his own hands to know I'd never inflict the damage I needed to render him unconscious.

On any other day, this position would have sent waves of lust flowing through me. I was tucked in tight against him, could feel the rising heat of his cock as it came to life beneath me. His warm breath skimmed over my breasts, his black eyes burning with desire.

I might not be able to kill him. But castration was an acceptable second choice.

"I won't let you do that, either," Arran said, shoving me off of him easily enough. I let out a scream of frustration as I plopped back onto my side of the bed.

I used the moment to roll off and come to stand. My daggers were at the bedside. I grabbed one as I planted my feet, rising into an offensive position.

Arran stared at me with wry amusement on his face, one dark eyebrow rising. "What do you plan to do with that?"

"Someday, I will sink this dagger into your throat," I promised.

I turned over the possibilities in my head. If I threw the dagger, he'd move in time. If I tried to attack him again I might draw blood, but ultimately he'd have the advantage. We were close enough to evenly matched, and he hadn't been knocked out for the last—

"How long was I out?"

Arran's eyebrow returned to its place above those mesmerizing dark eyes. "A few hours."

"Where is the human?"

He sighed, sliding his legs over to sit on the edge of the bed. His back to me—cocky bastard.

"Imprisoned," Arran said.

"Where?"

"What will you do if I tell you?" Arran's voice sounded tired. He was tired of dealing with me? The feeling was more than mutual.

"I will kill him," I snarled.

"Then it is better that you do not know."

"How dare you! You are not king yet! You are not my master! You are the Brutal fucking Prince!" I threw my dagger across the room, the feel of it in my hand suddenly unbearable, knowing it was useless. Useless, just like I was useless.

Arran's eyes followed the knife where it lodged in the wall. Then they turned to me. "And you are supposed to be the Princess of Peace. Or do you prefer the Queen of Secrets?"

"I did not ask for either of those titles," I said.

The Princess of Peace was my parents' way of selling my unusual existence to the realm. A second heir, to ensure the peace of Annwyn.

The Queen of Secrets... well, there was really only one secret that mattered. The one that would tear my kingdom apart. My powerlessness. A fae without power. A thing that had never existed in the history of Annwyn. An abomination.

Arran turned to face me fully and I could see the same exhaustion written on his face as had echoed in his voice. Strands of his dark hair had come loose from the knot at the back of his head, falling down around his face. His brows were knitted together, the heavy brow ridge shadowing his already dark eyes. The stubble on his chin was a visible shadow, where that morning it had been smooth and undetectable. Somehow it made him more handsome, this vulnerability. I wondered who else had ever seen it.

The Brutal Prince was worried. If only he knew the full truth...

Arran dragged a hand over the strong line of his jaw. "We have to question the human. Find out why he's come to Annwyn. Why are any of them coming to Annwyn? Passing through the rifts is dangerous for humans, there must be a reason they are risking it—"

"To kill us! To wreak destruction! That is the only reason they ever come!" I cried. How could he not see it? Was Arthur's murder not proof enough?

"We need peace, Veyka! That is our charge—yours and mine! That is what it means to be High King and Queen. We are stewards of peace in Annwyn, whatever the cost!"

Whatever the cost.

He was wrong. Revenge first.

"You speak of peace, but what do you know of it?" I sneered. "You are the Brutal Prince!"

If I kept saying it, maybe it would be easier to see only that image of him, rather than Arran, the male standing before me.

His hand dropped away, so he was staring at me unencumbered as he said, "I know that if you'd killed that human, it would haunt you."

I blinked. "Haunt me? I am already haunted! Everywhere I go, I see the traces left by my brother. I cannot take a single step without being compared to him." I did not speak of the other shades, the ones I saw hovering just outside of reality. The flash of wings at the Offering.

"Veyka—" He stepped toward me, one hand reaching out into the empty space between our souls.

"No! Do not speak as if there is tenderness between us." I was nearly screaming. But I didn't care who heard, whether it be my guards in the antechamber or the courtiers on the verandas beyond my own. "Gwen told me about how you beheaded those humans in the Shadow Wood."

Arran's hand dropped. "I was within my rights."

"And taking that man's life was within mine." It was one tiny blip of revenge.

He took another step toward me, close enough that if he dared to reach out again, we might touch. "You would regret it, Veyka, your soul—"

"That is your mistake, Arran. You assume that your soul is the only one that is ruined. But listen when I tell you... this thing within me, if it is a soul, is blacker than the starless night above the Split Sea. And no one can save me—not even you. Because I do not wish to be saved."

I could not read his face. He'd gotten so much better at hiding his feelings in the time he'd been here, but not now. Now, there were so many conflicting feelings playing over the handsome planes of his face I doubted either of us could untangle them. My own chest felt like it was being cleaved apart.

This is why I drink the tea and fuck Parys and hide in my rooms, I thought forlornly.

Except that I must have said it aloud, because Arran reached for me again.

"Do not take another step," I warned, hands up. "Go. Leave me."

"Make me, Veyka."

I raised my hand to strike, but he caught my wrist, holding it tight enough between his fingers that I felt the thrumming of my own blood.

With wretched slowness, he twisted it up above my head and slowly guided me backward until I was pinned against the wall. Then he crushed his mouth down upon mine.

He tasted exactly how he smelled—like fresh earth and spices, foreign but heady upon my tongue. But the power of him when he took what he wanted, what both of us wanted so badly, that I was not ready for.

My insides were on fire once again. Had they stopped burning since I awoke?

They'd been aflame since he arrived, since that meeting in the forest before either of us knew who the other was. Because some part of me knew him, called for him—even when I hated him with every fiber of my being.

I hated him, but the feeling of his tongue sliding across my lips was perfection.

His hands curled around my hips, those dangerously long fingers playing across the soft flesh as if I was an instrument. I'd been told from a young age that there was too much of me—my belly too soft, my hips too wide, my breasts too large. But the way that Arran's hands skimmed reverently over every curve made my knees weak with desire.

"You are fucking perfect," he said against my mouth, as if he could hear the echoes of self-consciousness and was determined to beat them back.

"What is perfect? Tell me," I demanded as his sharp canines nipped at my chin, his tongue dragging along the sharp angle of my jaw until it reached my ear.

Arran circled each amorite-studded earring with his tongue, making love to the tender bits of flesh on my earlobe hiding behind the armor of silver and gold jewelry.

"This ass," he breathed into my ear, sliding his hands down over my hips and taking me in his wide palms. "I want to fill my hands with it, to spank you for every damnable stupid thing you've done." He held on so hard, his nails dug into my flesh through the layers of my silk skirt. The pinpricks of pain sent my hips forward, searching for the hard length of his cock. "I want you bent over in front of me, this round ass wobbling while I pound inside of your cunt."

He pushed my bottom upward, and that was all the encouragement I needed to wrap my legs around his waist. He held me easily, as he'd done a few times before. Every bit of him was corded strength. I clung to his shoulders, marveling at the shifting of his muscles beneath my fingers.

Sometime since the throne room he'd removed his woolen tunic, leaving behind only the black linen undershirt. I gathered a fistful of it and then yanked, groaning in satisfaction as the fabric gave and his muscular shoulders and chest were exposed to me.

"These legs," he stroked up and down them, pushing me harder into the wall. "They were made to be wrapped around me."

My skirt was riding high, keeping me from thrusting fully against him. One quick flick of his hand, and that was gone. I was bare to him, my legs wrapped around his waist, my pussy wet and quivering. No matter how thick those trousers he wore were, I knew he would be able to feel the dripping heat of my cunt before long.

This was Arran Earthborn, some small part of my mind recalled. This was the Brutal Prince—the male who represented everything I hated about my life and my position, everything that had been taken away from me.

I hated him, but I wanted him inside of me.

Arran was done with my ear, now scratching his teeth and lips across my throat. The stubble of his chin burned against my pale, sensitive skin. I'd have marks come morning. Morning? Night? What hour, what day? I did not know, I did not care. All I wanted was him, this.

This escape.

My hands climbed his shoulders, the column of his neck, tangling in his dark silky hair. But I couldn't stop and enjoy the feeling of those locks wrapped around my fingers. My core was pulsing with need. I grabbed his chin, my thumbs pulling at his bottom lip while my fingers splayed across his stubbled cheeks.

"Now," I said, looking straight into those dark, fathomless eyes.

Arran didn't hesitate. He used one knee to keep me pinned tight against the wall so he could use his hand to free himself from his trousers. I felt the tip of his cock hovering at my entrance. But by the time I looked down between our slick bodies, determined to finally see that proud length, he slammed inside of me.

I hated him, yet I could have lived in that moment forever.

My head went back so hard it banged against the wall. Yet the feral scream that ripped from my throat was one of pure passion. Arran's mouth was on my throat, his canines dragging lazily along my jugular even as he pounded into me. My pussy clung to him, the wetness of my desire sliding down his cock, creating a loud sucking sound each time he pulled back and then thrust back in.

But that sound was nearly eclipsed by the animalistic sounds tearing from my throat with each thrust. My clit was on fire, rubbing against the wiry curls of hair around the base of his cock. My breasts—Ancestors, I wanted him to touch them, but I couldn't form words. Arran was too busy ravaging my neck. No, now he was on my collarbone. Sucking on it so hard, I could almost feel my blood rising up to pool beneath the skin.

Would he nip my skin with his sharpened canines and taste my blood? Did he want to?

My instincts told me the beast within him wanted nothing more.

The thought of it, of my blood on his tongue as he drove it into my mouth once more—it pushed me right over the edge. I felt the flood of moisture, felt my cunt tighten over him.

Tears or sweat or blood, I didn't know. I buried my hands in his hair and held him tight against me as my climax spilled through me, burning trails of fire through my veins.

It lasted longer than I'd ever experienced, my legs wobbling. Arran's hands were strong, around my waist now, caressing the outsides of my thighs. I expected him to hold me there against the wall, taking his own pleasure. But instead he eased my legs down, off of his hips, until my toes touched the floor.

Fear took over me. I didn't want it to be over. I didn't want the feelings to come back. I wanted to live in this suspended animation forever.

When the pads of my feet touched the floor, I gave into the weakness in my knees. I slid down his body, letting my tongue drag along the ink of his talisman until I was kneeling before him. My eyes landed on what I wanted and my breath caught in my throat.

Feeling the hard length of him inside of me was one thing, but seeing it before my eyes, erect and dripping with my juices... I nearly came again right there.

"Veyka," Arran growled softly as my hand came up and formed a circle around the base. I could only just manage it, the tips of my fingernails barely grazing one another as I fisted him.

He'd had me at his mercy. I dragged my tongue over the head, licking away the drip of thick cum that formed at the slit.

Now he was at mine.

I would not be weak before him, I told myself as I slid my tongue along the underside, taking him deep into my throat.

I hated him, but the feeling of his magnificent cock inside of my mouth was a decadence I would long for long after this moment was past.

The taste of my own pleasure on his shaft was intoxicating. He'd done this to me, elicited that sweet, slightly spicy rush of wetness from my tortured pussy. Now his precum was dripping down my throat as I worked him in and out, my hand circling the base where even my generous mouth could not reach.

I felt a tug on my braid, realizing he'd wound the tail of it around his wrist while also threading his fingers through the strands near my skull. With every bob of my head, his fingertips caressed my head and hair.

Arran was silent, but the beast inside of him was growling, low and steady, just for me. I could feel it in my bones, in the hollow place inside my chest where my heart used to be. This power over him... I was determined to savor it, to drink it down like sustenance I couldn't live without.

I felt him tense, the fingers buried in my hair tightening to the point of pain.

But I didn't stop. I pushed past the gagging, past the tears rolling down my cheeks, until I felt him explode inside of me. The heat of his cum filled my mouth, pouring down my throat, dripping out of my lips as I tried to swallow every last drop of him.

"Fuck." Arran's harsh whispered cry cut across the room.

When I was satisfied that every last drop of his thick nectar was safe between my lips, I rocked back, resting my back against the wall. My head dropped back as well, my face tilting upward. Arran's forearms were braced against the wall, his head between them. I expected his eyes to be closed, but they were staring right down at me.

For a second, I thought there was tenderness between us. At the very least, vulnerability. Perhaps there was something there... something that hadn't existed before. Something new.

Maybe some shriveled part of my soul, buried deep beneath the ruins of my heart, remained alive. Waiting to be rekindled.

Then Arran shoved away from the wall. My eyes drifted closed, but my hearing was sharp, even if not a single bead of magic lived inside of me. I heard every step he took; the rustle of buttons being shoved through fabric holes—his trousers being refastened. The soft whisper of linen as he picked up his shirt, judged it to be ruined, then tossed it into the ever-burning hearth.

I counted the footsteps as he walked out of my bedroom and through the antechamber, closing the doors behind him. Softer footsteps circled outside my door—Gwen, the only one he trusted to guard my door in his absence. She was in her dark lioness form, if the padded footfalls were any indication.

I sat there for five minutes, then ten and twenty. I waited for the flood of feelings, the hate and rage and grief to come crashing back to claim me. But my head was blessedly silent, my pussy still throbbing pleasantly.

After an hour, I managed to stand on still-wobbly legs and make my way back to the bed. I collapsed into the sheets, the ones that still smelled like Arran. No doubt from those hours he'd spent watching over me in my unconsciousness—an unconsciousness he had caused.

But still, the rage did not come.

I closed my eyes and fell into a dreamless sleep.

38
ARRAN

If I didn't tear myself away from her, I would never leave. I'd carry her to that massive bed of hers and spend the next week taking her in every way I knew how. We'd be sore and aching, and more satisfied than either of us had any right to be.

I would be caught in her spell, her mysterious magic that she managed to keep hidden, even from me.

Maybe her powers were ethereal.

I dismissed the thought with a hard shake of my head. Those gifted with ethereal magic had the ability to read minds; to look inside the heads of those around them and see their most private thoughts. It was a lost power—like void magic, its twin. Both had disappeared seven thousand years ago, around the time the Ancestors had forged the treaty that united the Elemental and Terrestrial Fae Kingdoms under the singular crown of Annwyn.

As a younger male, lying alone in my bedroll the eve before battle, I'd questioned whether those powers had ever truly existed. It seemed just as likely to be part of the fairytale mythos surrounding the Great War.

Whether those lost powers had ever existed did not matter, I scolded myself. They did not exist now. If Veyka could read the thoughts in others' minds, she'd have extracted her revenge already.

What revenge would she seek for what had just happened between us? She'd been more than willing. But when her mind cleared, the rage would return. The burn of Veyka's rage on my skin was becoming a familiar, comforting pain. I'd never imagined myself a masochist. But she'd crawled inside my consciousness and now refused to leave.

Even if I could not get her out of my mind, I could distance myself physically. At least as far as the antechamber, where I found Gwen.

How long had she been here?

Was my mind so fucking lust-addled I could not even detect footsteps?

She lounged on a gold velvet chaise, legs crossed in front of her, using a tiny, child-sized dagger to clean her nails. I'd known her long enough to recognize the ruse. Gwen was never truly relaxed. She was always calculating the best moment to strike her prey.

"Get out," I snarled. I was in no mood for whatever conversation she'd positioned herself here to have.

Her mouth curved into a feline smile, even as she continued nonchalantly picking at her claws. "I expected you to be in a better mood after finally slaking the lust that has been burning in your eyes since we arrived in Baylaur."

My beast roared within me. He was so close to the surface after fucking Veyka, clawing to get to her. It had taken every bit of my control to keep him leashed inside as she sucked my cock.

I clamped down on that memory, frustration replacing the memory of lust.

"Get out, Gwen, before I—"

"Before what?" Gwen cut in. She rolled her shoulders and her feigned nonchalance vanished.

Her challenge was clear. If my beast wanted to fight, her dark lioness would oblige.

Not wanted—needed, I realized.

Gwen was waiting in this room—and had probably sent all others away—to forestall me, to give me the chance to shake off the latent magical energy peeling off of me in waves. Better she bear the weight of my brutal magic than an unsuspecting servant.

I'd killed dozens in those early decades, when my gifts surged beyond my control. But I'd never lost it around Gwen or any of the armies I'd commanded over the last three centuries. But that proof of my mastery of my powers did not matter. The stories persisted, whispered over fires. Gwen had no doubt heard them. Maybe she'd told a few herself in the years since our first acquaintance.

My magic cooled, spooling up inside of me. I willed control through my limbs, then my veins. When I flicked my gaze back to Gwen, her posture had softened. She judged the danger to be past.

Her deep gold eyes, set against her matching chocolate skin, were clear when they met mine.

"Where did you put the human?" she asked.

I was suddenly so fucking tired.

I turned away and kicked loose my bedroll from its spot before the doors to Veyka's bedroom.

"He is secured," I said without looking back at her.

I didn't miss the low growl. "I have as much right to him as Veyka."

"Tell her that. I'd like to watch the bloodbath." I reached for my shirt by habit, only to remember Veyka shredding it in her desperation to get her hands on me.

I could hear the sound of Gwen's teeth grinding together. "What if I give you my word not to kill him?"

I grabbed the blanket and pillow that were neatly folded against the wall, tossing them down onto the now-flat bedroll. Still not looking at her. "Would you promise not to harm him?"

Silence.

I knew what Gwen wanted—the same thing as Veyka. To torture the human into divulging information, to try to sate the gaping hole in their chests left by Arthur's death. Veyka, for the brother she'd loved and lost. Gwen, for the future she'd worked so hard for only to have stolen for her.

But I trusted neither of them. Not in this. I would not have trusted myself in the same position.

"No," I said softly.

Long beats of silence stretched between us. When Gwen spoke again, her voice was deadly even. "Go find your bed. I will stand guard over the queen."

I sighed heavily. Why was every moment of my life an Ancestors-damned argument with a headstrong, stubborn female?

"I am a Goldstone Guard now," Gwen said simply.

She was right. Before, I'd left her to guard Veyka in my place because she was the only one I could trust, but she'd done it as a favor to me. Now it was her duty.

"Fine." I kicked my half-made bedroll off to the side and stalked to the exterior doors to find my long-neglected suite of rooms.

Gwen's silky whisper followed me in the corridor. "Enjoy your soft bed. If the queen did not invite you to share hers after that thorough fucking, I doubt she ever will."

39
VEYKA

For once, I woke early. Whether it was the lingering sexual satisfaction or the fact that my sleep was unusually dreamless, my eyes slitted open with the sunrise. Elegant shades of gold overtook the blue of dawn, spilling across my open terrace and onto the floor. Dust motes danced in the shafts of sunlight.

How strange, that they could shimmer gold and white as they hung there, each individual speck suspended in space and time. But when they all settled on the ground, they became that deep orange-red that covered most of the elemental kingdom.

At times, it shifted character. The dunes were covered in fine granules of sand as tall as mountains and much more treacherous for their ever-shifting nature. As the dunes gave way to the mountains that circled the Effren Valley, orange-red clay prevailed. A mixture—sand and clay and secrets—made the goldstone that had built the very palace around me. Only in the highest reaches of the mountains, where the goldstone palace was built, did the ground become thick enough to support trees and other flora.

Of all the places to build the seat of power in the Elemental Kingdom, it seemed a strange choice. Why choose to build the palace in one of the few places within the entire kingdom where flora-gifted terrestrial fae were able to call upon their powers? Our two fae races had been enemies for thousands of years.

Maybe the Ancestors knew. Or maybe the knowledge predated even them.

I stretched my arms above me, noting the twinge in my jaw. I was naked, I noticed, as the sheets slid down my body. Slowly, my mind catalogued the reason my jaw was sore. My fingers drifted toward my throat, where Arran's mouth had sucked so hard just above the collarbone. The skin felt no different. But I had a strong suspicion that when I found a mirror, I'd see the evidence of Arran's attentions. Unless I applied cosmetics, so would everyone else I encountered in the goldstone palace today.

Did it matter? He'd been sleeping in my rooms for weeks now. Neither of us had tried to hide it.

In a court that was notorious for gossip and trading in information, I was certain that every fae here knew as much. What I did not know was how many realized he was there to protect me, rather than bed me—and what the implications of that knowledge might be.

Some would think I was weak, unable to protect myself. Others would think he did not find my full figure attractive. There were probably a dozen other explanations and rumors. Perhaps I ought to ask Parys.

I sighed and rolled onto my side, missing the convenience of having him next to me. I'd never asked him about all the court rumors and gossip when I'd had him close to hand. Now, Arran had scared him away.

Not quite able to get comfortable, I shifted onto my elbow, the weight of my breasts pulling me down toward the mattress. As I wedged my arm underneath my head, a glint of gold-streaked brown flashed in my vision.

"Parys!"

"Good morning to you too, Veyka," his voice floated in from the veranda.

I could just make him out in the bright morning sunlight—

sprawled out, his limbs hanging off the side of the lounge chair. He was facing away from me but moving now.

I grabbed for the sheets, dragging them up over my breasts—as if Parys hadn't seen them a hundred times. Until last night, he'd been my lover.

No, that was not quite right.

He'd been my partner in despair, in release and in escape.

What did that make Arran?

My betrothed. Beyond that, I didn't dare analyze my feelings. But for once, I didn't try to shove them into a locked box inside of me either. I doubted there would be any point—Arran would simply rip the box open the next time I saw him.

Parys' eyes glimmered with wry amusement. "Good idea. I don't want your Brutal Prince finding me staring at your considerable assets."

I heard the soft whisper of wood—the door to my handmaiden's chambers opening, Cyara slipping out. I turned back to Parys.

"Is that why you are sitting all the way over there?"

Parys smiled, and well... he looked damn handsome. I realized I hadn't seen that genuine smile in a very long time. Not since before Arthur died. I wondered what had conjured it after all these months.

"That, and your lovely handmaidens had not yet laid out breakfast," he said, extending the grin to Cyara, who'd just reappeared from the antechamber with a tray laden with pastries and fruit.

"Did you sleep here?" I asked, wondering how he'd gotten in.

Gwen had been guarding my door. She must be still. Arran would never have admitted Parys. But Gwen was just salty enough—especially if the argument I'd heard bits of last night was any indication of the state of things between her and her terrestrial commander. She probably let Parys in hoping that Arran would discover him here.

Parys turned his back as Cyara circled the bed with a dressing robe.

"I came an hour ago. Couldn't sleep, and the library isn't open yet," he said.

I blinked. "The library?"

"You were aware we had one here?" He must have heard the Cyara stepping away, assuming I was dressed, because he cut a line straight to the table of food.

I rolled my eyes, approaching slower but with no less hunger in my stomach. "Of course I was. I was not aware that you frequented the place. Frankly, I'm shocked you find the time. You were quite busy yesterday, whispering your way across the throne room."

I selected a chocolate croissant. The smell was heavenly. The first bite was better.

"It is one of the few places I can escape the rumors," Parys said.

The pastry turned heavy in my throat. The rumors he collected, and the ones whispered about him and Arthur.

There was no rule against males loving other males here, not like in the human realm. Sex and love transcended gender and identity, just like magical gifts. But Arthur had been the elemental heir, with a duty to wed and reproduce. In a court built on lies and scheming... *Oh, Parys.*

I'd never imagined. Just like I'd had no idea what was happening with the missing children.

Guilt snaked through me. As familiar as the anger and thirst for revenge, I realized. Guilt for still being alive when Arthur was dead. Now, guilt that I'd been so fucking selfish. Exactly like Arran said.

Ancestors above and below. It was too early for this.

Parys took a hearty bite of the buttered scone in his hand. But the pain of his words lingered in the air between us.

Cyara watched us as she moved around the bedroom, making the bed, stoking the ever-burning hearth. I could practically feel the weight of her eyes upon me.

"Would you like to join us, Cyara?" I asked.

I could not believe I'd never asked her before. Parys and I gorged ourselves on the finest food that Annwyn had to offer almost daily, and Cyara, Charis, and Carly merely watched. Of course, I knew they were well-fed. No one in the goldstone palace went hungry. Though beyond it... I'd seen some disturbing things while sneaking into the streets of Baylaur.

But Cyara merely flicked her thick copper-colored braid off her shoulder to keep it free of the flames she tended. "No, thank you, Your Majesty."

I frowned. "Where are Charis and Carly?"

The corner of her mouth twitched. "They will be along shortly."

I found myself turning in my chair, looking at the door that led to their chambers. "Are they ill? Stop troubling with me and call a healer."

Cyara straightened, brushing her hands off on her white, flowing dress. Somehow, it remained unstained with soot. That smile that had played across her face was even more evident now.

"They suffer from nothing but their own foolishness."

Parys huffed a sympathetic laugh. "Too much aural?"

"No," Cyara shook her head. "They are rather embarrassed to look Her Majesty in the eye after last night's events."

I choked on my pastry, delicate flakes of buttery sweetness lodging themselves in my throat. Parys pounded me on the back, but I waved him away, coughing my way across the room and out on to the balcony. I'd never been embarrassed by my own sexuality. I'd certainly never thought twice about my handmaidens—or even my guards—overhearing my fucking with Parys.

I wasn't embarrassed about being overheard with Arran, exactly. But somehow, it felt different. Private.

Except that now the notion of fucking Arran with an audience had entered my mind. And that lust I'd thought so thoroughly slaked? It was raging hot and wet between my legs.

I coughed again, swallowing down the last painful dregs of what had been a perfectly delicious croissant.

Parys took a very loud bite of apple. "I thought I smelled another male's scent in the air," he said around his chewing. "For your sake, I hope it was your betrothed and not some other—"

He dodged the vase, but only just.

Cyara had taken to grinding tea at the little table in the corner, her smirking smile hidden from view. But if the twitch of her delicate feathered wings was any indication, it was still there.

"My sisters are foolish and young," she said. I refrained from reminding her that both Charis and Carly were at least twice my age. "Pay them no attention. If they do not come out here soon, I shall make them do the washing alone for the next week!" she said loudly in the direction of their closed door.

I drifted back toward the table. Parys offered another croissant, smirking. I swatted his hand away and reached for water instead. I gulped it down, trying to cool the heat that had suffused my body.

"You received a message this morning with your meal," Cyara said, snapping her fingers. The flame beneath the teakettle sprung to life.

My stomach tightened. My mother was determined to torture me even—

"It is from Councilor Roksana, renewing her invitation to dine with her any evening that is convenient to you," Cyara repeated, using words I could easily imagine Roksana herself saying.

My habitual response rose to my mouth, but my teeth caught my lower lip at the last moment. Esa's desire for power was out of control. The receiving of petitioners the day before had made that abundantly clear. She would be loath to give up control of the council when the time came.

It didn't really matter to me. Once Arthur was avenged, I would leave. That had always been the plan, half-formed in the back of my mind. But now that Arran was here, with all his proselytizing about peace and duty, there was no need to hide the truth from myself.

A fae queen with no powers could not hold Annwyn. Not even with the Brutal Prince at my side as king. It would tear the kingdom apart. Any children I bore would be threats, my own deficit of magic tainting the bloodline forevermore. There were few things that mattered more to the elementals than bloodline. Perhaps it meant that a Pendragon would never again sit the throne.

But with me gone, Arran at least stood a chance.

If he could wrest power from Esa.

Which meant I needed to start bringing her to heel now.

Slowly, I set the empty water cup down on the table with the rest of the forgotten meal.

"I accept her invitation."

This time, it was Parys who choked.

I pounded him heartily on the back, refilling my cup with water and handing it to him. His eyes were wide as he drank, but for once he said nothing.

Cyara's face had flattened, the little smile gone, replaced by the unreadable elemental mask worn by so many of my court.

She inclined her chin. "I shall send word. Is there anything else?"

Checking that Parys was not actively chewing or drinking, I turned back to Cyara and nodded. "Yes. Summon Lyrena. I wish to go for a stroll through the palace."

※

Lyrena walked right past me.

I'd allowed Charis and Carly to drape me in silk and chiffon, a deep fuchsia gown gathered at my shoulders with gold clips and cinched at my waist with a gold-braid belt. They had frowned when I insisted on adding the twin scabbards, but I was loath to go anywhere without my daggers. At least the scabbards Arthur had gifted me with on our twentieth birthday were heavily jeweled.

I even sat and let them twist my hair into a more-ornate-than-usual braid, threaded with strands of garnet and mother-of-pearl that made my moon-white hair shimmer. I didn't think of myself as vain, but even I could admire the effect in the mirror. I looked like a queen, even if I would never feel like one.

It would serve my purpose today. After making such a scene in the throne room, I needed to be seen around the goldstone palace as composed and regal. I needed Arran to see me and think I was unmoved by our interactions—both adversarial and sexual. But mostly, I needed to convince Lyrena.

But it felt awkward and strange. I'd been so deep in my grief for so long, I'd been unable to think of anything but food, fucking, and revenge. The grief was not gone. No, it was there in the pit of my stomach, deep and black and demanding. But it had sharpened into a blade that I would wield against my enemies. Starting with the human hidden away in the castle dungeons.

Apparently, it was strange for Lyrena as well. For when she entered my chambers, tall and confident in her uniform, she strode right through the antechamber and knocked on the bedroom door.

"Prompt as ever," I said drolly from the corner, where I sipped the tea that Cyara had brewed earlier. Sweet and delicious, if lacking in any of the intoxicating properties I preferred.

Lyrena did not jump. She was much too well trained for that. As she turned, her impish smile was already in place.

"Finally dragged your lazy bones out of the bed?" Lyrena said, grinning.

Gold gleamed in the corner of her mouth—she'd added a cap to one of her teeth. She was studded in gold from head to toe, woven into her long golden braid, capping the toes of her boots. On anyone else, it would have been garish. But Lyrena had always seemed to shine with an internal light that her penchant for gilding only enhanced.

"My lazy bones thrashed you in the training yard last time, if I recall," I said, unfolding myself to stand. I set aside my tea. "Care to have another go?"

Lyrena raked her gaze over me, appraising. "In that gown?"

I flicked the skirt to show the high slit. "I can move just fine," I said, fingering the hilt of one dagger. The temptation to spar was strong; I hadn't trained yet today. But I had other reasons for summoning Lyrena.

"I'm at your service, Your Majesty," Lyrena said with an irreverent half bow.

A heavy male sound came from the door to the corridor—Gawayn, clearing his throat. I rolled my eyes.

"You must drive him to distraction," I said with a conspiratorial whisper I was certain the head of my Goldstones could still hear perfectly well.

Lyrena's grin stretched wider still. "Someone has to keep him from getting too old and crotchety."

"Little chance of that." I nodded toward the door, indicating that Lyrena should follow.

As soon as I stepped out into the corridor, Gawayn fell into place as well. Two Goldstones, one at each flank, every time I stepped out of this door. But that could not happen today.

"I will take a circuit through the courtyards and return directly," I said to Gawayn over my shoulder. "Lyrena shall accompany me."

Lyrena huffed a laugh. Gawayn breathed in sharply, ready to argue.

I watched his face, waiting for him to argue. For a moment, he reminded me of my father. The sandy blonde with shots of gray was not the same as my golden-haired father, but the tiredness in his eyes... that I had seen so often when he visited me in the water gardens. Gawayn had been Captain of Arthur's Goldstones before me, and my father's before that.

Unfailing loyalty to the Pendragon line.

Which meant when I gave an order, he would follow it. Even if he disagreed.

"When should I expect your return, Your Majesty?" he asked, voice heavy with resignation.

"No more than an hour, I'm certain," I said, setting off before he could change his mind.

I hoped it would not take that long to wheedle the information I needed out of Lyrena. But in the court of the elemental fae, who knew what would happen in the next hour.

Lyrena waited until we were three turns away, far enough that even the sharpest of fae ears could not follow, before letting out a billowing laugh.

"He'll have a new streak of gray by tomorrow morning, I guarantee!" she hooted, slapping her thigh as we walked.

I tossed her a half-smile over my shoulder but kept walking. We entered the first courtyard, the one nearest to my rooms. There was a fountain in the middle, bubbling merrily. Palace guards on each corner. I didn't linger.

"Are you insinuating I am responsible for Gawayn's premature aging?" I said once we were inside another covered corridor.

"I'd hardly call it premature. He's nearing eight hundred years," Lyrena said.

I hadn't realized he was so old. A fae of strong magic and power usually lived to a thousand. The most powerful among us might reach fifteen hundred years old. Arran, the strongest fae born in millennia? He'd reach that at least. If I didn't kill him first.

As for me? I was lucky to have made it to twenty-five.

Or unlucky. Each of those years had been marked by pain.

I could feel the specter of darkness pushing closer, threatening to claim the unusual clarity I'd had since waking. I must not fall back into the pit. Not now.

I forced my attention back to Lyrena.

She still hovered a half step behind, off my left shoulder. Guarding my back.

I waited beneath the arch to the next courtyard. She stopped short, of course.

"Walk *with* me, Lyrena. It's impossible to talk to you when I have to look back over my shoulder."

I could feel her hesitation. Even without Gawayn here to admonish her, even with her customary irreverence, she was still a Goldstone Guard. She'd been looking after me since the moment I emerged from the water gardens.

Just as she'd looked after Arthur.

Ancestors, he was too present in my mind this morning.

He always hovered there, a spectral ghost just beyond the edges of reality. But today I seemed to see him every place I looked. In Gawayn's blond hair. In the gold and emerald band that held the end of Lyrena's braid in place. The one Arthur had gifted her; the same one she'd worn the night of his murder.

Had she been wearing it all these months? Had I really been so deep in my own despair that I hadn't noticed her subtle, unending tribute to the lover she'd lost? She couldn't grieve like I could; she had a duty to perform.

So did I, I realized.

Right now.

I reached out, clasped my pale fingers around her golden skin, and pulled her to my side.

She didn't fight me. This time, when she smiled, it was a softer thing, lacking any of her customary flippancy.

"This is the route you used to walk with Arthur," she said softly.

Of course, she remembered. I'd been flanked by Goldstones then as well, though they'd been focused on my brother rather than me.

There was Arthur again.

I had not done it intentionally. But my feet seemed to remember the path, even if my mind had stubbornly forgotten. Arthur and I had walked together nearly every day after my release, arm in arm, finally free to be the brother and sister we'd always been in our hearts. Despite my mother's determination to keep me isolated, and my father's cowardly inability to defy her, Arthur and I had loved one another fiercely.

But I was not the only one who had loved him.

The glint in Lyrena's eyes reminded me of as much.

And instead of leaning into that shared grief, letting our half-friendship grow into something closer—something real—I exploited it instead.

"I know precious little of the goldstone palace, I'm afraid. Only what Arthur showed me," I said, letting my voice ring with sadness.

Lyrena's warm hand covered mine. I still gripped her arm. I hadn't realized. But the warmth of her fingers against my own, ever cold, was eerily soothing. Had she warmed them with the fire that surged through her veins, the mirror of my brother's?

For a second, it almost overwhelmed me. The similarity between them, the unspoken connection.

But I forced my eyes away, across the courtyard. I forced my feet to move, along that route my brother and I had walked a hundred times in the life I led before. The brief glimpse of a happiness that was never to truly be mine.

"Now, with this lingering threat, I hardly get to leave my rooms. Beyond the council chamber and the training yard, I know embarrassingly little of my own home..." I trailed off meaningfully.

I hoped Lyrena could not see my lie, did not realize that I'd reconnoitered the entire palace years before, when I'd first snuck out of the water gardens. But she was looking ahead then back, scanning, still in her role as guard even as she walked at my side.

"What would you like to see?" she asked, eyes flicking down one corridor even as we passed into the next.

"I wish to know what precisely I am ruling over," I said as we walked through a dim corridor connecting the last courtyard to the next. I could see the light ahead, knew another palace guard would be waiting there. I had precious few moments before others could hear us once again. "Not just the shining, gilded bits. But the less savory as well."

We were twenty steps from the courtyard.

I could feel the weight of Lyrena's eyes upon me, pausing in their perpetual sweep.

"The goldstone palace is open to you, Your Majesty. Where do you wish to go?" she said. But the tone of her voice didn't match her words. There was warning in every syllable. She'd take me, I sensed, to the bowels of this palace. The torture chambers and prison cells. But she would not relish doing so, and she'd try to convince me otherwise.

Someone else hell-bent upon protecting me, because they thought they knew better. Because they thought I was too precious, too innocent, to handle the truth.

Midnight black eyes flashed in my mind.

I refused to acknowledge the sharp jerk in my chest in response.

Ten steps to the light.

"Take me to the human," I said simply.

Lyrena did not break stride. The laugh that bubbled out of her throat lacked all of its usual warmth. It sounded like it would choke her, choke the joy right out of that beautiful, golden face.

"I cannot," she said. "Arran Earthborn has hidden him away even from us."

I blinked in disbelief, even as my feet continued forward. "How can that be?"

"It seems your Brutal Prince has learned a few tricks over the centuries," Lyrena said. I hated the begrudging admiration in her voice. "Wherever he has hidden him, none under your command know. Which, I suspect, is what he intended."

Of course it was. The fucking, Ancestors-damned bastard was determined to keep the upper hand, convinced that he knew better—

The bright sunlight flooded over us. We'd reached the next courtyard.

As expected, palace guards were posted at each corner of the huge square.

Sunlight flooded in from the square of exposed sky, bright blue as my own eyes and unmarred by a single cloud. The goldstone pillars that lined the perimeter of the courtyard were not gilded in gems but with an intricate inlaid mosaic. Blue eight-pointed stars, diamonds of carved mother-of-pearl, a green marble that must have been mined from some faraway land, all carefully placed together to create a repeating pattern around the cylindrical columns.

In the center, not a fountain bubbling away, but a raised platform, the edges painted with an alternating pattern of gold and turquoise. Once, a statute had graced the platform, raised several feet in the air. Or so Arthur told once told me—he'd also told me about how he'd blown the thing to smithereens with a blast of fire when he was ten years old and still learning to control his power.

Now there was nothing but the raised, flat platform.

Or there ought to have been.

If not for the two figures dueling in the middle of it. One wielded a mighty sword, her brown skin gleaming under a sheen of sweat. The other swung a battle axe.

I didn't stay to watch. If I did, I'd likely try to swipe Arran's legs out from under him so that Gwen could land a painful blow. One that, of course, would not be fatal. Because even though she was my Goldstone now, she would not harm Arran—not fatally.

As I turned away, a gleam caught my eye.

I paused, blinking against the bright shine of Lyrena's layers of gold accessories, catching the radiant sunlight. But it was not her golden cuffs or braid or tooth that was glowing. It was her eyes. They were ringed with desire as she stared at the spectacle unfolding on the raised platform.

The fire stabbed through me with such ferocity that for half a second, I thought some seed of magic had finally burst to life within me. But in the next heartbeat, I realized what it truly was.

Jealousy.

40
ARRAN

The days crept by. One, then two, then three. I hardly saw her. We spoke not a word.

The hate that burned in her eyes every time she passed by was enough to put paid to the notion that something had shifted between us. Veyka hated me as much as she ever had.

And I… perhaps it was not quite hate, not any longer.

I would never respect her decisions. I would never forgive her for leaving her kingdom to the treacherous Royal Council. Nor would I ever forget finding another male lounging in her bed as if he had any right to be there.

But some part of me could understand the rage that burned inside of her, the consuming need for revenge.

I'd once been brutalized.

Held captive and punished for the things that were a fact of my birth and beyond my control. I understood what it meant to need revenge, to be consumed by it. But I'd been a child with no responsibilities beyond my own survival.

She was Queen of the Elemental Fae.

She wanted to avenge Arthur—deserved to, even. But not at the cost of everything else. I had to get her to see that she was being shortsighted. That *she* could be the ruler that Arthur would have been.

Veyka could be the future of Annwyn. The Princess of Peace.

If only she would give a damn about something other than herself.

41
VEYKA

The festival of Lugnasa was three days away. Mabon would follow six weeks later. Which meant the Joining...

That was not something I could think about.

By Mabon, I would be gone.

Time was not working in my favor.

I had to get to the human.

The preparations for the festival were ramping up by the hour. The Royal Council was overseeing them, of course. I'd thought about asking Arran to do it—for all his posturing about duty and being stewards of peace, I did not think that party planning was among his background as a commander of deadly armies. It was almost too tempting an opportunity to miss.

But I had other plans for him.

So, I strapped my scabbards around my waist and the long, curved blades across my back. I checked that my braid was secure, and then I slipped out the secret balcony passage.

Last I'd checked Gwen and Lyrena had been standing guard in the antechamber. Since Gwen had been appointed one of my Goldstones, Arran had given over sleeping outside my door. But an instinct in my stomach told me that he was never far away, that he was guarding me still, though less conspicuously.

That instinct was rewarded around the three hundredth downward step.

I slowed my steps, pausing on the next landing. It could hardly be called that, really. It was double the width of the other narrow stairs, marked with a tiny slat cut into the goldstone that allowed in a thin shaft of light. It was not quite dark yet. Lugnasa marked the end of summer in the elemental kingdom. Sneaking out was always easier in the winter, when the days were shorter. But I didn't have the luxury of waiting.

I leaned back against the goldstone, letting its perpetual warmth permeate my skin as I listened.

Ten more steps, and he'd round the curve. I'd kept my steps silent, but I doubted he would be surprised to find me waiting here. He seemed to anticipate my movements, to hover right outside of my field of view, waiting and watching. Most of the time, I hated it. But today, I would use it to my advantage.

I watched through narrowed eyes as Arran appeared.

He was impossibly tall when we stood on even ground. Now, several steps above me, he was nearly as imposing as the beast he so carefully kept hidden within. The wool tunic cut across his chest, this time a deep brown color. He'd left the top two buttons unfastened, leaving a triangle of his chest visible. I briefly wondered if that was intentional—was he trying to play against the lust between us?

I'd thought of it as I dressed, selecting a tight-fitting bodice held in place with leather straps. My breasts were cinched down by necessity, but I knew the leather straps accentuated their curve.

Of course, that part of my plan backfired. Arran's eyes might have been on my breasts, but I didn't know it. I was too busy remembering the way his mouth had felt as he dragged it over my tortured flesh.

When I did manage to drag my eyes up to his, they were vaguely amused. Damn him.

"Who are you sneaking out to kill tonight, Veyka?" he said, his voice sounding vaguely bored.

"I only killed the Shadows informant because he tried to stab me first," I said innocently.

Arran barked a harsh laugh. "Liar."

He was right, of course. But I didn't intend to tell him that.

"Why should I tell you?" I asked instead. The words could have come out as petulant, but I was careful not to let them. I wanted them to be wary. I *was* wary. Trusting Arran, even in this measured, calculated way, was dangerous.

But I was running out of time and options.

His hand caressed the head of his battle axe, those long fingers that had caressed me so many days ago. "I can help you," he said simply.

It was the answer I'd expected—the one I'd hoped and planned for. But I was still not prepared for it. The force of the words was one thing. I knew they were true. Arran couldn't lie. He could help me. I knew it as well as he did.

But it was the earnestness in his face that truly shook me.

His brows knitted together, his dark stare intense even in the low light creeping through that slivered opening to the fading daylight beyond our secret staircase. He'd gotten better at dissembling, but he wasn't even trying now. I could see the conviction in every line of his handsome face.

The shredded remains of my heart whispered into the black void inside my chest—*What would it feel like, to stand at his side as an equal? To trust him fully?*

It is not a luxury I have, the darkness said back. He would betray me—he would leave. Like everyone had before. Even Arthur had been torn from me.

But my body betrayed my mind, allying with my heart. The space we occupied, this half-landing balanced between a steep ascent and a neck-breaking fall, forced us close together. I wanted to reach for him. I wanted to mold my soft curves against the hard planes of his body. I wanted to hear more of the words he'd given me that first time—speaking of my perfection, his adoration for my body.

My chest heaved upward, my lungs clawing for air. I hated the trembling shake as I exhaled that breath. I dug my fingers into the goldstone wall behind me, forcing myself to focus on the pricks of pain where my fingernails began to break against the immovable stone.

I forced my next words out, past the clawing in my chest and the tightness in my throat. "Why do you want to help me?"

Arran shifted his weight, moving fractionally closer to me. A battle tactic, if I'd ever seen one. "What answer would satisfy you?"

"The truth."

I couldn't give it to him. Not entirely. I'd share my quest for vengeance because I could no longer avoid him. I could not tell him the truth of my powers—or lack thereof. It would throw everything into chaos, and I couldn't afford to lose the time it would take him to grapple with that irrevocable truth. But I knew that he would give me the truth, even if I could not reciprocate.

Arran's fingers flexed at his side. I found myself waiting, expecting him to reach for me. Instead, he gave me the truth. "Because I know you will think of nothing else until Arthur is avenged."

Good.

He understood that, at least.

I took another breath, steadier this time, as I returned to the firmer footing of the plan I'd laid out. "I will let you help me—" Arran snorted, as if to remind me I had no choice in the matter. "—if you will take me to the human prisoner."

Arran stilled. He hadn't been expecting that.

I couldn't decide if that was helpful or harmful to my prospects. If he'd anticipated the request, he could have resigned himself to it. But he also could have found a way to dodge it. But Arran wasn't an idiot—he had to know that I would continue my quest to find the human, to bleed him. It was why he'd been so careful in hiding the prisoner away, out of my reach.

"I will not let you kill him," he finally said.

I bit out a laugh, harsh enough I hardly recognized it from my own lips. "Does that mean you intend to?"

Arran raised one dark eyebrow. "Perhaps."

That did surprise me—even after what Gwen had told me about the merciless way Arran had beheaded the humans in the Shadow Wood.

"Let me question him first," I said.

"You mean torture."

I inclined my head. "If necessary."

He didn't respond.

"You want to help me avenge Arthur. That human may have information." *You have to let me question him.* I didn't say it aloud, but I knew that Arran heard the words clearly, as if I'd spoken them directly into his mind.

He was silent for so long, I thought he would not answer. I half expected him to grab me by the arm and drag me back up the steps to my bedroom. If he threw me down on the bed, I knew I'd open my legs for him first and seek revenge later.

"Fine."

I blinked twice, not sure I'd heard him correctly, that I'd imagined the clipped word. But the expectation in his face as he tilted it down to me convinced me it had been real. I responded with a sharp nod.

I was already down the next ten steps when I heard Arran's next words.

"Where are we going?" he asked.

I paused long enough to glance back over my shoulder, touching the goldstone wall to keep myself from pitching forward as I smiled wickedly back at him. "Keep up."

42
ARRAN

Down the staircase to the narrow opening at the bottom. We slithered through on our stomachs, no better than serpents, our bellies coated with red dirt. My beast wanted to lick it off of Veyka's soft stomach. I wasn't much better.

Instead of slaking my lust, that one night had set fire to the desire that had been burning within me since that first meeting in the clearing. I'd never experienced such desire. I'd wanted females, of course. Lusted after them, even. But always, that need fizzled out once it had been met. I'd never bedded the same female twice. I'd never needed to. There was nothing interesting enough about them to warrant it.

But I wanted to know every curve of Veyka's body. I wanted to hear every sound she made and feel the way her climax shuddered through every limb. I told myself I'd have a lifetime—a fae lifetime, at that. Hundreds of years. Perhaps a thousand, if her hidden powers were even close to those passed down by the Pendragon line for centuries.

Now, I needed to focus on Annwyn. I needed to get her through this scourge, drag her from the depths of despair, and onto the throne.

If that meant following her through the mountains surrounding Baylaur as darkness fell, then so be it.

After the second hour of climbing, I asked again, "Where are we going?"

Veyka flicked her moon-white braid as she turned and gave me that wicked smile of hers. My cock hardened instantly.

"You recall what Jax said. The Blasted Pass is not the only way through the mountains," she said, smile still in place. As if that statement made any sense at all.

"You are tromping through the mountains, looking for... something... based on the words of a male who tried to gut you in his next breath." I stopped, folding my hands over my chest. I'd help her avenge Arthur. I would not allow Veyka to get herself killed running through skoupuma territory on a whim.

She seemed to read my mind, for when she paused, she glanced around the sparse trees, scanning for threats. Something I'd been doing every minute as we'd walked for the last two hours. Stubborn ass princess.

"If there is another way through the mountains, then we must find it. The Shadows are smugglers—and if what I've gleaned so far is correct, they've smuggled humans more than once."

The determination was set in every line of her face. The clear blue eyes, softened by the moonlight, the lips that pursed now in a straight line. She placed a hand on each hip and squared her body to mine in silent challenge.

But I didn't want to spar with her—not now, not here.

But there was an obvious flaw to her logic. "Why would they smuggle humans into Annwyn? They cannot be sold at market."

Veyka glanced to the side, unable to meet my eyes as she said, "You are the Brutal Prince. I'm sure you can imagine."

Humans were inferior to fae in every way. They were smaller, less muscular, most lacking in even a drop of magic. I'd encountered them now and again. It was impossible not to, having lived as long as I had. Until they'd somehow managed to sneak into the goldstone palace and murder the King of the Elemental Fae, I'd regarded humans the same way most fae did—as little more than vermin to be exterminated when they wormed their way into our world.

But there were others...

They called me the Brutal Prince. But I was far from the cruelest fae living.

"The fighting pits were exterminated by the Ancestors," I said, hating the thickness of my own voice—the seed of doubt.

On other far-flung continents, beyond Annwyn, they were still kept as slaves, used for entertainment. But not here, not since the time of the Ancestors.

Veyka tipped her head forward so that her entire face was illuminated by the moonlight that slipped between the fronds above. "And you call me naïve?"

The shock must have shown on my face.

She laughed then, and the sound was so cold, so merciless, it threatened to shatter something inside me—the illusion that Veyka was innocent. That she was selfish and spoiled and naïve. The belief I'd held since meeting her—the judgment that might be wrong.

Veyka advanced toward me, her steps sure even on the uneven mountain terrain.

"Humans are smuggled through the rifts, through the mountains, and into Baylaur. Jax all but told me as much. My council was more than happy to execute the humans who murdered my brother —too happy. Too quick. No one questioned how they made it to Baylaur in the first place." With each word, I watched the fury build on her face.

Wrath only enhanced her beauty.

I swallowed down the desire to drag her to me and spoke instead. "You think the Shadows smuggled them in?"

Veyka nodded. "Yes. If they've done it before, they'll do it again. I will find out where, I will find out how, and then I will find who. When I find who is doing the smuggling, I will know who on my Royal Council paid to get those humans through. Who is really to blame for taking Arthur's life."

My understanding of Veyka was being reshaped around me. I also realized what she had not said. "And who is responsible for the attempt on yours."

She shrugged, as if her life was trivial.

I felt the slinking of my beast nearer to the surface. I'd shifted this morning, for Ancestor's sake. He should have been satisfied. But the threat to Veyka had awoken him. "You are the Queen of the Elemental Fae. If you are killed—"

Veyka stepped right up into my space then. My body thrummed to awareness, but if the desire rolled through her as well, she didn't let it show—as usual.

"You said you wanted to help me," she reminded me, tone threatening.

"I want you to live long enough to sit on that Ancestors-damned throne," I ground out, my hands curling to fists at my side.

Her eyes were fierce. How had I ever thought she was weak?

"Then watch my back," she said, turning away as suddenly as she'd advanced. "We keep going."

We did. For another hour, we climbed. I stopped Veyka a few times, pointing out potential passes that *might* be exploited. But upon closer inspection, they were too treacherous, even for elementals. A fauna-gifted terrestrial fae might have been able to navigate the sharp crags in their animal form. But humans? Impossible.

When I told her as much, Veyka didn't argue. She nodded and turned back to the invisible path she seemed to be following. Only when the moon started its downward descent, marking the midpoint of the night, did she finally turn back.

Baylaur had just appeared in view, a twinkling of yellow firelight far in the distance, when she stopped suddenly.

My eyes went upward by reflex, looking for the gap she'd spotted and wished to inspect further. But there was nothing—

nothing beyond an impenetrable red-orange mountain, turned black by the night.

But Veyka was not looking up.

She was staring down the slope. Into a ravine, I realized as I tracked closer. We were poised above it, the path we'd taken earlier —were retracing now—rimming the edge. The path was only a few feet wide. Dangerous, by most estimations. But even in the dark, I'd hardly noticed it. Veyka was so sure-footed, the idea of her falling into it was preposterous.

So why was she staring so intently now?

"What is it?" I breathed, some deep animal instinct instructing me to keep my voice quiet.

She didn't speak but lifted her finger and pointed instead. Down into the ravine, my sharp fae eyes acclimated to the darkness so that what was at first glance a wall of black began to show shades of nuance. I strained my ears to hear, to see if I could match what my eyes saw.

A river, at the bottom of the ravine, rushing softly.

And at the riverside, tucked in among the tall boulders, was a tent.

"Who—"

But Veyka was already moving. She'd chosen a path and was picking her way down the treacherous slope of the ravine. She had to go slowly, or risk upsetting the rocks and alerting whoever waited below to our approach. I could no more hurry after her than yell for her. I could shift. But little good it would do me—my beast was not winged.

I had no choice but to follow her down, step by agonizing step.

She reached the bottom of the ravine a minute before me, but I was ready. She was damned fast, but she didn't have the advantage of surprise. I grabbed her arm, one hand going around her mouth to stifle the cry of surprise.

The damned queen bit me.

I kept in my own curse, lowering my hand slowly. "I was only trying to stop you from crying out," I whispered against her ear, still holding her firmly back against my body. She gave up struggling, thankfully. My cock did not care about the danger of the situation.

"Let me go," Veyka hissed.

I didn't relax my grasp even a fraction. "What is your plan?" I countered.

"To find out who the hell is in that tent and what they are doing all the way out here," she said back.

"What will they say when they realize it is their queen questioning them?" Whatever anonymity she'd been granted by her sheltered upbringing was gone since that afternoon in the throne room. Petitioners from all over the elemental kingdom had come. Word of the gorgeous, white-haired queen would have reached even the terrestrial kingdom by now.

She exhaled very slowly. "Who says they are fae?"

A shift in the breeze, and I knew she was right—we both did. For the scent that drifted across the dark red clay was unmistakably human.

It wasn't coming from the tent, either.

A shape moved in the darkness.

He made no attempt to soften his footsteps, scraping across the muddy clay riverbed. But there was something wrong. Veyka must have sensed it as well. She shifted her weight back, moved her hand for one of her daggers.

"Why have you come to Annwyn?" she said sharply, her voice brimming with authority.

No answer came. She drew her knife.

"Who brought you here?"

Still, no response.

But the shifting in the darkness was faster, more urgent. Another few seconds, and the moonlight and our adjusted eyes would reveal the human intruder to us.

"Answer my questions or you die," Veyka said. There was not a single ounce of mercy in her voice. I was not inclined to it either.

Then the man lurched into the pale moonlight.

Not a man—not anymore. One leg stuck out at a terrible angle, bent at the knee. Still, it advanced forward. Half of its face was missing, nothing more than a gaping hole of black. It was moving faster now, dragging that ruined leg through the mud. No limp, no sign that the human felt the pain.

Because it was not human, not now. It was something else, something other.

And it sprung for our throats.

I lunged forward, shoving Veyka behind me. I ignored her holler of protest, pulling my axe free from my belt and swinging it above my head in one fluid motion. The human-thing had no weapons. I'd fell it easily. But there was no recognition or hesitation in its eyes— in the one eye that remained, the other half of its face a ruined mess of red blood now dried to black.

I didn't hesitate.

The blade of my axe cleaved deep into its chest, deep enough that a woman would have been split in half, a fae felled to the ground. But the man kept moving, as if it hadn't felt the blade at all. It reeled back from the impact, but then it was on me again, closing a hand over my arm where I still gripped the handle of my axe.

As it touched me, my entire body filled with cold. It was reaching inside of me, burrowing past the physical to the center of me, where my magic dwelled. Just like that night in Veyka's bedchamber. The assassin.

But the assassin had been fae, not human. He'd moved with precision and intent.

There was no time to think of it, not now. Not with the very core of my being, my magic under attack. I brought my knee up hard, slamming into its chest, trying to knock the axe free. The force of it was enough to send me back hard onto the ground. A second later I was up, dagger pulled from my boot, launched through the air.

It landed in the center of his face, lodging directly between where two eyes ought to have been.

The abomination did not even pause.

But neither did Veyka. She moved like the wind was at her heels, so fast I could hardly make out her movements in the half light. She swiped with her curved blade but missed. Ducked, then kicked the monster's leg out from under it. The bad leg, the one that was already broken. But it didn't roar in pain or clutch at the wound. It simply pulled itself back up and advanced again.

Veyka drew the other blades from her back, one wickedly curved rapier in each hand. I opened my mouth to bellow that the blades did nothing, to try to behead it, but it was too late.

She shoved forward with all the force of her body, skewering the half-human, half-monster onto the twin blades. I was already on my feet. I grabbed her shoulder, yanking her back out of its reach.

But it didn't attack again.

It fell back onto the clay with a slap that might have been comical if Veyka and I weren't both breathing so heavily, the only sounds in our stunned silence.

We both stared down at it—what had once been a human man, now nothing more than a heap of ruined body and blood turned black by the night.

I took inventory of each limb, each wound. I'd landed two killing wounds. The ones it had when it emerged from the darkness should have done him in already.

"Why was it your swords that felled him?" I said, crouching down to pull out one blade and then the next. I handed the first to Veyka.

The second, I held up the moonlight, inspecting closely.

They were beautiful blades, to be sure, an alloy of multiple metals with a swirling pattern imbued at the time of forging. But there was nothing remarkable about them that I could detect.

Veyka frowned and held out her hand for the second blade.

I gave it to her, turning back to the ruined corpse. It bore no similarity to the assassin who had attacked Veyka, none at all. Other than that feeling.

I glanced over my shoulder, expecting her to be staring as well. But Veyka was already walking away.

I was the only one affected.

Why?

She went to clean her blades in the river. I stalked around the site, pulling back the flaps of the ramshackle tent.

"A bedroll and a bit of food," I reported as I straightened. Nothing unusual.

Was I imagining it? My mind had tricked me before, long ago. It had tricked me into seeing what was not there, to killing when I might have stayed my blade. I'd accepted that death because it had never happened again. But now... this...

I shook my head, trying to clear it of the memories that had no place here. They would only distract me, make me weak.

Veyka needed me strong.

She was already halfway up the river, staring up the ravine and to the mountains beyond. "How did he get here?"

I followed her gaze, shaking my head again. "And what happened to him once he did?"

She glanced behind us, to where the ruined corpse lay. "Should we bury him?"

My stomach lurched. She claimed that her soul was black. But then she asked this.

"I don't think it was a 'him,' anymore," I said, though I did turn. "I'll take its head off, just to be sure it stays down. Then we have to get back before your handmaidens awaken. It will be daybreak soon."

For once, Veyka didn't argue with me.

43
VEYKA

Arran made good on his promise the next day.

I slept most of the morning, chucking a pillow at Charis when she tried to wake me. Cyara came in and tried to rouse me, no doubt worrying I'd stay in bed all day. But I threw the other pillow at her and then used my forearms to rest my head.

In my half-delirious, half-waking state, I mumbled something about preferring to sleep with my head on Arran's chest. I was too tired to wonder whether anyone heard me.

But when I did eventually deign to rise, bathe, and dress, Arran was waiting in the antechamber, showing Lyrena different techniques for throwing the axe he always wore on his belt.

The massive thing, its head as big as my face, spun past me as I opened the bedroom doors.

I rotated slowly, tracking the path of the axe to where it was wedged in the nearer of the two pale wood cabinets that flanked either side of the sweeping window. Just as slowly, I turned back to face the two of them.

Lyrena, at least, had the wherewithal to look sheepish. Arran just looked downright delicious.

"An entire palace at your disposal, and yet you choose my chambers for target practice?" I drawled, crossing my arms over my midsection, thrusting my breasts upward.

Arran shrugged. "Perhaps you shouldn't take so long dressing."

I flicked my wrist, sending the long drape of fabric that hung over my arm whirling behind me. Lyrena moved away as I stepped closer. I hadn't forgotten the gleam in her eyes that day watching Arran and Gwen spar atop the platform. My more logical consciousness reminded me that she could have been lusting after Gwen as easily as Arran. But the feral thing in my gut did not care.

It wanted to make a statement.

I'd dressed for Arran today, though I would never have admitted it aloud. I was showing off all the parts of my body he'd admired during that one too-brief interlude. My legs in particular. They were practically bare—a bejeweled belt slung low around my waist, one rectangle of fabric secured just below my navel, draped between my legs, and then tucked up on the back to cover my bottom. Every inch of my legs, save for the very inner thighs, was exposed. I knew the weapons strapped to my waist and across my back would only inflame him further.

To saunter out and find him so chummy with Lyrena? Unacceptable.

I waited until I was right in front of Arran, stopping just short of actually touching him. But instead of speaking to him, I lifted my chin over his shoulder.

"Fetch the axe," I said to Lyrena.

Arran's eyes flicked over my shoulder now, following Lyrena. I could not stand it. I reached out and grabbed his chin, dragging his face down to mine. The surprise widened his dark eyes instantly. There was the little ring of fire around the pupil—the one I'd come to think of as mine. A flame that burned just for me.

"What do you want, Princess?" he asked, a mockery of the line that had drawn the truth from me weeks ago.

We wanted each other, badly enough that we didn't care what witnesses stood around and saw it.

But before I could retort, Lyrena was back at our side, axe in her hand. I took it before Arran could.

"Show me," I commanded.

As his arms closed around me, I heard his beast growl in appreciation.

That's right, I heard myself crooning back to it. *You are mine. Only mine.*

Another growl of approval.

Then one from Arran himself. "Lift the axe slowly," he said, grasping my wrist loosely.

Slowly, he showed me the path my arm would take, starting off level with my breast, then smoothly lifting up behind my shoulder.

"It's heavier than a dagger," he said against the pointed shell of my ear, sending shivers down my neck. "Use that to your advantage, but don't lose control."

He repeated the motion twice more, then released my hand. Only for those long fingers to fall to my waist. His thumbs stroked over the arches of my hips. I had to bite hard on my bottom lip to keep from moaning. But then he stepped back, out of range, so I could move unhindered.

I carefully repeated the motion he'd shown me, slowly one more time. Then fast.

The moment I released the axe, I knew it would fly true. Just like when I released my knives. I was built for weapons. Or rather, I'd built my body for weapons.

I might not have magic, but I would not be powerless.

The axe lodged in the cupboard with a satisfying *thunk*, a few inches to the left of where Lyrena's had landed. I turned my face to Arran, waiting for praise.

He rolled his eyes at me instead. "A decent first attempt," he said, crossing the room to retrieve his axe.

I reached out my hand for it, but he slid the handle into his belt instead. "Another time. We have somewhere to be." *Someone to interrogate,* his eyes said to mine.

I glanced at Lyrena, who'd taken up a post at the door adjacent from Gwen. The latter opened the doors to the corridor, where Gawayn was posted. Ancestors above, three of them? Normally Gawayn was satisfied with two, if I was in my own rooms.

The two females stepped forward, ready to fall into place behind me.

They were the ones officially on duty, then. So, why was Gawayn lingering as well? But I didn't have time to contemplate it; Arran was striding to my side.

"I shall accompany the queen," he said to Gawayn, not even sparing a glance for Lyrena or Gwen.

If any of them had a comment, they didn't voice it until we were well out of hearing range.

I followed Arran through the corridors, marking familiar locations as we went. What I'd said to Lyrena was true. The goldstone palace had at least ten occupied levels, plus at least a dozen more carved into the stone mountainside and used for various purposes from kitchens to dungeons. I'd explored some on my own, in those early days when I'd first figured out how to sneak out of the water gardens. But soon enough, I'd discovered the joy of freedom outside the palace walls. After that, I was intent on finding ways to get out, not to explore within.

I counted the staircases as we descended.

After the seventh level, I was unable to recognize a thing.

By the tenth stairwell, I was shivering. There were no more windows, courtyards, or terraces. We were in the subterranean levels of the goldstone palace now, in the depths of the mountain itself.

I'd dressed for seduction, not warmth. There was hardly a need for such a thing in Baylaur—at least in the parts I occupied.

Arran paused on the next landing. "That is what you wear for an interrogation?" he said, gaze sliding none-too-slyly over my scantily clad figure.

"I have never interrogated someone," I admitted. "Do you think the human will find me distracting?"

"I think he will find you terrifying."

I smiled wickedly. "Good."

"How much further?" I asked, looking past him. We'd reached a crossroads of sorts. Several corridors branched off from this landing. One was another set of stairs down.

"We aren't going down any more," he said, following my gaze and looking amused about it. Bastard.

"Aren't the dungeons in the very bowels of the mountain?" I'd never visited them, but I was not an idiot.

"They are," he agreed. "But I knew better than to put him where you could find him."

By instinct, my hand landed on the hilt of my dagger. Arran's eyes noted that as well.

"Try it," he said softly.

Slowly, chewing my bottom lip viciously, I dropped my hand. "Yet you know I am memorizing this route," I said.

His eyes met mine steadily. "By the end of this interrogation, I doubt it will matter."

Because I would kill the human. Or he would.

What had changed, I wondered? He'd been so adamant I not kill the man in the throne room. Had it been because there was an audience? Or he wanted me to get a handle on my emotions? The latter seemed most likely. But he ought to know by now that when the rage bubbled over, I had little control over it. I didn't *want* to control it.

I could feel that anger rising to the surface now. The desire to make the human pay, to exact revenge against an entire race. It rose within me, heating my veins. My eyes had flitted closed. I opened them now, finding Arran staring at me intently still. A smile curved my lips.

"What have I done to earn that wicked smile now, Princess?"

My mouth was impossibly dry. My lips as well. "Your eyes are glowing," I said softly.

It was impossible, but the black fire burned brighter at my words.

I licked my lips, unable to pull my gaze away from those

mesmerizing eyes. "Does the thought of my bloodlust arouse you, Brutal Prince?"

"Everything about you arouses me, Veyka."

I wondered if he heard the trickle of wetness sliding down my inner thighs.

"Let's go," he said, turning down the dark corridor. He knew I'd follow.

44
ARRAN

Half hidden away and entirely forgotten, the closet where I'd stashed the human was hardly big enough for me to shove myself into. But it was perfectly adequate for a human prisoner. I wasn't surprised when Veyka paused in the corridor, immediately sensing something was amiss. I'd cloaked the place every way I knew how, but still, that wasn't enough to fool her.

She paused, hands settling on her impossibly wide hips. Hips I'd thought about endlessly.

"A closet? You stuck the human in a closet?" She shot me a look of vaguely impressed disbelief.

I shrugged. "Would you have gone looking inside a closet?"

She swayed those hips, and I almost pushed her up against the wall. Let the human hear my beast ravage her. It would only add to his fear and make him more pliant to our questions.

Veyka could read the desire in my eyes. She flashed that wicked smile, dragging her tongue over her perfectly white teeth, the same pearlescent color as her hair. Ancestors, I was so fucked.

No, I needed to fuck her. Again. A hundred times. Maybe then I'd be able to think.

But she'd shifted her attention away from me, toward the closed door. I waited, half expecting a burst of power to explode out of her and decimate the door. Instead, I watched her chest move up and down in a steadying breath. Then she reached for the handle.

The scent of human hit hard, but I'd smelled every offensive odor that existed on the battlefields over the last three hundred years. It knocked Veyka back a step. She grabbed for the door to steady herself.

Humans were always so easy to read. Fear always drenched their scent, coming off of them in waves. This man was no different. Fear, unwashed grime, the excrement bucket I'd left in the corner. But there was something else that was harder to name. Something not quite as dark as all the other fetid stenches seeping from the small space... something, perhaps... hopeful?

The human blinked in the darkness, his eyes taking longer to adjust to the low torchlight of a single flame halfway down the corridor. But the second they did, we knew it. He fell forward, prostrating himself on the dirty ground before Veyka.

"Your Majesty," he mumbled into the rough cobbles.

"Groveling will not save you." Veyka's voice was as cold as ice, as cold as her hands, or the phantom wind I'd not felt since dismissing Evander days before.

The human's head rose a few inches, enough that he could peer up at Veyka through the matts of dark hair that hung over his forehead.

"I have... I..." he sucked in a ragged breath. "I have no regard for my own life."

Veyka bit out a harsh, merciless laugh. "That makes you either quite wise... or very, very stupid."

I knew this side of her existed. Of course, I did. Revenge—it was all she cared about. It was the dark twin to the apathy she'd bathed in before. It was terrifying to see her blue eyes so full of hate. Different from the hate she'd directed at me. This—the way she looked at that human—it was bone deep. Deeper, maybe. In her soul.

Exactly as she'd told me.

But I was not afraid, and I was not repulsed.

It was another dimension of her unlocked. My beast wanted every facet Veyka had to offer, as well as all the ones she'd rather keep hidden.

Veyka raked her eyes over the human, still flat on the ground before her, and drew a dagger from her waist. She didn't lower it to him, but rather lifted it level with her face, tilting it to catch the scarce light.

"Why did the humans kill King Arthur?"

The human's shoulders twitched. "I don't know."

Veyka slid her finger down the length of the blade, then pulled the pad away. Not a drip of blood to be seen. A performance, that's what she was doing. "Wrong answer."

In less than a blink, she'd flipped the dagger in her hand so the blade pointed straight down. She released it, letting it fall straight for the human's exposed neck.

Only to catch it an inch from piercing his paper-thin skin. "Why did the humans kill my brother?"

She may not have ever interrogated someone before, but she was damn good at it anyway.

The human's shoulders were shaking now.

"We heard about the death of the golden king," the man said quietly. "You have my condolences, Majesty. There were many of us who hoped... hoped that he might hear our petition."

"I do not want your condolences." She spat on the dirty ground at his feet. "I want to know who ordered my brother's murder."

The human was wise enough to say nothing. Veyka drew herself back up to her full height, towering over him. She was losing control. I could see it in every line of that magnificent body. Her knuckles, whiter even than her pale skin, were nearly shining with the force of gripping that dagger. Her legs, exposed from hip to ankle, were quivering ever-so-slightly. She was a predator about to pounce.

My beast wanted to watch her tear the man apart. Ancestors, so did I.

But we needed information. It was the only reason I'd allowed this.

I touched her arm. The briefest, lightest touch I could manage when what I really wanted was to yank her back.

The look she shot me would have melted a lesser male on the spot. But I glared back at her, letting the darkness swallow my eyes, letting my body shift forward into the stance that had intimidated and massacred thousands of lesser males and females. Veyka didn't cower, not a bit. But that burning desire to kill in her eyes softened, just enough.

"You are not a citizen of Annwyn. You have no standing to present a petition to the High King or Queen," I said, dropping my gaze to the quivering human.

He struggled to his knees, a feat with his hands fettered behind him. But the feral gleam in his eyes, the fear that drenched his scent, propelled him upward.

He thought I was the bigger threat.

A mistake.

One I could subvert.

"I have nowhere else to go," the man said through chapped lips.

"There are human courts. You have your own kings and queens." I knew little about the human realm. It was of trifling interest compared to the threats here in the fae realm. But I did remember that.

The man nodded jerkily, the irons clanging. "There is nothing they can do. The threat is magical."

Veyka laughed, spinning on her heel, the vicious sound echoing through the close corridor. "There is no magic in the human realm! You expect us to believe a word from your wretched mouth, and you feed us this trash." She spun again, dagger ready. "I think I will kill you now and be done with it."

"Please, Majesty," he cried, eyes rocketing to me. "Highness, please. I speak the truth. Magic has come to the human lands. There is a darkness, it creeps through the night, stealing the men—"

"Sounds damn helpful to me," Veyka sniped. "Why should I care? Fewer humans to sneak through the rifts and wreak havoc upon my kingdom."

My stomach lurched. Or maybe it was my chest. *Her kingdom.*

But the human stammered on. "It steals the men and leaves something else in their place. Something not of our world. Something *other.*"

I'd thought his voice was trembling before. But those last two syllables barely made it past his lips.

Veyka stilled. Only for a moment; she wasn't willing to let the human see any more than that. She picked at the edge of her bodice, fitted tight against her breasts with one of those enticing gold brassieres she liked to torture me with.

But the glance she shot me, with a quick flick of her eyes, was enough.

We'd met something *other* in that ravine.

A human, but not.

Not in the human realm, but in Annwyn.

I could tell she was dissatisfied. He was giving plenty of information, yes. But too easily. She'd *wanted* to torture him. I could hardly blame her, though I could also be glad it wasn't necessary. She might think her soul stained black already; but her world was infinitesimally small. She had no idea what three centuries of killing could do to one's soul.

"Why did you come to Annwyn?" Veyka asked, her voice passing for bored. I knew better, and I suspected the human was canty enough by now to realize it as well. But he answered.

"I was sent by my village—Eldermist. It is just on the other side, tucked between the peaks, through the mountain rift. We came to beg help. To beg the kingdoms of the fae to summon back their darkness. To make whatever offering you require to stop foisting this plague upon us—"

"What mountain rift?" Veyka hissed.

There was no pretense of indifference now. Every muscle in her body was taut, ready to spring or implode or sunder the world apart.

"Between the—"

A flash of bright light filled the cupboard, so fierce and brutal it forced my eyes shut. I felt the whoosh of air, of wings in flight. I willed my eyes to open, axe already warm in my hand, ready to kill.

But there was nothing left to kill. No one.

The human was still on his knees, staring up at us. But where his eyes had once been was nothing but black. Not like the dark of my eyes, still swimming in that sea of white and reflecting back color. No, true black. Black that reached the corners of his eyelids. Black that swallowed the light around us, sucking it away into nothingness.

Then the black spilled out. Rivulets of thick black fluid that should have been blood but smelled like nothing of this world ran down his cheeks and splattered to the floor.

Veyka lunged with her dagger but I yanked her back, flat against the wall.

The man's body seized up, his mouth wrenching open in an empty scream, that black venom filling his throat and bubbling out through his nostrils. I waited for the sounds of pain, waited for him to lunge for us like the human terror in the mountains.

But there was only eerie silence.

"End it," Veyka whispered, her voice shaking.

I was all too ready. But as I stepped forward, the tension fell from his body. He collapsed to the floor, writhing, rolling in the black viscous substance until it coated his wretched form. Every orifice leaked, that noxious darkness filling the space with its fetid scent.

Veyka dragged in a breath.

Shallow. Too shallow.

I stepped forward into that darkness, feeling it reach out for me. The same terrifying cold I'd now felt thrice, trying to get inside of me. I spun for Veyka's curved blades. She already had them up, ready, realizing at the same time I did that whatever this was, it would not be felled by my axe.

Still, the human did not attack. No, this was not quite the same as the assassin or the thing in the ravine. The human was being attacked from within, destroying itself rather than us. But I couldn't take the chance on that instinct.

I darted forward, crossing the daggers over each other, and in a single, brutally efficient swipe, I parted the man's head from his body.

The writhing stopped.

We watched in silence, our breathing heavy with shock and adrenaline but raggedly muted as we tried to avoid breathing in the horrid stench of that darkness.

Finally, the flooding of black stopped as well. The waves of cold eased, retreating and hovering within the closet. Though I doubted closing the door would truly contain it.

Veyka held out her hands.

I blinked, confused.

Then I realized—I still held her blades. They dripped with a mix of thin red human blood and the black death that had poured from him. But she took them, nonetheless. I understood completely her need to be armed in that moment.

"No magic like that exists in the kingdom of the elemental fae," Veyka said, staring at her blades. The question in her words was clear.

"None that I've seen in the terrestrial kingdom, either," I said.

"Then where?"

"There are other places... other continents beyond Annwyn," I said carefully. Places I'd done battle. Places forgotten to time. "But I've never seen this."

"The humans think we are wreaking a plague upon them, is that..." Veyka's voice shook. "Is that why they killed Arthur?"

"It is possible." Because it was. It seemed unlikely—how could the humans have gotten to Annwyn, into the goldstone palace, without magic? Without fae help?

"The mountain rift," Veyka said softly.

I settled the axe back into my belt, trying to find normalcy. "What of it?"

"There is no mountain rift."

My head snapped up.

Veyka was staring at the decimated human body. "The rifts to the human world are known, protected. There are none in the mountains surrounding Baylaur—at least, there are not supposed to be."

"The Shadows," I said, realizing even as Veyka was nodding.

"That's how they are smuggling humans in. The human in the ravine... we must have been close. He must have passed through the rift in the mountains." Veyka's eyes were clearing, the shock of the human's grotesque death giving way to calculation. "Whoever is behind Arthur's death knew about the rift in the mountains. They knew how to get the humans through undetected."

"What about," I paused, gesturing to the otherworldly tableau. "This?"

Veyka chewed her bottom lip. Any other time, I might have been inflamed. But the expression on her face summoned something else instead—worry.

"This is a human problem," she said icily. "I am the Queen of the Elemental Fae. I do not care what happens to them."

The mask of cold hate was firmly back in place as she shouldered past me. "Let's clean this up. I don't need anyone else finding out about the human treachery until I am ready."

45
VEYKA

I was shaken.

Stubborn as I was, even I could admit it to myself.

The human's death, while gruesome, was not the cause of my nightmares. I'd endured terrible things before, and I was beginning to suspect that I would again before this was all over, my vengeance satisfied.

What startled me awake at night was the enormity of it.

Arthur's death. The secret mountain rift. The darkness haunting the human lands. I insisted to Arran that I did not care about what happened in the human realm. And mostly, that was true. They could rot in that disgusting bile, each and every one of them, for what they'd done to my brother. But if that darkness came to Annwyn...

I stuffed the thought down. I didn't have time for it. Mabon crept closer and closer, and I had not yet found Arthur's killer. I could not afford to wait for things to unfold; it was time to force them forward.

Which was how I found myself in a library, of all places.

I didn't mind books, really. But they were a luxury. They couldn't stop a blade. They couldn't keep me alive. They couldn't protect me from my mother and her schemes to imbue me with a magic that didn't exist.

I'd learned swordplay so I could slaughter the monster she brought to the water gardens. I taught myself to wield the daggers, hidden behind the crashing of the waterfalls, so that when the chance came, I'd be able to punish her. So that one day, I'd be strong enough to defend myself.

I had no magic.

Now I had no family.

But I had my blades.

However, they would do me little good amid the stacks of books. So, they remained in their jeweled scabbards at my hips.

When I'd asked after the location of the library, Gawayn described a multi-level fortress within the palace, cut into the side of the mountain. After my foray into the lower levels, I'd dressed more warmly.

While the library was indeed down farther than the residences, it was nowhere near as deep as the catacomb of hallways where Arran had stashed the human. I turned a corner, expecting to see yet another long corridor, and found myself instead in a cavernous hall.

The ceiling stretched far enough above my head that the corners were concealed in shadows. Huge torches burned on the walls, casting orange shimmers across the goldstone walls, none of the cooler daylight permeating this inner cavern.

Two statues, carved not from goldstone but from the red-orange clay that coated the mountains, flanked each side of the massive library doors.

The first sent a shiver down my spine. Female, tall and shapely, the body could have been mine. But the face of the statue was entirely different. The eyes slanted more and the cheekbones were higher. A curtain of perfectly straight hair covered the right half of the face. She looked regal, but unnerving. Something about the sculpture was wrong, as if the proportions did not quite fit.

The second statue was worse. Slender as a reed, though just as tall as the other. The form was almost fluid, as if caught halfway in an undulating motion. Here, the face was familiar. Not quite the same as mine, or my mother's, but undoubtedly some Pendragon female of history. Again, however, that same sense of wrongness permeated.

Maybe it was the existence of the statues at all. There were so few in the goldstone palace. Most of the decorations were geometric patterns created with colorful tile or actual gemstones. I had enough faces staring at me every time I emerged from my apartment; seeing those lifeless eyes watching me as well was damned unnerving.

I forced myself past them—to the massive doors that reached nearly to the ceiling, where they joined at an arched point. Such grandeur, even for a bunch of books. Ridiculous.

Once I opened the doors, I realized how wrong I was.

I barely heard Gawayn and Lyrena taking up their posts at the doorway behind me. I was much too focused, being drawn in.

A bunch of books.

Ha.

Walls of them. Buildings. An entire city built of books came into focus around me.

I took a step forward, then another. Until I was standing in the center of a huge, circular blue carpet. Wrapped around it were bookcases, built to caress the curve of the rug. Two aisles broke off like spokes in a wheel, or rays of sapphire night.

It should have been dark. We were in the lower levels of the goldstone place. Except that instead of a wall of books, like one might expect, my eyes lifted past the tall bookcases to an even taller wall of windows.

Light flooded in from the Effren Valley, washing the entire room in brilliant shades of gold and warm tawny. The water gardens were famed for their beauty, but this...

I could see why Parys spent so much time here.

The cavernous library must hold thousands of tomes. Tens of thousands, maybe. But I saw no one. Of course, that didn't mean there weren't occupants. However many of my courtiers were here, they were so dispersed across the space that standing there I felt entirely alone.

Except for Gawayn and Lyrena. The former of which cleared his throat.

"Would you like us to find something for you, Your Majesty?" Gawayn said.

I rolled my eyes, even though he could not see it. "No," I said, taking a step forward. Toward the left of the two aisles. A few more steps, but then I slowed. Because the reality was, I did not actually know where I was going.

"Parys?" I called hopefully, if a little too quietly. Heat flooded my cheeks. I couldn't very well ask for Gawayn and Lyrena's help now.

But fae ears were sharp, and Parys' were trained to hear whispers.

He popped his head out from between two cases of books, fifteen yards ahead of me.

"Veyka?"

I hurried forward, waving away Gawayn and Lyrena with a shooing motion. They stayed in place near the library doors.

"Hush," I chastened Parys, sliding between the two tall bookshelves. "Do you want the entire library to know I am here?"

Parys chuckled. "In case you haven't noticed, there's no one here."

I glanced around the row, finding it as empty as Parys said. "There must be someone here, somewhere. This place is massive."

"Figuratively, there's no one. Practically," Parys waved his hand dismissively, "there are perhaps five of us who regularly haunt the library."

I shook my head, still disbelieving. "There are a thousand courtiers here in the palace. Five of them are in the library?"

Parys' smile was wry. "Depressing, isn't it?"

Depressing, but perhaps not as surprising as I'd initially

thought. Elementals loved to gossip and connive, not broaden their minds.

I raised an eyebrow and looked down the row again. Books lined the shelves, two stories tall, complete with ladders to reach the tomes stored up high. Not a single book was out of place—other than the small stack on the floor, next to a goblet of wine and a half-eaten slice of cake.

"Who cares for this place?" I said, edging around Parys and closer to his little cocoon on the floor.

"The librarians. They're surly old goats, the pair of them, so mind you don't do any magic in here. They say it's dangerous for the books," Parys said, not bothering to bow or scrape before settling himself back into the cozy nook he'd created for himself on the carpeted floor.

No danger of that.

Parys held out a hand, and I accepted, folding myself down onto the ground beside him. He leaned back against the shelves behind him, not seeming to worry about the books he pressed up against. If he could be that cavalier, then I could too. I mirrored his stance. Then I reached for his cake.

He tried to swipe it away from me, but I was faster. I'd learned to be. Speed had kept me alive more than once.

I shoved a bite into my mouth, savoring the decadent chocolate and rich buttery frosting. I even let a low moan escape my lips.

"Do you have a reason for coming here? Other than stealing my cake," Parys complained.

I chewed that delicious cake thoroughly, took another bite for good measure.

But I was concerned Parys might try to stab me with the fork if I finished it off entirely. And I had a purpose.

I set it aside, begrudgingly. Parys didn't hesitate, grabbing the plate and shoveling the remnants into his mouth before I could change my mind.

Smart male.

"I need you to research the rifts."

Parys was not mid-swallow, so he did not choke. But he did let his mouth hang open comically, masticated chocolate cake filling the otherwise gaping hole.

"That's gross." I reached out and tapped his chin upward.

He finished chewing with agonizing slowness. Swallowed with the same, then reached for his wine goblet and drained it. Only then did he speak, and even then it sounded strangled.

"The rifts? To the human realm?"

I picked up his goblet of wine, frowning to find that it was, indeed, totally empty. "Yes. Everything you can find about them. Where they are located in the elemental and terrestrial kingdoms, how they work, who can pass through them, what sort of protections there are, how they are formed." I set the wine back down, attempting casualness. "If they can be hidden."

There was no cake or wine left, so Parys stared at me, warm brown eyes wide.

I stared right back.

Parys finally broke the tension, glancing over my shoulders, then up at the towering walls of books around us. "It could take weeks. I can ask the librarians, though they'll give me hell—"

"No," I said sharply. "You cannot ask anybody or mention this to anyone. And we don't have weeks."

He frowned.

"Days, Parys. As fast as you can manage." I paused, sucking in a breath. "It's about Arthur."

I watched him begin to curl in on himself. That same retreat that I'd made, again and again, to the darkest places within me. But I couldn't let him do it. For months, I'd helped him—we'd helped each other. We'd fucked each other into the oblivion of release to hide from our pain. But now I needed him to help me in a different way.

I grabbed his hands, hauling him close, so that we were knee to knee, squared off, our faces inches away from one another.

"What about Arthur?" Parys' voice shook over every syllable.

"You know as well as I... a handful of humans could not have killed the greatest king to sit on Annwyn's throne," I said.

I prayed to the Ancestors I wouldn't have to say more. There may be hardly anyone in the library, but the walls of the goldstone palace had ears. There were shifters here now. Who was to say that one of the terrestrials was not creeping down the next row disguised as a mouse? I didn't want to take the chance to explain, but I needed Parys' help.

Inch by hesitant inch, Parys nodded his head. "I... I know." Then a sob. "I know."

I closed my eyes, forcing down the pain. I couldn't cry. I wouldn't allow it. I squeezed his hands so tight, trying to will strength into him, into us both. If I let the pain in, it would swallow me whole. If I opened my eyes and saw my friend go to pieces, I wouldn't win the fight raging within me.

I leaned forward and pressed my forehead to his, anchoring us both together.

That one sob ebbed into slower tears. Still, my cheeks remained dry. The dam of despair inside of me had cracked open, but it wasn't flooding free. Not yet.

Finally, Parys rocked back, pulling his hands away. He wiped at his eyes with his sleeve, turning back and staring at the empty plate and goblet accusatorially.

I knew how he felt.

"I'll have some more food and wine sent down to you," I said, getting to my feet.

Parys nodded, shifting his eyes to the books stacked at his side.

I wasn't sure what else to say, so I didn't. I turned back to the aisle, that main artery to find my way back to my ever-present guards.

"Wait."

Parys peered down at the pile of books for a full minute before selecting one and gently tugging it loose. His other hand caught the top of the pile, steadying it from teetering over.

"Take this," he said, holding it out to me.

The deep amethyst cover was embossed with gold, a little stag stamped in the center of the cover, gold swirls emanating out towards the rectangular edge of the book.

"What is it?" I asked, turning it over in my hands. I wasn't quite sure what to do with it.

"It's a book," he said, grinning mockingly.

"I will throw it at your head."

"Read it," he suggested instead. "I think you will enjoy it."

I stared at the little book. Better to stare at it than to stare at him, to let him see the thoughts and emotions swirling in my eyes. He could already probably guess too much.

"It won't bite."

A felt a smile play at my lips. If nothing else, Parys could help with that. "Alright," I said softly. "Thank you."

My eyes lingered on the book, but I was aware of Parys straightening, his head pointed in my direction. When I lifted my eyes, he was staring at me intently.

"No, Veyka," he said firmly. "Thank you."

46
VEYKA

That little purple book stared at me from my dressing table as Carly finished braiding strands of aquamarine into my hair. Lugnasa was upon us, the festival of purification and light. Another instance when nearly every elemental—male and female—would be dressed in symbolic white.

I had no idea what the terrestrials would wear, or how they marked the occasion.

But as I swathed myself in deep teal, I wondered if I would have more in common with them than my own courtiers.

Once Carly stepped away, Charis stepped into her place and fixed a diamond choker around my throat. She reached for my ears, but I waved her away. They were already sparkling with the amorite studs and silver hoops that pierced the flesh from the rounded lobe all the way to just below the pointed tips.

"Go," I insisted, waving toward the door. "Enjoy yourselves."

They exchanged a look. "Your Majesty, we cannot possibly neglect—"

"I will see to her needs tonight," Cyara said, breezing in from the washroom. "So long as you two promise to find other beds for the night. I will not have you disturbing the Queen."

The two handmaidens looked between me and Cyara in shock, as if not certain whether to believe what they were hearing.

Cyara crossed her arms, wings flaring behind her. "Go before I change my mind."

The two younger sisters needed no further urging. The bedroom doors had hardly closed behind them before their squeals echoed back to us.

Cyara rolled her eyes and adjusted the shoulder strap of my gown. I smiled despite myself. "It would not bother me if they came back tonight, they are quiet enough," I said.

"Not after a glass or two of aural," Cyara countered. She brushed away some invisible speck of dust and then stepped back to examine me. "It is Lugnasa. I'm certain they will find company for the evening."

She was right, of course. The festival symbolized purification, but there could be none without corruption. While the sun was high in the sky, the fae court would dance in swirls of shining white and glowing lights cast by the fire-gifted among us. But when the sky turned the many courtyards of the goldstone palace dark, so too would the activities of those who danced beneath it. Light was for cleansing. Night was for debauchery.

I had no doubt that my beautiful handmaidens, freed from their duties for one night, would find more than one willing partner should they wish it.

Apparently finding my appearance acceptable, Cyara turned to the little corner table, returning with two steaming cups of tea.

"Will you be partaking in the evening's festivities, my lady?"

I sipped my tea and avoided her eyes. "I am duty-bound to attend."

Truth.

But I'd also been thinking about what might happen after the sun faded from the sky.

"Is your betrothed familiar with our customs?" Cyara asked, sipping serenely, as if we were discussing the weather.

I shrugged, the gold and silver bracelets on my wrists jangling. "Gwen is, I'm certain. Perhaps she has filled him in."

"If not, it would be your duty to do so."

I bit on my lip to keep from laughing nervously. Ancestors, why was I nervous? "I suppose so."

Cyara looked at me with such knowing in her eyes, I felt five years old and five inches tall.

"It is nothing," I insisted. "Arran and I are... nothing."

"You and Parys were nothing," Cyara observed, astute as ever.

"Precisely. It is the same."

Now I could see Cyara biting her lip. "If you say so, Majesty."

"I do."

Cyara only nodded mildly. "Very well. I will await you in my chambers," she dipped a curtsey. "Unless you need something else?"

"No," I said, setting aside my tea myself. "I am ready."

Judging by the desire burning between my legs and the nervousness flitting in my stomach—

Lie.

47

ARRAN

The human realm was being infected by some sort of disquieting darkness, my betrothed was coming out of her skin with the need to avenge her brother, ready to stab anything that looked at her wrong, and I was so fucking repressed my cock felt like it was about to explode.

So, of course, the elementals threw a party.

Lugnasa was observed in the terrestrial kingdom as well. But nothing I'd ever experienced in my homeland was as opulent as the celebration unfolding around me in the goldstone palace. I shuddered to think what Mabon would be like, when Veyka and I were finally and irrevocably joined.

That would take place in the throne room, I assumed, in a similar configuration to the Offering. But for Lugnasa, the courtiers spilled out into the courtyards instead.

I wondered what I would see if I was in the streets of Baylaur tonight. Would the citizens of the elemental kingdom dance under that biting Annwyn sun without the promise of a magically cooled palace to retreat to? Perhaps this was a celebration only observed by those gifted with wind or ice powers.

Or perhaps the rest of the fae were smart enough to not risk the consequences of their magic on a hedonistic festival. I snorted into my aural. That wasn't likely in any kingdom of the fae.

A presence approaching my left side.

Gwen—no. She did not have that freedom anymore. She was leashed to Veyka, watching and guarding. It was a comfort, really. I could sleep in a real bed, knowing that Gwen was standing guard. But her place at my side—it was empty.

I certainly didn't have any fondness for the male that sidled into it just then.

"Your Highness," Parys said, dipping his chin and sending his dark curls swaying rakishly over his forehead.

"Go away." I'd been thinking about sinking myself between Veyka's thighs since we climbed back up from the bowels of the palace and I had to watch her hips sway up ten flights of stairs.

The last person I wanted to talk to was the one who had been fucking her last.

Even if I'd made a promise to myself not to kill him—for Veyka's sake. Whatever the hell that meant. Because, apparently, now I cared about her wellbeing.

Fucking Ancestors.

I took another gulp of aural.

"Do you know what to expect from the afternoon's festivities?" Parys said mildly, visibly unruffled.

Bastard.

"I can figure it out."

Parys smiled slyly.

He knew I was clueless.

My fingers caressed the head of my axe as I considered where would be the most painful place to bury it in his body.

Gwen had trained for this. She'd fought to become the terrestrial heir. She knew about the customs and traditions of the elemental court. Me? I was the solution to an unprecedented problem. I'd been trained for battle and bloodshed. I had no fucking idea what the ceremonies and nonsense would entail, and I didn't care, either.

All I cared about was getting my cock in Veyka as soon as possible.

If the subtle grinding I was already seeing in the bright sunlight around the aural fountains was any indication, Lugnasa in Baylaur was not that different from Wolf Bay.

"I'm certain you can, Brutal Prince," Parys said, taking a wise step away. "If not, I'm sure the queen would enjoy explaining to you."

I drew my axe, ready to swing. But by the time I turned, all that remained of Parys and his sly smile was a rush of wind. If he'd been born a terrestrial, his animal form would have been a fox, I was certain.

That wind swirled unnaturally, propelled by Parys' magic even as he disappeared into the crowd, urging my head in the other direction. To the other side of the courtyard.

Where the Queen of the Elemental Fae had emerged from the shadowed corridor to stand in the sunlight.

She looked good enough to eat. Male and beast alike, every part of me wanted to devour her.

I had no idea how the dress—if it could be called that—stayed on her body. Maybe through magic—though what sort I had no idea.

The deep teal was the color of the dark holly that I'd seen only in the wettest hollows of the Shadow Wood. Fitting, that she was dressed in the color of Annwyn's most fatal poison.

If I didn't get inside of her soon, I was going to die.

A single piece of fabric looped around her neck, either end coming down to cup her full breasts before twisting behind her once again. I couldn't tell if that long strip ended there or if it was somehow incorporated into her skirt. But I knew when she turned, her back would be bare—a sharp contrast to her legs. For once, the flowing panels of her skirts completely concealed her legs. I already missed the view.

Expanses of navel and back and tantalizing curves of the underside of her breasts were on full display—and not a hint of the shapely round ass and legs below her waist. She was actively trying to kill me now, I decided.

Diamonds sparkled at her throat, even brighter amorite at her ears. There was a faint bluish glint buried among the strands of her intricate braid. As she turned to speak with a royal councilor I vaguely recognized, I saw a gleam from her stomach as well. Her hair was usually the color of the moon. But today, in the scorching afternoon, it seemed to be the color of the sun's very center. White hot, like the burning in my loins.

Around her, all the beautiful females dressed in flowing white paled and faded away. Their supple, slender bodies were nothing to the bold, buxom siren before me. She was soft and rounded, her stomach full, breasts generous. But I'd felt the corded muscle beneath, both wrapped around me in passion and straining against me in the training courtyard.

Across the courtyard, over an aural fountain brimming with gold liquor and a hundred undulating bodies dancing to lazy music, Veyka's eyes found mine.

She was too far away to see my eyes burning with desire. But her mouth curved in that wicked smile, nonetheless.

Instead of putting me out of my misery, she turned to speak to her councilor, leaving me there to die.

48
VEYKA

"The priestess will begin soon," Esa was lecturing. "Your Majesty should ensure that you are at her side. She's given to vanity. You should not allow her to occupy the stage alone…"

I ignored her and sipped my aural.

Ambitious priestess? It sounded like a problem for *after* Mabon. As in—not my problem at all.

My main concern at the moment, given that I could not do anything on this particular night to advance my quest to avenge Arthur, was to make it to nightfall. Once the sun dipped below the horizon, I intended to drag Arran back to my bedchamber bodily and squeeze every ounce of pleasure I could from his magnificent body.

I was done dancing around him.

We both knew what we wanted.

As I'd told Cyara—there was no emotional entanglement between us. But physical need? Oh, Ancestors, yes.

If I didn't come around his cock soon, I was going to melt into a puddle, and then I'd be no use to anyone, living or dead.

"Your Majesty," Esa intoned, her voice sharper.

I didn't even look at her. "You are dismissed, Councilor."

Maybe she blinked in disbelief. Maybe she pulled a face. But either way, she left my side. Unfortunately, she was replaced almost instantly. At least this time, it was Roksana.

"Councilor Esa makes valid points, Majesty," Roksana said smoothly, calmly. A soothing coolness filled the air. I knew if I looked down, I'd see her fingers flexed, ice swirling around her palms.

"Esa needs to learn to enjoy a party," I said, swigging back more aural. Two cups would be sufficient to get me drunk enough to throw consequences to the wind and drag Arran back to my bed.

"Is that what you're doing now, Veyka? Enjoying yourself?" Roksana said carefully.

I slid my eyes to her. I wasn't bothered by her familiar use of my name; the female was eight hundred years old, for Ancestors' sake. But the implication in her voice... I could not quite read it.

I knew she couldn't see any lust burning in my eyes, but that didn't mean she couldn't read the signs emanating from my body. Somehow, I didn't think that Roksana was judging me for my attraction to Arran. Fucking was a daily pastime more popular than reading in the elemental court.

But I still couldn't read the fathoms in her dark eyes. She shifted her gaze away from me, toward the full courtyard. By sundown, every courtyard in the goldstone palace would be a mass of writhing bodies.

As she turned, a spark of silver caught my eye. Threaded among her dark black braids, there was indeed the evidence of aging so rare among our kind. It was sharply visible against the deep brown of her skin. How long had it been there—worse, what did it mean?

"You accepted my invitation for dinner," Roksana said.

"I did."

"I was surprised, after all of this time."

I kept myself from biting my lip, from revealing too much. "The arrival of the Brutal Prince has changed many things."

It was the best I could settle on.

Roksana's eyes traveled across the courtyard, snagging on Arran.

He stood in the opposite corner, drawing me in and then pushing me away like we were two magnets in constant rotation.

"Indeed it has," the matron said quietly.

But her eyes were not on Arran any longer, but another terrestrial.

Gwen—not at my side, or hovering, guarding the rear—but coming to stand before me, to address me formally. The same way that Gawayn had that day when he joined his brothers, to beseech me about the missing children.

A deep sense of foreboding sputtered to life in my belly, spreading steadily through my chest and into my limbs. I was vaguely aware of Arran, moving now, navigating the perimeter of the courtyard in my direction. Roksana was gone. I stood alone—as Gwen dropped to her knee before me.

This couldn't be good.

❦ 49 ❦
ARRAN

I realized what was happening as soon as Gwen fell to her knee.

Damn it all, she should have discussed it with me. She should have done it in private. She should have told Veyka what was coming.

"Your Majesty," Guinevere began. "I was not the first of my family to train for the Offering. For many thousands of years, our strongest have been put forward for the throne of Annwyn, only to fail."

To die brutally, my mind filled in as I skirted around curious onlookers.

My beast started to growl—not with desire, but menace. When had my presence here become so usual and expected that courtiers stopped jumping out of my way? I needed to remind them why I was called the Brutal Prince—but not now.

Now I had to get to Veyka before she said something damning.

"My father's table has stood in the halls of my ancestral home for seven thousand years, awaiting the worthy heir. Its stone is mined from the sacred ores of the Spine and blessed with the magic of the terrestrial kingdom. Flown into the Effren Valley by the strength of no less than fifty terrestrial wings."

As if summoned by her words, those fifty beating wings came into view, silhouetted against the blazing sun. But the round table blotted out the sun itself. Only for a moment—but a moment was all it took for the grandeur and importance of the moment to be cemented.

The courtyard cleared as the elemental courtiers realized what was happening. The airborne terrestrials were lowering the mighty stone table into the center of the courtyard.

The sound of the pale gray stone hitting the rich orange-red goldstone tiles jolted Veyka enough that her jaw popped closed. Her knuckles were white around her aural, her eyes pinned to Gwen, refusing to look at the table.

"It was to be offered to my betrothed," Gwen said steadily.

I waited for a quiver of her chin or a flash in her eyes. But she was cool and composed as ever as she lowered her head to Veyka. "As I have pledged myself to your service, I offer it to you now, Veyka Pendragon. Queen of the Elemental Fae and soon to be High Queen of Annwyn."

Gwen's chin may be still, but Veyka's was not. She understood the significance of this moment. From the glint in her blue eyes, the tick at one corner, I could guess that the legendary round table had made it into the lore of the elemental kingdom. For Gwen to gift it, to pass it out of her family line, meant she found Veyka worthy.

Veyka Pendragon might want many things. But I knew one for certain—she did not want to rule this kingdom. She did not think herself worthy of it. I wasn't sure I thought so either, for all that I admired her commitment to her brother's legacy and her luscious body.

But Gwen had made her decision, and now we would all have to live with it.

"I thank you, Lady Guinevere, for your generous gift," Veyka stammered.

Courtiers looked at her curiously. Her royal councilors, huddled off to one side, wore matching, carefully indifferent faces. Every one of them was calculating what this might mean in the machinations of power.

To the terrestrials lingering on the edges of the festival, it was a gesture of peace and reconciliation. A way for Gwen to show that she was fully committed to Annwyn, and that she'd moved on from the loss of the throne herself. It ought to have been a powerful moment, a symbol that could be wielded for obedience, like carrying the head of one's enemy on a spike into battle.

But Veyka was hardly managing. I stepped up to her side, ready to make a declaration on her behalf. It was eerie how similar court machinations were to battlefield ones.

I wasn't the only one who noticed.

The priestess, dressed in an ombre red gown, stepped forward and laid a hand upon the table. Gwen hissed through her teeth at the audacity. Veyka nearly spilled her aural, her wrist flicking dangerously. Maybe she was considering throwing it on the female.

But then the priestess' entire body jerked, her head snapping back, eyes skyward.

"A table of destiny," she cried in an otherworldly register. *"Five shall be with you at Mabon. One is not yet known, but the bravest of the five shall be his father. When he comes, you will know that the time for the Grail is near."*

I'd never seen so many fae robbed of words, all at once. Every eye was on the priestess, her body arched unnaturally. Silence beat on, long enough that gazes drifted, mouths opened to whisper and wonder.

But she wasn't done with her performance.

"The last is the Siege Perilous. It is death to all but the one for which it is made—the best of them all—the one who shall come at the moment of direst need."

Three beats of silence, then the priestess gasped in a breath, straightening, an air of normalcy returning to her countenance.

"My apologies, Your Majesty." She dropped into a pool of red silk, sinking to her knees. "The prophecy..."

Veyka's eyes looked like they were going to pop right out of her face. That aural was definitely about to be thrown on the priestess. I snatched the cup from her, lifting it in Gwen's direction and ignoring the priestess entirely.

"To the peaceful union of Annwyn! For all that has been and all that will ever be!" I didn't wait for the response before gulping back the aural.

A hundred goblets lifted in response, then drank. Gwen rose, returning to her post. The priestess was glaring, still kneeling on the floor, awaiting an acknowledgement that would not come.

I thanked the airborne fae who had delivered the round table, offering them aural and food. I considered asking them to transport it somewhere else, but the table was massive and they'd flown far already. The revelers gave the table a wide berth, clearly aware of its import. I'd have to remember to set some palace guards to watch over it once night fell. If enough aural was consumed, that reverence would give way to desire to be one of the few to fuck atop the legendary round table.

By the time I'd seen to all of it, Veyka was gone.

Not far.

I found her lurking in the corner of the next courtyard, watching the courtiers dancing in the sun. She already had another goblet of aural in her hand, half drained. That was how she was going to deal with the onslaught of pressure—the reminder that even after Arthur was avenged, she still had to rule this cursed place —by getting systematically drunk.

I decided to offer her another alternative.

"In Wolf Bay, we do not wait for the darkness," I whispered into her ear. She must have heard me coming or caught my scent. She didn't jump at all.

"The entire day is spent in fornication and lust." I dragged my finger down the exposed column of her spine. "So that when the sun rises anew, we are ready to be cleansed."

I reached the edge of her gown, nudged it aside, and settled my finger into the gap between the generous twin curves of her ass. Veyka breathed in sharply, her teeth sinking into her full bottom lip. I wondered briefly if anyone had ever touched her there.

As soon as the sun dipped below that damned horizon, I would.

"Would you like me to show you, Veyka?"

No response. But she didn't move away.

I shifted closer, bracing my hand on the pillar above her head so she was framed in by my body.

"I think you would," I said softly, rubbing the bulge in my trousers against her soft ass. "I think you want to fuck me right now, in front of everyone. I think you want to throw every tradition to the wind, every arcane vestige of this kingdom, and damn it all to hell."

I leaned in, brushing my lips against the curve of her neck, breathing her in. A low, dark chuckle rumbled up in my chest. "Oh, yes. I can smell how much you want it. But we must observe the traditions, at least until darkness falls."

Veyka ground her hips backward against mine—revenge, and a challenge.

How many ways could we touch each other, without giving in or being noticed? I tugged on the end of her braid, hard enough that her head tilted to the side, exposing her neck. I dragged my canines along the smooth column, careful not to break the skin.

Veyka's answer was to catch my hand in hers. She skated my fingertips over the curve of her breasts. She let me feel the heat of her stomach, soft and exposed and waiting for me to worship. Then she lifted those fingertips to her lips and kissed them. With the pads pressed to her lips, she darted out her tongue, where no one else could see. Then her teeth. Just a little nip. A promise, and a reminder, that two could play this game.

My eyes went skyward. The sun still had a painfully long way to go.

By nightfall, I wasn't certain that either of us would still be standing.

50
VEYKA

I hadn't breathed normally in hours. Every breath was a desperate pant for air, to get what I needed into my lungs before Arran's next assault. His clever, cruel fingers took me apart piece by piece. The aural loosened my reserve.

Every time I thought of that blasted round table, I arched into Arran's touch. When the darkness threatened, I let myself sink into him instead. Dark, yes, but pleasurable. So pleasurable, I was a breath away from coming just from his hot hands on my skin.

I was on my third goblet of aural. Or was it my fourth?

It didn't matter. I couldn't think, which was the entire point. The only thing anchoring me to reality, keeping me from becoming a drunken puddle on the goldstone tiles, was Arran's never-ending touch on my body.

Then the sun dipped below the horizon.

The priestess tried to say something, but it was lost to the wet sounds of kissing and moans of pleasure. Arran and I weren't the only ones who'd been teasing and touching all day. My entire court was a second from combusting.

And as the furor of lust took over the goldstone palace, I gave myself over to it willingly.

I reached for Arran's hand, ready to drag him back to my bedroom.

But he grabbed me first, slamming my hands onto the wall of the pillar. I ricocheted back against him, his hard body caging me in against the wall. Warm goldstone tickled the tips of my breasts while Arran's hard, hot body ground against my back. I was nothing more than a blazing inferno, a candle lit at both ends and ready to melt.

Arran didn't give me time to catch up. His hand was on my pussy, shoving my skirts aside roughly as he slid a finger inside of me, then another. And then... oh, Ancestors... a third. I was powerless to stop the deep moan ripping from my throat.

"You like that, do you," he said into my ear, tearing at the lobe with his sharp teeth. "Let your entire court hear how I make you moan."

He fucked me with his fingers, too fucking slow but so wonderfully deep. I bit hard on my lip, trying to hold it in, not wanting to give in to him. Defiant to the last. But I was so full of him, so impossibly full. Then he curved his fingers inside of me, scraping his fingertips over that soft spot inside of me only I'd ever been able to find.

I threw back my head, howling my pleasure to the wind. Arran caught it, his fingers curling tight around my throat. "Oh yes, my Queen, let me serve you."

My orgasm was so close. Ancestors, it was all happening so fast. So fast, I couldn't stop myself as my hips began to ride him, demanding release. My roars of passion soared through the air, but I didn't care if there was one person watching us or a thousand. Not as that pressure released, as a flood of liquid spilled out of me, covering my thighs and splashing into a puddle on the floor.

Shock rolled through me—I'd realized such a thing was possible, but I'd never done it before. I grabbed Arran's forearm to keep myself upright, legs shaking treacherously beneath me. I tried to maneuver myself around to see his face, but I was met instead with a searing kiss.

His tongue swirled around mine, demanding and fast. Then his tongue was gone, replaced by his fingers as he forced them into my mouth, forcing me to suck my own juices from his fingers, turned wrinkled with the force of my orgasm.

I gave up entirely then. I was going to let Arran take me wherever he wanted to go, whatever he wanted to do.

So my squeak was of surprise, but not of resistance, when he pushed me back up against the pillar. For once, he didn't go for my breasts, intent this time on torturing my pussy instead. The force of his body held me against the wall while one hand probed at my dripping opening. I felt the other behind me, then the length of his cock pressed against my gown.

A rip, and there was nothing but his hot, velvety skin against mine.

But instead of sliding into my pussy, he pulled back that hand dripping with my juices and rubbed it over the tight puckered opening of my ass. He massaged my juices around and around, even as his other hand began to mirror the motion on my clit.

He wasn't tentative, but he was waiting. He was giving me an opening.

I didn't need it and I didn't fucking want it. I wanted him inside of me, any way he wanted.

I told him as much with a demanding thrust of my hips.

I was rewarded by the low rumble of his chuckle and the brush of his lips on my shoulder before he eased his thumb into that forbidden cavern. It wasn't entirely a new sensation for me, but everything with Arran was different. It was *more*.

One finger continued those punishing circles on my clit as the other explored gently. Then he eased his hand away and replaced it with his cock.

Inch by glorious inch, he eased into me. His hand dipped back to my pussy, then to my mouth, then his mouth, finding the lubrication he needed to go in, in, in. Until I felt the warm press of his balls against my ass, his cock fully seated inside of me.

"Veyka," he groaned.

I glanced over my shoulder, and seeing the look of pure ecstasy on his face almost had me coming right there.

"Fuck me."

He did. He slid that perfect, huge cock out and then back in, filling me again and again. It was tight and tense, and every now and then there was a tiny twinge of pain that just sent me arching harder against him. His fingers on my clit were relentless. I screamed my orgasm—once, twice, I completely lost track.

My entire world contracted to the feel of Arran's body inside of mine. I felt the shift, the moment he lost control and pounded into me. Three strokes of that punishing pace, sharp edges lancing through my body, and he was spurting inside of me, cum leaking down my back, coating my thighs. It was enough to send me crashing over the precipice again, both of us screaming until we were nothing more than a tangled mass, held up only by the planes of our bodies pressed together and that blessed wall.

51

VEYKA

I had no memory of making it to my bed. My first thought was to reach across the soft expanse, expecting a hard male body —nothing.

My second was drowned out by the pounding in my head.

Ancestors.

I'd never drunk so much aural in my life. I knew better than this.

It's fine. I'll stay in bed until the pounding stops.

I rolled over, dimly aware of my tangled garments hanging off of me in shreds.

Oh, no.

No. No. No. No. No.

Moving was a terrible idea.

I hurled myself out of the bed, pure instinct driving me in the direction of the washroom.

Somewhere around the fourth or fifth heave, gentle hands pulled back my hair.

I tried to lie down right there on the cool tiled floor. But those same hands guided me to lean against the wall instead. Another pair laid a cool, damp cloth over my eyes.

"I'm dying," I moaned, certain of the fact.

"Isn't that what you've longed for these many months?" Cyara's dry voice cut through the fog wrapped around my brain.

She wasn't wrong. Not entirely.

Revenge and oblivion. Those were the only things I'd wanted after Arthur's death.

And now?

Ancestors, I couldn't think. I could hardly swallow.

Anticipating as much, Carly arrived with a cup of cool water. I gulped at it greedily.

"Slowly, Your Majesty, or you'll see it all again in a few minutes," she warned.

I let her offer the cup again and again, taking tiny sips, waiting for my stomach to revolt. I kept my eyes closed beneath the cool cloth, and thankfully, none of them tried to speak with me. The pounding between my temples couldn't stand it.

But that left me alone with my thoughts, which were decidedly worse.

The humans, the rifts, that creeping darkness. The throne of Annwyn, waiting empty, taunting me. Arran.

Arran.

I'd let him save me—again.

Stupid, stupid, stupid.

I was letting him closer. Each secret, each shared glance... each time I let him bury that magnificent cock inside me. Eventually, I'd let him too close, and it would all fall apart.

I could not let it happen.

Revenge for Arthur's death. Then get far away from Baylaur, as quickly as possible. Maybe that was the reason the rifts kept coming up. Not because they'd played a significant part in Arthur's murder, but because the Ancestors were trying to send me a message. The rifts could take me out of Annwyn altogether—to the human realm. Where everyone was as powerless as me.

But I wasn't going anywhere today.

Hell, I might die on this very floor and save myself from the decisions.
But, of course, I was not that lucky.

"They've sent up a lunch tray, Your Majesty," Charis said tentatively from the direction of the door.

"No."

"Yes." Cyara commanded as I moaned.

I cracked my eyes open enough to glare at her.

She was half my weight, a fraction of my height, and stood across the washroom with an imperious stare that dared me to countermand her again.

"You need some food to soak up all that aural," she said, wings flaring.

I didn't have the energy to argue. Maybe if I ate, she'd let me go back to sleep. Though my bed seemed impossibly far away and the washroom tiles were still entirely too inviting.

"No, you don't," Cyara muttered, grabbing my arm before I could tumble sideways.

I shook her off and clambered to my feet unsteadily, all of my warrior's grace utterly deserting me. My stomach roiled threateningly, but there was nothing left to heave up.

Still glaring, I slowly found my way back into the bedroom. I perched on the edge of the bed and let Charis feed me toast while Carly brushed my hair and re-braided it into a simple three-strand plait. I stood long enough to shrug off my dress, sticky with aural and the remnants of Arran and I's minutes spent pressed against the wall. By the time they'd draped me in a fresh silk nightgown, my eyelids were drooping once again.

I was more than ready to give in, to silence the pounding that had softened marginally to a dull but persistent thud.

Thud.

Thud.

Thud, thud.

Except it wasn't inside my head. Or at least, not only inside my head.

I stared at the enormous table in utter disbelief.

I must still be asleep. I'd never woken from my aural-induced stupor at all. That was the only way to account for the ridiculousness of the scene unfolding before me. It had to be a dream—or a nightmare.

"What the hell am I supposed to do with it?" I said stupidly.

The Ancestors-damned thing took up my entire antechamber. Someone had removed the table that had been there before, an ordinary rectangular thing that had sat innocuously off to one side.

But there was nothing ordinary about the table Gwen had gifted me. And it certainly couldn't be set to the side. It had taken four full-bodied fae guards to deliver the damn thing. Shreds of the priestess' prophecy floated betwixt my pounding temples.

Thud.

Table of destiny.

Thud.

Siege Perilous.

Thud.

Moment of direst need.

It's just a table, I told myself stubbornly. The priestess is a power-hungry elemental, like all the rest of them, just like Esa had said and Roksana had implied. It meant nothing.

The guards who'd delivered the table retreated, leaving behind Lyrena inside the door, on guard duty, and Parys standing at her side, grinning like he hadn't drunk as much aural as me the night before.

"Planning to host some grand dinner parties, are you?" Parys said, walking the perimeter of the table.

"Not likely," I bit back, raising my index fingers to my temples.

"I thought the penchant for ostentatious dramatics was endemic only to the elementals." Parys ran a finger over the gold scrollwork cut into the surface of the table at intervals, counting aloud. "Eight seats. But the prophecy only speaks of seven."

My hands froze on either side of my face. "I don't want to hear a word about prophecies, or dire needs, or brave fathers," I said sharply, turning away and walking to the window. But even as I tried to focus on the scene outside, the sharp red angles of the Effren Valley, I could feel the round table behind me like a presence all its own. "It is just a stupid table."

"Don't let Gwen hear you say that," Lyrena said. I could hear the mischievous smile on her lips.

"I'm not afraid of Gwen."

If Parys and Lyrena exchanged a look, I didn't see it.

Feather-light feet came from the bedroom.

A pause. The soft thud of a tray being set down.

"A lovely gift befitting of a queen," Cyara said softly.

A long scrape across the tiled floor.

When I turned around, I saw my half-eaten breakfast tray obscuring one of the gold engravings. Parys had dragged up a chair and was resting his feet on the edge of the round table, chewing on a chocolate croissant my traitorous stomach wouldn't allow me to even nibble at. Only Lyrena kept her distance, standing at the door to the corridor. I wondered if Gwen was on the other side.

A shiver ripped through my spine, turning my stomach and setting off a series of explosive, painful fireworks in my head.

"No!" I cried.

All three of them jumped.

Comical flakes of pastry rained over the round table. Except that it wasn't comical at all. It was sacrilege. Which was insane because it was *just a table*.

But before I could stop myself, my feet stomped over and my hand was scraping the crumbs off the table and into my hand, my elbow shoving Parys' feet off.

"No one sits at the table," I said, dumping the crumbs onto the tray. I picked that up too, shoving it into Cyara's surprised hands. "We don't use it for storage either."

They all blinked, stunned into silence—probably by the fact that I cared at all.

They could chalk it up to my hangover. I didn't care. I just wanted to go back to sleep. So, I left them to exchange looks and whispers and aimed for the refuge of sheets and pillows.

52

ARRAN

The sun was tracking downward, casting the sky in golds and pinks. The elemental kingdom was different than any place in the terrestrial, or any of the others I'd visited in those hundreds of years of battle and bloodshed. It had its own beauty, I could admit.

Though none of it compared to the female hiding in the shadows at the edge of my balcony.

I was exercising my magic.

While the elemental fae controlled fire, ice, wind, water, and weather, to varying degrees, the terrestrials fell into just two camps: fauna or flora-gifted. Fauna—the power to shift or to control animals. Meanwhile, the flora-gifted among us could bend the trees and grass to our will, or coax deadly plants to grow. When a terrestrial child was born, families waited on tenterhooks to see where their affinity would lie. Flora or fauna. Never both.

Until me.

If I'd been born a female, I would have been the heir presumptive for the Offering. But with a male elemental heir foretold early in Uther and Igraine's reign—Arthur—my gifts had been put to other uses. Killing, mainly.

But despite all of that, here I was. Offered to Veyka, reluctant Princess of Peace and reigning Queen of Secrets.

The beast inside of me made his needs known, demanding to shift. But the other side of my magic, for all that it was steady and quiet, was no less deadly. It had saved us from the skoupuma. My vines had held enemies in place while I tortured them, as good as any shackles. The roots I summoned from the ground had ripped armies limb from limb.

Tonight, the victims were all inanimate.

Pink-studded fuchsias swung from hanging planters on either side of my veranda. With a flick of my fingers, the delicate blooms tripled in size, the vines thickening and multiplying until they formed twin columns that stretched to the floor.

The spiky cacti in planters—everything was in planters in this damn palace. I focused on the spikes, channeling my power until each spike was the size of a rapier, longer than my arm and wickedly sharp.

It started systematically. I'd had two dozen various plants brought into my chambers. I started with those that seemed the most threatening—the cacti and carnivorous flowers. But as my magic surged, building within me, my movements became erratic, motivated by instinct and desire. Innocuous flowers turned deadly, big enough to swallow a male and squeeze the life from his body. What were once beautiful, potted rose bushes turned into spiky instruments of death.

But there was no one to strangle the life out of, to kill and maim. My brutal gift strained at the edges, wanting to burst from the veranda and through the doors to find a victim. This power inside of me wanted one thing, always—to kill.

What would the cost of this magic be? I already knew.

Others paid for the magic with aches and pains, with deep sleep lasting days, or the loss of something valuable—an object or wager. I knew the cost of this magical 'gift' that lived inside of me, had paid it a thousand times over.

My soul.

The slithering of a vine caught my eye. Of course, I'd had half an eye on her for the last hour, as she crouched in the darkness, watching.

As her slippered feet hit the floor soundlessly, I turned to face her. My breath was coming in heavy pants from the exertion. I didn't bother trying to hide any of the emotions playing across my face as I met her clever blue eyes. She knew I'd been watching her, I could read that easily as her lips curved into that wicked smile that spoke right to my darkest desires.

She wore the palest color I'd ever seen her in, a light orangey gold that reminded me of the goldstone palace itself, though a bit more muted. For once, her garments clung to her body rather than draping over them. No long, loose trails of fabric. Just that close-fitting pale gold, right down to her matched slippers.

Not ideal for climbing or trekking through the mountains, but perfect for silence. Which meant whatever she was up to this evening, it would take place within the walls of the goldstone palace.

Veyka tipped her head toward the pillar of fuchsia nearest her. "Impressive."

I rotated my wrists, working out the tension. "You should see what I can do when the plants are actually rooted in the ground, rather than stunted in clay pots."

She tested the sharpness of the edge of one of the cactus spikes. "Such an exhibitionist."

"Not everyone keeps their powers as close as you," I said, letting my feet take me closer to her.

Those blue eyes flashed. "Queen of Secrets, remember?"

Of course, I did. But she hadn't liked the moniker when she first heard it, and I doubt she did now. "Are you ever going to tell me? Or will I wake one morning to find myself being drowned by a punch of water down my throat?"

Devastation darkened her face. But she turned away quickly, trying to hide it.

Wha—why?

Was that why she didn't use her powers? Had she unintentionally harmed someone, and now she was afraid of her magic? For a female who enjoyed stabbing so much, it seemed unlikely. But perhaps it had been someone she cared for. The Ancestors knew, I'd hurt plenty of innocent bystanders before I'd gained full control of my beast.

If that was it... well, I couldn't broach that. She'd spit in my face —literally.

We might be willing to fuck one another, but that didn't give me any sort of claim to her emotions. She'd allowed me to help with her quest for revenge, but even that had been begrudging.

Did I still hate her?

Part of me did.

She might have revenge in her mind, but she'd made one reckless, stupid decision after another. I still hated that she thought her life was worth nothing, that she thought she didn't need to concern herself with running her own damn kingdom.

But hating her didn't stop me from seeing the vulnerability and pain. And it certainly didn't stop me from wanting to shove my cock into every cleft and crevice of that magnificent body.

But neither hate, nor lust, nor whatever else I felt for Veyka gave me the words I needed just then. I was a male of battle and bloodshed. Comfort was as foreign to me as the human realm.

When Veyka turned back, shoulders squared and eyes set in dark determination, I realized that wasn't what she needed from me, anyway.

"I decided I'd spare you the failure of trying to tail me without getting caught," she said, lifting her chin in challenge.

I caught her jaw in my hand, dragging her across the two feet that separated us, and claimed her mouth. I slammed my tongue into her, past the surprised lips, deep into the recesses of her throat. I took and took and took, demanding that she give herself to me. I couldn't comfort, but I could distract. I could spin her up into challenge and fire and vitriol. Veyka met every thrash of my tongue, grazing her teeth along the insides of mine.

When I set her back down, ripping my mouth back and gnashing my teeth, canines begging to tear into her skin and taste her blood, we were both panting.

"Lead on, Princess."

I realized very quickly the real reason she'd come to lurk on my veranda and invite me along.

Veyka needed my help.

More specifically, she needed my powers.

If she'd had any doubts in her mind, watching me turn my quarters into a veritable jungle had surely dispelled them.

She led me over the edge of the veranda, down to the one below. Then horizontally across three more of diminishing sizes. I didn't know who they belonged to, but by the confident way she moved, I guessed that Veyka did. It was suppertime; many of the courtiers joined the communal hall in the throne room, though I never had and I knew Veyka didn't either. But she must know who could be counted on to desert their rooms.

At the edge of the third balcony, she turned to me and pointed.

"We need to get up there," she said simply.

There was another veranda, larger than any of the ones we'd scaled, including my own. It looked to be almost as large as hers, which likely meant it belonged to someone important. Someone whose quarters we were about to enter.

But unlike so many of the balconies, which were close to others or had decorative carved goldstone that could be used for climbing, this one jutted out sharply before giving way to a sheer drop. I glanced down, noting the distance. If we fell, neither beast nor fae form would save us. Fae bodies could heal almost any wound, save decapitation, but without the assistance of a healer, we would almost certainly die from the fall.

However, our salvation was apparent.

"Ancestors be damned," I cursed under my breath.

The balcony was crowned in a mass of sweeping ivy.

Whoever occupied those quarters must have water magic, given how bright green and lush the ivy was. Several long vines already curled around the balustrade before hanging down off the sheer edge, swaying romantically in the wind.

But lush and vibrant as they might be, those vines wouldn't hold Veyka's considerable weight, and they certainly would snap the instant I challenged them to mine.

Veyka lifted one pale white eyebrow. "Up to the challenge?"

"You are a menace."

She dropped the hand that had pointed to the center of her chest. Her eyes gleamed wickedly as she traced the outline of her breasts, down over her stomach, to the apex where her legs joined. "If you do this for me, I'll let you have a taste."

Sexual favors in exchange for my magic.

I wished it was the worst bargain I'd ever struck.

My eyes must have given my answer—burning with desire—because Veyka drifted back a step to give me better access.

Summoning my magic was like breathing. I could not remember a time before it had been a part of me. Even before I knew how to wield it effectively, I'd felt its hum. My earliest memory was sinking my hands into the soil of my mother's rose garden and watching the bushes burst into bloom, in the dead of winter. I was four years old.

I lifted one hand, extending my middle and index fingers. I traced a spiral in the air, slowly, watching and waiting. Far above our heads, the vines of ivy began to move. At first, it looked like nothing more than a strong wind, swirling around them. But then the vines thickened, multiplied, stretched.

In less than a minute, they'd reached my hand, curling around my extended fingers, then my wrist and my arm, down to my shoulders so they held me fully. I heard Veyka suck in a breath—whether she was surprised or impressed, I didn't know. But when I turned back to her and offered my hand, her eyes were bright.

Not quite glowing.

But the nearest thing I'd seen.

Oh, yes. My Queen liked power. That was why she trained so hard in the sparring ring, and why she was always so damned wet for me. It was why she didn't turn away from my beast when he growled his need for her. I took a deep inhale, scenting the tang of her arousal.

Veyka sunk her teeth hard into her lower lip, enough to add the scent of her blood to the thick air around us.

She placed her hand in mine, let me pull her tight against me, and we were off.

I'd often wondered what it would have been like to be gifted with wings instead of fangs. This was as close as I'd ever come, soaring over the edge of the Effren Valley from one balcony to another on the strength of the vines I'd fortified with my own magic. I willed them to shorten, to contract so that we travelled up, up, up. Veyka clinging to my side was another element of delicious torture.

She resolutely kept her face turned out instead of burying it in my chest, unwilling to show even a modicum of fear.

But when our feet touched the balustrade, she slithered free of my grip too soon. Not from the desire to be away from me. But to stand on solid ground.

She crept over the edge, planting her slippered feet firmly on the goldstone floor of the balcony. I did the same, taking more care with my booted feet, sending the tendrils of ivy that had transported us spiraling away silently.

The entrance from the veranda to the apartments was framed with a wide, colorfully painted arch, a gemstone the size of my fist embedded in the goldstone at its apex. There were a few feet on either side between the edge of the arch and the balustrade. That was where Veyka went, pressing her back flat against the goldstone wall.

I followed, attempted to do the same, and found the space severely lacking.

Veyka made no sound, but I could feel the tension in her body as my hands closed around her shoulders, urging her to stand perpendicular to the wall so I could slip in behind her. Even this way, we were packed together to avoid being seen.

Curtains billowed across the open arch, partitioning the balcony from the rooms beyond. But they were white and transparent and would provide no cover for two large, muscular forms such as ours.

Between those strips of translucent white, a conversation floated on the wind. I tensed, channeling my magic to summon those vines once again and spirit us away. But Veyka leaned fractionally closer, angling her head so her delicately pointed ear, studded with sparkling amorite, was able to hear more easily.

We were not sneaking in, I realized. The room was already occupied. The way that Veyka settled herself against the wall, letting it take some of her weight, told me that she'd expected as much.

It took me a while to recognize the two voices.

"Health to the queen." Male.

"To the royal councilors who run our fair kingdom." Female. Followed by the clinking of glasses.

Esa. The one who'd been so clearly flustered by my presence at the council meeting. She'd been holding court over the petitioners herself for months, until Veyka and I took the dais. Not just a royal councilor, but *donna*, its leader.

"You should be more careful. The Queen of Secrets has ears everywhere," the male voice said.

The pulse just below Veyka's temple began to tick.

She really hated that name.

Several seconds of silence, the splash of more wine, then Esa spoke again: "She's too easily swayed. We need to get her back. The more time she spends with the Brutal Prince—"

"Who will be our king in a few weeks' time." A slight shift in the temperature. I glanced to where the sun ought to be dipping near the horizon. But it was obscured now in clouds—clouds that had come in unnaturally fast.

The male had storm magic, and powerful at that.

"What of it?" Esa drawled.

"He's made it clear he intends to rule."

I imagined the male counterpart shrugging. I couldn't recall his name, though I saw his face in my mind clearly enough. He was hulking, powerfully built, the sides of his head shaved and a long, dark braid that draped straight down his back.

The female sniffed haughtily. "He's done nothing of the sort. He wants power? I can give him the illusion of that. He's a battlefield commander, not a king. Let's give him a battlefield to go command."

A soft rumble of thunder in the distance. "You mean to start a war."

"If necessary."

Ancestors, Esa sounded almost bored. As if she wasn't suggesting treason, ripping apart Annwyn's fragile peace. I wished I could see Veyka's face, to judge whether any of this bothered her at all, or if she was merely waiting for Arthur to come up in the conversation.

Several beats of silence passed. More wine being poured.

It was Esa who broke it, her voice carefully measured. "Many a high king or queen of Annwyn has left their Royal Council in charge while they ride at the head of their armies."

The male was silent. So far, other than entertaining this conversation, he'd done nothing to explicitly incriminate himself. Crafty, just like his elemental brethren had surely trained him to be.

I, however, was ready to draw the dagger tucked in my boot and start slashing throats.

I must have shifted without realizing it because Veyka's fingers closed around my wrist. A silent command to hold my tongue and my place.

"You still might not get what you want," the male finally said.

Teo.

The name flashed from the recesses of my mind.

"Do we leverage the Dowager?" Esa asked.

Veyka nearly crushed my wrist.

A long silence.

"Not yet."

I knew the relationship between mother and daughter was bad. Every person in the elemental court did. But the anger, the unmitigated strength in that grasp of my hand, told me more than words had thus far. Veyka hated her mother as vehemently as she was set upon avenging her brother.

Another piece of the mystery of Veyka slid into place.

"So you will not take any action until the Joining is completed," Teo was saying, the voices suddenly seeming much more distant, even though the councilors hadn't moved.

"Let her pour the wine. She hasn't the intellect nor the interest to do anything more."

Veyka's hand released mine. She tilted her head just enough that I could see her profile—and the wicked smile that climbed her face.

Understanding crashed down onto me as the first raindrops began to fall.

There it was—after all this time—the plan. Her plan. The thing she'd held so close to her chest. She'd become a cupbearer for the Royal Council so she could listen in, study them, deduce who was to blame. She'd given up control of her kingdom so she could not only avenge her brother, but find the traitor in their midst, who was a danger still.

She was everything I'd suspected.

And more. So much fucking more.

I wondered if she'd acknowledged it to herself, if she even realized it. That this was not just a quest to avenge Arthur, but to protect Annwyn after all. The kingdoms of the fae would not be safe until she discovered who was responsible.

My hands landed on her waist, tightening.

Veyka twisted in my arms, lifting her eyes to meet mine. I didn't hear the rest of the conversation, though I noted the glasses being set down and footsteps and a door. But my eyes were on Veyka, on those clear blue eyes of hers that at times seemed so impossibly young, but right at that moment were ageless and deep. Understanding flickered in the inches between us, so intense she tore her eyes away from the force of it.

The voices disappeared. We were alone, pressed together from shoulder to hip.

I leaned down, my lips brushing against the pointed shell of her ear. "Why didn't you tell me?"

I heard her loud swallow. "You hated me."

I grazed my canines along her hairline. "What makes you think I don't, still?"

She shifted her hips so that the rounded cheeks of her bottom caressed my cock, hard and needy through my tight-fitting trousers. Her implication was clear enough, though we both knew that hate and fucking had plenty to say to one another.

"You're not my enemy," she said softly. "I don't know what you are."

Truth between us. Finally.

Veyka jerked her ear out of reach, even as she ground her hips back against me.

"Incorrigible tease," I huffed, summoning the vines of ivy once more.

Our feet touched down on the smaller balcony, still one level down and three over from my own. I paused for half a breath, to listen and check that the connected rooms were still unoccupied. The rain was increasing steadily, masking sounds. But we were alone, for now at least.

What I wanted wouldn't take long.

I shoved Veyka up against the wall, fell to my knees, and feasted.

53
VEYKA

As Arran slid into place beside me, I remembered the way he'd slid his tongue over my navel.

As he flashed me a smile that was equal parts menace and lust, I remembered the nip of his canines on the lips of my pussy.

How I was going to survive this dinner with Roksana without throwing him down on the table was a question I'd been asking myself ever since I'd asked him to come along.

There didn't seem to be much use in keeping him out of the machinations anymore. He'd seen and heard it all. Maybe he would notice some thread that I had missed. He was also a convenient distraction. If I felt Roksana getting too close, pushing too hard, I knew just which words would send my Brutal Prince into a fit of temper.

If he knew the same about me... well, I wasn't going to think too hard about that. Not just then.

Roksana's apartments were located in the older part of the goldstone palace, built more than seven thousand years ago before the Great War. The suites were huge, ten or more rooms each with sweeping balconies that faced outward over the Effren Valley.

Arthur had offered me one of these suites when I first emerged from the water gardens. As a demure servant admitted us, I could almost hear Arthur's offer in my ear. *Choose whichever one you like. Nothing is too grand for the Princess of Peace.* I'd argued back that it was idiotic for a newly crowned king to kick one of his highest-ranking courtiers out of their apartments. Though, I knew he'd have been happy to do it.

However, making enemies had not been on my list of ways to spend my newfound freedom. I selected my smaller but still lovely suite, on the opposite side of the palace. What would I have done with ten rooms, anyway? Besides, my apartments had the added benefit of being on the complete other side of the palace from my mother.

Though even from my bed, I'd still imagined I heard her pounding on the door Arthur had sealed, trapping her in her wing. For months, the nightmare had haunted me. Until Arthur died and a worse one came along to replace it.

The servant led us through an antechamber lined with portraits of various elemental kings and queens. Some I recognized, others had faded from my memory in favor of fighting maneuvers. The next boasted an exquisite stained-glass window depicting the elemental powers—water, ice, wind, fire, and weather.

I was torn between the impulse to roll my eyes at the grandeur and just staring outright at the beauty. I'd seen so little of the palace, I realized uncomfortably—given that I was its queen.

I glanced to Arran, silent and scowling at my side. He wore as many weapons as I imagined he did into battle. Not that I was much better, my knives in their scabbards a comforting weight on my hips. But at least I was decked out in jewels and silk. Arran looked more likely to kill our host than talk to her.

"You could smile," I said quietly.

"I said I would accompany you. I didn't say I'd play nice."

"Well, one of us has to."

"Go ahead, Princess. I'd pay good gold to see it." He flashed his canines and my traitorous knees went weak.

Which, of course, meant that was the moment we rounded a

corner and Roksana appeared. She stood in the middle of a richly adorned living room. The furniture was old but well maintained, clustered in little groups around tables to encourage conversation, the favorite currency of the elemental court. A tall wingback chair upholstered in gold velvet caught my eye. A lovely, luxurious thing I wanted to drop myself into with a goblet of wine.

It was very carefully set in a corner, as if it was just another piece of furniture. While Esa would have had it front and center, would have stood before it to imply her own power, Roksana was a thousand times subtler. She was grand and important. This trot through her suite was meant to convey that clearly. But as she lowered her head, she sent the other message as well—she was loyal.

"Your Majesty." Roksana dropped into a curtsey, graceful despite her eight hundred years. "I did not anticipate the honor of your presence as well, Your Highness."

Arran offered no excuse. Because why would he? He was the Brutal Prince, the Terrestrial Heir. Roksana was an ancient and wise member of my Royal Council, but she was still a rival. The smile she offered, the respectful inclination of her head—she knew it as well as he.

Fuck, I was already so, so over this whole endeavor.

I shrugged irreverently, pretending to ignore Arran. When in reality, every movement of his body spoke directly to mine.

"I suppose I shall have to get used to having him at my side," I said casually, looking past Roksana's shoulder to where a grand table awaited, already set for dinner and filled with covered dishes of food.

"Please, let us eat. I've invited you for dinner, not scheming," Roksana said, motioning us through.

I did roll my eyes then.

Arran's beast growled a warning. *Guard your face.*

Behave, or I'll put you on a leash, my eyes shot back.

Roksana had a surprise of her own—Elora waited just beyond the table, hovering near the window holding a frost-chilled glass. I wondered if it was an intentional use of magic, to chill the wine, or an extension of Elora's passionate nature.

I'd never seen an elemental with as little control of her emotions as Elora. I found it endearing, honestly. As much as I could, for someone who sat on my Royal Council and was a suspect in my brother's murder.

I knew I ought to hate her. I did hate the others—Esa, Teo, Noros.

But Roksana and Elora... I wanted to trust them, even if I knew better.

I hoped this dinner would give me some direction, something more than a guess. The skepticism etched unapologetically on Arran's face told me exactly what *he* thought.

"Good evening, Elora," I said to her dark braids as she bowed.

Like Arran, she was a soldier, the commander of the small army kept by the elemental kingdom. But that was where the similarities ended.

I sat, then Arran, followed by Roksana, and finally Elora.

Propriety *be damned*. I was a half breath from issuing a royal decree banning all the ceremonial bullshit when the servant who'd shown us in stepped forward and started revealing the dishes beneath the silver covers.

Long, delicate noodles in creamy sauce, sprinkled with spring peas and thin, crispy slices of meat. Pomegranate and plum, swirled with buttery cheese and drizzled in honey beside toasty slices of baguette. Layered squash in an aromatic red sauce whose sharp acidity cut through the air.

My stomach gave a very un-queenlike growl of appreciation.

"I sent down to the kitchens and asked that they prepare all of your favorites," Roksana said with a gracious smile.

It was meant to make me feel at home, I realized. She'd been asking me to join her for months, and when I did, she made sure the table was filled with comfort.

A genuine offer of kindness, or a ploy to disarm me. Maybe some strange combination of both.

My stomach didn't really care either way. I inclined my head to Roksana, all the thanks required of a queen to her subordinate, and dug in.

We'd barely taken our first bites when Roksana turned to Arran, pouring his wine herself. "It was a welcome change to have you join us for our council meeting, Your Highness."

He accepted the goblet, sipping it before answering. Making her wait for his response. For a terrestrial, he was not half bad at this game. "I wish to learn about the running of my new home."

"Indeed. Is it much different than the terrestrial kingdom, then?" Roksana asked amid a delicate bite.

Arran's brow tightened, just for a moment. But it was smooth again as he admitted, "I was a battle commander. Not a politician."

Elora perked up instantly, seeing her opening. "Do the terrestrial forces—"

"Perhaps you can teach Elora a thing or two," Roksana said with a razor-sharp smile to her daughter.

I'd sensed the undercurrent between mother and daughter before. Not the unequivocal hate the Dowager and I shared, but certainly not a loving or close relationship, either.

"Perhaps they can start in the sparring ring," I said with a grin, around a bite so glorious my stomach almost cheered. "I'd enjoy wagering on that."

Arran's eyes glittered—not that dark fire he reserved for me, but the promise of a challenge. "Anytime you like, Councilor Elora."

Roksana drummed her fingertips on the tabletop. The conversation was straying, and she wasn't pleased. Interesting.

What *did* she want to talk about?

"I am sure you are busy with preparations for the Joining," Roksana said. "Do you intend to take back command of the council soon, or wait until after Mabon?"

A bold question.

My face must have shown what I thought of it, because Roksana's face transformed into a conspiratorial smile.

"I only wonder how much energy I should spend holding Esa in check in the interim, you see. She is very..."

"We know quite well what she is," Arran said sharply.

We.

I swallowed hard, forcing the surge in my chest to quiet so I could speak. "Politics. A great way to spoil a delicious meal."

A chill crept into the room. I knew if I glanced toward Elora, I'd see her fingers wreathed in frost. What that meant, though, I didn't know.

"You promised me once that should I accept your invitation, you would not push me to speak of anything that would make me uncomfortable," I said quietly, staring at my plate.

Arran shifted in his seat beside me. I didn't need to glance over to know he was moving to get better access to his weapons. One word, and he'd strike down anyone who threatened to touch me, to cause me harm. Physical or emotional.

And I was more than capable of taking care of myself. I'd taught myself to fight in the shadows of those waterfalls. I'd trained with Arthur and his Goldstones until my palms bled and I could barely walk.

But having him at my side... it felt good. Even my shattered heart could admit it.

I'd never rely on him, not really. That was too far, too much. For now, though, I'd take advantage of his menace.

"Stand down, beast," I ordered softly, knowing neither Roksana nor any other elemental had seen the beast of legend that lurked beneath Arran's skin. "Roksana understands."

Her eyes didn't widen, no fear trembled on her lips. She was the most skilled elemental I'd ever met at concealing her thoughts and feelings. But she blinked once, and I knew that Roksana understood the warning.

She changed the subject to cuisine, asking Arran to compare the food in the elemental kingdom with typical fare in his homeland. It was as neutral a topic as any.

Roksana offered dessert. I was too full to accept. We didn't linger for drinks, and she didn't invite us to. A small mercy, that.

We said goodnight and left Elora glowering and Roksana with her serene smile back in place.

Arran waited until we were well away before speaking. "They could both be the threat."

"Or neither," I sighed heavily.

Nothing had been revealed. Even Elora, who was worse at playing the game of hiding emotions than me, was impossible to judge. I was so tired. This sort of parrying of words and smiles for which Arthur had been so well suited exhausted me. More than sparring in the ring or running through the mountains.

But as the doors swung open to my rooms, Gwen and Lyrena stepping aside, twin guards of night and sun, I realized I was about to be denied the rest I craved.

54
ARRAN

"I believe I warned you about loitering in the queen's chambers."

It was the only warning I'd give. The beast in my chest was demanding I shift, that I tear out his throat.

Arrogant trash, sitting on her chaise like he had any right to be there.

Cool fingers closed around my arm, their temperature infiltrating my skin even through the tunic I wore. "I told you, he is my friend," Veyka ground out.

"Which is the only reason he is still alive."

Veyka cursed under her breath. *Mule-headed terrestrial bastard.*

She could curse all she liked as long as she let me tear the limbs from Parys' body. Starting with the one he'd been foolish enough to insert inside of *my* Queen.

The elemental courtier was making a good show of smiling, flipping that ridiculously long mop of brown curls over his forehead. If I commented aloud, Veyka would point out that my hair also reached my shoulders. But it was always tied back.

He could play the roguish courtier.

But I could smell his fear.

Apparently, so could Veyka.

She released my arm, only to plant her other hand in the middle of my chest and shove me bodily backward. I felt every inch of that contact, too.

Even with her considerable strength, I could have held my ground. But I allowed her that bit of control. She craved it, I'd begun to realize. Though why, I hadn't yet deduced.

The more space between me and Parys, the better.

Veyka shot me a look, all command. *Stay, dog.*

I flashed my canines.

She rolled her eyes and turned back to Parys, scrubbing a hand over her face. She was tired—and the bastard was disturbing her. That dinner with her royal councilors had been its own particular sort of torture. Not that I'd intended to leave her at her door.

But for what I'd had planned for her, she could be flat on her back.

A shiver snaked down Veyka's spine, her shoulders shifting slightly, her wide hips giving a delightful wobble, as if she'd heard my thoughts.

Or the growl of my beast.

"I'm tired, Parys," she sighed, crossing her arms over her body. "What is it?"

Parys made a show of stretching his arms above his head. "I know the feeling," he said with an exaggerated yawn. "I've been in the library for hours."

Veyka's shoulders tensed. The motion was so slight, anyone else would have missed it. Because no one else was as obsessed with her body as me. I knew every line of muscle and shifting curve of soft flesh.

The tension held for several beats, then eased.

Her arms dropped to her sides, hands softening so her fingers hung slack. "You may speak freely in front of Arran."

The male's wide brown eyes grew wider still. For all his courtly manners, he actually leaned over on the chaise so he could see past Veyka's wide figure and peer at me more clearly.

"Decided he's trustworthy, have you?" Parys said, the muscle on the left side of his cheek twitching.

"Do not question your queen," I snarled.

That muscle twitched again, but the male wisely swallowed whatever smartass comment played through his mind and directed his attention back to Veyka. "You might want to sit down."

Veyka needed no further encouragement. She flopped onto the oversized settee, laying all the way back and staring up at the ceiling. Parys' eyes slid to me. I remained standing, one hand on my axe. Not that I'd need it to tear such a pretty male limb from limb.

I knew the threat was clear in my eyes. Parys straightened, all pretense of casualness gone.

"I cannot definitely say I've found everything the library has to offer. There are well over a hundred thousand tomes," he said, looking at Veyka, still reclined and staring at the ceiling. "But I've found a fair amount about the rifts."

Still no movement from Veyka.

She'd asked for his help. Smart, if he was trustworthy. The fact that she believed he was had me looking at the foxlike courtier with keener eyes.

"There are three tiers of rifts to the human realm. The ones we all know—the northern dunes, the southern coast, and the one near Skywatch. There is less information about those located within the terrestrial kingdom..." Parys slid his eyes cautiously in my direction.

"The northeastern foothills of the Spine, the entrance to Wolf Bay, and in the Shadow Wood," I rattled off the locations of the known rifts in my homeland.

Parys nodded confirmation. He'd already known them.

My hands curled into fists.

Wily, pretentious, fucking bastard.

"Then there are the ones that are documented, but not well known. They were a secret held only by the priestesses before the Great War. When the Ancestors stripped them of their power, they took that information as well. It's documented, though harder to find," Parys continued.

Veyka twitched, another shiver running through her—this time, not sensual.

"How many?" Her voice punched through the air.

"One in each territory," Parys said steadily.

"Eight rifts in Annwyn," Veyka said. I'd been counting as well. "You said there were three tiers."

I felt the tension creeping into my own muscles, bracing for what was coming, knowing it would be bad.

Parys' sigh was heavy enough to fill even the cavernous room. "There are unmarked rifts."

Veyka voiced the question on my lips. "How many?"

"I don't know."

All the air was sucked from the room on those three words.

"There may be only a few. Based on the accounts of disappearances and reappearances, I can guess at a handful of locations. But more remote ones would be less well documented." Parys' voice was half-strangled.

But my eyes were pinned to Veyka.

Slowly, she rose up to sit, those blue eyes sharp as shards of ice.

"How is it," she paused, sucking in a breath through her teeth, "that I did not know there are *so many* damned ways for humans to sneak into my kingdom?"

The anger seething in those words, burning in her eyes, in the quivering muscles of her shoulders and arms, sent a spear of pride through me. There she was—the queen Annwyn needed. The one I wanted standing at my side.

Parys steadily met her gaze, no humor or artifice in his eyes. My estimation of the male nudged upward—begrudgingly.

I spoke for the first time, stepping forward. "We know there is one in the mountains. We must have been close when we stumbled across the human."

"That's how the Shadows are smuggling humans into Baylaur. They know about the mountain rift." She threw up a hand in frustration. "Assuming there are not multiple. Ancestors, how has this been kept a secret for so long?"

"It's probably not," Parys said grimly. "If the Shadows know about them, so do members of this court. Members of your Royal Council, surely. Nothing is a secret here for long, if one has the will and skill to find it."

I realized then why he was such a powerful ally. His magic—wind, I thought—was not the reason. It was his head for intrigue.

My cunning, beautiful Queen.

I traced the bob of Veyka's throat with my eyes.

"Someone on my Royal Council used the rift in the mountains to smuggle in the humans. The ones who murdered Arthur." Her voice was trembling.

I didn't reach for her. Instead, I drew the axe at my waist. "Tell me who to kill."

Veyka tilted her head in my direction, vague amusement in her eyes. "So bloodthirsty, Brutal Prince. We don't know who the traitor is."

"So we cut down them all. It would be an acceptable loss."

"You hate political dinners that much, do you?"

"Yes."

"Me too." That wicked smile flashed over her face, and my cock hardened instantly. Veyka's eyes flicked downward. Oh, sly Queen. She knew exactly what she was doing.

"I hate to interrupt," Parys said, voice half-strangled. "But there is more."

Veyka's blinked. I watched her attempt to leash her lust. My beast growled in appreciation at the heavy-lidded eyes, the scent of her.

"Of course there is," she said heavily.

"You've heard of the Void Prophecy."

My head snapped to the side, eyes pinning Parys. Veyka rolled her eyes. "I don't believe in prophecies."

"I'm not talking about prophecies made by power-grabbing priestesses in the throne room. The Void Prophecy is much older."

"Yes, yes, we've all heard it." Veyka crossed her legs, smoothing her skirts. She did not think this information of any importance. "Voids of darkness, faerie queens, blah blah blah."

For once, Parys' eyes did not sparkle with mirth. *"Then comes a queen, in the age of uncertainty, when shadows cast doubt upon the realm. Born under a double moon and marked by a radiant star, a faerie queen shall rise to command the depths of the voids of darkness."*

Veyka uncrossed her legs. "It doesn't say anything about rifts."

"What do you think a void of darkness is?" Parys challenged.

He thought this was something, I realized. He thought it was important, even as his queen was ready to dismiss it, her eyes already flitting to the bedroom doors over his shoulder. For once, I was inclined to agree with him.

"You think it is a reference to the rifts," I said, ignoring Veyka's bristling.

"Maybe," Parys said judiciously. "But that is only the first part of the prophecy: *Twice blessed, the realm of shift and mist, when comes the awaited queen who shall possess ethereal might. With a touch, she will feel the heartbeat of her subjects, and she will unlock the secrets they guard within.*"

"That is the Ethereal Prophecy, not the Void." Veyka pushed herself off the settee, clearly impatient now for the conversation to be done.

"They are one prophecy, split into two by simple-minded fools." Parys' voice was brittle. "I found the original text, recorded by Nimue herself."

I didn't know much about the elemental kingdom, but I knew my battle history. I was a commander. Nimue was one of the Ancestors. She'd fought in the Great War, commanded an army of elemental fae and become the first High Queen of Annwyn.

Veyka stilled, her hand on the back of a chair. "My Ancestor had her own motives. As does every queen." She gave Parys a pointed look. "If you have nothing else, I'm going to bed."

Based on her tone, I doubted I'd be invited to share it. My beast grumbled his disappointment.

Parys caught her arm.

My beast roared.

I didn't shift, but he was fully in command as I leapt forward, that string I'd felt a few times before pulling at my chest. I ripped his arm away from her, twisting it back. Parys was on his knees, swallowing back a strangled cry of pain at the angle of his arm.

Veyka didn't intervene. She stared down at Parys, then slowly up at me, as if seeing things clearly for the first time.

Her expression shattered mine. I released Parys, stumbling back.

Fuck. Shit. Ancestors.

I hadn't lost control like that... not in years.

Parys was her *friend*, and my beast couldn't handle seeing him lay a hand on her. Even in passing, entreaty. She'd wanted to go to bed. He'd tried to stop her, and my beast took that as enough of a reason to punish and maim.

Slowly, Parys climbed back onto the chaise. He didn't reach for Veyka again, but he didn't hold his tongue either. "This is something, Veyka, I can feel it."

She cut her eyes back to him. I wished I could see inside her mind as she contemplated.

"I will consider it," she finally said, turning for the bedroom doors.

Parys' sharp intake of breath froze her once again.

"What else could you possibly have to keep me from my bed?" she hissed.

"I will keep searching the library," Parys said. "But that is not the only place we should be looking. One of the books mentioned the carvings. Those predate the Great War, just like the rifts."

"What carvings?" Veyka's back said, each syllable wearier than the one before.

Parys stared at the ground. Again, that rising unease in my stomach. "In the water gardens. They are the oldest part of the goldstone palace, originally built on a natural spring."

Veyka went still.

She'd been standing before, her muscles twitching, a stretch here or there as she waited for Parys' last bit of information.

But now, she was truly still. Unmoving. As if she'd turned to stone, a lovely glowing white statue, unable to move. Not even the quiver of breath in her body.

She'd spent most of her life in the water gardens, in seclusion. I'd learned as much in my first weeks in the goldstone palace.

I learned more from the pain etched in every line of her body than I had in all my weeks of questioning.

"I am going to bed."

She didn't wait for a response from either of us. As the bedroom doors closed behind her, I turned to look at Parys. But he was staring down at the floor, still, his own body tight. I stared at him, knowing he could feel the weight of my black glare.

But still he didn't lift his eyes.

"I don't know," he finally said, unmoved. "But it was bad."

55
VEYKA

Make it stop.
Bed—a bed. I couldn't sleep. I couldn't stand.
I had to move fast. Faster than those pretty winged handmaidens, listening for me. To preen, to primp, to make me into something I was not.
Not a queen.
Lost, scared, alone.
I tumbled through the secret door. Not a secret anymore.
I didn't care.
Out, out, out. I had to get out.
I couldn't see a thing. My eyes blurred with tears. I lost my footing, tumbling down the ragged stairs. I scented my blood as the tender flesh scraped along the jagged edges. My nails tore as I grappled at the walls, trying to find purchase, trying to stop the fall.
I couldn't make it stop. I couldn't.
But then I did. On the little landing, where Arran had pressed his body against mine in promise and threat.
Then I was on my feet again. I savored the burn of the scrapes and bruises as I spiraled down, down, down. Dragging myself

through the mud, faster and harsher than ever before so I earned more wounds. But I kept going.

Until the sky was open above me, dark and sparkling.

But instead of lying there, panting on the ground, I shoved myself to my feet.

I ran.

I ran and ran and ran until each breath was a ragged grasp, and the skin between my thighs burned with chaffing. Still, I ran on, determined to get away.

If I ran fast enough, I could escape the pain and the memories. If I ran fast enough, I could make it stop.

No one else had ever been there to help me, to save me. I was alone in this fight, had always been alone. Arthur had freed me, but not soon enough.

Wetness coated my face.

Tears, streaming down my cheeks as I cried for myself like the pitiless, worthless princess I was.

Except I was not alone.

Through the trees, I saw the flashes of white. A mass of fur and fangs, claws and violence. Tracking me, running with me.

For the first time in my life, I was not alone.

56

ARRAN

The message came sooner than I'd expected.

From the pain I'd seen etched in her body and the fear I'd scented as she ran through the forest, I'd thought it would take her days to muster the strength—maybe even weeks.

But the message came mere hours after her return to the goldstone palace, to meet her in the water gardens.

I strapped my broadsword across my back, tucked a dagger into my boot, all in addition to the battle axe ever present on my belt. I suspected the terrors of the water gardens were mental, but I felt better with the steel kissing my body.

Veyka must have felt the same.

She wore her customary dark-hued, flowing combination of scanty clothing. A kind of armor all its own, I'd come to realize. Her body was so different from the thin, supple forms prized by our kind. But she refused to cover herself. Wore more seductive, more distinctive gowns and confections than any other female in the elemental court. She dared them to look at her and judge her wanting.

I looked at her, and all I did was want.

I hadn't visited the water gardens since my arrival at the goldstone palace, though I'd walked past the entrance a few times. They were located near the rear of the castle, where the goldstone palace abutted the mountains. Like everything, they were connected to a courtyard. Though, I'd noticed, this one was always conspicuously empty.

The entrance was barred by a wide golden gate, each long vertical bar twisted into a decorative design—vines, waves, flowers, clouds. An odd mixture of elemental and terrestrial symbols. Perhaps a reference to the age of this place, to a time before the kingdoms were divided, before the Great War and the treaty that had followed.

Veyka had already pried open the gate.

Maybe she'd arrived before me, just so she could do it in peace—tackle that challenge on her own, without an audience.

I raked my eyes over her, noting the familiar daggers in their twin scabbards at her waist and the wickedly curved blades crossed over her back. A breeze caught her skirt, and I saw two more knives—one strapped to her thigh, the other small as a child's finger and slipped between the lacings of her slippers.

"Are you ready?" I asked.

I wouldn't ask for more. Never. Not until she was ready to offer it.

Her chin jutted out in determination. "Let's go."

I followed her into the gardens, waiting as she paused to lock the gate behind us.

I'd never seen a lock as intricate as the one that Veyka's fingers systematically closed. It wasn't one lock, but three. The levers were curved at unpredictable angles, one lock component feeding into another. They had to be opened and closed in sequence, I guessed, but that sequence wasn't easy to follow.

Veyka's fingers flew over them with familiar ease. That told me enough—these locks had been in place for a long time.

When she turned back to face me, her face was impenetrable. She'd snapped on that indifferent mask she'd worn for weeks after I first met her.

For once, I didn't try to work my way past it by infuriating her, poking at her rage.

If that ruse of implacability was what she needed to survive the coming minutes... I'd done as much myself, in the early days.

The shell that Veyka had formed herself into led me down steps, each one wider than the next, until the arch above our heads gave way and the full grandeur of the water gardens came into view.

The sight stole the breath from my body.

The sound of rushing water filled the air, creeping over my senses, into my keen ears, the mist curling, cool and refreshing against my skin.

One tall waterfall dominated the space. Two stories high and as wide as the courtyard we'd just left, it descended in varying levels and drops on each side, creating a treacherous stairstep effect.

The center fell straight down, creating a cloud of white responsible for the mist that coated everything.

Veyka walked past the magnificent waterfall as if it did not exist.

She followed a stone path cut through the middle of the pool, made slick by the mist, but her steps were steady. Smaller waterfalls and pools, drops and stairwells, branched off from the grand waterfall at the center.

Through the mist, I sighted the buildings. Squat enough I knew I'd have to stoop to enter them, they were cleverly incorporated among the flowing water and stone so that they blended in rather than detracting from the beauty and grandeur.

A lovely place.

And yet, Veyka moved with more tension in her shoulders than I'd ever seen.

She led me past the buildings, past the waterfalls, her eyes determinedly facing forward, refusing to look from side to side.

Finally, she cut to the right.

Straight into a solid wall.

Before I could ask, she lifted a hand to a stone even with her shoulder and pressed.

What had seemed like an impenetrable wall of stone shifted, creating a passageway.

"After you," she said, voice still emotionless.

I ducked to get in, but once I was through, I was able to stand easily. She slid in behind me, leaving the way open.

On one side of us, a wall of water. The backside of that grand waterfall, I realized. On the other side, a stone wall that reached up and up and up. Every inch of it was covered in carvings.

"What is this place?" I stepped back, craning my neck to see, minding the edge that plummeted to the pool below.

"Forgotten," Veyka said succinctly. "The water gardens are forbidden to courtiers. They have been since my mother and father's reign. Perhaps longer."

I noted the slight tremor in her voice, but she was trying so hard to cover it that I didn't acknowledge it. "Why keep them hidden?"

I watched her bite down hard on her cheek. "It was incidental."

My eyes tracked over the carvings at my eye level, as well as those that Veyka could easily see. "It looks like a depiction of the Great War."

I could make out the shapes of the Ancestors—Nimue and her consort, Accolon, the first two fae from each kingdom to fulfill the Offering. Higher up on the wall was the Battle of the Roses, where so many of my own bloodline had fought and died.

Veyka's face lifted higher, scanning above her own head. "Parys said this is the oldest part of the palace. This existed before the Great War."

I followed her line of sight. Sure enough, the events of the Great War gave way to less familiar representations.

"This is Annwyn," Veyka said, tracing an outline in the shape of the continent, then pausing at a similar outline carved right below it. "Is this the human realm?"

I looked closer. The landmarks were the same, but the symbols marking them were different. "It must be. They are mirrors of each other."

That was how the rifts worked. The human and fae realms existed on different planes, but their physical attributes were the same. The Effren Valley, the Split Sea, the Spine... all of those landmarks existed in the human realm as well, by different names, used differently by the humans who lacked the magic, speed, and the long-life of the fae.

The rifts allowed one to travel between the planes. If one passed through the rift in the mountains that surrounded Baylaur, they would emerge at the same place, but in the human realm.

I followed Veyka's hand as it drifted upward. To another outline of Annwyn, above our own. Then another. And another.

Nonsense, all of it. Without the historical reference points, I couldn't begin to decipher what any of it meant. I moved farther along the ledge, studying the carvings. There were two armies, facing off against one another. One had the pointed ears of the fae, the other the rounded of the humans.

I knew no history of a war between humans and fae. Humans were too weak, too easily put down.

This was a waste of time.

The carvings were rough, impossible to glean any real meaning from. The eyes of the humans were little more than black smudges, their bodies carelessly rendered. While the fae were perfectly wrought, here and there a human arm or leg stuck out at an odd angle.

I recalled an adage my mother said once, during those brief years she'd thought to school me for a life of royalty rather than bloodshed. Something about history being recorded by the victorious. Whatever fae scholar had etched these carvings, they didn't think much of the humans.

A belief I shared.

I made my way back to Veyka. She'd drifted from side to side, examining the carvings, but was now back as I'd left her—tracing the repeated outlines.

"Anything?" she asked, eyes not leaving the wall.

"Depictions of a human-fae war."

Her eyes flicked to me in question. I could only shrug.

"I'll ask Parys to look into it." Then her eyes were back on the wall.

Her empty expression had given way to something else, something softer. Her brows were furrowed slightly, lips pressed outward in the slightest pout. I watched her fingertips moving—first over the human realm, then Annwyn, then higher to the repeated image.

"Do you suppose... that the rifts could open to other realms? Beyond the human realm?" she said softly.

My eyebrows followed the direction of her hand—up. "There are no other realms."

She cut me a scathing look. "None that we know of."

"If there were, then wouldn't the rifts open to them as well? Wouldn't Parys have found some mention of it?" I watched her trace the third and fourth mirror images, an unsettling tension taking my shoulders. I rolled my head to either side, forcing my muscles to stretch and relax.

"He didn't mention a human-fae war, either," she pointed out.

But she lowered her hand and didn't try to press the point further. She could ask Parys to look into that, as well. None of it seemed pertinent to Arthur or the hidden rifts.

As she turned back for the opening, that tension that had lived in her shoulders during our descent returned. I followed her out silently, waiting for her to seal the passage behind us and lead back through the maze of waterfalls.

We made it as far as the dwellings when she stopped again.

I didn't see what caught her eye. But I recognized the instant she began to come apart.

57
VEYKA

How dare she.

I would flay her alive.

I would use my daggers to cut a systematic pattern into her skin, deep enough it would not heal without intervention. If I ever found my brother's blasted sword, Excalibur, I would drive it through her heart—if the twisted thing in my mother's chest could still be called that.

I hadn't set foot in the water gardens since the day after my father's death, when Arthur became the King of the Elemental Fae and unlocked the gate. But sometime since then, in the months since I'd found freedom, the Dowager had come back.

I never should have looked. On the journey in, I'd kept my eyes purposefully straight. I knew if I let them stray, I'd never make it to the wall of carvings tucked behind the grand waterfall. The one my mother had strengthened to cover the sounds of my torture.

But as we climbed out, with Arran's steady presence at my back, I could not resist the urge to glance to the side. To look at the squat dwelling that had been my home for twenty years.

Only to find it ransacked.

No, not ransacked.

Empty.

Systematically cleansed of every remnant of my existence.

Through the open door, into the singular room that had been my bedroom, schoolroom, playroom, and personal torture chamber, I looked, expecting to see things exactly as I'd left them.

But there was nothing.

Not a single piece of furniture, not a book or a scrap of clothing. No evidence of me.

No evidence of what I'd endured.

I knew it was her.

Arthur would have asked me. Or at least, kept my things and asked me what I wanted, if I wanted any of it. Or if I'd rather it was all burned.

Only my mother would dare to take the choice from me. A message—that she was still in control. That she could still hurt me, even as I sat on the throne.

I was going to be sick.

I stumbled, tripping over the force of my own emotions. I anticipated the crash of my knees, still bruised from the night before, the sharp lances of pain.

But I didn't hit the ground.

A hand caught me. Two hands—around my shoulders, pulling me back up and into a solid wall of warmth.

Arran.

His arm hooked around my chest, holding me firm against him in case my legs gave out. I gritted my teeth, stifling back the tears that threatened. I thought I'd cried them all out the night before. But somehow, here they were.

The scent of him filled my nostrils, stronger than the wet damp of the waterfalls and pools. I felt the scrape of his canines against the shell of my ear.

"They do not get to win," he said, low and sharp. A growl rumbled through him, through me. "Not like this."

I dragged in breath after breath. I anchored my being to the heat of his body behind me, the scrape of his teeth on the point of my ear. I let his strength be my strength; let it remind me that I held plenty of my own.

Somehow, Arran knew when I was ready. His arm eased away, and I stood solidly.

"The Dowager did this," I said, my voice clearer than I expected.

Long silence. A long breath. "Tell me."

Not a command, but an offer. One I could walk away from, if I wanted.

But I didn't.

"She took everything. I lived in that room for twenty years, and she took every scrap of my childhood and did the Ancestors' only know what with it. As if it was hers to take—as if I was hers."

Arran's beast growled, low and deep. *You are mine*, it said.

I belong to no one, I whispered back, though with less conviction than I might have a month ago.

Whether Arran the male heard that silent conversation, I did not know. I could not begin to explain that strange, silent channel of communication that had opened between me and the beast. But I saw the understanding in his furrowed brow as he eased around to look at my face.

He'd seen the locks on the gate. And now, this pitiful cell.

"You were a captive," he breathed.

"As good as," I agreed.

"Why didn't your father free you? Or your brother?"

I could see his mind shifting behind those dark eyes, trying to make sense of it. Uther Pendragon had been a powerful terrestrial shifter, taking the form of a larger-than-life horned owl, sharp beak and talons more than capable of shredding flesh and bone.

"My mother was stronger," I said. Images flashed in my memory. Raging waterfalls. Torrents and spirals of water that could choke and drown. "My father would visit me sometimes. He'd always promise to convince her that I should be freed, or at least brought out more often. But it came to nothing. It was Arthur who opened the gate as soon as my father died."

For though my mother still lived, one could not rule without the other. The treaty was predicated on a partnership, an alliance—one elemental, one terrestrial—on the throne, ruling together at all times. With my father's death, the faerie crown of Annwyn passed to my brother, and the cycle of heirs and Offering and Joining began anew.

Arran studied my face, the questions still heavy in his eyes. What? Why? Questions I knew he would not voice.

There were those within the goldstone palace, within my orbit, who knew details of my captivity. Who suspected what might have occurred, even if they did not know precisely. I'd wondered more than once how much Arthur had confessed to Parys, his closest friend. Or to Lyrena, his lover and the one he'd entrusted with my protection once I'd been freed. But none of them said anything. Especially not after Arthur's death. None of them dared to ask.

Perhaps they were scared to know the details.

But not Arran.

The offer in those dark eyes was clear and sure. Whatever I told him, he'd be able to withstand. And though there was concern and the beginnings of rage in his gaze, there was no pity.

So I told him.

"I was an abomination from the moment I was born. There were sometimes second children born to the High King and Queen, but never a twin. A twin was dangerous. My brother was supposed to have killed me in the womb and absorbed my power. The fact that I lived to be born cast suspicion on my brother's power, his fitness for the throne."

I had often wondered if the reason I lived at all was because I'd had no power for my brother to steal, even as fetuses inside our mother's hostile womb.

"No one doubted Arthur," Arran said quietly, eyes still focused intently on me. As if there were no crashing waterfalls, no goldstone palace beyond. No revenge.

"The Dowager would argue that is because she kept me hidden from sight. An oddity to be trotted out for state occasions, but nothing more. Nothing dangerous." I bit down on my tongue, holding back the confession that had almost sprung forth. The other reason she kept me hidden—so that no one might suspect my lack of power.

I couldn't give Arran that truth. It was too dangerous to the fragile trust growing between us. It would derail the mission to avenge Arthur. It would change everything. I was running out of time, and I could not share that secret.

But all the others spilled out of me.

"The... violation... it began when I was eight years old. I was not an obedient child. I failed to please the Dowager again and again. So she punished me. Or rather... she brought in her courtier, a powerful magic wielder, to punish me."

I'd thought Arran's eyes were black. But the darkness that filled them then... it was not like the one we'd seen take over the humans, dead and unfeeling. It was the sort of darkness that promised to hunt and kill, to choke out every last bit of life—to end the world.

"What sort of violation?"

"The sort no child should have to endure."

Beats of time passed.

Heartbeats. The water beating against the wall, the ground, the pool. The sun overhead, beating down. My blood thrummed in my veins, until the pressure of it threatened to explode out of me.

Then movement.

The stroke of Arran's hand over his axe.

"I will kill her."

I covered his hand with my own, feeling the vulnerable core inside of me hardening once more. "You will do no such thing. Vengeance, should I ever desire it, is mine."

He stared long and hard, midnight dark eyes boring into me. Just when I expected him to turn and make for the gate, ready to ignore my edict, he blinked. His chin dipped a fraction—the only acknowledgment I would get.

In that moment, I felt more seen than I ever had before.

Even Arthur, who loved me as much as I loved him, had not

truly been able to understand. But the Brutal Prince... whatever he had seen and endured, it allowed him to truly know. To understand without pity. To recognize that kill was mine.

What had he survived, to grant him this grotesque empathy?

Arran stared down at where my hand covered his, my pale skin a sharp contrast to his bronze.

He breathed out, the air rattling in his chest as he exhaled three centuries worth of pain.

"You have heard the stories about my... history," he said, voice low.

My chest tightened. "Of course."

"There is more to the story than is usually told."

The cascade of waterfalls drowned out any noises beyond the water gardens. No one could hear us.

So, I made the same offer he'd given me. "Tell me."

My heart began to break as he spoke.

"My powers manifested early—much earlier than other terrestrials. I was no more than a babe in arms, squalling as my mother walked in the garden. She took too long to feed me, and I turned every single one of her precious rosebushes to shriveled stems." His voice was so even, so painfully emotionless.

I wondered how mine had sounded, moments before. I was the child of the elemental court, ought to have been able to keep a mask in place to cover useless emotions. But Arran was the unreadable one as he spoke.

"My power grew quickly. By the time I was ten years old, I was the Heir presumptive. Although no elemental heir had yet been born or foretold."

I knew all of this, of course. Not the bit about the roses. Impressive, for a babe. I might have been surprised, had I not seen the force of his magic firsthand. The image of him subduing the deadly skoupuma using nothing more than blades of grass flashed in my mind. But he had not mentioned his fauna-gift. The presence of both kinds of terrestrial magic—that was the thing that made him truly unique among the fae.

"There were those in the terrestrial kingdom who believed I was a danger. My power too great, from too young an age."

I sensed it immediately—there was more to those sentences. More than he was ready to tell me, I realized just as quickly. Had it been as clear when I spoke, that I too held back? But it wasn't retaliation that stilled his tongue... but understanding.

That the pain inside each of us—it was too big.

If we opened that door more than a crack, it would take over.

"Our kind are vicious," Arran said. An unequivocal truth.

"They decided to eliminate me."

My fingers tightened over his.

"I was stolen away from Eilean Gayl on the eve of my eleventh birthday. They tried to kill me." My breath caught, even as his voice remained steady. "But I would not die."

My eyes snapped up, ready to meet his. But those dark eyes stared determinedly down, fixed on our hands where they overlapped atop his blade.

"That is when my beast awoke. They held me for forty-seven days. On the forty-eighth, I shifted for the first time and killed everyone in my path. I did not care who or what or why. I did not care for degrees of innocence. I killed every being that crossed my path for the week it took my beast to travel north, to return to Eilean Gayl. Until I stood before my mother once again, and shifted back into the male."

My heart ached for him. My torture had been contained to myself. But Arran, his power had been used against him. Tortured from him until its only instinct was to kill—an urge I understood. What was dead could not rise again to torture and maim.

For a second, I wanted to tell him everything. To complete the circle—he'd been tortured because of his magic. I'd been tortured for my lack of it. It was the cruelest sort of irony, that in this twisted way we were perfectly matched.

But I could not bring him anymore pain. I could not make this any worse than it already was. I could bear the secret. I'd borne it my entire life.

Just a bit longer.

I could do it, just a bit longer.

But what I couldn't do was let go of him.

I threaded my fingers through his, lifting our hands off of the head of the axe and bringing them to my lips.

A strand of long, dark hair had fallen free of the knot at the back of Arran's head. It made him look younger—a ridiculous notion. He was a three-hundred-year-old fae warrior. But it was an effort to drag my eyes away from the thick, dark lock to his eyes. Unreadable, unfathomable eyes. Not glowing with lust—for once—but thick with emotions neither of us dared to name.

I pressed my lips to the back of his hand. I whispered against his skin. "I see you—all of you. And I am not afraid."

A second of thanks—a flash in those dark eyes—and then the fire returned.

A low, feral growl ripped from Arran's throat as he hooked one arm under my knees and the other around my shoulders. He carried me out of the water gardens, using his magic to sever the locks, kicking the gate closed behind us.

Over his shoulder, I glimpsed what he'd wrought.

The way was barred—the majestic waterfalls and bridges completely obscured by a jungle of deadly vines and thorns.

58

ARRAN

I unleashed my power. Let it flow around me in terrifying waves, clearing our path. The growl of my beast traveled on the wind, vines springing from every potted or hanging plant, chasing away any courtiers.

This moment was ours. Veyka's and mine.

The only ones standing firm were Gwen and Gawayn, at the doors of Veyka's apartments. The former knew my power, would have recognized it. The latter was too damn loyal and noble to be scared away.

But I didn't care about them. I kicked in the doors to the antechamber, then the ones to the bedroom. None of the winged handmaidens came running.

Veyka turned those clear blue eyes up to me as the doors closed behind us. No glowing of desire in them. Whatever her power, it must be weak. I'd surmised as much from the story of her torture. Weak enough she hadn't been able to fight back, weak enough it could be stifled.

It didn't matter, I'd decided in a breath.

I would protect her. No one would ever get close enough to test the strength of her magic. I'd kill anyone who tried to touch her and offer her their severed heads as a gift. We'd bring each other to climax with the scent of our enemies' blood swirling around us.

"If you are that skilled at scaring away courtiers, you may carry me everywhere," Veyka purred, catching her lower lip between her teeth. Dropping her eyes to my mouth.

I peeled away her clothes, inch by inch. I worshiped every new stretch of skin revealed to me. Before, it had been hasty. Clothing torn, pushed aside, the desperate need to get as deep within one another as possible.

Not now.

I wanted her naked and writhing beneath me. I wanted to see every inch of that pale skin shimmering beneath the torchlight.

I started at the tip of her delicately pointed ear, nipping at it with my canines and then dragging my tongue along the outer shell. Veyka trembled deliciously below me, like she always did when I played with her ears.

"Do you like that, Princess?" I whispered to the hollow of her neck, meeting her arching hips with my own.

I was still fully clothed. Veyka seemed to realize it as she slid her hands up over my shoulders, then down my back to grip my bottom and demand the intensity she craved.

"Ah, ah, ah," I said, shrugging her hands away and catching her lower lip between my teeth. I sucked hard, until she had to lift her neck off the pillow or cry out in delicious pain. "Me first."

I released her lip, and her mouth fell open. She expected me to press my cock inside of it, I realized. I felt the wicked, carnal smile climb across my face. I slid down her body, pressing kisses and licks as I went. I paused at her nipples, nipping them between my sharpened teeth enough to draw gasps of pain, but not blood. Then I covered those small hurts with a swipe of my tongue.

When I finally reached her pussy, quivering, wetness already spilling out of her, she was near the breaking point. But I wasn't quite ready to shove her over. I dragged my nose along the seam where her thigh met her abdomen, inhaling the rich scent of her arousal.

I groaned in appreciation, loud and deep, letting her hear every drawn-out syllable. Another rush of wetness in response.

"Such a good girl," I said, laughing ruefully.

She squirmed beneath me, but I held her pinned, tracing my thumbs over the dip between her rounded stomach and the curve of her hipbones down to her glistening pussy.

I eased my fingers around to grip her full ass, then flipped us both so that she was straddling me.

Her hands went right to my trousers, working at the lacings to get me free. My cock strained in response, wanting nothing more than to get inside her dripping cunt. But I kept myself under control, just barely, using my hands still on her waist to urge her hips forward, up over my chest until her lust-glazed eyes flicked down to me uncertainly.

I didn't hesitate as I urged her down, the pink lips of her pussy begging for my kiss.

"Now sit on my face, Veyka."

59
VEYKA

Oh.

Oh.

I grabbed onto the headboard, certain my legs were going to give out any moment. "How do you intend to breathe?"

"I've been waiting for you for too long," he growled—half Arran, half beast. "*Mine.*"

Not an answer. But I didn't try to stop him as he dragged my hips downward, his eyes turned to nothing but raging black flames. I could have stopped him, if I'd tried hard enough.

But I didn't want to fight, I didn't want to test the strength of those arms around my waist. I wanted to give into it. Such strength —he threw me around like I weighed nothing.

With that first swipe of his tongue, wide and flat across the seam of my pussy and right up to where my clit begged for him---

"Oh, Ancestors, yessssss."

I felt his chuckle of appreciation reverberating between the layers of tender flesh. Slowly, I started to move atop him, letting my hips rock back and forth. His tongue responded immediately, finding different repetitive rhythms, shifting as the tones of my cries changed.

When he flicked his tongue over my clit a hundred times in rapid succession, I nearly exploded. But then it stopped, replaced by grand, sweeping ovals like he was trying to taste every crevice.

I glanced down and had to grab the headboard for support. My thighs quivered terribly as I saw his wet face. Wet, with my juices. Fuck.

I stilled, determined to get ahold of myself. But Arran's hands came back to hips, urging them to resume those gentle thrusts. A few seconds, and they weren't gentle anymore. I was grinding my pussy against his face, desperate for his tongue.

"Don't stop," he commanded, dragging me even further down.

I clung to the headboard, my nails surely digging dents into the carved wood. I was so fucking close. His teeth scraped over my clit again and again while his tongue burrowed inside of me, fucking me as I rode his face.

"I...I..."

"Yes, Veyka."

"I... can't," I whimpered. I was going to die. I was going to take Arran with me. We were going to dissolve into nothing but pleasure.

"Yes, you can," Arran said, his dark voice muffled against my pussy. "Come right now," he commanded.

My body obeyed him without consulting my mind.

Orgasm stole the breath from my chest, the thoughts from my mind. Reality shifted, distorting around me as I struggled to find a pinpoint of reality. Then I found it—Arran. His scent, mixing with my own. His voice, heaping words of praise as he gently licked my tortured flesh.

I eased back so I was sitting on his chest, my weight balanced partially on my knees, my forehead resting against the headboard. I took in huge gasping breaths, but I doubted I would ever really catch my breath. Not after that.

Sure enough, before my heartbeat could steady, I felt the gentle nips and licks of Arran's mouth on my inner thigh.

"Oh no you don't," I said, easing myself back and sliding down his body. "You'll kill us both."

He sat up on his elbows, dark hair a mess around his shoulders, the unforgiving line of his jaw stretching into an animalistic smile. "Then I will die a happy, sated male."

My hips encountered his cock at the same time the word sated dropped from those wicked, beautiful lips of his. Reminding me that though my body was still quivering, he was very much not sated yet.

But I intended to make him pay for every tremor in my body.

I leaned forward, pressing a kiss to his lips that almost bordered on chaste. But I knew the smile I gave him was anything but.

"There's that wicked smile of yours," Arran breathed, lifting one fingertip to trace the outline of my lips. I caught it between my teeth, nipping, then sucking hard until his eyes started to glaze over again.

I released it, my cunt clenching at the little 'pop' sound it made. Arran dragged his wet fingertip down the side of my face, into my hair, tangling it in the length of my braid. He lifted his thick, dark eyebrows in challenge.

Oh, yes, I'd make him pay.

I tore away his clothes. The two of us would keep the palace seamstresses busy, it seemed. But I didn't think about that. I needed to see that sculpted chest beneath me.

He was huge, I thought as I gazed down at him.

I was not a small female, not by any means. Not even a regular-sized female. I was tall, wide, with a soft belly and an ass that wobbled when I walked, breasts that swung and enticed. I'd looked at more than one male, potential bedmate, and worried I might be too much.

But not for Arran. Never for Arran.

I was tall, he was taller. My breasts were wide, but his shoulders were broader. And while my powerful muscles were disguised by layers of soft flesh, his were on display for everyone to see.

Not everyone.

Me.

Mine.

"Mine," I said it aloud, savoring the sound of it. His beast growled in approval.

With his body bare before me, I leaned down and touched the tip of my tongue to the northernmost tip of his tattoo. He'd told me only the bare facts when I'd asked—how old he'd been when he received the Talisman, whether it had hurt. I knew the rest. That the terrestrials considered it an important rite of passage, to receive the Talisman—a tattoo that reflected whatever power the individual bore.

I didn't know what it meant to him, precisely. But from the story he'd told me in the water gardens, and the way his chest had trembled when I first saw that personal part of him... I could hazard some guesses.

Tonight, I wanted all of him.

So I dragged my tongue down the branch to the first split, then back up again. Then down, down, nearly to the trunk just above his belly button. I curled my tongue around the knot etched into the wood, then back up over his granite-hewn pectoral muscles to where the outermost branches reached.

I teased him again and again, each time I traveled down the trunk of the tree towards where the roots splayed across his navel, my tongue ventured a bit lower. But then always upward again. Until the time I got so low, his cock rubbed against my throat. I couldn't resist darting out my tongue to lick the top as if it were the most delicious thing I'd ever tasted.

"Fuccckkkkk," ripped from Arran's throat.

His hand in my hair became a demand, and then he was dragging me back up his body.

He didn't wait, didn't give me a chance to tease. One hand in my hair, tight enough to send sharp pinpricks of pain through my scalp. The other on my hip, centering me. Then he slammed me down and buried his cock inside of me.

It was fucking glorious, the massive length of him pounding up into me. I rode his cock like I'd ridden his face, grinding my clit into the dark curled hairs above the base until I was burning and climaxing, and a flood of my pleasure covered us and the bed around us.

My legs were shaking so hard, I could barely keep myself upright.

Arran noticed immediately that I was flagging, that the force of my orgasm had me trembling. In a breath, I was beneath him again. His strokes stretched out—longer, harder.

"Arran, Arran, Arran," I chanted his name like a prayer.

"Veyka, I can't..."

A hysterical laugh bubbled up in my chest. I managed to rally enough strength to grab his shoulders and drag him down to me, catching his mouth in a scorching kiss.

"Yes, you can," I murmured, sure I was grinning wickedly as I pressed our foreheads together. "Come, Arran."

He did, and the heated force of him spilling himself inside of me, thrust after thrust, giving me all that he had, pushed me there one last time as well. Until finally, my soul left my body and I was nothing more than thought and pleasure and bliss.

60

ARRAN

She came apart in waves, letting go of another piece of herself. For each new layer of her soul, I gave her something of me in return. So that by the time we were done, our bodies aching from release after release, I felt like a new being entirely. And curved against my side, drifting to sleep, Veyka shined like a beacon of holy light.

It was a trick of the light, I was sure. But her hair, always the color of moonlight, seemed to actually shine. Her skin, so pale and delicate, stretched over a warrior's body, was softer than velvet. I'd felt the weight of her in my arms, on my face, as I licked and fucked her to oblivion. But she'd turned strangely weightless, as if she might drift away on the breeze that snaked through from the veranda.

I pulled her closer, so her soft stomach molded around my muscular hip and her breasts pillowed out against my chest. I held her tight and told myself that I would never allow anyone to take her from me. Ever.

That thread I'd felt in the center of my chest, pulling me toward her again and again, had transformed into something new. Stronger. Tenuous, still, but more. More than I'd ever imagined was possible.

61

VEYKA

Warmth suffused every limb, right down to the tips of my toes and the rounds of my fingertips.

How can my toes be relaxed?

Hours upon hours of sexual satisfaction, climax after climax, followed by a dreamless sleep—that was how. When I woke, Arran was gone. But I was glad of it. We'd shared so much... almost too much.

Enough that we both needed to come up for air.

I tried reading the book Parys had given me. I was already more than halfway through the fictional epic—at least I hoped it was fiction, given how gruesome it was—set in the terrestrial kingdom before the Great War. While I'd been enjoying it earlier, I couldn't read more than a page before my mind drifted off. Setting the book aside for later, I called for a bath instead.

I settled into the lusciously warm water, letting the heat soothe my ever-cold hands, the scrapes from the day before barely stinging. The miracles of fae healing. Not a drop of magic in my veins, but at least I was still blessed with the most mundane features of my kind.

My eyes drifted closed as I listened to the soft movements around me. The crackle of flame as Charis lit a brazier to warm the towels for when I was done. A soft whistle—the teakettle in the bedroom heating the water for tea. Cyara's low voice as she issued directions to the other two. Slowly, the sounds faded away until only the soft bristle of a singular set of wings remained.

The scent of jasmine and sweetberry drifted over me at the same time that a steady warmth appeared at the head of the tub. I was ready when Cyara's fingertips touched my temples, skating over my scalp and gently massaging.

I leaned into her touch, a soft groan slipping from my lips. A slight pressure, then she dipped my head back to wet my hair.

"I have not seen you this relaxed."

Not in the months since Arran's arrival, nor during Arthur's brief reign before that. Never was the word that Cyara meant but didn't quite say.

Guilt quivered in my stomach, but I kept it small as I leaned into the stroke of Cyara's hands.

"Sex has a way of releasing one's tethers," I said flippantly.

Cyara's hands continued their steady massage. I heard the brief sound of a cap popping, then the sharper scent of the shampoo filled the air. "Is that why you kept Master Parys around?"

I flinched. Only from the sharpness of her nails, I told myself. Cyara eased her touch in response.

"Parys is my friend." It was the answer I'd given again and again, even when I hadn't meant it. *Friend* was a dangerous word. It implied caring and emotion I hadn't been able to express or endure. It meant I could be hurt.

Cyara continued to massage in the shampoo, reaching for the long strands that drifted away in the water. "I hope that you consider me a friend as well, Veyka," she said quietly.

My chest tightened.

I was so, so bad at this.

For most of my life, I'd been deprived of all company except those chosen by my mother. I'd never known which nursemaids actually cared for me, which ones would be complicit in her torture, and which were as twisted as she. When I emerged from my captivity, the only person I dared to trust was Arthur. His brutal murder had not improved my wariness.

But now...

"I consider myself lucky to count you as my friend," I said past the emotion in my throat. Maybe I could have a friend. I could stand the pain of it—of that inevitable goodbye.

I'd withstood much worse, I reminded myself.

"Friends help one another," Cyara's mild voice said.

"You are currently washing my hair," I said blandly.

Cyara flicked my ear. "I can help you."

Unease settled in my chest. "What do you mean?"

"You have tasked Parys with investigating the rifts. Allow me to do the same."

That seed of guilt sprang to life, loud and punishing. How she'd found out... there were enough opportunities, I supposed. I should have been better at hiding it. But I was so damned tired. When all the rage was stripped away, I was just... tired.

I scrubbed a hand up over my face. "Do Carly and Charis know as well?"

Cyara emitted a delicate, ladylike scoff. "You were not *that* obvious. Carly is too busy spending all of her spare time lusting after a mid-level water-wielder who's taken an interest in her, and Charis spends every extra minute strumming at her harp. She fills the silence with music and is careful not to listen past it."

Small mercies, I supposed.

But Cyara was not an acceptable loss. "You help me enough."

Those steady hands continued their work, lathering every tendril of my waist-length white hair. "A queen knows how to delegate, to use her resources."

A mirthless chuckle fell from my lips. "I thought you were my friend. Now you want me to treat you as a sentinel."

"I can be both."

"No."

"Your Majesty—"

"I will not risk it." I wished I sounded more like a queen and less like a petulant child.

But Cyara continued on smoothly, unfazed. "Let me go to my family. My father was a librarian in the palace, a century ago. I can question him without raising suspicions, see what he knows to assist Parys in his search."

A real offer of help. A real way to gain more information. To avenge Arthur.

I didn't wait for Cyara to nudge me down toward the water. I dunked myself, all the way under.

She didn't reach in to wash away the suds from my hair. I guessed that she knew I couldn't bear to be touched, just then. She understood so much. All these months of quiet observation... I should have been more careful.

Not because I did not trust her... but because she was inevitably putting herself in danger.

But hadn't she been doing that from the moment she became my handmaiden? I was always a risky bet. After Arthur died, with the attempts on my life... a horrific realization rolled through my gut.

Everyone who knew me, everyone who came close, was in danger.

Make it stop.

Just a bit longer.

I was getting close. I could feel it with whatever preternatural senses the fae had—I was very close to finding out who was truly responsible for Arthur's murder. Then I would leave. I would get far, far away from Baylaur and everyone within it. I would stop putting others at risk with my choices, with my deadly secret.

I would be free.

Once, it had beckoned so persistently, I could think of little else. But now, a thread in my chest pulled and pricked—straining at the thought of leaving this place.

My air was running out. I could hold my breath for a long time, but I'd been under long enough that my lungs were beginning to burn. When I crested the water, I had to have a response ready. A decision. A queen's decision.

I grabbed the sides of the tub to steady myself, water streaming down my face and into my mouth as I gulped for air. I relished the burn of it in my throat, my nostrils. It was nowhere near punishment enough for the words that left my lips.

"Go to your father," I said.

62

VEYKA

The waiting threatened to tear me apart. So, I tore through my Goldstones instead.

One by one, I challenged them in the training ring. I watched their bodies fall in the compacted red-orange dirt. Only Gawayn held himself apart, staring past my swaggering with his ever-aloof, ever-wise gray eyes.

Gwen was doing a decent job kicking my ass when Arran appeared.

"Don't think that pretty-faced prince will save you," Gwen said with a wicked upward thrust of her sword.

I spun out of range, tensing my muscles to parry her next strike.

"Did he teach you all your best moves? Or do you have any of your own?" I countered, snagging the dagger from my waist. It was clear from her fighting style that they'd spent many years—perhaps decades—training together.

Swipe, thrust, she was down.

But in one powerful movement, Gwen flexed the muscles in her back and leapt to stand.

"Now *that* is a trick I'd like to learn," I said slyly as I met her, steel to steel.

"How long have they been at it?" I heard Arran ask Lyrena.

"Fifteen minutes," she answered. "We've started placing wagers."

I *felt* Arran's dark chuckle.

"My gold's on—"

"We can hear you!" I hissed, just dodging Gwen's fist.

"Good. Maybe that will motivate Gwen to end it," Arran crooned.

He wanted a show.

Bastard.

I knew his dark eyes would be burning if I spared him a glance. But I didn't dare, not with Gwen on the other end of that vicious sword.

I clenched my teeth, summoning every bit of strength—

A swirl of white flashed in my periphery.

The blow came down hard enough to knock me off my feet, down to my knees, scraping in the unyielding red dirt.

I didn't expect an apology. And, of course, none came.

But a dark-skinned hand did reach out, hovering at the edge of my vision as I struggled to regain the breath Gwen had knocked out of me.

I slid my pale hand into Gwen's, letting her tug me to my feet. But I barely noted the half-smile of triumph on her face. My eyes caught on the figure standing behind her—that flash of white.

I was before Charis in a second. Her bare arms were covered with gooseflesh despite the warm evening, and her pale wings were trembling.

I felt Arran arrive at my shoulder as I asked, "What is it?"

Her lower lip trembled. "Cyara has not returned."

I ignored Arran's sharp inhale.

"She said she would be gone for the day," I said.

A jerky nod. "But she ought to have returned by now. She planned to be here to serve your dinner."

I glanced over my shoulder, finding Arran's expression closed.

"Is it possible she elected to stay the night with your parents?" I asked Charis, channeling that emotionless veneer I'd worn for months. It was the closest I could come to calm.

But Charis shook her head, lovely copper hair shaking as the trembling overtook her entire body. "She'd never leave you alone, Majesty."

Shit.

This was why I didn't have friends.

"Why didn't you tell me?" Arran demanded over the thundering of our footsteps. Down, down, down that spiral staircase.

"I haven't seen you," I bit back.

"And apparently all the palace messengers have gone missing, as well as your handmaiden."

"I don't report to you. I am not a common soldier under your command," I shot back.

The bickering was a distraction against the fear building in my chest. Maybe Arran knew that.

"So much for trust."

"No one ever told me the Brutal Prince was so damn whiney."

"Let's find your missing handmaiden and then I'll show you what it's like to—"

"Enough!" I ignored the tingle of lust in my spine. Ever-present, when Arran was around. "Her father used to be a palace librarian. She was only meant to talk to him, then return here. I would never have sent her into danger."

"I'm glad you deem *someone* worthy of your consideration. Even if you don't extend me the same courtesy."

I snarled over my shoulder before throwing myself flat on the ground to wriggle free of the tower.

Arran's beast growled right back.

I felt Arran blast the wards apart. I didn't need to remind him to seal them behind him. He was always careful, always in control. My opposite, in so many ways.

I ran through the trees, circling the base of the goldstone palace. Cyara would have gone out the servants' entrance. With her wings, she didn't need to worry about taking the wide route around the Gremog's territory. She'd be on a direct path from Baylaur.

I shouldn't have sent her.

"This is what it means to be a queen."

Whether his beast heard it on that unspoken frequency between us, or I'd said it aloud without thinking, it didn't change my answer.

"I never wanted to be queen."

Those words echoed in my head again and again. I was ready to scream them to the sky, to the world, to the Ancestors above and below.

But another scream wrenched from my gut instead.

She was nothing more than a heap of white and red.

The coppery tang of blood filled my head, making my senses swim. It was everywhere. In a pool around her, staining the simple white gown she wore, and on her wings.

"Ancestors," Arran breathed behind me.

Her beautiful wings...

Where they had been, there was nothing but a mass of bones and bloodied feathers sticking out at all angles. Whatever had attacked her—or whoever—had targeted them specifically. My stomach roiled, threatening to spill its contents.

But her shoulder quivered, and I forgot myself entirely.

I fell to my knees, gently skimming my hands over her body to check for more wounds. Gashes, scrapes, but nothing fatal. She was breathing, though unconscious. But her wings...

"They might not be able to heal them," Arran said.

I looked up at him through the tears in my eyes. It was a mistake. The expression on his face was hard. Experienced. He'd seen bloodshed like this before. Of course, he had. He was a commander. He'd led legions of terrestrial shifters into battle. He'd surely seen wings in worse shape than this. The realization of just how much brutality he'd witnessed over the past three hundred years turned my stomach anew.

"We have to get her back to the palace," I yelped.

I began shifting my position to carry her myself, but Arran nudged me aside.

Better, some still functioning corner of my brain said. Faster, for him to carry her and me to lead the way. We couldn't go up the spiral staircase, couldn't shove her beneath that narrow entrance. But we could take the door hidden in the ivy.

I led the way back, having to restrain myself from running. Arran couldn't run with Cyara in his arms, he'd risk jostling her and injuring her further.

It took forever, that painful walk back in silence. There was nothing to say. I didn't dare ask for reassurance, and Arran wouldn't offer any platitudes. There was at least that much respect between us.

The wall of ivy appeared and I felt my knees tremble beneath me in relief. A few more minutes, and she'd be safe within the palace. I'd give her my own bed, call for the best healers. Anything, everything, to save her—

"What the hell?"

I froze, my hand already on the door. I started to spin, knife in hand, ready to meet whatever new threat—

But there was nothing. Just me and Arran, Cyara unconscious in his arms.

And my hand was on the door.

He hadn't opened the wards.

He knew that I hadn't either.

No. No, no, no, no. This could not be happening. Not now, not with—

Arran stared at me blankly, his confusion written all over his achingly handsome face. "How?"

I swallowed hard, but let the words come. "The wards do not recognize me. They never have." I was able to move in and out of the goldstone palace without dismantling the wards, because they didn't even detect my presence.

It was a twisted joke, that the very reason I'd been locked away was the key to my ability to sneak in and out undetected.

"But surely, after your brother—"

"The wards are keyed to power." I took one last sharp breath before finally breaking loose that piece of my soul. "And I have none."

I'd been so careful. Whenever I came in or out of the palace with Arran, I let him break apart the wards, or I was far enough ahead he assumed I'd opened and closed them myself.

I watched the understanding ripple through him. His body stiffened, fists contracting into tight balls and feet shifting into a defensive stance. Readying for battle, even with Cyara's battered body in his arms. Understandable, given the extent of my treachery, though unnecessary. But his face... something inside me died as the openness that had grown between us shuttered, the trust gone in an instant.

"You... you are human," Arran said carefully, a sharp, guarded mask covering his face, betraying nothing.

"No. The wards detect humans, even before what happened to Arthur," I clarified, hating every word.

He did a magnificent job of masking his emotions, but I detected the slight widening of his eyes as he said, "You are a fae without power."

Slowly I exhaled that breath I had been holding.

"The one and only."

He was shaking his head. Slowly, then faster, then stopping entirely as he remembered the burden in his arms. "How... how can that be?"

I swallowed hard, revealing the final piece of the puzzle. "Why do you think my mother kept me locked in the water gardens?"

"You didn't tell me." The final nail in my coffin. "You lied to me."

My throat was closing. My heart, barely pieced back together, was burning away to ash. My weapons, still in place from sparring in the ring a lifetime ago, were so heavy I almost couldn't stand.

But then Cyara shifted slightly, a terrible moan falling from her lips.

"We have to get her to the healers," I said in a voice that belonged to someone else, because I was certain I no longer had the ability to speak.

I turned for the door, wrenching it open and not letting myself look back. "Don't forget to seal the wards behind you."

63

ARRAN

Queen of Secrets.

It would have been better if she'd died, ripped to shreds by the skoupuma. It would have spared me from having to keep this secret. A queen without power. No such thing had ever existed.

The Ancestors had accounted for everything in their blasted treaty. Everything except this.

No one would trust her. No one would follow her.

She'd be torn limb from limb. Killed in the middle of the night, sleeping helplessly in her grand bed, in her grand apartments.

A court—a kingdom—a blasted realm where power was more important than anything. The only currency that mattered. And Veyka had none.

I could have lived with it, maybe.

There'd been weak kings and queens on the throne of Annwyn before. I had enough power for the both of us, to protect the kingdom.

But she'd lied. Not just to me—to everyone.

Every breath she took was a lie.

They would punish her for it.

Arthur would not be the last to die.

The traitors within this court would wrest power from her, then make her watch as they systematically killed everyone she cared about. Parys. Cyara. Gawayn. If I'd marked the affection she tried so hard to keep hidden, so had others.

Footsteps.

The shift was instantaneous, not even a thought. Wholly outside of my control

The snarling growl gave way to a howl that turned into a roar.

Running.

Run, run, as fast as you can.

Run away from the Brutal Prince.

Recognize me for the beast that I am.

Be afraid.

Fear would be the only thing to keep her safe. Fear of the unknown. Of secrets and lies.

I didn't shift back. I didn't know if I could. The beast held sway. He looked around the room, the lavish apartments fit for a king. I'd never wanted the crown. I'd hated my power from such a young age. My power had ripped me from my family and my home. My power had made friendships impossible, connections impossible, isolating me until I was nothing more than a weapon honed for battle and bloodshed.

But I would do it. I would sit on that cursed throne, for the good of the kingdom and family I'd left behind, for the good of Annwyn.

For a brief moment, I'd thought Veyka would sit beside me. Truly. Not as a figurehead, but as my Queen. My partner. My equal.

How wrong I had been. Not a Princess of Peace, but a Queen of Lies.

I'd been right to hate her. I hated her still.

I hated everything she stood for—her selfishness, above all. Not a care for her kingdom, for the families in Baylaur and beyond who depended upon her. All Veyka wanted was revenge and to save her own hide. A selfish princess, and nothing more.

And she'd made me complicit. I would have no choice, now, but to keep her secret. To guard it, to maintain the fragile peace between our two kingdoms. Another burden, laid at my feet, because I was powerful—because I, above all others, could handle it.

Fuck that.

I tore apart the sofa. Then the bed. I ripped through the vines I'd created days before, my massive, beastly body shattering the clay pots that held them until the floor was covered in the wreckage.

More footsteps—these ones almost feline.

I paused in my destruction, the growl starting low in my throat. Growing, growing, until it vibrated through the entire room.

But she nudged the door open anyway.

She stood there and surveyed the destruction, her golden eyes heavy. There were worry lines around her eyes and mouth. She looked tired, despite the perfectly polished gleam of her Goldstones uniform.

I allowed her the grace of one minute to look at me, to take the measure of the situation, and to get the hell out.

But Guinevere thought she knew what was best for everyone. She always had.

I snarled in warning. The only one she would get.

She stepped into the room and closed the door behind her.

Time's up.

I lunged for her, my powerful haunches launching me across the room while my jaw hung open, fangs eager to tear into something meatier.

My jaws closed not around a delicate, deep brown neck, but a thick black mane. Wickedly curved feline claws dug into my skin, flipping me to the ground.

Our beasts battled, snarling and scratching in a blur even my fae-honed beastly eyes could not make out. What was left of the room shattered beneath the swing of paws, the lashing of powerful tails. Gwen's lion threw back her head and roared; my beast bellowed in response.

We tore at each other until there was not a single unbroken piece of furniture. Until the walls dripped with blood and gore, our fur matted with it.

When unconsciousness came, I welcomed it.

64
VEYKA

The room was small. So small—smaller than the cell I'd called home for twenty years. How had I not realized it before? I'd lain in the bed for weeks, while Cyara slept in mine, awaiting an assassin whose origin was still unknown.

It was unforgivable, that I'd ever been willing to trade her life for mine.

She lay on that narrow bed, her body unmoving. Her beautiful, shining white wings were shredded away to nothing but delicate, light bones.

Broken bones.

So many of them—broken, splintered.

Because of me.

Make it stop.

The healers came. Magically gifted elementals who could use delicate wind to set bones. Highly trained terrestrials who could coax the healing power from medicinal plants. But it was slow. Brutal.

Eventually, there was nothing to do but wait and watch. To stare at the carnage my quest for revenge had wrought. Carly and Charis couldn't stay and watch, their tears and worry too heavy. Which left me, sitting in a hard chair at the bedside.

Knowing that every tremor of pain, every low moan, every fracture was my fault.

This is what it means to be a queen.

I didn't want it. I'd never wanted it. All I'd ever wanted, my entire life, was freedom. But I'd gone from one cage to another. From the torture of the water gardens, to the agony of watching those I cared about suffer for my sake. First Arthur. Now Cyara.

It was only a matter of time before the rest were taken as well.

Like everything was taken from me.

I was being clawed apart, piece by piece. I could feel the invisible hands touching me, pulling me down, down, down into the abyss. I thought I'd escaped. But that had been a lie too.

Lies. Secrets.

They swirled around me.

Queen of Secrets.

This is what it means to be a queen.

I'd always known the price. Me—I was the price. My soul. My lack of magic. My secret would doom my throne, my kingdom, thrust us into another war. The Ancestors had planned for everything. But they hadn't planned for me.

One night fell. Then another. Then I stopped seeing the daylight, stopped looking for it.

I looked into the night instead, letting the darkness into my soul, where hollow emptiness had always lingered. Let the darkness take me, let it dull the pains and the edges of emotions too strong, too much.

Make it stop.

But even the darkest night has stars.

Pinpricks of light.

Parys, curls unkempt, familiar body pressed against mine from hip to shoulder.

Lyrena, curling flame from her fingertips to light the darkness.

Gwen, a creature made for darkness and loyalty.

Even Gawayn, steady and true as always.

The darkness tried to consume me. But this time, I looked up and saw the stars.

65
VEYKA

There is a difference in moans.

Moans for when pleasure rolls through you. One for when that pleasure comes at your own hands, and a second when there's an audience to hear it.

Moans that border on groans to express annoyance or disapproval.

Moans of pain.

We moan for help from the Ancestors or whatever higher beings the humans and priestesses pray to. Deep, guttural cries as the blood tears from our bodies and the soul demands its own outlet as well.

Then there are the moans you only make when you're alone. The expression of agony that is for no one but yourself—when you're certain the higher beings have deserted you.

I heard all of those moans of pain from Cyara's mouth in the days I sat by her bedside.

I thought I'd heard them all.

And yet, when she shifted on the bed and let out a low moan, I realized I was wrong. Because this one told me that she was finally awake.

I fell to my knees at the bedside, my fingers curling around the bedsheet tight enough to tear. "Don't move! I'll send for the healers."

"Veyka? I beg your pardon—Your Majesty—"

"You *must* hold still, you'll tear—"

"Wha—ouch!"

I'd pinched her arm cruelly. But it got her to hold still. "You must stay on your stomach. Your wings are healing, but the damage was..." I bit hard on my lip to still the trembling.

Ancestors. How I missed the cold emptiness of indifference.

Cyara slowly turned her head to peer over her shoulder. Her copper brow, turned darker by the low light in the small room, furrowed as she tried and failed to see the extent of the damage.

"It's probably better that you can't see," I said bluntly. I'd never been much good at soft, comforting words.

Cyara swallowed, a wobbly smile rising to her mouth. "What a tender nursemaid you are, Majesty."

"If you wanted flowery words, you ought to have been nicer to Parys." I flicked my eyes toward the door. "He's been here, by the way. Lyrena, Gwen, Gawayn, as well. And your sisters, of course."

They'd come for me as much as Cyara, I suspected—to try to keep me from jumping off the edge where I'd teetered for so many months.

Arran hadn't come, and I couldn't blame him for it. Even if the organ in my chest ached at the knowledge. He'd surely realized what I'd known all along.

I was better off dead—for the good of Annwyn.

She rolled her eyes, the motion in her shoulders as well. She flinched at the pain, the wounds that were just now knitting together, even after all these days. "Blood makes Charis retch. And Carly has always been overly-sensitive where her wings were concerned. I apologize that they left the tending to you, Your Majesty."

"I think you've more than earned the right to address me as

Veyka," I said, my chest tight. "And they couldn't have pried me from your side."

"Did you see your attacker?" I hated to ask, fragile as she was, even though I expected the answer.

She shook her head slowly, eyes clouding over. "I was knocked down, then I remember the pain," she paused, gulping. "Then nothing."

I reached out and took her hand in mind, squeezing gently.

Cyara smiled softly, appreciation in her eyes. It seemed like such a small, insignificant thing to offer her after what had happened. I forced myself to hold her gaze, even when the shame bade me to turn away. I let her have that piece of me—my friend.

So, I saw the shift in her eyes before she said, "We must speak."

About the rifts.

I sucked in a breath, easing myself back up into the chair that had been my bed for the last several days. My backside ached, the narrow wooden chair made for my delicate handmaidens and not my wide hips. But I'd take that and more, if I could spare Cyara the pain written on her face as she shifted to prop herself up on her elbows.

"I spoke with my father—"

"Hold a moment," I said, forcing myself to my feet. My muscles ached from disuse. The cavity in my chest ached more. "I am not the only one who needs to hear. Would you like tea? I will bring you some tea. Rest." The words tumbled out of me, awkward and unsure.

I'd never taken care of anyone. First, there'd been no one but me and my captors. After that, I had thoroughly isolated myself as a means of self-preservation.

"Tea would be nice," Cyara said mildly, settling back onto the pillow.

I opened the door to my bedroom, finding it empty. No surprise there. Charis and Carly had taken up residence elsewhere in the goldstone palace, worried about disturbing Cyara. They checked on their sister every hour or so. But I knew that at least one of my

Goldstones would be lurking in the antechamber, close enough to hear if I so much as squeaked. Surely, they heard me coming.

Which was why I was surprised to find the antechamber lacking a single gleaming goldstone badge. But that didn't mean there was no guard.

⁂

I should have felt awkward. Or angry. Sad, at the tentative bridge between us that had shattered.

But when I looked at Arran's dark face, closed off from me completely, I just felt tired.

It's almost over.

Then I would be gone. Then my secret would not matter. That fragile thing that had existed between us... its destruction was as inevitable as the revenge that I would exact.

"Where are the others?" I heard myself say, exhaustion lining my words.

"Gawayn and Gwen are stationed in the corridor. Parys is in the library. Your handmaidens have not returned," Arran said, voice devoid of all emotion.

I'd felt the brunt of his hate and his lust. But this was worse.

He looked at me as if he didn't care if I lived or died. It was no more than I deserved.

But was it?

Didn't I deserve to keep my secrets? After everything that had been done to me, all that I'd survived... didn't I deserve to share the layers of myself in my own damn time?

This is what it means to be a queen.

To have no secrets. To put the wellbeing of the kingdom before my own.

That was exactly what I was doing—had been doing all along. If anyone knew that the queen—the queen no one had wanted to begin with—lacked even the tiniest drop of magic, it would tear Annwyn apart.

I was doing the kingdoms of the fae a damned favor. Hunting down the traitor in our midst and then promptly faking my own death. It was the only real option. As a martyr, I might be useful. As a powerless queen, I was a destabilizing threat.

But none of that was why I hadn't told Arran my secret.

He'd given me all of his, and I'd held back.

Arran, who stared at me with a face entirely closed off. A face I'd learned to read over these past months, now slammed closed. Now looking at me as if I'd grown a second head.

"Do you have something to report?"

I tilted my chin upward, letting my eyes fill with challenge. My hands slid down to my waist, hooking casually around my daggers. Arran fingered his axe. This was how we'd begun. It was only fitting to descend back here once again.

"Cyara has awoken."

His hand stilled. "I will send for her sisters." His shoulders eased slightly—glad the conversation was over so quickly. He wasn't as indifferent as he'd like to seem.

"Not yet."

He paused, tightening instantaneously.

"We must speak with her privately before Charis and Carly come."

Arran's eyes went to the closed doors to the corridor, where Gawayn and Gwen no doubt heard every word of our conversation.

Without a word to me, he turned and strode through the antechamber into the bedroom, aiming for the door I'd left ajar and Cyara waiting beyond. As I followed, I realized—he hadn't been there in that close little room while I stood watch over Cyara.

But he hadn't been far.

66

ARRAN

"My father is eight hundred and ninety-seven years old," Cyara said, positioned carefully on her forearms.

I didn't glance at her wings, what remained of them. I'd seen enough battlefield wounds, inflicted plenty of them myself, to know better than to look at the gore when you didn't have to. No matter how hardened you were, it chipped away at something inside.

This was a battle, I'd realized as blood seeped from my veins, matting my white fur and staining the lush rugs of my suite. Arthur had been the first casualty. Everything since then had been tactical movements from different regiments and legions on the field. The Royal Council, the Shadows smuggling humans, Veyka herself. Long and drawn out, but bloody and devastating, nonetheless.

The delicate handmaiden had been a willing foot soldier deployed by her queen. Now she'd make her report.

"He served Uther and Igraine Pendragon for most of his life. But he was originally granted the position by the previous High King and Queen."

Veyka's grandmother, I dredged up from history lessons I'd definitely slept through. I didn't glance her way, either.

But she shifted in her seat, a too-small chair that creaked under her weight. Her scent drifted over me, primrose and plum flooding my senses and waking my slumbering beast.

"What does he know about the rifts?" Veyka asked.

"More than he wanted to tell me," Cyara huffed. "My father is a learned male. Not much in this world can shake him. But when he spoke of the rifts..." A shiver snaked through her shoulders. I watched her face tense as it no doubt moved through her back and the damaged wings.

I waited for Veyka to say something to ease her fear or pain. But the female at my side was silent.

"He encountered mentions of them in his early years. His role as a librarian was to look after the tomes, but also to aid anyone who might come to the library. Therefore, he must be knowledgeable about its contents," Cyara continued.

A soft, forced chuckle. "The library must have gotten more use in centuries past," Veyka said.

Cyara's smile was barely there; the merest acknowledgement of an attempt at levity where none belonged. "Someone came to the library, a courtier. He asked about the rifts and asked my father to compile every book that mentioned them. My father left him with a stack of books and went home. When he returned the next morning, there'd been a fire. An entire row of shelves had been destroyed, including where the courtier had been working. The books were destroyed."

A sharp, unsteady inhale. "But Parys found references to the rifts in the library." Veyka's voice was steady, but a note too high. I wondered if Cyara noticed it as well.

Cyara swallowed hard. "My father's memory... he is very old," she paused, looking down at her hands. "He gathered as much as he could. But it was near to the end of his tenure, and he acknowledged that he may have missed some."

"The ones that Parys found," Veyka said quietly.

The small, close room lapsed into silence. I could not let myself look at Veyka, though I was sure that sharp and cunning mind was running through all the possibilities. Still, I couldn't hold my tongue while I waited for her.

"Who was the courtier?" I asked.

Pain clouded the handmaiden's face. I recognized that pain—not the specifics, but the shape of it. Damage to the soul, rather than to the body. "He does not remember."

Veyka's eyes cut to mine, her hand reaching—stilling, hovering over my knee.

She stopped her hand just short of making the entreaty, but she did let it show in her eyes. A plea, to not pry any further.

A powerful fae could live a thousand years. To have reached nearly nine hundred, Cyara's father must have been quite blessed. But sometimes, the mind did not endure as well as the body.

Veyka needn't have tried to stop me.

I understood Cyara's pain all too well—a mind taken by forces beyond one's control.

Those clear blue eyes, turned nearly sapphire in the low light, considered me closely. I'd avoided looking at her, but she seemed bound by no such compunction. She studied every inch of my face, and whether she found it wanting or not, I didn't know. Only that she turned back to Cyara and folded her hand safely back in her own lap.

"This is not a coincidence," Veyka said grimly. "Though I do not understand precisely how it all fits together. I must speak with Parys."

I didn't want to agree, but I also couldn't argue with her logic.

"I have sent word to your mother and father," Veyka continued. "Two palace guards have gone to help them pack and escort them back to the palace. Your father served this kingdom with honor; he should enjoy the comforts the goldstone palace has to offer for the time that remains to him. No more travelling into Baylaur for you, not until you're well enough. And no more dwelling in this ghastly little room. I'm arranging for apartments one floor down for you and your family."

"Your Majesty," Cyara breathed. "This is inappropriate. Your courtiers—"

"—will bend to my will or find themselves broken," she said with finality. "Rest, my friend. Later, I'll have your sisters help you to your new quarters as well."

Her hand hovered uncertainly over the female's shoulder, then dropped to her forearm instead. A gentle squeeze.

"Rest." An order.

An order from a queen to her sentinel.

67
VEYKA

Cyara moved to her new apartments. Arran disappeared, leaving me with my Goldstones. He'd insisted on guarding my door himself until Gwen had become one of my protectors. Apparently, he trusted her to guard me, even if he didn't believe I was capable of doing so myself.

I went to sleep.

Not that endless, bottomless sleep that I'd used to hide from reality in the months after Arthur's death. But actual restoration. I'd been at Cyara's bedside for days, and as the door closed behind me, I realized how bone tired I was.

My consciousness bid me go to the library, seek out Parys and tell him what Cyara had found. But my body demanded rest, and I was in the bed before I could think too hard on it.

When I awoke, morning had broken. Carly and Charis were there to help me dress, and if they were extra attentive, I was also murmuring more thanks than I ever had before. I emerged from my bedroom, set on my destination and ready for whomever was on duty to fall in at my shoulders.

Of course, Arran was there instead.

How was he always there? Did he have some sort of otherworldly terrestrial sense that alerted him to when I was awake?

I didn't know what to say to him. We'd barely exchanged a sentence as we spoke to Cyara. By the dark expression on his handsome but unforgiving face, I doubted he was in the mood to talk.

Fine. Neither was I.

"I am going to the library," I said to no one in particular.

Let them squabble about who would guard me. I didn't care. I swept through the doors and down the corridor. I hated that I recognized instantly that it was Arran's footsteps that followed me.

I opened my mouth. Then closed it.

I didn't have anything to say to him, I reminded myself. Nothing that I wanted to apologize for. I'd lied to protect myself and to protect Annwyn. If Arran couldn't understand that, then I'd misjudged him from the beginning, and it was for the best that the tentative understanding between us had been sundered early on, before it grew into something more dangerous.

Neither of us spoke as we descended into the goldstone palace, into that cavernous entrance chamber with the two strange statues standing sentinel on either side of the library doors. I paused long enough in the doorway to see if Arran would follow me. But he was already going to stand beside one of the statues, arms crossed over his broad chest, glare firmly in place.

Fine.

It was all fine.

I didn't need him to talk to Parys anyway.

68

ARRAN

For someone I hated, I was having a damn hard time staying away from her.

That string in the center of my chest pulled, a silent demand, and my feet were walking to her apartments. Whatever instinct that was, it proved true as always. Veyka appeared a few minutes later, every curve of her delectable body on display and determination in her blue eyes. It had taken no more than a look to pin her Goldstones to their posts at her door, rather than following us to the library.

When we arrived, Veyka disappeared behind the massive doors without a backward glance.

I stood beside the unnerving statues, trying not to look at them, trying not to think. Breathing was an effort these days.

Maybe that pull in my chest was a reminder from the Ancestors. While I may hate Veyka, resent her for her lies, our futures were inextricably linked.

Things were changed between us. But the world around us, the threats within the elemental court, to Annwyn—those persisted. We still needed to find out who had ordered Arthur's death and eliminate the threat. We needed to find out how the rifts—known and unknown—fit into that plot. Whether they fit in at all, or were a waste of time.

We were being watched now, I had no doubt. It was unspoken between us, but the weight impossible to miss. Cyara's attack had not been random. It had been a contrived attempt to eliminate the handmaiden and whatever knowledge she carried.

I started ticking through the members of the Royal Council, the likeliest suspects, as I had a hundred times now. Esa, power hungry and willing to start a war to hold on to it. Teo, a possible conspirator, but also hedging his bets. Elora and Roksana... both wildcards, for their own reasons. Elora was young and impetuous. Roksana the opposite, ancient and wise and skilled in political maneuvering. Both were equally dangerous. The only one I didn't have a real sense of was Noros, the fox-faced councilor who sat beside Esa, but thus far hadn't shown himself as an ally one way or the other.

Then, of course, there was the Dowager. Igraine Pendragon.

Veyka had mentioned her brother sealing her mother in her wing, but I'd seen the Dowager at a distance walking through the court. Whatever magic Arthur had used, it must have faded with his death.

Veyka had not listed her mother as a possible suspect in her brother's death. But after hearing about the water gardens, about the torture Igraine had overseen... I did not think murdering her son was beyond the realm of possibility.

I couldn't broach it with Veyka, though. Not yet. I'd planned to, but then...

It didn't matter.

I squared my shoulders and settled into the space, standing guard as I'd done thousands of times in my three hundred years. I let the weight of my feet anchor me to the ground, let my eyes close to slits so I could inventory my other senses. Not closed entirely. That was an unforgiveable weakness. But enough that I could hear and smell and feel.

Which was how I sensed the footsteps, long before even the most sharp-eared fae would have heard them.

I was poised and ready to face whoever rounded the corner, to send them on their way with a snarl. But it was not a faceless courtier who rounded the corner.

It was the Dowager.

I'd seen her before. It was unavoidable. But in the filtered light of that cavernous room before the library, it felt like the first time I'd truly *seen* her. Her hair was a pale blonde that some described as platinum. At first glance, some might think it a match for Veyka's. But where gold teased the edges of Igraine's long plait, Veyka's was pure moonlight.

Where Veyka's body was soft curves covering powerful muscle, the Dowager was slender to the point of waifish, as if a strong elemental wind could send her toppling. If not, of course, for the defiant tilt of her chin as she looked me over.

"Step aside, Prince," she ordered.

"The library is occupied." It took every bit of control, mastery of my magic and my beast, to keep me from tearing her bodily limb from limb. This was the female who'd hurt Veyka. Who'd held her prisoner. Allowed her—nay, commanded—her to be violated beyond what any person, let alone child, should ever endure.

I knew without Veyka telling me that this female was the reason Veyka's steps were silent, even when no one was listening. She was the reason Veyka trained so hard with the blades and always wore them strapped to her body, no matter how mundane the courtly task. Arthur had meant so much to her, because of the shared childhood the Dowager had stolen from them.

Her defiant chin lifted. She'd come alone, assured of her power. Alone, so that none might witness whatever cruelty she planned to inflict upon her daughter.

"Let me pass. I wish to speak with my daughter."

"The queen is not to be disturbed."

She lifted her hand, a tendril of water curling between her fingers. She watched it with a half-smile, before splaying her fingers wide and sending it spraying into a fine mist. Then she folded her hands before her and met my gaze once more.

A petty little display, to remind me that she was a powerful elemental. Dangerously powerful, more powerful than her husband had been, Veyka had told me.

I snarled at her, and there was nothing of the male I was in it. Only the beast.

"You think your power is a match for mine," she said with a cruel, cunning smile. "I saw what you did to the water gardens. Very impressive, Prince. But why did she take you there in the first place, I wonder?"

She knew. She knew about the carvings behind the waterfall. She knew we'd gone to look at them.

It ought to have been impossible... but then, how careful had we really been? Someone could have easily seen us as we entered the courtyard. And reported it back to the Dowager.

Dangerous, still desperate for control. Veyka had been right about that.

I didn't reach for my weapons—didn't need to. Only a fool would think that the steel blades were the most dangerous weapon in my arsenal. The Dowager High Queen of Annwyn thought a lot of herself and her own powers—enough to underestimate me.

Her mistake.

"Touch her, speak to her, breathe in her direction—and I will hold you down while she shreds the skin from your body slice by slice."

Igraine opened her cruel mouth to respond, but then suddenly stilled.

I watched the confusion spread over her face, the horror of realization. I drank it in like the finest wine in the realm.

She tried to jerk away. My vines tightened around her calves, rooting her to the ground.

The nearest courtyard was on the next level. But she'd forgotten about the windows, the curling ivy that I'd ordered Osheen to bolster along the palace walls, for just such a moment as this. So that my flora-gifted soldiers might have the powerful, mighty plant to command.

"Bold, to try to kill me now," the Dowager bit out, that sharp chin still high in defiance.

I laughed. Let the dark, mirthless sound fill the cavernous chamber, let it echo off the walls as the vine tightened around her throat. Fear flashed in her eyes—a pale, watery blue that had nothing of Veyka in them.

"That honor belongs to the Queen," I growled, letting my beast a little looser from his tether. "I will enjoy watching her exact her revenge. By then, I will have schooled her in all the ways a brutal prince can inflict pain."

Her chin dropped a fraction of an inch.

I wouldn't break her now, though the temptation was real. This creature, who had punished Veyka for her very existence, did not deserve to live. It would be easy to bend her, break her, until she was begging for mercy. I could see it all there in those shallow blue eyes, a shadow of the bright, powerful ones I'd come to regard so highly. Power the Dowager might have; but power was not the same as strength.

From somewhere deep inside of me, perhaps where my beast's instincts held sway, a warning sounded.

I tightened the vines, one last look of warning, a snarl from my beast. Then I eased them away.

The Dowager's eyes flared, as if she didn't quite believe it. Then hardened, considering. Part of me wanted her to try it. Let her lash out with her power, try to drown me where I stood. I'd enjoy punishing her.

"Go," I said. Command, warning, promise—all wrapped into one.

Her eyes flashed. But in a swish of silvery skirts, she was gone. Nothing more than receding footsteps caught in a dying echo to mark that she'd ever been there at all.

They faded away to almost nothing when the massive library doors opened.

"Are you speaking with someone?" Veyka's brow furrowed, eyes darting around the chamber and finding nothing, no one.

"No." I stared straight ahead, not letting myself get caught in the bright blue eyes, the curious tilt of her mouth.

I didn't see it, but I could picture the way her eyes shuttered, her lips thinning to a line. Ancestors help me, I could imagine the wobble of her breasts as she crossed her arms beneath them or squared her shoulders in challenge. My cock and my beast grumbled their opinions; I shoved them down mercilessly.

"Fine. I am done here."

She strode past me without a backward glance. Knowing, as well as I did, that despite what had happened between us, I'd follow her anywhere.

69
VEYKA

Time was going too fast, progress too slow.

Parys combed through the library, researching the rifts and how to access them. I spent hours dawdling at his side, wandering the aisles of books, while Arran stood silent guard outside the massive wooden doors. I chatted up the grouchy librarians, attempting to glean who might frequent the library, if anyone else had been interested in the same books as Parys. To no avail. Grumpier bastards, I'd never met. My own betrothed included.

I sparred with Lyrena and Gwen. I visited Cyara as she healed, meeting her parents and instantly understanding how three such sweet, loyal handmaidens had come into existence. Arran and I attended Royal Council meetings, dissecting each word spoken in terse exchanges afterward.

We were stuck.

My current, most appealing idea for how to break the tension was to cut down the entire Royal Council and start fresh. Let Arran start fresh.

Of course, I also had a plethora of less reliable, wilder, and arguably reckless ideas swirling around in my mind.

His dark gaze hadn't softened. The tightness in my chest hadn't eased.

My entire world was at an impasse, yet still the festival of Mabon crept closer, and with it, our Joining.

I was sifting through my list of reckless possibilities as I strode from another Royal Council meeting to my bedroom. To find it occupied.

"Why does there always seem to be someone lurking in my bedroom, uninvited?" I drawled, crossing my arms.

Lyrena stilled, her golden braid swaying as her body froze in place, halfway to the fire burning in the hearth, hands extended. The flame that seconds before had flowed from her fingers sputtered out.

"Your Majesty," she said, broad smile in place, quick as a whip.

She straightened, her eyes flicking to the hearth—burning brightly—before turning to me with her hands casually on her hips and that gregarious smile growing with each second.

"What are you doing, Lyrena?" I asked, settling my own hands on my hips—sans smile.

"I'm tending to the hearth," Lyrena said brightly.

I blinked in confusion. "I told Cyara to let it die."

"There's no need for that, Majesty. It is little effort, little dent to my magic," she countered. She shifted her weight forward, as if she would return to her post outside my chambers, where I'd passed Gwen a few minutes before.

"I am so sick of this Ancestors-damned fire. It's hotter than the suns out there," I tossed my hand in the direction of the open veranda. "I've told Cyara a hundred times as she rubs her damn wrists, this stupid fire is not worth the cost."

"There's no cost—"

"Lyrena! Let it die!"

"It cannot die," Cyara said from the doorway.

I spun, my eyes raking over her as I noted every detail. The perfectly draped white gown, the neatly braided copper hair, and the lovely wings rising gracefully above her shoulders. The feathers were smaller than they had been, less full, but the promise of healing was there to see.

As she stepped further into her room, her movements were unmarked by pain. An explosion of gratitude burst in my chest.

Ancestors, be thanked.

But that didn't stop my terse words. "And why is that?"

"Arthur ordered it," Cyara said steadily, holding my gaze.

I blinked. I must have misheard her. "Arthur?"

"When you emerged from the water gardens. He ordered that the hearth here always burn," Cyara explained.

I still struggled to understand. "Why?"

Cyara's shoulders tensed as if she might shrug, but then thought better of it with her still-healing wings. "It is charmed. A protective fire, to guard you while you are in this room."

I laughed, a borderline hysterical sound. "Goldstones at my door day and night, my own blades never out of reach, wards on the palace walls, airborne terrestrials circling my courtyard. It's a miracle I can take a breath without someone marking it."

"You can't," said Cyara and Lyrena in unison.

Oh, fuck me.

They knew so much more than they'd ever let on. All these months I'd imagined myself working in secret, playing this cunning elemental game, and they'd known all along. At least, some part of it. And Arthur, he'd snuck around behind my back and charmed my damn fireplace. It was all a sick fucking joke.

I threw my hands up in the air and cursed filthily.

The doors behind me sprung open again. This time, a soft feline growl filled the room.

Gwen looked from Lyrena to Cyara, then back to me. Her queenly face revealed nothing, though her hand lingered on her sword belt. "I heard raised voices."

I scrubbed my hand over my face. "It's nothing."

One black eyebrow rose.

They were going to drive me to distraction, one by one. "Well, since all of you are here already, we might as well summon the others. Someone fetch Arran and Parys and let's get on with it."

※

"Why am I here?" Gwen said carefully.

"Because Arran will tell you everything anyway, or try to avoid telling you, which will make you mad until you beat it out of him. This is the easier way." I sat on the chaise in my antechamber, arms crossed over my chest, annoyance flaring in every muscle.

Gwen and Lyrena stood on either side of the doors, standing guard. Where Gawayn was, I didn't really care. So long as he wasn't outside the door, listening. I didn't doubt his loyalty, not for a second. But it felt wrong to involve him in my intrigue, when he spent every waking breath worrying about whether I was going to get myself killed. Ancestors, he probably had nightmares about it, too. It was a mercy, then, that he wasn't here to hear the foolishness I was about to propose.

But the rest of them were—because I needed their help.

Parys was sprawled on the sofa across from me, looking thoroughly put out. Cyara had found him not in the library, but on a veranda with a dozen other courtiers sipping wine. I shuddered to know what sort of nasty rumors he'd heard while sitting there, schmoozing the vapid creatures that populated my court.

Cyara lingered near the window, eyes on the valley and mountains beyond. I wondered if she missed flying. I doubted her wings, newly healed as they were, would hold even her slight weight.

None of them sat at the round table, perpetually mocking me on the other side of the room.

Arran wore the darkest expression of them all. He was all darkness. Black pants, deep green tunic buttoned across his chest, ending at his shoulder. The terrestrial style, still, after all these months. A black tunic underneath, the thin linen open at his chest to reveal a triangle of muscle I wanted to run my tongue over.

His black hair was pulled back into a knot at the base of his neck, as always, silken strands gleaming. It had been too long since I'd had him inside of me. But I doubted he had any interest in coming to my bed these days. Sure, the lust was still there. His eyes were always burning when I was around.

But what had started as hate fucking had turned into something more, something I'd killed when he learned I'd been lying to him all these months.

Enough bemoaning my own sexual frustration. I had them here, and I had a limited amount of time.

I stilled my fingers, which had been toying with the diaphanous sleeve of my gown, and sat up on the edge of the chaise.

"You all know, to some degree, what I've spent these last months doing."

Five stares, of varying degrees of emotion, varying shades of guarded appraisal.

"Humans may have swung the blade, but someone within this court was responsible for Arthur's murder. Someone who has not been brought to justice."

Cyara's eyes flicked back out the window. Gwen's jaw clenched.

Lyrena's eyes widened, then began blinking rapidly, holding tears at bay. She'd avoided talking about Arthur, not letting that grief anywhere near her, because of those tears, I realized. I'd thought her joyous personality too bright to be dimmed, even by the loss of her lover. How wrong I'd been, about so many things.

"They used a rift in the mountains—an unknown, unmarked rift—to smuggle the humans into Annwyn. Either on their own, or with the help of the Shadows, the black-market runners in Baylaur. Parys has torn the library apart researching the rifts, but someone has removed most mentions of them from the library, years ago. Whatever this is, whoever is behind it, they've planned carefully. And they know I am onto them—they attacked Cyara already."

Silence, as each of them fit the information I'd shared in with what they'd gleaned themselves in their various capacities. It was a huge leap, a huge risk, to bring so many into my quest for revenge.

They might get hurt. They might betray me, wittingly or by accident. But I was out of time and options.

"You didn't mention the darkness in the human lands. The... possession... we witnessed," Arran said, eyes dark and unreadable.

Possession. Not quite the right word for that dark, lifeless mutilation we'd twice seen. But better than nothing.

"We don't have time to worry about the problems in the human realm," I said sharply. I'd decided that much for myself during these last few weeks. "If that darkness truly spills over to Annwyn... it will be dealt with then." *By you,* I didn't add.

Because by then, I would be gone.

This wasn't the time to think about that, either.

"I have considered the possibilities. But we need to know who is behind this, before someone else gets hurt. They've tried to kill me. They've attacked Cyara." I gulped down a deep breath, hoping it would give me the courage to keep my voice steady. "They didn't want Arthur as High King, and I doubt they will let me be enthroned as High Queen. Mabon is near. Time is short." Another deep breath. "It is time to seek out a witch."

Arran blinked. "A witch? Are you out of your mind? It is banned."

"With good reason," Parys put in.

"Horribly tricky creatures," Lyrena agreed.

I sighed heavily. "Yes, but a witch could answer these questions."

Silence. Utter silence.

They all knew what I meant.

Witches had been banished from Annwyn by the Ancestors, when the original treaty was made to finally bring peace after millennia of endless war between the elemental and terrestrial kingdoms. The Ancestors felt they had too much power, their boundless knowledge giving too much advantage to one kingdom or even one individual.

But there were two places the witches remained—if the legends were to be believed. Held captive, really, should the fae ever decide they were truly needed.

One was said to be confined deep within the mountains of the Spine, in a cave that no fae living had ever seen or visited.

The other was in the Tower of Myda.

I could see it from my balcony.

"I got this idea while reading that book you gave me," I said, cocking an eyebrow and summoning the sly grin Parys wore so well. He didn't return it, his face draining of color.

"Three questions," Parys finally said. "A witch could answer three questions, if you have her at your mercy."

Lyrena choked on her disbelief. "The particulars do not matter. We cannot actually be considering this."

I looked to Arran. He was silent.

An omen—but of what, I was not sure.

I bit my lower lip, staring into the fathomless depths of his black eyes. I tried to speak to his beast, to appeal to the feral part of him that had called to me long before the male.

Please. If you support this, they will go along with it. They will think it a worthy idea, rather than the plea of a desperate young queen.

Arran's brows softened, just slightly. The broken shell of my heart fused a bit more.

"We will have to get the questions just right," he said.

I could feel the eyes of our companions upon us. But I could not sever the connection, not until I let him see the answer in my own eyes. *Thank you.*

Arran blinked again, then turned to the others.

"Short of killing our way through the elemental court one by one until we find the traitors, this is the only way."

Parys swore under his breath. "The witch will be well defended. I'll give up on the rifts, for now, and see what I can find about what we might face in there."

We. My heart thudded. A painful, unfamiliar motion in my chest.

Cyara spoke for the first time, drumming her fingers on the windowsill. "We must craft the questions very carefully. Practice them on one another, so that we might see if there are any loopholes. If the wording is wrong, the witch might answer the question but still leave you without the information you truly seek."

I blinked up at her in surprise. So did everyone else.

Cyara merely shrugged, her wings—those beautiful, delicate, *healed* wings—fluttering softly. "My father was a librarian. I like to read."

Lyrena laughed softly. Gwen and Arran exchanged a look I couldn't read, but when they turned to face me, there was no argument in their eyes. Only steady acceptance.

I let out a long, measured exhale at the group assembled around me.

My friends.

"Let's begin."

70
ARRAN

The second terrestrial delegation arrived. The third, I realized as I watched from an unoccupied veranda, marking the faces of those who stalked across the tenuous line of safety through the Gremog's territory.

The first had come to negotiate the details of Arthur and Guinevere's Offering. The second was my own. Now the third, nearly the size of the one that had traveled with me, all come to celebrate the Joining and angle for positions in our soon-to-be-formed court.

If Veyka had been thinking about the Joining, beyond what it meant for finding Arthur's killer, she hadn't let on. I wasn't privy to her wicked smiles anymore.

Maybe I didn't deserve to be.

I was angry, and justifiably so, I'd decided. She'd lied, when she could have trusted me. I could have protected her better, if I'd known. I would have kept her secret, for the good of Annwyn.

But that was why she'd kept it a secret all along. For the good of Annwyn.

In a world in which power was everything—used to bend others to your will, to maim and punish—weak powers could be hidden, stored up and expended in quick shows of force. Powerful magic caused as many problems as it solved; I knew that better than anyone. But to have no magic at all... it would mark her forever. It would cause ripples of shock throughout Annwyn, even into the human realm. It would make her a target for the rest of her immortal life.

After everything that she'd been through, everything Annwyn had been through with the sudden loss of its king, she'd known that her secret could mean the end of peace. It could mean death and destruction. War.

She should have known I would keep her secret, for the good of Annwyn.

And maybe that was why she hadn't told me. Because I wouldn't keep the secret for her sake, but for the good of the kingdom. And that made me unworthy of knowing it at all.

But I couldn't explain that to her. I could hardly reckon with it myself. At least, for now.

For now, we needed to avenge Arthur. Get through the Joining, and then we would have the next thousand years to sort through the rest.

After hours of discussion, we'd agreed on the three questions for the witch. We'd discussed the plan for taking the Tower of Myda, prepared with the scant information Parys had found about it in the library. Tomorrow night, under the cover of darkness, we would make our move.

Until then, we would go through the motions of court life as if nothing were amiss.

So, I stood at Veyka's side as we waited in the same chamber she'd dragged me into after the Offering. Where we'd lingered before meeting the petitioners and the human who would die that horrific death, blackness eating him from the inside out.

Veyka didn't bother with a smile as she accepted my arm to enter the throne room and join the feast welcoming the terrestrial delegation.

She was beautiful, mesmerizing as only she could be. She'd chosen a deep forest green that the elementals would roll their eyes at, and the terrestrials would take as a nod of respect. For once, most of her luscious body was covered, the only skin on display the square neckline and a sharp triangle cutout on each hip, just above the jeweled belt that held her scabbards and knives. But this garment was not one of the flowy, voluminous gowns she favored. There were no layers of fabric to sway with her curves.

Only a perfectly cut column on fabric so thin, I could see the shadow between her legs and the points of her breasts. It looked as if it had been sewn right onto her body. How else would Cyara and the others have gotten it on her? Magic, perhaps.

And damn well worth whatever cost was demanded in exchange, I decided. She was the vision of every wet dream I'd ever had. My cock strained in my tight leggings, demanding that I worship those curves.

She'd implied more than once how unfavorably her mother looked upon her fulsome body, how out-of-fashion her rounded, generous curves were. But this ensemble was meant to be a battle cry. Let anyone look upon her and dare to deem her less than magnificent. I'd cut them down myself.

A thin circlet of diamonds and amorite sparkled at her brow, a nod to the crown she'd wear in mere days.

I led her into the throne room and watched with satisfaction as every being in the cavernous, open-air space took a deep, collective inhale.

Every elemental sank into a bow. Even the terrestrials inclined their heads. If I'd had the gift of wind, I'd have sent a whipping gale to remind them to kneel. One look to Parys—and I watched the surprise flicker on the delegation's faces. Then bend.

Veyka's arm tightened on mine. She'd been terrified of this sort of reverence when Gwen had gifted her the round table. But when I glanced over, her face showed none of that fear.

The gentle tilt of her chin, inclining her head in acknowledgement, was as regal a movement as any I'd ever seen from Guinevere. Something like pride surged through me. After everything... a queen did indeed stand at my side.

Veyka's chin returned to its usual station, and the throne room dissolved into discussion and dining once more, the moment over. I could feel lingering eyes upon us, but I didn't seek them out just yet.

"Aural," Veyka squeaked, already tugging me toward the foundation in the middle of the room.

I escorted her down the dais, around the tables that had been brought in for the feast, crowded with courtiers and guests. I dipped one goblet in the fountain, passed it to her, filled my own, and then let her guide me back toward the edge of the room.

I sipped the golden liquid, its flavor reminding me of how it had tasted on her tongue the night of Lugnasa. My eyes slid to hers, wondering if I'd see the memory stamped here as well.

But Veyka's eyes were wide with shock, her mouth falling open.

Her eyes darted across the room, horror blooming on her face.

I watched in confusion as she marked Parys, seated on the other side of the aural fountain, facing the dais. Her eyes found Gawayn, positioned near a pillar a few yards away from us. Then Lyrena, at the rear of the dais, watching the collection of royal councilors seated in a neat line.

I moved closer to her, every protective instinct in my body waking. "What is it?"

"It's exactly the same," she rasped, her fingers clutching the aural in her hand so tightly I could practically see her bones beneath the taut skin.

"The same as what?"

"The night Arthur died."

I followed the path her gaze had taken moments before. I hadn't been there that night, but I'd heard reports. Detailed ones, from the terrestrials who'd been in attendance at that feast. Realization formed in my gut, a black, burning flame that would only be extinguished by bloodshed.

I only needed to know who to kill.

Whoever it was, they'd done this on purpose, to unhinge her. Maybe the Dowager had a hand in it. It didn't matter, not now.

Whoever had done it would play this evening out without revealing themselves. But Veyka could not crumble, not now. Not with the Tower of Myda looming over us.

I leaned in close, until my lips were a breath away from her ear.

"We will kill them," I promised her. "By the time the sun rises in two days, we will have our answer. It will be over."

A shaky exhale.

I scraped my canines over the pointed tip of her ear.

Her inhale was sharper still, her teeth sinking into her lush lower lip.

"I promise you. They will pay." A vow. Truer than the one I'd made at the Offering. I felt this one in every corner of my consciousness.

Her eyes softened, drifting closed. I stepped in front of her, so no one would see the way her lips trembled as she drew in a ragged breath. But when she opened her eyes again, the blue was clear, her brow set.

She nodded, echoing back my words with such vicious conviction, a chill snaked down my spine. "They will pay."

71
VEYKA

Arran's hand at the base of my spine was a constant, steady presence throughout the feast. I sipped that one goblet of aural all night, letting it slowly ease the pressure in my veins. Oblivion beckoned, an escape I needed more than ever. But not now, not so close to our assault on the Tower of Myda.

That was what it would be, I'd realized as we planned. Each level was guarded by a different horror. That was as much as Parys had been able to find in the few days allotted to him. If we'd had more time, we might have discovered what at least some of those horrors were. But the terrestrial delegation was here, Mabon was days off and the Joining with it. There was no more time to wait.

And yet, the feast dragged on and on. Until I was staring at the bottom of my goblet, grieving the lack of aural. No more than a droplet remained. A dreg, really. Still, I tipped my head back and tried to coax it into my mouth.

"I think we've stayed long enough," Arran's voice said against the shell of my ear. Sending shivers down my spine, as I recalled the scrape of his canines there hours before.

I didn't glance around to see if plates were cleared or if anyone planned on making a toast. If Arran, the prince of propriety and duty, deemed we'd met our quota for useless interactions with even more useless courtiers, I was not going to question him.

We walked back to my apartments in silence, Gawayn and Lyrena's steady presence trailing us. I didn't have any words. Too many had already been spoken. More were caught in my throat. The need to thank Arran for staying at my side, steadfast for the hours when I otherwise might have drowned. The desire to rage at him, for not understanding why I'd kept my secret. Some twisted part of me wanted to demand that he confess his feelings for me, whether it be hatred or admiration or lust.

Lust.

That was the one thing that had always been clear between us.

Tonight, on the precipice of a new world... I could cling to that.

I could let it fill me up. Let him fill me up.

One last time.

We were at my door. Gawayn and Lyrena followed us into the antechamber, ready to take up their posts on either side of the door outside of my bedroom. Gwen was not on guard tonight, which meant that Arran would stay. Even after all this time, she was the only one he trusted to guard me while I slept. He pulled his hand away, the heat of it tattooed on the small of my back.

I was powerless to let him go.

He took a half step toward the chaise. I caught his hand.

I caught his eyes.

Stay.

I was floating.

Weightless, the cool night air kissing my skin. The cold season was coming. In a few months, the tips of the peaks ringing the Effren Valley would be capped with snow. But already, the alternating kisses and nips were persistent.

It wasn't the cold air, I realized as another quiver of pleasure seized my body. It was Arran's mouth, the wet trail he left across my body, that caught the breeze, shivering and shimmering. Those nips were not the cold, but his canines against my skin, teasing at the barrier.

My scabbards were on the ground, my gown with them. There was nothing between his mouth and my skin but his hot breath as it skittered and sent gooseflesh rising.

How could I be so hot, so cold, so completely undone by one male?

Arran lifted his mouth to mine, kissing me slowly, thoroughly. He caught my lower lip and pressed down hard enough that my flesh yielded, so little pinpricks of my blood filled our mouths. Then he feasted on that blood, his tongue picking up speed, darting into the recesses of my mouth to taste every drop of it.

He was a male crazed.

Tasting my blood had done something to him. Those long, languorous touches of the past half hour were replaced by a desperate frenzy.

Good.

Take it, I urged him with the lift of my hips.

Take me, I begged as I hooked a leg around his waist to draw him closer.

Let us be joined, this one last time.

"Veyka," he moaned, the head of his cock nudging at my pussy.

I ground my hips against him, desperate to hear it again. "Tell me," I said, taking control.

He tried to shove his hips forward, tried to work his head past that initial resistance, to where my walls would tighten around him. But I wouldn't let him, denied him that final push. I relished the feeling of his cock stroking up and down my slit, pausing so the head could tease my clit again and again. A delicious torture that I wanted to burn into my memory forever, to erase everything bad that had ever happened to me.

These were the moments I would remember, exiled in a foreign land. Not the pain and the loss. But this male and what he'd given me. The way he'd made my body feel, and how he'd made that sick, dead organ in my chest quiver to life once more.

"Veyka, please," Arran rasped, his nails digging into my shoulders.

I scented the blood—my own blood. Suddenly, I was as desperate as he was.

If I'd been born a terrestrial, I'd have thought a beast of my own was awakening inside of me. I raked my fingers down his back, drawing blood as I went.

Arran roared against me, half male, half beast. But then my fingers were closing around his tightly muscled ass, shoving him forward as I lifted my hips and finally welcomed him inside of me.

Every inch of that magnificent length tore me apart, sundered my sanity. I lifted one hand to my mouth and sucked the fingertips between my lips, savoring the thick, coppery taste of his blood on my tongue.

Then my orgasm was upon me, my climax driven by the brutality of his thrusts, the stars above our heads, the taste of his lifeblood as it slid down my throat. I heard the deep growl building in Arran's chest. He was close, too.

I held on, not knowing what else to do. I clung to his shoulders, my tongue licking over the tracks I'd raked through his deep golden skin. I fucked him as hard as he fucked me, until we both came in an explosion of sound and sensation.

Arran collapsed on top of me, his head resting on the arm of the lounge chair.

I couldn't open my eyes to look at the stars above us, because I knew I'd mark their progress across the sky and count the hours. I pressed them closed instead, savoring the heat and weight of his body where it pressed into mine, relishing the way his cum leaked out around his cock, still buried inside of me, mingling with my own wetness and sliding down my thighs.

I would never find this again.

Whatever *this* was.

But I could walk away. I *would* walk away—because there was nothing else I could safely do. Not for myself, not for my kingdom. And ultimately, not for Arran. He deserved a queen who would be his equal, not a danger at his back.

Arran shifted slightly, and I couldn't help the cry of displeasure from my lips. I wanted to stay in the moment, forever. His fingers skimmed over my arm, and I half expected him to slide them down into my pussy, to coax another climax from me.

But instead, he slid something onto my finger.

My eyes popped open, down to where his hand now hovered just over mine.

A band of braided silver circled my fourth finger. I'd seen the ring before—he wore it on his pinky, on formal occasions. The Offering, the feast tonight. But now, it lay on mine.

I knew I ought to give it back. Just like I knew that Arran would keep Annwyn safe, even when I was gone.

I had no right to wear it, knowing I would be gone so soon.

But I couldn't take it off. Couldn't stop looking at it. Couldn't stop myself from leaning forward and kissing him. Kissing him until our bodies began to awaken once more, the need for each other persistent, steady, a promise of a future that would never come.

It was damn selfish, but I kept that ring on my finger, the metal still warmed by his skin. As he kissed me, I prayed.

I prayed to the Ancestors that Arran would understand.

All of it was for Annwyn. For him. For the future.

Even if I could not be a part of it.

72
ARRAN

The screams began just after midnight.

I thought it was a dream. A nightmare conjured from one of the all too real battlefields I'd fought on over the last three hundred years. But when my eyes sprung open, I was not on a bedroll in the dirt. A soft, warm body was curled at my side, leg draped over my hip, hair scattered across my chest.

The screams were not echoes in my memory.

Veyka knew it too, rolling away from me and coming to stand on the other side of the bed, daggers already in hand.

"What is it?" she asked through the darkness.

The hearth had gone down to embers, no more than a tiny, flickering flame.

Veyka's eyes went to the small, waning flame as well, some kind of realization playing across her face. "They let the fire go out," she said softly, momentarily transfixed.

Another scream rent the air, this time from outside, beyond the balcony. Her eyes snapped back to mine. I was already pulling on my trousers. Her gown was in shreds on the floor from earlier in the night. I tossed her my shirt.

She buckled her scabbards over it, already halfway to the door, swinging on the harness that held her curved blades across her back. My axe was ready; my sword as well.

We paused inside the doors, exchanging a singular look.

"Don't bother telling me to stay," she growled, tossing her loose hair over her shoulder and out of the way.

"I wouldn't dream of it," I said. I let myself take one last look at her. She had not a shred of magic to defend herself with. But she had her blades, and she'd proven more than once that she knew what to do with them. "Try not to get yourself killed."

She flashed that wicked grin I loved so much. "Likewise."

Then she kicked open the door.

73
VEYKA

It was a massacre.

We got through the doors, only to find the antechamber deserted. Eerily quiet, in contrast to the screams echoing around us. Our sensitive fae hearing only made it worse. I could hear the sounds of blades sliding in and out of flesh. The groans of the dying were worse.

I glanced to Arran, but he was completely unfazed. He'd lived his life on a battlefield. While this was my first true test.

I would not fail.

The next doors were harder to open. Gwen, Gawayn, and Lyrena stood, holding the line. Blocking me in.

They caught one glimpse of Arran and stepped out of the way. Just long enough to let him through before closing ranks again. Over their shoulders, I watched him shift, then disappear down the corridor, his beast leaping over the hallway already filled with bloodied bodies.

I strained to see the wounded, to identify them, but Gwen was already pressing the doors closed.

"Let me out!" I demanded.

"Your Majesty," Lyrena appeared at Gwen's shoulder. "You must stay inside—"

I drew my daggers, spinning the left one in my hand once. I cut them both a look, summoning every drop of regal command in my Pendragon blood.

"Let me pass, or I will cut you down where you stand," I said steadily.

Gawayn was there, the Captain of my Goldstones, my most faithful protector. And his face was truly, actually, pained. Not from a physical wound, but from what I asked. But I didn't back down.

"We have vowed to protect you," he said, entreaty in every word.

I'd anticipated them. I jerked my head to the side. "Then fight at my side. Guard my flank. Make them pay for every life taken."

He looked at my knives.

I didn't know if I could beat him.

Lyrena, yes. Gwen... yes, but it would take too long. But Gawayn had never stepped into the sparring ring with me, and maybe this was why. Because he'd feared this test of skill, and what knowing its outcome would do to the two of us.

But he held my gaze and then bowed his head.

I lifted my knives and tilted my head down the hall. "Let's make them bleed."

Who were we making bleed?

We'd fought our way across two courtyards, and I hardly knew. Elementals and terrestrials both alike were cut down. But the enemy was made of elementals and terrestrials as well. Most often, the only differentiating factor was who was still in their bedclothes.

My Goldstones recognized more of the faces than I did.

With each swipe of my blade, I realized how greatly I'd failed my kingdom. When Lyrena had to shout to me which of the pair of dueling fae spinning tendrils of water at each other was a member of my court, I knew. I'd thought of my courtiers as conniving, vapid, and shallow.

They were all of those things.

But they were my subjects first. And I ought to have known their faces at least well enough to protect them. To not waste precious seconds glancing to my Goldstones for confirmation as I interceded in duel after duel.

Magic swirled around me, used as often as blades. For every blast of fire, there was an answering wind shoving it away. An Ancestors-damned lightning strike came down in one of the courtyards and struck three dead. I didn't wait to see who'd summoned it before continuing the fight.

If my Goldstones noted my lack of magic, my complete reliance on my blades, they said nothing. There was no time, anyway. We were alone only for the brief seconds when we ran between courtyards, where most of the fighting was happening.

I hadn't seen Arran since he left my side. At some point, Gwen shifted into her dark lioness. Lyrena's fire burned at my back, lighting the night. Gawayn's wind pulled the air from his victim's lungs and knocked them from their feet.

And still, we fought on.

Endlessly.

That was what I was not prepared for—the driving relentlessness of battle. Killing was no chore. I relished the dying gasps, the spurts of blood as it drained from my opponents. But on and on it went. Longer than any training session in the courtyard. Longer even than the abuse I'd endured in the water gardens.

My muscles strained, but every face I recognized drove me on. For Annwyn. For Arthur. For the goodness he'd dreamt of, but been cut down before he could see. I couldn't be the queen he'd have wanted, but I could protect our kingdom. I could keep going.

I dodged a plume of fire spearing for my back, the dagger an extension of my arm as I whipped it out, sending it straight into the male's chest. He roared, fire wreathing his hands for a second attack. But I was there with my curved rapier, the wickedly sharp blade cutting through sinew and bone with startling ease. I didn't see his head hit the ground. I was already searching for my next target.

But through the fray, I recognized where we were.

Horror and fear and a thousand unthinkable emotions ripped through me.

I cleared the yards to their door. Slice. Behead. Thrust. Kill.

Then I was standing at the door, my Goldstones at my back. It was already open.

"Veyka," Lyrena warned, her voice low. She was at my shoulder, Gwen and Gawayn watching the courtyard should anyone try to follow us. But I was fixed on what was ahead—on what was inside.

The sprawling set of apartments I'd given to my handmaidens and their parents were in total disarray. Walls were singed—all three of them possessed fire magic. My heart gripped; they'd battled here. Chairs overturned, shards of pottery and glass covered the floor.

I forced myself to keep walking. "Cyara? Charis?" I stepped over a dark-skinned body. "Carly?"

The rest of the apartment was the same—worse, maybe, because for each room I passed through, I saw only more wreckage and no evidence of my friends' survival.

Finally, I saw it. The door to the bathing room was closed. The only one in the entire suite. Two heavily burned fae bodies lay before it, weapons nothing more than melted metal around their hands.

"Cyara! Charis! Are you there?" I cried desperately, pounding on the door.

For a second, nothing. My heart was ready to break.

Then it cracked open, a flash of copper hair and turquoise eyes.

Relief poured through me as the door swung open fully. I drank them in, counting bodies. Cyara, Carly, and Charis, my three stalwart handmaidens, standing in a line before their parents, who'd taken refuge against the back wall in the small room. Not powerless, but old. Too old for this sort of fight.

I looked closer at the three sisters. Their white gowns were singed in places, torn and hanging off of them in others. But there was no defeat in their eyes.

"You've done well, finding yourself a defensible position," I said, looking at each of them in turn.

Only Cyara managed to smirk back. "I've learned some things, all these months tending to you."

I smiled, because she clearly had. But that did not make her a warrior, and it would not save them if they were truly overwhelmed by the intruders.

"Stay here," I ordered. "I will guard your door. No one will get through," I promised, praying to the Ancestors that my tired muscles would make good on that promise.

I closed the door firmly, kicking the two charred bodies in front of it as a makeshift barrier. Then I strode back through the destroyed rooms, to where they opened on the chaos of the courtyard, still raging in bloodshed beyond.

I turned to Lyrena and Gwen, bastions of day and night, warriors. Friends. "Go."

Lyrena opened her mouth to argue; Gwen growled, flashing those deadly lioness fangs.

"I will not leave," I promised. "I will stand guard here until..." I forced my voice to steady. "Until it is over."

More attempts to argue. I shot a look at my captain. "Gawayn will stay to guard me. But I will not leave them defenseless. Nor can I have three guards standing watch over me while my kingdom is bleeding. Go. Defend Annwyn."

Lyrena still wanted to argue. But Gwen's deep, gold eyes were different. They were warm. Lined with approval. She lifted her massive, powerful maw to the ceiling and roared. When she turned on her haunches and leapt back towards the battle, Lyrena was at her side.

I huffed a breath of relief. Gawayn was already closing the exterior apartment doors behind them. I grabbed an overturned armchair and started dragging it towards the doors.

"We should block each set of doors with as much debris as we can, to slow anyone who tries to break in—"

"There is no need, Your Majesty."

"Wha—" The kiss of steel at my throat kept me from turning, my body realizing what was happening even as my mind grappled in disbelief.

"I am sorry, Majesty. But your reign ends now."

74

ARRAN

As I ripped out throats, I took the measure of the attackers.

A powerful elemental whose blood tasted like the wind. A terrestrial who shifted into a leopard and tried to run away at the sight of me. His flesh was particularly sweet between my jaws.

The force they'd assembled was a mix of elemental and terrestrial, some skilled with blades, some skilled with magic. They'd attacked the court while they slept. How had they snuck in without raising the alarm?

The same way the humans had the night of Arthur's murder, my animal instincts told me. Whoever had plotted his murder had orchestrated this massacre as well.

I passed more than one palace guard, battling valiantly. The invading force hadn't dispatched them through poison, which had been my first thought. The secret entrances... that was possible. Likely, even. Veyka had shown me two. Did she know of more? Even if she didn't, it wasn't far-fetched that there might be others she didn't know about.

The elemental courtiers fought, on and on as the hours dragged towards dawn. I recognized the faces of the terrestrial delegation, fighting at their sides.

The goldstone palace would not fall. Not today.

I didn't see Veyka or her Goldstones, but some instinct buried deep inside of my beast growled that I'd know if some grievous injury befell her. So, I fought on, tearing through courtyard after courtyard. With every kill, I expanded my sense of the battle.

I fought across one courtyard, then took a flight of stairs in a single bound before leaping on the shoulders of an attacking water-wielder. Instinct alone told me who was friend and who was foe. After three hundred years on the battlefield, I knew better than to question those instincts.

The attackers were being beaten back. Slowly, but steadily.

They were disorganized, no sort of rank that I could discern as my eyes scanned while my beast tore out throats. They didn't seem focused on advancing toward a particular place. They weren't even trying to take the palace, I realized as I bounded through the deserted entry hall where Esa had greeted me on my first day in Baylaur.

Which meant this attack had another purpose.

A distraction.

Veyka.

I never should have left her alone. A fool's mistake, to trust her guards. We could not trust anyone. Perhaps not even those in the little cadre we'd assembled. The very ones I'd trusted to guard her and keep her safe while I killed my way across the goldstone palace.

I had to get to her. I didn't pray to the Ancestors; not after three hundred years of being ignored. But I sent out entreaties to whatever beings might exist in this realm or the human realm, begging them that Gwen was still at her side, still keeping her from harm.

Finding her in this melee would be hell. Where would she have gone? Who would she have chosen to defend in a court of treachery and lies? But even as my mind tried to scramble, my beast caught her scent on the wind.

Four powerful legs churned beneath me.

Hold on, Veyka.

EMBERLY ASH

I'm coming.

75

VEYKA

Did I deserve this?

When the blade touched my throat, the sharp edge pressed against my jugular with only a thin veneer of my pale skin to stop it, that was the first thought that sprung to my mind.

The next was shock. Deep, plummeting through my heart and stomach to the depths of my soul, as I realized who held the blade to my throat.

"Gawayn," I heard myself croak. "What is this?"

"This is for the good of Annwyn," he said, and he sounded so tired as he did. An exhaustion I'd read in his face so many times since I'd become queen. Ancestors, I'd actually felt guilty for all the worry I'd caused him. But this?

"You truly mean to kill me? Who will rule in my place, Esa?" I threw it out there, my only coherent thought. That he must have been working with the traitor hiding on my council.

"None of the royal councilors are fit to rule. I knew that the day you surrendered control to them," he said. Gently, he nudged my shoulder. Too gently, for someone who held a sword to my throat. "Come, stand. I would not have you die on your knees like a criminal."

My eyes darted around the room frantically as I released the chair I'd still been stupidly holding onto and got to my feet. There were two more sets of doors separating us from Cyara and the others. Not that I wanted them to try to come to my aid. No, I'd rather they stayed safe.

It would be easy, I realized, to let him kill me. I'd never planned to stay, to rule over Annwyn. I hadn't avenged Arthur, but I knew that Arran would. I'd set him on the path, I'd made him see that revenge and protecting the realm were inextricably linked.

It would be so easy, to let that blade slice across my throat and end the agony I'd lived with for months. Years, really.

But it was only with the blade pressed to my throat that I realized the truth.

I wanted to live.

For the first time in months, I wanted to live. Not just for the sake of avenging Arthur, but for myself.

My eyes darted around the room with renewed purpose, searching for anything I could use to my advantage. I was armed, my knives in the scabbards at my waist, but I couldn't reach for them. Gawayn would slit my throat the second my fingers twitched that direction.

I had to distract him, buy myself precious time to think.

"Then who, Gawayn? Arthur is dead. Did you have a hand in that as well?" I couldn't control the words coming out of my mouth, didn't bother to try.

"Never," he hissed. He threw an arm around my chest, pinning my back against his chest and pressing that blade ever tighter against my throat.

"But you'd kill me? His sister, his twin? So that some distant, unknown Pendragon cousin can sit the throne in my stead?"

"I wanted it to be you, Veyka," Gawayn said, voice softening. Through the doors, in the corner of my vision, I saw a flash of movement. My gut twisted horribly.

No, no, no. I couldn't let this happen.

"I hoped that you would step up and fill the gap left by Arthur. I hoped you might become half the ruler he might have been. For months, I watched you waste away, content to do nothing but fuck and eat and fight. But then the Brutal Prince arrived, and I thought that maybe, just maybe, you would fulfill the promise of your Pendragon name." A heavy sigh. A tightening of the blade. No more movement from my periphery.

"But you've proven again and again that you only care about yourself, Veyka. Sneaking out of the palace. Cavorting with Arran Earthborn. Pouring wine at Royal Council meetings as if you're not the Ancestors-damned Queen of the Elemental Fae."

The same judgments that Arran had made about me. But Arran had drawn me up from the darkness, walking at my side as I found something to live for. While Gawayn was ready to kill me for it.

But it didn't quite fit. "You sacrificed all of these courtiers, elementals and terrestrials alike, just so you could kill me? Where's the nobility in that?"

For a second, Gawayn's face was pained. "I didn't want this. I would have killed you in your sleep, if your prince ever left you unguarded. I made a deal." He jerked his chin back toward the sounds of battle, still waging wildly behind us. "This was the cost, and I will pay it. For Annwyn."

Someone had helped him. Whoever had killed my brother, who'd tried to kill me... they'd seen in Gawayn what I'd been too naïve to realize. It wasn't worry that turned his hair gray, it was guilt at what he'd been plotting.

A plan formed in my mind, the steps like an intricate combination of movements in the training ring. But I had to try one last time. To beg.

"Please," I breathed. "Please, Gawayn. You're right, I was so very selfish. But everything I've done these past few months has been for Annwyn. For Arthur, I—"

"Enough!" The blade pressed into my flesh hard enough that it should have drawn blood. I cringed at the pain, the realization that there was nothing more I could do—nothing except fight.

"I won't let you try to charm me, like you've done the other Goldstones and your handmaidens—"

Fire burst through the door, throwing them open. Three plumes of it, glowing and bright. Cyara, Charis, and Carly.

I spared half a second for a silent prayer of thanks that their parents had not tried to come to my aid as well. They must be safely back in the bathing room.

I'd scold my friends later. If we survived.

Because that was Gawayn's warm wind, meeting the flames, creating a wall of hot air around himself as a shield. Their first shots had landed. Burn marks marred his chest, shoulder, and upper thigh.

I hit the ground hard, my knees screaming at the impact even as I used them to roll away, clear of the flames and the sword still gripped in Gawayn's hand. I swung upward, daggers in hand.

"Get back," I yelled over my shoulder, edging into that space where flames met wind.

"No," they said simply, in unison.

My heart cracked.

"This is between us," I said to Gawayn instead, edging closer. I could feel the heat of the sisters' flames. The near-invisible hairs on my arms started to burn away.

"If they will not stand down, then so be it," Gawayn said. He sent a pulse of magic, pushing their flames back farther.

I could see Charis beginning to flag. She was the weakest of them, her magic limited. Carly would last longer, then it would be Cyara alone. But she was still healing, still weakened from the attack on her wings.

Wings.

Cyara could not fly yet, but the other two could.

I lunged to the side, out of the way of the flames. "Charis, to me!" I commanded.

Gawayn sighed heavily but didn't move, didn't pull back his magic. "Enough games, Veyka. It is only a matter of time before I wear them down. If you truly wish to spare them, then give yourself up."

Charis paused, but did as I said, peeling away from her sisters and edging to my side. I couldn't whisper. It would be of no use. We were all too close, our hearing too sharp for secrets in this small space.

But as I made a show of sheathing one of my knives and drawing the curved blade from my back instead, I dragged my hand purposefully along the outside edge of Charis' white feathers. Her eyes widened, and I knew she understood.

She looked to her sisters, and I knew she'd convey the message. They may not be twins or triplets, but I'd seen the unspoken language between them. Recognized it for the same connection Arthur and I had once shared. It felt like a final gift from my brother that the sacred tie between siblings would be what saved me once again.

I waited for Charis' eyes to return to me. A half breath to steady myself, then I dipped my chin.

Charis and Carly shot into the air, and I sprang forward on silent footsteps, praying the distraction would give me an opening.

But Gawayn was faster, more powerful than I'd ever imagined.

He shoved me back, a gust of wind whipping my legs out from under me even as another held Cyara's flames at bay.

It was the fact that she could not fly that saved Cyara.

That spared her, as Gawayn's brutal wind snapped her sister's wings and brought them crashing down in front of him. Two swipes of his massive sword, easy, unbothered swings that were almost casual.

And they were gone.

Their heads severed from their bodies.

Cyara's flame disappeared as the cry ripped from her throat. The same gut-wrenching sound I'd heard from my own lips when Arthur died. I remembered that moment. It had been Gawayn who pulled me to safety, who protected me when I'd been helpless.

But I wasn't helpless anymore. I'd never truly been, I realized as I flung myself through the air.

No strength, no magic in the world could have stopped me then, as I sank my dagger into his chest. The surprise in his gray eyes was lost to the darkness as death stalked nearer. I hooked that curved blade around his throat, ready to rake it across. To steal his lifeblood, as he'd been ready to steal mine.

But I was thrown back, my body careening over the lifeless bodies of my two felled friends, the force of it and the cracking of bones disgusting and wrenching.

I tensed the muscles in my abdomen, springing back up to my feet in the fluid, powerful motion Gwen had taught me. Her dark laughter as she'd watched me struggle, while we practiced again and again, was the power that fueled me through that next moment.

I gnashed my teeth, ready to go again, attack again.

But there was nothing to attack.

Where Gawayn had been, a huge white wolf stood.

A wolf I'd seen in my dreams. That had haunted my footsteps, ran at my side as I battled the demons and darkness inside of me.

Too large. Impossibly huge, twice the size of the animal it emulated, at least. Curved fangs that dripped blood onto the ground. It's massive head, too big for its body, the sort of feral nightmare that kept children awake at night. Claws too long, a tail too thick and powerful. Out of proportion, awful and terrifying.

Arran Earthborn.

At his side, a dark lioness, her deep brown fur turned nearly black with blood. But from the graceful, steady rise and fall of her chest, I knew it was not hers.

And on the floor between them, face mangled almost beyond recognition, were the remains of Gawayn's body.

76
VEYKA

Someone rounded up the royal councilors. Arran didn't leave my side, so it must have been Gwen and Lyrena. I doubted Arran would willingly leave my side anytime for the next decade or so. I didn't have the wherewithal to think about what that meant for my future, not yet. I had one thing on my mind.

"Who did this?"

Silence.

They each sat at their spots at that hideous, long stone table, their representative gemstones sunk into the stone itself. The gems gleamed in the early morning light that spilled through the carved archways.

For once, my Royal Council was silent.

I was having none of it.

I stalked to the table, to the throne at its head that Arthur's death had left unoccupied. I'd never been able to sit in it. I sure as fuck wasn't about to now. I kicked it over, my foot on the arm sending the awful, bejeweled thing careening sideways across the tiled floor with a horrific crash.

"My people are dead! My friends are dead!" I screamed, more unhinged than I'd ever become with Arthur's death. I didn't have the time or ability to dissect that, either. I slammed my hands down on the table, on either side of the amorite embedded at my seat. The seat I refused to take.

"Who did this?" I asked again, with deadly calm.

Still, no one said a word.

Their plan had failed. They'd wagered on Gawayn finishing me off, had snuck traitors into the palace using the same methods as they had months before, to facilitate Arthur's murder. But I was still breathing.

I looked at them each in turn. Esa, the supposed leader of my council, her fingers trembling. Noros, looking like he'd rather be anywhere but here, maybe the only one who realized the extent of my wrath. Teo was dead, cut down in the battle. I guess that exonerated him. Roksana and Elora sat side by side, mother and daughter. The latter's fingertips were coated in frost, her impressive ice magic still not depleted. At her side, Roksana looked on with those wise eyes, sympathy and pain evident as she met my gaze.

But none of them spoke, neither to confess nor to throw one of their peers upon my mercy.

I turned to where my friends stood against the wall—what remained of them. Arran, Gwen, Lyrena, Parys, Cyara. I couldn't meet Cyara's eyes. I didn't know how she stood there at all, straight-backed even as her chin trembled.

I still wore nothing more than Arran's shirt, long enough that it covered my ass and not much more, especially with my sword belt fastened around my waist. But I'd never felt more like a queen.

Arran's words flashed in my mind.

This is what it means to be a queen.

Yes, I understood now. And I fucking hated it.

"We go, now. We cannot wait for tonight," I said to them, the ones who would follow me into another battle, with blood still drying on their hands from this last one.

"Veyka," Arran said, the only one who would dare to challenge me.

"It is either that, or I kill them all right now." A visible tremor went through the remaining members of the council.

Arran closed his mouth, crossing his arms over his broad chest. The closest thing to agreement I would get.

I turned back to the council, pinning each of them with a stare. A promise. "If I do not find out who did this, I will kill each of you. Pray to the Ancestors that I do it quickly."

I strode from the room without another word, and hoped mine would cause them even a fraction of the pain they'd brought on my kingdom.

77

ARRAN

Around us, the goldstone palace slept. Many of the courtiers, exhausted from battle, had lain down right there amongst the carnage, their bodies unable to bear the cost of expending their magic any longer.

I followed Veyka back to her rooms, the rest a silent procession behind us. We walked through the doors into the antechamber, no Goldstones posted on either side. Another reality to face.

"The attack was a distraction so that Gawayn could get to you. They must have used the secret passages to disperse throughout the palace. Further confirmation that someone on the Royal Council orchestrated the attack. Based on what you've said, only they and the royal family have access to them." I didn't dare propose that the Dowager might have had some hand in it. Not yet, not now. It might unhinge Veyka beyond hope.

But when she turned to meet me, her eyes were clear. Cold. The blue in them frozen over to ice as frigid as the glaciers atop the mountains of the Spine.

She didn't falter, walking straight to the center of the room and then turning to face the rest, hands planted on her hips.

"We leave in an hour," she said. "Cyara, stay with your parents.

Gwen, guard the royal councilors. Everyone else, make whatever preparations you must. Then come back here."

Cyara hadn't stopped shaking. Her magic was depleted, her wings still shivering, not wholly healed. But I was unsurprised to hear her protest.

"Veyka," she said sharply. "Let me come. Let me avenge them."

But the queen was unrelenting. "I will not allow your parents to lose another daughter today. Use that strength to hold your family together." A swallow, a flash of knowing pain. "Trust me to avenge your sisters."

Cyara stared her down—half Veyka's size, in both height and weight, but almost as stubborn. But in the end, she bowed her head to her queen.

Gwen wasn't going to argue, but I was ready to. "I want Gwen at your side." After me, she was the best chance of protection.

The sharp line of her jaw softened slightly, her stance shifting. She knew she couldn't command me, so she'd appeal to me instead as one ruler to another. I supposed that was better than appealing to my baser instincts, though those might have been easier to move.

"The Royal Council must be kept secure, or all of this is for naught. They know Lyrena too well, understand the extent of her powers and how she might use them. Guinevere is still something of an enigma. They will be wary of her. Besides, if any of them step out of line, she can rip their heads off."

"Lyrena is more than capable," I argued back. "She proved it last night."

I should have accepted Veyka's reasoning. It was sound. But it meant putting her life at risk—even at the expense of Annwyn.

Something shifted within me. Understanding.

I'd let Annwyn burn, down to the last soul, if it meant Veyka's life.

I was as selfish as I'd ever accused her of being.

I was in love with her.

If she saw the realization playing across my face, or if she passed it off as exhaustion, I didn't know. But Veyka's eyes shifted away from me, and I was damned thankful for it. The weight of everything was suddenly suffocating, the world pressing in on me from every angle.

"I trust you fully, Lyrena." Her eyes flicked to Gwen. "And you as well. One of you to guard my back in the tower, the other to guard my revenge. I do not lie when I say I value them equally."

The two warrior females exchanged a look of understanding, then inclined their heads.

Veyka nodded sharply. "It is done, then. Go."

Just like that, they dispersed. Gwen shifted into her lioness form, bounding back up towards the council chambers. Parys mumbled something about food and left, Cyara at his side. Lyrena closed the door behind her as she took up a post in the corridor, still lined with bodies. Cleaning up would have to wait. Everything would wait.

Even my feelings for Veyka. *Especially* my feelings for Veyka.

"I'm going to take a bath," she said with a heavy sigh, stalking towards the bedroom. I followed her, noting for the first time how both of us were crusted in blood. "Care to join me?" she offered, tossing a glance over her shoulder.

Her eyes didn't glow with desire—couldn't, I knew now, because of her utter lack of magic. But I recognized the invitation in her eyes well enough.

I unbuckled my sword belt, tossing it to the side. My axe next.

Then the tunic, on the floor.

Veyka unbelted her scabbards. Released the harness snapped over her shirt.

Until we were both naked except for the blood and sweat that clung to our skin.

I understood the invitation her eyes, better than anyone. The need to erase the pain, to push it away just for a little while. As her arms slid around my neck, I read the desperate urge in her eyes to replace death with life.

The glint of silver caught my eye as she slid her hand down my muscled bicep. The ring I'd slid on her finger. I'd meant to tell her what it meant, where it came from. But the night had slipped away from us, only to be stolen by the bloodshed and brutality. To talk of my mother's ring now... it seemed blasphemous.

But I caught her hand anyway, holding it in place. Veyka turned her eyes up to mine, questioning.

"Don't run."

Veyka's nails dug into my flesh. "I don't know what you mean."

"Yes, you do."

She didn't argue that time, didn't lie to me.

"Promise me, Veyka." I had no right to demand it, not really. Not after I'd let her down so spectacularly, railing at her instead of standing at her side when her secret was revealed. Even now, I kept the words for how I truly felt away from her. Not for her wellbeing, but my own. I didn't deserve anything from her, and yet I made the demand again. "Promise me you will stay."

She bit hard on her lower lip.

So clearly, I could see the spools of thought unthreading and spinning within her mind. I couldn't read them, not unless she chose to speak into that strange shared space between our minds. But the sense of her thoughts unfurling before me was as real as the specks of blood on her cheeks and the tangled white hair I twined around my fingers.

"I promise to walk out of that tower and return to this palace," she finally said.

We both recognized it for what it was. A half-truth. A clever elemental twisting of words. But I also knew it was the most I would get.

I lowered my mouth to hers and took everything I could.

78
VEYKA

It took too long to skirt around the Gremog's strip of destruction and death, along the outskirts of Baylaur, to where the Tower of Myda loomed at the center of the Effren Valley. Every minute that passed, then lapsed into hours, I wondered if more of my courtiers were being butchered.

What if a second force had come while they slept, lost to the cost of their own magic?

How many would the healers be able to save? How many would die alone, their own well of magic too shallow to heal them without help?

Which of my royal councilors was the traitor, sitting there in the council chamber, savoring the sounds of my kingdom dying around them?

On any other day, the thoughts would have sent me toppling headfirst into the dark abyss. But not today. Not now, with so many depending on me.

As we walked and jogged, we debated what those levels of terror might hold. What enchantments would bar the door at the base of the tower? I'd never seen physical guards, but that didn't mean they weren't there, in hiding, waiting for someone to attack the tower before striking.

But in the end, it was all for naught.

The simple wooden door at the base of the tower wasn't even locked. It felt like a joke.

Or a threat.

For those arrogant enough to walk past the door deserved whatever pain and punishment they'd receive.

We climbed the staircase in silence, a spiral set into the interior of the tower, wrapping along the wall. Lyrena, Arran, and I held our weapons at the ready. Parys wore a dagger at his waist, but said his magic was the strongest weapon he had.

Ahead, golden candlelight heralded the arrival of our first challenge. But as we stepped into the circular room, all of our weapons slackened.

There was no beast or maze or warrior.

"It's a parlor," I said in disbelief, turning in the center of the room.

Plush, scarlet carpet lay beneath my feet. Padded, velvet-upholstered chairs stood against the walls. A silver tea service sat on a cart. And three portraits hung at equidistant intervals on the walls, all of crowned fae that looked vaguely familiar.

"Don't you recognize your ancestors, Young Queen?"

I spun to the voice, curved blade ready. But there was no one but my companions, and all three of them were staring at the portrait of a tall woman with dark hair and bright blue eyes.

"How disappointing," she said, frowning down at me in disapproval.

"I've been called a disappointment my entire life. You'll have to find a better insult if you wish to get a response," I said, lowering my blade. I jerked my head back toward the staircase. "There is nothing here. Let's keep going."

"I don't think—"

"Veyka—"

"You can try, Young One. If you wish to die."

I heard the slice of Arran's axe. I turned in time to see the gash he'd split through the canvas—and to see it stitch itself back together.

"If I cross that threshold, I die?" I asked directly, staring down the dark-haired queen.

She smiled cruelly, but did not answer.

Apparently, our kind were vicious even in death.

"Then what is the task? The terror?" I looked around the room, noting that the other two portraits moved as well, though they didn't speak. "Talking to my relatives does sound like punishment."

That wicked smile—so eerily like my own—remained in place for several more seconds before she straightened and spoke clearly, sharp voice filling the room:

In hues and strokes, our tale is told,
Seek the answer, let your mind unfold.
Look within our frames, secrets lie,
A hidden truth, which you must spy.

The first portrait speaks of wisdom's grace,
An owl perched high, with steady embrace.
In scholarly libraries, we find its trace,
Knowledge preserved in every case.

The second portrait boasts courage bold,
A beast rampant, spirit untamed and untold.
In valiant hearts, its virtues behold,
Bravery shines in stories of old.

The third portrait whispers secrets concealed,
Stowed within, a mystery revealed.

In shadows, the truth unsealed.
Unlocking the past, the present revealed.

My stomach dropped as I realized my steel would be of little use. Nor would my companions' magic. "It's a riddle."

"Wisdom's grace, courage bold," Parys repeated, raking a hand through his hair. "And secrets concealed."

"What happens if we get it wrong?" Arran asked, inspecting the portrait more closely now. Waving his hand in front of it, touching the canvas, probably trying to detect magic. But the knot in his brow told me that whatever secrets that canvas held, they weren't revealing themselves to him.

"A book," Parys said suddenly.

We all turned to look at him.

He nodded to the first portrait, the dark queen staring down at us. "She's standing in a library. The owl is a symbol of wisdom—probably the High King, a terrestrial shifter, if she's the elemental queen. The answer is in each portrait. *Knowledge reserved in every case*. Libraries preserve books in bookcases. The first answer is books."

I stared at the dark queen, awaiting her response. She inclined her head. Not even a 'well done.' Fucking bitch.

"Was it meant to be this easy?" Parys said warily, looking around the room.

Lyrena blinked. "That was easy?"

"He spends half his life in the library," I said. "We don't have time to question our luck. What is the second one?"

"A beast of some kind," Arran said. Of course, he'd pick up on that particular line.

"But it's a portrait," I said, examining the second painting closer. A bearded fellow with white blond hair like my mother's. A shiver of unease slithered through my spine.

"Maybe it has something to do with who is in the painting,"

Parys said, stepping up beside me. "I think that is Accolon," he said.

"You know my family history better than I do," I sighed, cursing myself for all the times I'd let my mind wander.

"Accolon was known for his courage," Lyrena said, nodding quickly. "He was the original owner of Excalibur."

Parys' mouth twitched, but he nodded. "Alright... yes. Accolon."

We all cried out in unison.

Pain lanced through my body, suffusing every limb. It felt as if my bones themselves were on fire. Beside me, Parys crashed to his knees, Lyrena's voice a keening moan as she buckled. Only Arran and I remained standing.

Then, just as suddenly, the pain was gone. Only flickering embers of memory remained. I turned immediately back to the dark queen, whose smile had grown to reach her eyes. "That is the punishment for a wrong answer?" I demanded.

"Eventually, you will stop guessing. The pain will get worse each time until you'd rather starve to death than risk another wrong answer." She looked as if she'd enjoy watching either spectacle.

I turned back to Parys. "You didn't think it was Accolon. Don't listen to Lyrena." She was staggering back to her feet, face white, but nodding emphatically. "Listen to your own instincts."

Parys' usually warm brown eyes had turned wary, his golden skin ashen. But he nodded as he turned back to the portrait of Accolon. He was silent for a long time—too long, longer than we had. A rumbling growl rolled through me. I ignored it, forcing myself to keep my eyes on Parys.

"I think Lyrena was right, partially," he finally said. "It does have to do with Excalibur. But the beast isn't Accolon, it is on the sword itself." He pointed to the carved pommel. "A lion."

"Accolon was a lion shifter," I said softly, the fact dredging itself up from the recesses of my memory.

Arran and Lyrena looked to the painted figure of Accolon for confirmation, but Parys and I turned to the dark queen instead. She inclined her head, blue eyes a shade darker as disappointment set in.

"You were wrong, Parys. Your strongest weapon isn't your magic. It is your mind. Now use it and get us out of this cursed room," I said, touching his shoulder.

"One more," Lyrena breathed, fully upright once more.

The third portrait was of a child.

Dark-haired, bright blue eyes, she looked like the miniature of the cruel queen. She stood in a massive doorway, darkness painted behind her. I didn't know her name, though I was certain I'd find it on my own family tree. But I felt that I recognized her all the same.

"Repeat the third riddle," I commanded, not taking my eyes off of the small, delicate female.

The dark queen's voice echoed through the room once more. *"The third portrait whispers secrets concealed, stowed within, a mystery revealed. In shadows, the truth unsealed. Unlocking the past, the present revealed."*

"The Queen of Secrets," Arran breathed.

I pressed my eyes shut, unable to look into those eyes any longer—*my eyes.*

"I know this one," I breathed, turning to face my dark-haired ancestor. Her eyes were heavy as she waited for my answer... as if she knew, and understood. "To unlock a secret, you need a key."

There was no visible change in the chamber, but we all felt the shift. Lyrena swung her sword over the threshold, and when nothing happened, stepped over it herself. The others followed her, myself included. None of us looked back at the dark queen or her daughter.

Arran's hand on my back was the only acknowledgment. There was no room for anything else. No time to question or wonder or go to pieces.

We went up, up, up, around the curving stairwell.

But this time, instead of being welcomed by candlelight, we walked into a wall of darkness.

79
VEYKA

"What is this? Lyrena, use your fire," I said into the black.

It was darkness like I'd never seen, meant to steal every shred of light and awareness. As if I'd suddenly been rendered blind. I could only assume my companions had as well. But why wasn't anyone saying anything? Why—

That was when I realized—sight wasn't the only sense that had been stolen.

I strained my ears, but I was met with absolute silence.

"Arran?" I called tentatively. But though I could feel the vibration of my own vocal cords, I didn't hear the words. I was certain Arran didn't either.

Which was why Lyrena hadn't used her fire. She had no idea where the rest of us were, and she'd risk injuring someone. Even a few flames around her fingertips... no, she wouldn't risk it. There might be consequences, like there had been for the wrong guesses on the level below.

We'd have to find each other in the darkness.

Arran would be the easiest.

As if in answer, a low rumbling growl filled my consciousness. Whatever magic had stolen our senses, it hadn't touched that deep, unnamable connection between me and Arran's beast. A second more, and I felt the heat of Arran's body, his hand skimming over me, checking for injuries. Then grabbing my hand and lacing our fingers tightly together.

A warm wind licked at my neck. *Parys.*

I stepped tentatively toward it, pulling Arran with me.

Then I felt Parys, his hand on my arm. I could sense his other flailing around in Arran's direction.

The rich scent of blood filled the air. Parys must have caught his hand on the blade of Arran's axe.

Then everything was in motion. It felt like a thousand rats were scurrying past my feet, a moving mass all around us. I gripped Arran's hand tightly, trying to make sense of what was happening.

Parys' wind was gone, his fingers slipping from mine.

Blood... more blood. A lot of it. It filled the room, flooding my nostrils and my other stunted senses.

Oh Ancestors... I couldn't even hear Parys, couldn't get to him to help.

Arran tugged on my hand, and I had no answer but to follow him. The movements around me were too much, too scattered. He stopped suddenly, catching me against him. I felt a tickle on my hand—hair. Long hair. Lyrena.

She must have recognized me as well, because a second later, a blast of fire filled the room.

I wished then that I couldn't see.

Hundreds—no, thousands—of shiny green lizards crawled across the floors, over our feet and around our ankles. But they weren't just on the floor. They covered the walls, the ceiling, so that we were surrounded by an undulating mass of shimmering green.

No bigger than my palm, they might have been kept as pets—if not for the inch-long fangs they sported. And the bloodlust.

That rush I'd felt had been them converging on Parys. I couldn't even see his body, it was covered in the vicious little reptiles, small streams of blood shooting from his huddled form. One might have been nothing... but thousands of them... they'd eat him alive.

I felt the bile rising in my throat, but Arran caught my chin. He shook his head and shoved my hand down to my waist. To my scabbards.

With one hand, Lyrena's fire lit the room while her other wielded her sword. We swiped and stabbed, ripping the filthy, vicious vermin in half. But it wasn't fast enough. There were too many of them.

It was Arran who realized what truly needed to be done. He grabbed Lyrena's sword arm, pointing across the room to where her pillar of flame was driving into the stone wall. Where a space had cleared, no more than a yard wide—but free of the little beasts.

She nodded, understanding immediately. She'd burn them away with her fire.

I turned back to Parys, determined to cut my way through the mass to get to him.

But Arran caught my hand. He dragged me away, even as I screamed. But he didn't hear a single one of the vile epithets I hurled at him. He tugged me over the threshold, and Lyrena's fire followed, sealing the vicious creatures inside. And sealing us out.

I opened my mouth to scream at Arran, but I couldn't.

Because while Lyrena's flame sealed the door, it didn't block out the sound. Parys' screams echoed through the stairwell.

Make it stop.

But Arran didn't let me stop. He shoved my weapons into my hands and pushed me up the stairs. Coward that I was, I ran.

80
ARRAN

Lyrena's fire chased us up the staircase, blocking the way for any of the vile little creatures who might try to follow. Veyka charged ahead, blades drawn, trying to escape Parys' screams. I filtered them out, like I had hundreds of times on the battlefield. To listen to your friends die... there was no room for the damage that would inflict. Not now.

We hit the landing, pausing long enough to search the room for threats. No smart-ass paintings, no looming darkness. The walls of the circular tower room were completely unadorned. No windows, either. Only a singular mirror, taller than Veyka, leaning against the wall directly opposite the door. I could see the glint of my axe reflected in it, Veyka's white hair.

Until we stepped into the room.

The image shifted entirely, a black-cloaked figure replacing our reflection.

Not a figure, I realized as I marked the shifting, the huffed breaths.

"What is it?" The chill in Veyka's voice told me she was making her own assessments.

"A creature," I said slowly. "Likely a deadly one."

"Says the male who killed a skoupuma with blades of grass," she said, a poor attempt at flippancy.

"Do you see any grass here?" I shot back, examining the room again for other potential threats.

"I guess I was technically the one to kill it—"

"Are you quite done?"

It wasn't a voice, because beasts didn't have voices. But neither was it a growl. Maybe it spoke directly into our minds, some bastard cousin of the lost ethereal magic.

Veyka and I both lifted our weapons, exchanging a silent look. Waiting would only raise our anxiety, make us sloppy. Best to attack whatever the challenge was directly.

"Yes," Veyka said, voice sharp as her blades.

The image of the creature in the mirror rippled.

The reflective glass pane of the mirror was gone. The creature leapt free, a mass of fangs and claws and death. I didn't hesitate, shifting into the snarling beast within me. That beast of bloodshed had time for one growl in Veyka's direction, one command that only she would hear.

Go.

81

VEYKA

Go.

One word was all Arran's beast could manage as it fought the ever-changing monster. First a darkling, with clawed feet and hands, a beast that stood on two feet and could kill with the cunning of a fae, but the brutality of an animal. Just as Arran got his fangs around its throat, it shifted. Now a long, deadly serpent, with glowing red eyes and sharp spines that promised poison.

I couldn't let him die, I couldn't leave him here alone, not knowing—

He is the most powerful fae in thousands of years.

I am nothing.

I can't do this.

Another flash of light, and a harpy replaced the snake, beating wings filling the room and knocking Arran to the side. But he was up before the harpy's talons could slash, his teeth aiming for those wings, recognizing them as the creature's weakness.

I didn't let myself look back to see how much of the blood I could scent belonged to Arran. He was ready to bleed and die for this, for me. I could not be a coward.

I forced myself up the stairs, each step painful and labored. My muscles ached from the battle in the palace, from watching my friends fall as we fought our way up this blasted tower.

Don't stop.

I could see the landing ahead, light around the curving wall.

Don't stop.

I was so very close, to finally finishing, to dousing the burning rage for vengeance that Arthur's death had lit within my gut. I pushed the fear aside, let that flame of vengeance consume it until there was nothing but determination.

If this was how I died, then at least I was not alone.

I stood on the precipice, looking into my own doom.

But my friends were with me still.

I could feel the heat of Lyrena's fire at my back, blocking the way behind me. Gwen's last roar still rang in my sensitive fae ears. I could only pray to the Ancestors that someone would hear Parys' clever laugh again.

Arran—I could not think it.

I pressed my thumb hard against the ring Arran had slipped on my finger. Let me go to my destiny with the etchings pressed into my skin. So that we might be together, if only in death.

Death and terror had been wrought upon my kingdom.

But I could make it stop.

With my friends seated deep in my heart, the place inside of me they had healed, the one and only place they were truly safe, I stepped over the threshold.

82
VEYKA

She was beautiful and terrible to look upon. A face untouched by time, even though she'd been captive in this tower for thousands of years. A curtain of perfectly straight, perfectly black hair fell past her shoulders, the edge as sharp and straight as one of the knives in my scabbards. How it stayed that way... how her clothing maintained its rich sheen... I didn't waste my questions.

I fought the urge to look too closely at any of the details. I could not be distracted; not now, when I was so close. I kept my eyes fixed on the witch. She was seated, staring at the ground, as if I wasn't there at all.

I curled my hands tightly into fists until my fingernails bit into the soft heels of my palms and forced the words out. Words we'd crafted so carefully, based on the scant information Parys had dredged up from the library and our own memories of childhood legends.

"I have conquered the terrors of the tower. I come bearing blades and power." Not magical power, obviously. But she didn't know that. Besides, I'd brought three powerful magic wielders with me, even if they had not made it all the way here. Just short of a lie. "You are at my mercy. You will answer my questions."

Slowly, so slowly I thought at first that she wasn't moving at all, the witch lifted her head. Her cheekbones were high, marked by not a single freckle or wrinkle. And her lips... so thin that they stretched to nothing as she fixed me with a horrifying smile. Each tooth was as sharp and pointed as one of Arran's canines.

But the eyes were the worst.

I thought at first they were pure white, like my hair. But as I adjusted to the sight, as I forced air in and out of my lungs, I realized there were irises and pupils the same as mine. But each was a shade of opalescent white that glimmered unnaturally.

A voice, ageless and wispy, filled the room, swirling through it, leaking in through my ears, my nostrils, my mouth. "Blades you have, and you wield them well. But you bring no magic to face me today, Veyka Pendragon."

"How—" I swallowed the word, refusing to be tricked. "You know my name."

A soft, approving laugh. "Very good, Young Queen. You have me at your mercy. Are you brave enough to ask your questions?"

Another trick. To try to get me talking, so that I might fumble and unwittingly let a question slip into the conversation.

"Hold your tongue and listen well," I said sharply. Parys had found that order in one of his books.

The witch grimaced, recoiling back. I couldn't quite make out what she sat upon, her thick, dark skirts billowing out and obscuring her legs and the seat as well. But she was silent, for now.

It worked, then, to still her trickery. But only for a few moments, that same text had advised.

We'd tried a thousand variations on the first question but had decided to keep the most important of our three queries the simplest, most straightforward.

"Who conspired to murder my brother, King Arthur?"

The witch started rocking softly on her perch. Back and forth. Back and forth. A vague, vacant expression on her face, as if she was not present in the room at all, but her mind had gone to a different place altogether.

My mind pricked in memory.

But then that eerie voice was speaking once more. "The one who has seen so much, seen too much, to make her still. The one who pulls you closer, to have you at her will. Roksana," she hissed, drawing out the 's' in a long whistle through her horrible teeth.

I didn't have it in me to be surprised, not after the events of the last twenty-four hours. It made sense, in some ways. But why... and could it possibly have been her alone? Not Elora, or any of the others? Such a massive plot, to conspire to kill first Arthur, then me as well—

"So many questions, swirling in that head of yours," the witch crooned. She spoke the word, 'questions,' as if it was a treat, a savory morsel on her tongue. "Ask me, Veyka. I will tell you what you want to know."

"You will trick me into wasting my questions."

"I only seek to help you, dear child. I can hear those questions that haunt you. So many mysteries in your young life. A mother who so desperately tried to change you, but why, oh why, would she visit such horrors upon her daughter? Arthur, dear Arthur, stolen from you so soon. Why was he taken? Why should you become queen?"

"Stop." *Make it stop.*

The witch could see into my mind. She could read the horrors of my past, name the feelings that even I couldn't acknowledge. This hadn't been in any of Parys' books.

"Perhaps you'd like to know about your betrothed, the storied Brutal Prince. Oh, how I've relished tracking him across the centuries. Such a beast, that thing that lives inside of him. You know that he burns for you, but do you want to know why? I could tell you, my sweet. I could tell you why you can hear the beast growl, why you feel yourself being pulled back to him, again and again. Why he's made you question every conviction, even your most jealously guarded quest for revenge."

The room began to swirl around me. The world itself. I could feel the darkness pulling me down. The darkness had taken me after Arthur's death. I'd stopped it after Cyara's attack, but only just.

So easy.

It would be so easy to give into it again.

"Why... why was Arthur taken?"

I fell to my knees, realizing what I had done. Wasting a question. But still, my ears strained to hear the answer to a question that no one else could give.

"To make way for you, Veyka."

"No." I shook my head, again and again, so hard I was going to careen sideways. I could feel the force of it, of my body's inability to keep up with the motion. "No. That cannot be."

A laugh so cruel, my bones turned to shards of ice. "Oh yes, Veyka. You and Arthur should never have been born. A duality in the world that was never meant to exist. You could not both be here on this plane of existence. It was only a matter of time."

Her words pricked my ears. I felt the slight swivel of those delicate points. But I stayed on my knees, clutching my dagger. Tears streamed down my face. I let all that guilt and self-hate pour out of me for her to see.

"Arthur does not exist here, but he could exist elsewhere," I said softly, hardly more than a whisper.

A sharp intake of breath. "Is that your next question?"

"This place... all places... they also exist in the human realm."

"There is no witch atop their feeble human tower, waiting to answer your questions. My sisters are gone from this world, thanks to your Ancestors."

"But not from all worlds."

Another laugh, this one shrill, nearly hysterical. "Your kind have never possessed that sort of power."

A spear of understanding, straight through my gut. "There are layers. I... I knew it."

"You have wasted another question—"

"No." I climbed to my feet steadily, spinning the knife once in my hand. "I asked no question. You gave the information willingly."

Her thin, nearly non-existent lips curled into a grotesque smile of razor-sharp teeth. "There are many layers. But your brother exists beyond those of even your reach." A taunt.

And a confirmation.

"Thank you," I said softly, letting the corner of my mouth curve into a smirk.

"Ask your final question and leave me to another thousand years of solitude."

She couldn't see everything in my mind, I realized then.

"Who within the goldstone palace is truly disloyal?" I asked. My third and final question. Originally, we'd phrased it to ask about my Royal Council. But Gawayn's betrayal had taught me I could not assume anyone's allegiance. Not anymore.

She did not answer immediately—merely stared at me with that vacant expression. I thought the corner of her mouth twitched. As if she would enjoy giving me the answer. A chill snaked down my spine. But then, it could have been a trick of the light.

"Power comes to those who wait, or those who do not hesitate. Your *donna*, Esa, will not wait much longer."

I swallowed. Esa was not the one to kill Arthur, but everything she'd implied in the meeting Arran and I had listened to was true.

But the witch was not done. "What once was free is now on the run. Oh, but how we witches and priestesses did have fun. Locked in this tower, I may be, but there is one clothed in red who remains free."

The priestess. I'd written her off as power-hungry, self-important. But not dangerous. Another mark on the tally sheet of the many things I'd judged wrongly.

I drew my other dagger, easing closer. I had to strike quickly if I wanted to avoid those fangs.

"Igraine." I froze at the strangled name that tore from her lips—as if she'd wanted to keep it from me, but some force compelled her. "Her loyalty shifts like the tides of the Split Sea. Trust her at your own peril."

I laughed bitterly. "I'll never make that mistake."

The witch stilled then. She'd been rocking again, but I hadn't realized. Her eyes drifted shut. This was my moment, to kill her and be done with it. So that no enemy might climb this tower, so that the answers to my questions died with her as well.

When her haunting eyes opened, the shades of white had gone. Transformed into empty black pits.

Her lips curved slowly. My heart thudded to a stop as she lunged.

I slashed my dagger across her face, knowing from the resistance on my blade that I'd found flesh.

But I was so worried about her teeth, I neglected to see the talons she withdrew from her cloak. Sharp as knives, but not. They were nails, I realized. Curved and sharpened into wicked points. One slash, and she'd cut through the leather straps that held the blades across my back and left a deep gauge in the flesh of my chest.

By some miracle, it didn't break the skin. But the scratch stung enough for me to wonder if she'd tipped those fingernails with poison.

Not she—*it*.

The witch was gone, and in her place was the sort of death and darkness that I'd seen twice before. Flailing, unpredictable movements that made no sense. She didn't cry out as I slashed at her hand, slicing down to the bone. I whirled, trying to get to my rapiers. But she'd flung them away, to the other side of the circular tower room.

I threw a knife, grazing the side of her face. But she moved too erratically, I couldn't count on my aim. I'd have to stab her directly.

The air had turned cold. Not just my hands, always cold, but my toes, the tip of my nose. Even despite the exertion as I whirled, dodging those wicked nails and defending, I felt the ice settling in my chest.

A brutal hit to my wrist—like a whip, she'd wielded those nails. My dagger clanged to the ground.

I was weaponless. Had only my fists against a being taken over by darkness, that did not feel pain. Death was coming for me, I realized then.

I leveled a kick, hard as I could, at the center of her chest. She clawed at my leg, even as she went stumbling backward. My teeth gnashed at the pain, eyes squeezing closed even as I fought against the instinct, knowing I couldn't allow even a blink of weakness.

Over her shoulder, a glint of gold caught my eye.

She careened into it, falling to the side from the impact of my kick.

It couldn't be.

She'd be up in a second, totally impervious to pain. I didn't have time to think or question how it could be there. How I'd missed it, when she'd been sitting on the stone the entire time.

I kicked her again, not looking to see if I caught face or teeth or body. Only knowing that I had to get myself up onto that stone.

My hand curled around the hilt, so much smaller and paler than the last that had gripped its pommel. But I didn't have time to wonder as I pulled Excalibur from the stone.

Heat flowed into my body from where I held my brother's sword, as if he'd left some piece of his burning magic there for me to find. It fought against the cold pushing in from all sides.

The thing that had once been a witch roared, throwing back her head and gnashing those wicked teeth, ready to tear me apart.

But I brought the mighty sword above my head, clinging to it tightly with both hands, and stabbed it down into her chest. Cleaving her apart.

She, it, the witch—fell to the ground.

I did too. The blast of heat from Excalibur's golden hilt ebbed away, replaced by that creeping cold.

I hoped it was enough. Did I need to behead her, the way I would a fae?

Was that ancient blade the same as the daggers, that faint swirl of mixed metals? I'd never looked before. Never cared.

Such a beastly sword, so heavy in my hand.

My hand couldn't hold it, my wrist shaking.

Everything shaking.

Cold. I was so cold. If I could open my eyes, I'd see frost on my fingertips, I was certain.

But I couldn't open them. Couldn't move.

Cold... I was so very cold...

83
VEYKA

Witches, claws, and a ray of golden light. Up and up I rose toward the star-flecked sky. My hands burned, my palms, the back of my neck. Flashes of emerald, undulating above me.

Arthur.

Close, so close I could almost reach out and touch him.

But fading too fast, slipping through my fingertips.

Darkness.

Not the cold, unforgiving dark. But raging black fire, flames that wreathed a heart, a hand. My hand. My fingers intertwined with his.

Then true darkness.

Oblivion.

Sleep.

My eyes cracked open, my cheek pressed against the soft white pillow. I saw my arm flung across the bed. Not just my hand, though. Those fingers intertwined with mine were golden. Calloused and strong. I knew them in an instant, like they were my own.

"Arran." My voice was hoarse, as if it hadn't been used in days. My eyes, fully open now, darted around the room, looking for any indication of the passage of time.

"A few hours," Arran said, his voice steady. My gaze tracked up from where our hands were joined, along his muscled forearm. He'd rolled up his sleeves to the elbow, exposing the golden skin corded with muscle, even more accentuated as he gripped my hand fiercely.

I let myself savor those muscles, the deep triangle of chest from his unfastened shirt. I could see the tips of the branches of his Talisman.

His hair was loose around his shoulders, unbound in dark waves. It looked like he'd been running his hands through it. "Have you been worrying about me?" I asked, amused.

Arran ignored the comment, dropping his gaze to our joined hands. He tried to loosen his grip. I held him right where he was. The ghost of a smile flitted over his face.

"You are still here," he said to our hands.

"I am."

He reached out with his other hand and flicked my nose. "Despite your best efforts."

"I didn't *try* to get myself killed."

"You promised you would walk out of that tower," he reminded me.

I cringed. "Did you have to carry me?"

"Down four flights of stairs."

"Next, you're going to tell me I should lay off the chocolate croissants."

"If you hadn't been half-dead a few hours ago, I'd be fucking you on this bed right now," Arran growled. "Don't change a single thing about that gorgeous body. Ever."

"I promise." I laughed, realized how tender my ribs were, and eased back down to the mattress. "On second thought, perhaps it is better if there are no promises between us."

Something like pain flashed in his eyes. But he covered it so quickly, I questioned whether I'd seen it at all. He sighed heavily instead. "We cannot stop the Joining, Veyka."

I nodded. "I know. But between us, here, not the High Queen and King, but... Veyka and Arran. No promises. Just truth. Whatever the cost."

I could see him struggling. He was holding something back. Something important, if the wrinkles forming around his eyes were any indication.

I decided to spare him thinking about it any longer. I grabbed his neck and dragged him down to me, slanting my mouth against his.

"Truth," he agreed against my lips.

He let me pull him down onto the bed, his knees bracketing my hips on either side. But when I tried to arch against him, several stabs of pain ripped through me. Wrist, chest, legs. Arran eased onto his left knee, settling in to lie beside me instead, head propped on his elbow. Not the hand that still held mine.

"You were injured. So cold, I could hardly feel you breathing or hear your heartbeat. There was not a single drop of blood on you. Scratches... yes, so many. Deep, hideous gouges. But no blood. How is that possible, Veyka?"

I stared at my leg, which should have been mutilated.

"I didn't have enough questions to ask," I said cheekily.

He wanted to push it, I knew.

It was luck, I was sure. I'd been damned lucky. For a few minutes, it had even felt like Arthur was there with me. Even if that witch had all but confirmed that was impossible.

Arthur.

His name speared through me, every muscle tightening. I opened my mouth to tell Arran, to demand he let go of my hand and go cut Roksana into tiny, little pieces—

"Roksana is dead," Arran said.

I stilled. "How?"

Arran stroked a fingertip down the inside of my arm. "Elora

began asking questions—about Arthur's death, the massacre on the palace. When her mother couldn't answer them, she beheaded her."

"I see." Part of me wished I'd been the one to inflict the killing blow. But the other half was just glad it was over. I'd have to question Elora eventually, to find out more about how she'd realized her mother's treachery. And reward her appropriately. But it all seemed too exhausting to contemplate.

"They are all still under guard. If that is not who the witch—"

"No, no. It was Roksana all along," I said, still struggling to believe it. It should've been easier, considering the betrayals and losses of the last few days. But it still felt like a knife wound in my gut, the blade rotated with each reminder.

Arran paused, but ultimately asked, "What else did the witch say?"

I told him what had happened from the moment I stepped into the tower room. How she'd tricked me, how I'd tricked her back.

"Layers," he said, rubbing at the stubble on his chin. The action made me desperate to find out what that stubble would feel like scraping against my inner thighs. "In the water gardens, all those outlines of Annwyn..."

"Multiple realms," I nodded. "Not just the human and fae realms. But more, maybe an infinite number. Stacked on top of one another, coexisting, without us even realizing it."

"And Arthur..."

"I don't know. She said he was unreachable." I bit hard on my lower lip, staring down at my hands, the wrist where the witch's nails had gotten to me red and raw. "When I saw the carvings in the water gardens... I hoped that maybe the afterlife was one of those layers. That maybe I could use the rifts..." I sighed, shaking my head. "But none of it matters, not really. We'll have to find a way to seal all of the rifts, to stop this darkness coming from the human lands."

Arran opened his mouth, closed it again. He had an opinion on that, clearly. But it was not a discussion we'd have today.

He leaned down and kissed me again, tracing each line of my

mouth reverently. I tried to shift beneath him, but still he held me fast. Our hands joined tightly, the ring he'd slid onto my finger digging into my skin.

A comfort and a promise, despite what I'd said.

But then he slid his tongue into my mouth and I let myself forget the rest.

84
VEYKA

I considered dragging the lounge chairs far back on the balcony so that no one would be able to see us, so that we might have a few days of privacy after the events in the Tower of Myda.

But then I remembered that I was Queen of the Elemental Fae. I sent an order to have the apartments of every courtier whose balcony overlooked my own reassigned. There was a lot of grumbling. I did not care. Nor did I hear it, for I did not leave my rooms.

We did not leave my rooms.

I also sent an order to the Royal Council. It was not difficult to retake control of my kingdom from the council, considering a third of them were dead. I had a plan for that as well, though I supposed I ought to talk it over with Arran first.

But for those first few days, neither of us wanted to talk.

Arran stayed in his wolf form most of the time. Only at night, when Cyara disappeared for the evening and dinner had been cleared away, only then did he shift. Then he took me into his arms and dragged me to the bed.

When the first rays of dawn came, he'd shift again. I'd wake to find him lying at the foot of the bed, keeping guard, as always.

When our quiet reverie was finally broken, we were sitting on one of those lounge chairs, basking in the sun and silence.

Well, I was sitting. Arran was sprawled out across me, his head in my lap, my entire lower body covered by his heated form. I'd taken to burying my ever-cold hands in his fur for warmth. Pure white. The exact color of my hair.

"Doesn't this paint quite the idyllic, peaceful picture of the next High Queen and King of Annwyn," Parys said, smirking.

A low growl slipped from Arran's jaws. I doubted he'd ever fully forgive Parys for having shared my bed in those empty days before the Offering.

I flicked his ear. Never mind that it was bigger than my hand.

But I leaned my head back against the cushioned seat and gave Parys a baleful look. "You come bearing neither food nor drink."

"I come with news," Parys said, his smirk faltering a bit.

I sighed heavily. "I feared as much."

The reprieve was over. Reality must be faced. Annwyn had survived something brutal and treacherous—a threat from within. A violation of the treaties of peace our Ancestors had fought and died for. Arran and I could not hide forever.

I flexed my hands, cold again as soon as I withdrew them from Arran's warm fur.

My secret... it was not a secret anymore. My companions all knew; impossible not to, after what had unfolded. But I trusted them to keep that precious, dangerous information close, at least for now.

Answers, the ones I'd so desperately searched for, vengeance... perhaps it was not wholly satisfied. Perhaps it never would be.

I felt Arran's shift. And in the next breath, his hand closed around mine—a silent offer of strength.

What I hadn't been able to say was that I felt stronger than ever before. All these days of silence, I'd come to terms with the guilt and grief that would never leave me. They had made me stronger.

So, though I did not want to hear what Parys had to say, I was at least ready for it.

"Tell us," Arran ordered, the quiet strength of his voice an echo of my thoughts.

Picking up an orange from the table and tossing it in the air, Parys began with all casualness, "Tomorrow is the eve of Mabon."

Arran's eyes slid to me.

"Is it?" I said, matching Parys' nonchalant tone.

"The priestesses seek to remind you that the day is symbolic and will not come to pass for another year," Parys continued.

"Does that mean if we miss tomorrow we can put this off for a whole year? I suddenly feel a headache coming on—"

"Veyka," Arran growled. Only he could say my name with that particular shade of exasperation.

"Alright," I groused, standing up and snatching the orange from the air. I dug my thumbnail into the tender flesh. "I assume the priestesses have arranged everything?"

"They have," Parys agreed.

"And all that we," I gestured with my orange-filled hand in Arran's direction. "All we have to do is show up dressed in our finery and the thing will be done?"

Parys snickered. "How romantic you make it sound, Veyka." He cast a glance at Arran. "You must be so flattered."

Arran's face gave away nothing. My passionate, fierce... what? Lover? Partner? Ally? There had been no words of love between us.

Betrothed.

It was the simplest and most inadequate word for what lay between me and my Brutal Prince. But it would have to be enough, because my heart would allow no more. I'd barely survived losing Arthur. I couldn't stand that sort of risk again.

"Be ready tomorrow evening and you shall appease the priestesses," Parys confirmed.

I stripped away the last of the orange skin, a neat single swirl. I walked to the corner of the room, disposing of it in the trash. A flash of memory struck my mind. Arthur carefully setting aside the cups that day in the practice ring, rather than chucking them away to be cleared up by a lesser fae.

My heart hurt.

But at least it was there.

"We will be there," I said, turning back to the balcony.

Parys' eyes went to Arran and found confirmation there, too.

"Good. If you'd argued, I would have left you to deal with the priestesses yourself," my friend said. "As for the Royal Council, they want to meet with you straightaway. What remains of them. After the Joining, of course."

"Of course," Arran grumbled, turning away and stalking out onto the balcony.

His mind had been as busy as mine these last few days. I knew that once Parys left, the words would start to spill out. The future we'd been avoiding had come to claim our lives as its due.

Parys stared uneasily at Arran's back, shrugging and loosening his limbs noticeably as he tried to fight off the anxiety. He, too, had travelled to hell and back. The fact that he stood here before me was a testament to the skilled healers of Baylaur and more than a little luck. Perhaps a bit of destiny, if the witch's words were to be believed.

"I'll spare you the rest of the gossip," Parys said, turning for the door. "For now."

"Wait." I tossed him the peeled orange, smiling at how easily he caught it, at the crinkle of his eyes. "Tonight, at sundown, come to my antechamber. Lyrena, Gwen, and Cyara as well."

Parys frowned. "For what?"

"You'll see. Tell the others," I said.

Parys nodded, throwing a questioning look at Arran. But he only shrugged, his eyes slipping to mine.

I have given up trying to uncover all your secrets, Arran's eyes said.

Good, my heart answered. *Because I have one more.*

85

ARRAN

For once, Veyka told me of her schemes without sneaking around first. And for once, I didn't feel inclined to argue with her. The plan she laid out had pride building in my chest with every word. I'd come so close to losing her in that tower. The cold, the wounds... I still didn't quite understand how the healers had managed to warm her body, to coax her organs back to working. If she'd bled from those wounds, it would have been even worse.

Fae could survive almost anything, save a beheading. But when I'd lifted her into my arms in that tower, I'd questioned the reality of that truth I'd lived with for my entire immortal life.

But she stood beside me now, fully healed, that wicked smile on her face as she watched everyone she'd summoned file in.

Four palace guards stood watch outside in the corridor, selected by Gwen and Lyrena. Four, to fill the void created by Gawayn's absence. It still didn't feel like enough. For all that she brandished that grin, I knew the pain of betrayal was heavy in Veyka's chest. But I didn't force her to talk about that, either.

Just like I kept the words to myself. The words that would change everything between us.

There had been too much change, too much upheaval. She was

stronger now than I'd ever seen her, but I wasn't foolish enough to think that dark precipice had disappeared from her mind entirely. Fear was an insidious foe. If I pushed too hard, too fast...

I shoved those thoughts out of my mind, focusing on the feel of my weapons instead. Even in her apartments, safe as we could be, I wore them. It still felt like danger could spring up at any time.

Maybe that feeling would fade. But it might take months. Decades, even.

Cyara glanced around the room, looking for something to put in order. She was straightening pillows on the sofa when Parys strolled in.

"If you're planning another dangerous conquest, count me out," he said, swiping a plum from a dish filled with fruit on the side table.

Lyrena laughed softly from just inside the door. Gwen's face was regal and impassive, as always.

"Not a conquest, precisely, but not necessarily less dangerous, either," Veyka said truthfully, her smile easing into seriousness. She lifted her arm and gestured to the round table. "Please, everyone, be seated."

They all stared back at her in silence.

No doubt, the priestess's words of prophecy sounded in their minds, as they did in mine: *a table of destiny.*

When no one moved, Veyka rolled her eyes and walked to the nearest chair, folding herself gracefully into it. She flicked her gaze to me, expectant. I did exactly as I'd told her I would—as I would always do. I took my place at her side.

The others followed slowly, Parys coming first. He left the half-eaten plum on the side table.

Gwen and Lyrena sat side by side, the former's face determinedly blank. This was her father's table. She'd meant to sit at it as a queen. But there was no resentment in the set of her mouth.

Cyara was the last to come. She lingered behind the high-backed chair, her fingers floating over the curved top. "Veyka, I am not sure—"

"Sit, Cyara. You have as much of a place here as anyone else." A queen's order.

The handmaiden sat.

"What is this?" Cyara asked immediately, wings flaring.

Veyka straightened her shoulders. She'd prepared herself carefully. A simple three-strand braid, a dove gray gown, and a singular golden circlet around her head. Reserved, for once.

"This is our new royal council. Though we've decided to toss out that name and all the treachery that goes along with it. I've decided on the Knights of the Round Table," she said steadily, before flicking a mocking gaze in my direction. "Arran, wisely, agreed."

I let her see me fingering the head of my axe. "Agreeing and deciding not to argue with you are not the same thing."

"You liked the name."

"I agreed that abolishing the Royal Council was a wise idea."

"I am not a knight," Cyara interjected, her voice several octaves higher than usual.

Veyka shrugged casually, though I knew it was contrived. "Neither is Parys."

"I am not a warrior," she insisted.

"I don't need another warrior. I have these three," Veyka motioned to me, Lyrena, and Gwen. "*I* am a warrior. What I need is a steady, wise advisor. I need *you*."

Cyara wanted to argue more, but Parys cut her off.

"*Five shall be with you at Mabon*," he mused, quoting the priestess's prophecy. "Does this mean you intend to fulfill the other parts of her prophecy as well?"

"I don't believe in prophecies," Veyka said sharply. "The priestess is power hungry and clever. Everything she says or does has a motive, and not one that is in the best interests of Annwyn. The witch told me as much."

A collective inhale.

Now we were getting to the heart of things.

"This is where we begin. I tell you everything that the witch revealed, and we discuss it together. A round table, where we each may share our thoughts without considering status or with fear of political retribution. I am sick to death of politics and maneuvering. I want truth—and I want you each to vow to give it to me—to us. Always."

Us. High Queen and King. Not queen and consort, not after tomorrow. But true, joint rulers.

I already felt a headache forming behind my temples. A thousand years of having to come to consensus with Veyka was a more daunting notion than going back up that tower.

"So you won't be holding a seat for the mighty '*Siege Perilous*,'" Parys tried to joke. But we could all read the seriousness that belied his question.

Veyka waved her hand at the two empty seats. "Who knows who will join us in the next few hundred years."

Parys dipped his chin, considering. But it was Gwen who unfolded her hands atop the table, her thumbs skating over the smooth stone surface.

"There are four elementals and only two terrestrials seated at the table," Gwen said, pinning Veyka down with her eyes.

But where Veyka might once have looked away, she stared right back at her Goldstone.

"There are still two seats open," Veyka pointed out.

Both had their futures stolen from them. Both queens, in their own way. And it was a regal stare down that passed between them. But also some sort of message, an acknowledgment.

Gwen inclined her head.

"It is settled then." Veyka looked to each of us in turn, then to me. *Satisfied?*

Let me fuck you on this table, and then, maybe.

She grinned wickedly.

But a sudden, flaring light drew both of our eyes away.

It wasn't from Lyrena or Cyara, their flames nowhere to be seen. It came from the table itself. Before each of the occupied seats, a low glow emanated. Growing, brightening, until suddenly there was a bright flash, and then nothing.

I read the words before me.

Arran Earthborn.

No mention of my legacy as the Brutal Prince, nor my future as the High King. Merely my name. A quick glance around the table told me the others were noting the same. The two empty seats remained unmarked.

"Any other tricks you'd like to tell us about, Gwen?" Veyka asked, feigning irreverence. But I could see the unease in her eyes.

"The table is ancient," Gwen said, shaking her head. "Whatever magic it possesses will be revealed in its own time."

"Lovely," Veyka said wryly.

She pushed away from the table just as a knock sounded at the door. She must have been listening for the footsteps.

"Enter," she called.

The doors sprung open to reveal servants bearing heavy trays of food. She motioned towards the sofa and chaise. She'd decided the table should only be used for official business; I was inclined to agree. Symbolism in command was always important.

Veyka wasted no time in swiping up a sausage roll, issuing her next decree. "First we eat, then we plan."

86
VEYKA

Thrice I had stood on this precipice, awaiting my destiny. Dressed in my finery, forced through the motions into a reality I hated.

First, for my coronation as Queen of the Elemental Fae. I'd barely been able to go through the motions as they placed my mother's crown up on my head. The memory still only came to me in fragments, as if it had been experienced by some other person entirely.

Then the Offering, where I'd been forced to give myself to Arran, a complete stranger, for the good of a kingdom I didn't plan to be resident in for more than a few months.

Arran was a stranger no longer. Was I prepared to be joined with him, to seal myself for the rest of my immortal life?

I didn't have a choice.

But I had chosen to stay.

I could have slipped away, during those days when Arran and I lingered in my apartments, healing and hiding. Even Arran could not have stopped me if I'd really wanted to go. But I stayed.

There was the choice, made.

So, I allowed Cyara to truss me up like a chicken, and I walked through the halls of the goldstone palace to meet my destiny one final time.

For once, I'd given up my scabbards in favor of a sword. Not just any sword—Arthur's sword. Excalibur.

I pressed my palm against the pommel, hoping for some bit of warmth like I'd felt in the Tower of Myda. Even a tiny bit of my brother's comfort, sent from whatever unreachable plane he existed on now. But it was just a sword, cool as my own fingertips.

A mighty sword, no question.

But it felt too big at my side, cumbersome as I walked, the opposite of the flowing gown I wore. Yet I understood the significance. Excalibur only bent to its true master. It had disappeared after Arthur's death. It's appearance in that stone, at the top of the Tower of Myda, was a validation that I was meant to bear it. That it had been waiting for me.

No one outside of my knights knew what had happened in that tower room. But every citizen of Annwyn, terrestrial and elemental alike, would understand what it meant when I walked into that throne room with Excalibur on my hip.

My mother's crown on my head. Arthur's sword at my waist. Arran's ring on my hand.

But when I stepped into the throne room, I was Veyka Pendragon.

87

ARRAN

Just like the Offering, we started on opposite sides of the throne room.

After today, we would always enter together. A unified pair, the High Queen and King of Annwyn.

Despite fighting together to defend the goldstone palace, our two kingdoms were still separate in that massive room. The number of terrestrials had grown with the arrival of the additional delegation, while the number of elemental courtiers had been thinned by the massacre. Even after we'd announced Roksana's treachery, each side remained wary.

Nearly equal in numbers now, our court, but they stood on opposite sides of the room. One huddled mass of wool and earth tones, another of flowing white and pastel. Unifying them would probably take the next hundred years, at least. If it could be achieved at all.

But that was not the task for today. Today, I was to finally join with Veyka. The female I loved. The female I wanted, with every breath I took, every thrum of my blood in my veins.

She stepped into the throne room, framed by a grand archway and the Effren Valley behind her, and I forgot everything else.

Her moon-white hair was braided, as always, with glittering jewels. But as my vision cleared, I realized they were not strands of rubies, but tiny jeweled clips. A hundred tiny red roses shimmered in her hair. The Dowager's gold crown sat atop her head, almost an afterthought compared to the beauty who wore it. Excalibur was at her side, its golden handle a sharp contrast with the gown she wore.

For a second, I thought she'd bowed to propriety. But then a phantom wind ruffled the dress and I realized she wasn't wearing white. No, it was silver. A silver gown that changed in the breeze and light like the inside of an oyster shell. First purple and then rose, then gold and blue. Iridescent, ever-changing, absolutely spectacular. Just like Veyka.

She was every inch a queen, and I would enjoy worshiping her for the rest of my life.

My beast growled in approval. Even across the throne room, I knew she could hear it by the slight smile that lifted her mouth. The little bit of challenge in her raised eyebrow as we walked toward one another.

The priestess, having traded her blood red gown for a darker garnet, was frowning. Whatever she'd expected from the queen, it wasn't this show of confidence and royalty. When Veyka and I joined hands without her permission, she seemed to remember herself.

Her hands shot towards the vaulted ceiling, a tower of water spinning up and up and up, drawing every eye—away from Veyka and I, toward her display. Cunning, this priestess. Bloodthirsty, if her choice of attire was any indication. After today, we could allow no more self-indulgent displays. But for now, I'd endure it.

Veyka's hand was in mine, her cool skin warming with every passing second.

I could endure.

"Our kingdom has survived a great threat. A spear to the heart of our race and our peace. We turn now to the Heirs who have pledged themselves to Annwyn, in hopes that they shall seal the treaty our Ancestors bled for..." a dramatic pause, "And usher in a new era of prosperity for the realm of the fae."

The column of water jutted apart into two different streams, spinning through the cavernous room in spirals and curves. The symbolism was impossible to miss. As was the length of time she kept those individual tendrils spinning on their respective sides of the throne room.

One glance at Veyka's face—she was glaring at the priestess, blatantly curling her fingers around Excalibur's hilt.

I dragged one finger over the head of my battle axe as Veyka crooned her threat in a velvety voice that promised death— "*Enough, Merlin.*"

The priestess's eyes flared. I hadn't realized—Veyka had learned her name. A mysterious, nameless danger no longer.

The two tendrils of water shot for the center of the room, spiraling together above our heads, back up towards the ceiling, until suddenly Merlin dropped her hands and the water exploded in a mist over the heads of every fae in the room. Rainbows shined in the fine droplets as they met the bright rays of evening sun streaming through the throne room's open arches.

Merlin flicked her wrist, and suddenly an object appeared in her hand. A jeweled dagger, though not the same one she'd used in the Offering. She turned to me first.

"Do you, Arran Earthborn, consent to join with the Heir of the Elemental Fae? To bind yourself to her for all eternity, in this life and beyond, first a thousand years and then a thousand more? To protect Annwyn as its High King, until your dying breath?"

Her words didn't shake me. They couldn't, so long as Veyka was at my side.

"I do." I offered her my hand, watching detachedly as she swiped her knife across it and my own blood bloomed, coppery tang filling the air, carried away on dozens of elemental breezes.

"Do you, Veyka Pendragon, consent to join with the Heir of the Terrestrial Fae? To bind yourself to him for all eternity, in this life and beyond, first a thousand years and then a thousand more? To protect Annwyn as its High Queen, until your dying breath?"

Veyka pretended to ignore the priestess. Merlin's eyes darkened dangerously, but Veyka only flashed me that wicked grin that already had my cock and my beast rising to attention.

"I do," she said, holding out her hand.

Another slash, this time without error. The scent of Veyka's blood mingled with mine, and I had to resist the urge to lift her hand to my mouth to taste her. Not quite yet, I soothed the beast inside of me.

Merlin lifted our hands by the wrists above our heads so that every fae gathered could see. "I join you," she decreed, and pressed our palms together.

Veyka's blood flowed into my wound, and mine into hers. Joined, in every way.

Heat blasted through me, more powerful than anything I'd ever felt before. So hot, it burned into every crevice of my body and my being. Through my soul, my heart, deep into the wells of my magic itself.

Suddenly the world sharpened. It was as if everything I'd ever seen had been through a thin veneer of fog, and with one brutal stroke, the fog had been wiped away. The vines of ivy that wound around the archways were not green. They were a deep, otherworldly emerald that sparkled as the sun's rays hit them. That sun... it was infinitely brighter than it had been a moment before. So bright that I tried to close my eyes against it. But I could not.

Because that would have meant tearing my eyes away from her. From the female inches away, her defiant chin trembling.

The realization hit me a fraction of a second later. I lunged forward—

But in the next breath, my mate erupted with power.

A flash of light as bright as the fire that had burned inside of me, wrapping around Veyka until she was consumed by it. Then, just as suddenly, it disappeared. The light was gone.

And so was my mate.

THE END

Veyka and Arran's journey continues in *Throne of Air and Darkness*, Book 2 in the *Secrets of the Faerie Crown* series. Starting reading now!

Can't get enough of Annwyn? Sign-up for my newsletter to receive a FREE steamy bonus scene. Get an extra peek at the tender moments between Arran and Veyka after the massacre of the goldstone palace and before the taking of the Tower of Myda. You'll also be the first to find out all the official release details for upcoming books from Emberly Ash—including exclusive excerpts, cover reveals, and more.

ACKNOWLEDGMENTS

This book has been, without a doubt, the most painful and gratifying of my writing career. While it is terrifying to start a new pen name, it is even harder to put your own traumas on the page and leave it for others to judge. Veyka's story is not mine. But her pain, betrayal, and darkness—I know those all too well.

So many people deserve acknowledgment for this book. Bryan—my husband, my confidant, my rubber duckie. This last year has been one of the hardest of my life. But with you standing at my side, I've found the courage to write my way out of the darkness. Thanks for all the coffee, snacks, and never making fun of me as I talked out the intricacies of this fantasy world. I hated filling the holes you poked in my magic, but this book is better for it.

Britt—my little sister and stalwart defender, even when we made each other bleed. Having you at my back for the last thirty years has made me who I am. Having you in my corner the last year has kept me standing. I love you.

Thanks to Kathleen Ayers, my work mom and this book's first reader. Without you, this story would have been way less spicy and way less dark. Thank you for pushing me to go there and give Veyka and Arran the story they deserved.

To Mel at Made Me Blush Books, my friend/beta analyst/developmental editor extraordinaire. Look how far we've come! Thank you for the love and care you always give my characters.

And finally, for E. Every book is for you, baby girl.

ABOUT THE AUTHOR

Emberly Ash stole her first romance novel off her mom's bookshelf at the age of ten and never looked back. The author of 12 romance books under her first pen name, Emberly craved something darker and steamier--enter the world of fantasy romance. Her books are dark, twisty, and not for the faint of heart. In the real world, she manages a fire-breathing five-year-old and a grumpy mage of a husband. But you'll most often find her in her hot-pink writing cave, dreaming up your next book boyfriend. Spoiler alert: he's fae.

Find Emberly online at:

https://www.emberlyash.com
https://www.amazon.com/stores/author/B0C55YXHS8
https://www.instagram.com/emberlyashauthor/
https://www.tiktok.com/@authoremberlyash

www.ingramcontent.com/pod-product-compliance
Lightning Source LLC
LaVergne TN
LVHW091232240525
812087LV00001BA/115